Nerd of the Year

By: Supraja I.R.

ISBN: 978-1-68030-831-0

Please feel free to send me an email. Just know that my publisher filters these emails. Good news is always welcome.

Supraja I.R. - supraja_ir@awesomeauthors.org

Sign up for my blog for updates and freebies!
supraja-ir.awesomeauthors.org

About the Publisher

BLVNP Incorporated, A Nevada Corporation, 340 S. Lemon #6200, Walnut CA 91789, info@blvnp.com / legal@blvnp.com

DISCLAIMER

Praise for Nerd of the Year

Awesome book I would totally recommend it for shifter-romance fans! It is a hilarious book and I couldn't stop reading once I started. I can assure you that I'm planning to buy it once it gets published. Also congrats Supraja! I love the way you write and I can be honest when I say you deserve this, your book is amazing!! :) Good Luck in the future.

- Karen, Goodreads

One of my favourite books, I would definitely recommend and can't wait for it to be published so I can buy it! Congratulations!! I've read this book since it first started and it was a very magical journey. Very proud of the author achieving her dream.

- Lareb, Goodreads

I read this book when it was on watt pad and let me tell you when I heard it was going to be published I was ecstatic. This book just sucks you right in you cannot put it down. Neviah was so unlike most of the heroines in werewolf books she was her own person and never let Easton get the best of her. Now Easton at the beginning was a cocky little snot but he grew on you especially when Nev got done with him. This story had a little bit for everyone and trust me it does not disappoint I cannot wait to read more from this amazing author.

- Melanie, Goodreads

Table of contents

PROLOGUE 1

CHAPTER 1 5

CHAPTER 2 22

CHAPTER 3 35

CHAPTER 4 47

CHAPTER 5 59

CHAPTER 6 69

CHAPTER 7 80

CHAPTER 8 88

CHAPTER 9 99

CHAPTER 10 110

CHAPTER 11 117

CHAPTER 12 126

CHAPTER 13 138

CHAPTER 14 149

CHAPTER 15 161

CHAPTER 16 178

CHAPTER 17 189

CHAPTER 18 199

CHAPTER 19 214

CHAPTER 20 222

CHAPTER 21 231

CHAPTER 22 242

CHAPTER 23 251

CHAPTER 24 263
CHAPTER 25 270
CHAPTER 26 278
CHAPTER 27 286
CHAPTER 28 294
CHAPTER 29 305
CHAPTER 30 317
CHAPTER 31 328
CHAPTER 32 336
CHAPTER 33 348
CHAPTER 34 357
EPILOGUE...370

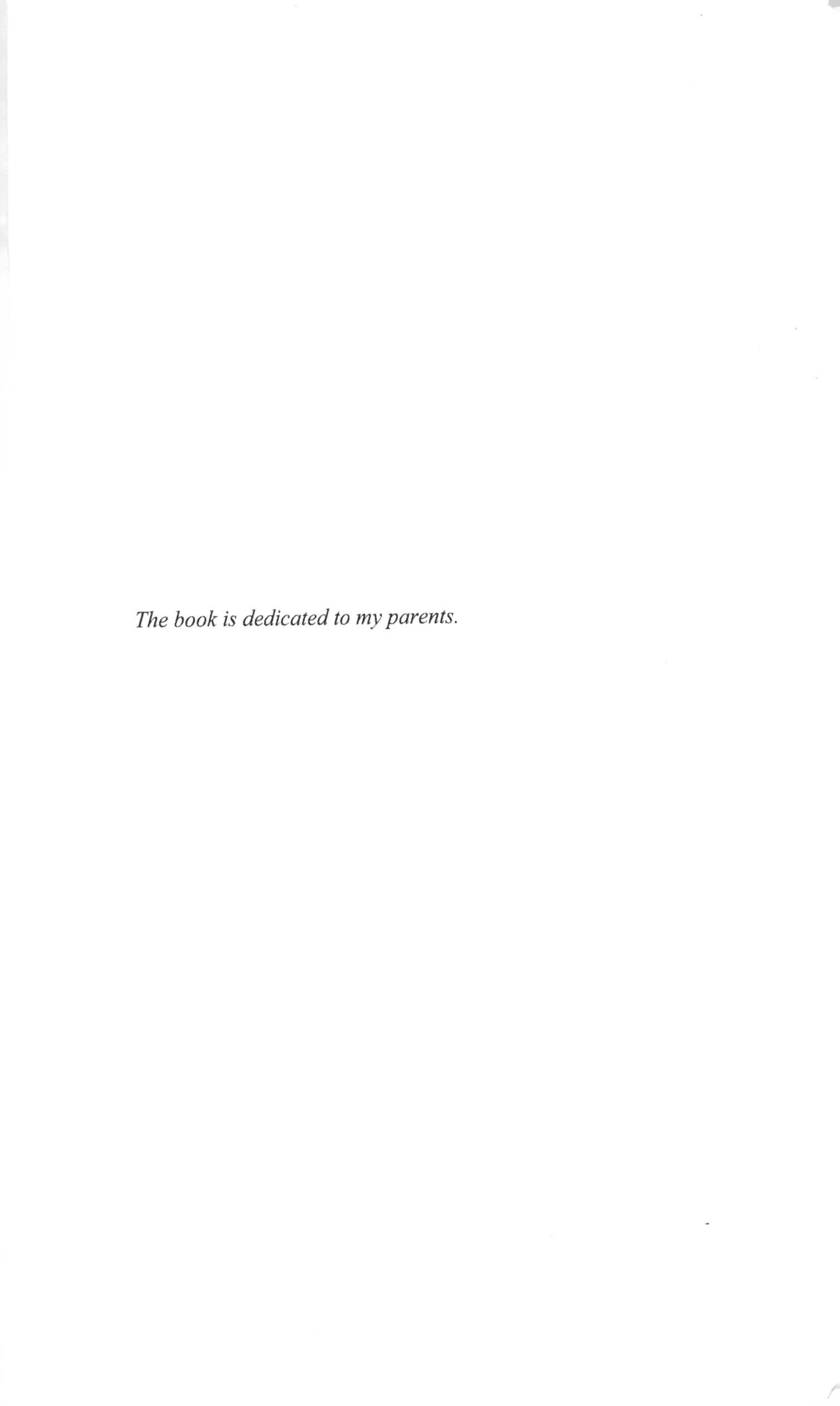

The book is dedicated to my parents.

FREE DOWNLOAD

Get these freebies and MORE when you sign up for the author's mailing list!

supraja-ir.awesomeauthors.org

Prologue

Easton

"Easton, you are paired with Neveah for this project," the chemistry teacher announced.

Neveah? Why her? She was probably the only person in this whole wide world who didn't give a damn about me.

Soon after the announcement, the bell rang.

At the lunch room, my beta, Xavier, and I were talking about the pack when Melissa turned up. She was the head cheerleader and my personal stalker.

She was always eager to do *stuff,* and I was always eager to turn her away from me. Many people believed that something was going on between us, but it was so far from the truth!

I couldn't bear to be near her in that manner. I made it clear to her that there was nothing between us, yet she didn't understand. That was the problem with girls, they stick to you like a stupid glue.

Xavier *entertained* her for some time in the janitor closet before disposing of her. I didn't understand why he did it. He needed to set a bloody standard. She was hot, but no one was that desperate to be with her.

It was my eighteenth birthday today, and the title of the alpha would be passed on to me tonight. I might also find my mate on this day among my pack. I didn't have to do any searching. Once I see her, I would know.

The girls were apparently very excited about it.

I had no specific expectations from her. Heck, I wasn't even sure what kind of girl I wanted to be with for the rest of my life. I trusted the fates. They would pair me with someone suitable, someone worthy of standing by my side… as the alpha female.

I have fooled around a lot till now. It was now the time to take up my responsibilities and act like a man capable of handling them.

We were all in the parking lot during the latter half of the lunch break. It was our usual hangout place in the school.

"Hey man, found the girl?" my third in command, Alden, asked.

"No, dude," I replied. I was even confused whether I wanted her in my life right now.

I knew that I had to grow up, but I wouldn't mind spending some more time alone.

Alpha responsibilities, I was sure I could handle. Having a mate? Not so much

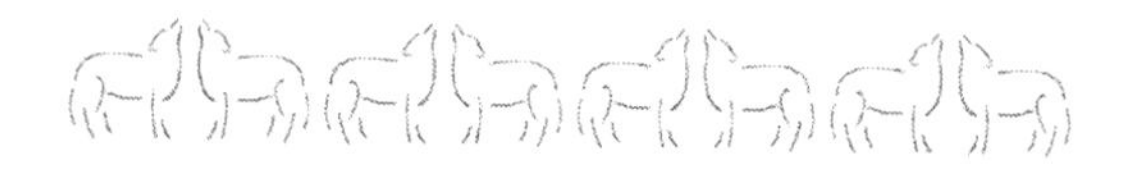

I was still in the parking lot when I heard someone call my name.

I turned back to see Neveah rushing over to me. What does she want?

She came near my car and looked up, meeting my eyes.

I wish she hadn't done that.

I barely heard the words.

"Listen, Eugene, I need marks. The only reason you are paired with me is because you are brainless, and you need marks to pass. Do both of us a favour and don't show up till I tell you to. I'll complete it on my own and just make sure you are with me when I give the final draft."

Shit! Bloody shit!

I was looking at her pink lips while she was talking. They were so beautiful.

She was wearing a brown dress which reached up to her knees, allowing me to perv on her smooth olive-toned legs.

She was short, I have always known that, but right now, I loved that trait of hers. It would make it easier to hold her in my arms. Her brown eyes held so much warmth, and her long black hair that gorgeously framed her face only emphasised them. Suddenly, I wanted nothing more than to bring her retreating figure into my arms and hold her there.

My wolf wanted to mate and mark her now, but that was not possible.

She was human and telling her my secret was highly unacceptable.

The worst part yet was that she was "the school nerd." She and I do not belong together.

Besides, how could I expect her to accept me after our *not so good* history?

I made a conscious decision of resisting the bond. It was not like I couldn't live without her.

What was wrong with the fates? But at least, she didn't know anything about the bond.

I decided that I was going to ignore her despite the deep longing of my wolf.

I was checking her ass when Xavier who was suddenly beside me asked, "What did she want?"

I turned to see him looking at her legs, too.

"MINE."

That was when I realized that I could never stay away from her, and she would never keep me near her. My plans for a happy single life were going down the drain.

Chapter 1

Neveah

"All the best, honey, and be careful." My mother, Gina Huber, kissed my forehead and wished me luck for the first day of my last year in school.

I looked at my watch before getting into my Toyota car. I was already fifteen minutes late. By the time I reached school, I would be around forty minutes late for school.

I was not like the others who were always late. This was only the second time I have ever been late to school. Late for classes is a different question now. I parked the car in the only available space and entered the school building. The name of the school was painted in bright orange colour:

ALGER HIGH SCHOOL

It was named after John Alger, the first mayor of Baxtell, a small town in Kansas State. It only had two more schools. One of them was a girls' convent, and the other was filled with delinquents. Then again, the population was just over seven thousand.

I entered the office and asked Miss Whitney for a late slip. Since I was a very good student and the only one who somewhat respected her, she gave me one. Just like that!

I entered the class twelve minutes before the next lecture. The teacher looked at me surprised, but I just showed her the slip. There were snickers throughout the room, but only one boy spoke up.

"What happened, Neveah? Why so late?"

6 years ago

I ran as fast as my small legs could take me to reach school in time. I was really short for a girl in grade six. I was nowhere near five foot and was, most of the time, a slow runner.

I pushed my legs harder while checking my watch.

Big mistake!

I ended up tripping and, luckily, on my knees. I somehow balanced myself and looked at my scraped palms. When I looked up, I could see two guys surrounding me.

Oh no! Not now.

"Well, well. Look what we have here?" Xavier's voice sounded so sick that I wanted to puke. I managed to keep quiet somehow and did not show any kind of response. I just hoped that it would be all over soon.

I kept my head down and looked at the grass below. Suddenly, I felt a pair of hands grasping me and pulling me up.

I looked up to find Xavier holding my shoulders tightly and staring at the mud on my clothes.

Please, don't let it be what I am thinking! Please, God.

It looked like God wasn't listening to my prayers because the next second, I felt ice cold water pouring all over me.

I shivered from the cold and glared at Xavier. Behind him, the others were laughing loudly. Among them was Easton, his best friend and leader.

"Now, she is clean," Xavier announced as if he was proud of his handiwork. Knowing him, he really was.

"Come on, let's go. We don't want to be late for class." There was a dirty smirk on Easton's face as he pulled Xavier to class.

I quietly went to my locker and took the change of clothes I always had prepared since I realized that circumstances like this were likely going to occur. I quickly changed my clothes and ran to the classroom. Looking at my watch, I realized that I was twenty minutes late, so I just hoped that the teacher would take me in.

"May I know the reason for your tardiness, Miss Huber?" she questioned me. I showed her my red and aching palms. I cleaned them already so that there was no blood and mud. The teacher didn't say anything and just motioned for me to get in.

"What happened, Neveah? Why so late?" Xavier asked out loud in a very polite tone. I gritted my teeth. Starting a fight would not help me now.

"Nothing, Xavier. I just had a small accident." My tongue curled on the word 'accident.' I swore to myself that one day he and his group of bullies would suffer for this.

Someday, I would get back at them

It was the same guy and the same question, and he still had that same irritating smirk. Behind him, Easton was staring at me. He was clearly enjoying the show and waiting for my reply.

"I had a nightmare about you and some guy in bed, Xavy. I was distraught," I replied in a totally innocent good girl tone. I mentally compared my response from the last time, and I was damn proud of myself.

It showed how far I had come. I was now a lot braver than before while he was still acting like a twelve-year-old kid who never grew up.

Xavier's smirk fell instantly. Well boy, he should've thought before opening his useless mouth.

Behind him, Easton roared with laughter, and I glared at him. Some other jock commented, but I preferred to not waste my time on them.

There wasn't a time when they left me alone, and recently, I was starting to enjoy these conversations.

All the lectures passed in the same monotonous manner.

At last, lunch time came, and it was definitely my favourite time. I didn't have a big group of friends. Wait, let me correct that. I actually had no friends, but that didn't mean that I sat in a library corner and wept my heart out.

I usually sat alone in a table. However, I had company today. Melissa, the head cheerleader, was in my usual spot. Apart from being the queen bee, she was also by ex-BFF. She was just like any other stereotype cheerleader. She was a blonde with large blue eyes, plump lips, and small hips. She was beautiful, but that beauty was just in her physical appearance.

We were best friends till eighth grade. Even though she was at the height of dumbness, I actually liked her.

However, everything changed in high school. Her hormones became out of control. She became the use and throw toilet paper of the class while I became the loner nerd. Not that I had a problem with it.

She was absolutely smitten by Easton Dale, the royal head jerk, and thought that they belong together. She apparently *associated* with him a few times. When she is not with him, she was busy with the other idiot, Xavier. Whenever she was upset or free, she sat with me for lunch.

We never spoke, though. It was kind of a mutual agreement.

She was busy filing her nails. She was never one to eat lunch, trying to maintain her bones and whatever little flesh was stuck to it.

I, on the other hand, was enjoying my full plate of food. I wasn't plump, but I wasn't skinny either, and I was happy the way it was.

Lunch passed by silently.

Next was my least favourite class— gym. It was the only class where I didn't shine. I was the last person on earth to finish laps.

I changed into my gym uniform which was a white tank top with the school logo and red hot shorts. Pathetic!

"Come on, kids. We are playing volleyball today. Girls and boys, go to opposite sides of the net." The coach motioned me and the few others who took their sweet time to go to him.

I took my place in a corner and internally cursed the coach. How in the hell could we compete with the hulk like guys?

Easton, Xavier, and their other friends were huge with unnaturally bulky muscles. I swear it was not normal. They must've been on some drugs or something.

The game started and, one by one, everyone in our team started quitting. At last, only Melissa and I were left. Both of us were bad at the game. We sucked big time, but I somehow made sure that the ball didn't end up near me.

Easton then hit the ball to Melissa. She managed to return it, but it ended up bouncing off the net so she was obviously out. Xavier then looked at me and gave me the smirk of a devil. He took the ball and aimed at me.

Luckily, I was able to hit it back. The ball went over the net and into a boy. Sadly, the boy unintentionally struck the ball towards Xavier who wasn't looking and hit him in between his legs. The impact apparently hurt a lot. And here I thought that jocks had better reflexes.

Xavier was writhing in pain, and I would be lying if I said that I didn't feel good. Coach Sir came towards us and asked, "What happened? Where is the ball?"

"That's what he is searching for." It was not my intention to say it aloud, but since the room was silent except for Xavier's grunts of agony, my comment was heard by everyone save for the coach who was already examining him.

The whole class roared with laughter, even the head jerk. What kind of a best friend was he?

I hated Xavier with a passion. Not only did he lack brains, but he also thought bullying was cool. News flash: it is barbaric to bully people. I thought him a lesson, but that was a story for some other time.

Luckily, the game was declared over. Otherwise, those hulk-like guys would have chewed me alive.

After school was over, I stayed in the library to complete my homework and work on my projects. Most of the time, I worked on my projects alone because none of the students wanted to get stuck with me. I didn't blame them. I would just do them a favour by helping them, anyway.

At about six, I returned home, three hours after school was done.

My mom was busy preparing food for her new boyfriend. The guy was actually decent, unlike the past ones. It was just Ma and me. My a-hole of a father ran away after learning that Ma was having me. Ma had me by the end of her first year at college. I have never met my so-called father.

Ma was a lawyer and a very good one. Her new boyfriend, Bryan, was a colleague and was two years younger than her. But since she had me young, she was still wrinkleless and really gorgeous.

We had the same long black curls, olive skin, oval-shaped face, and not so high cheekbones. We pretty much looked similar except for our lips and eyes. Ma's lips were really thin and pretty while mine were a bit plumper. Also, her eyes were blue while mine were brown. They were the only things I inherited from that bastard of a man.

"Baby, Bryan will be here in an hour. So dress nicely." She meant it in a caring way, but I read in between lines.

“Okay, Ma. I’ll leave after he comes. I am going to the mall with the guys, anyway. I will be back by ten. Wear that hot red dress and put less make-up. Also, please make sure that you’ll be in the bedroom by the time I’m back if you’re going to be busy tonight.” I wiggled my eyebrows, enjoying the scene way too much.

It felt absolutely gross saying this, but seeing them together would be bad and hearing the sounds would be even worse. I secretly hoped that they would go to his place. He lived alone and had no children.

Ma turned to a shade of a tomato instantly. She was probably the only mother who would be blushing at that statement. Unlike me, she was a good girl. She never spoke in a loud voice, let alone pass comments. I liked that about her. Someone had to be mature among us.

Seven pm came, and Bryan arrived. He brought me chocolates and cookies and pecked me on the forehead. I liked anyone who brought me anything to eat. Food was my weak point. You want to impress me? Buy food and never complain about how or how much I eat.

“Hey, kiddo. How’s school?” Bryan was always interested in my life.

“School is… well, school!” I replied, not knowing what to say. It was the same routine again and again. “Any boys?” He made his question seem casual, but I knew that he genuinely wanted to know the answer.

I shuddered before replying. “Nah.” The idea of me with someone from school was a very bad one.

After exchanging news, I went to the mall. I was happy to be out of that place. They looked so lovey-dovey. *Yuk!*

I was currently at the mall entrance waiting for the boys. They were late, as usual. I usually come half an hour after our agreed time, but since Bryan was at home, I had to leave early. Finally, two of them turned up.

"Hey, Nev." Broody greeted me with a hug, his six-foot frame completely swallowing my petite one. He let me go and gave me one of his 'charming' smiles. With his blond hair and blue eyes, he had one of the prettiest faces I have ever seen.

"Where's Dan?" I asked them.

"He is busy," Ryder answered. I only had three friends: Ryder, Broody, and Daniel. Broody was eighteen like me but in a different school— the delinquent one while Danny and Ryder were nineteen and were studying in college. The two were cousins and had some identical features with their same dark hair and eyes, but the similarity stopped there. Ryder was equally handsome as Broody while Danny was more the normal looking type.

We have been friends since childhood. We used to hang out a lot when we were younger, but things just grew apart. Now, we just met a couple of times a month.

Danny boy just got a new girl, so I guessed he must've been busy. The four of us grew up together and were neighbours before Ma and I moved to my grandma's place. Looking back, I realized that I never had many friends except them, Melissa, and some occasional acquaintances. Not that it ever bothered me.

We were going to watch a movie. To my utmost disappointment, Melissa was there along with some people from our school. Melissa had a huge crush on Ryder and used to find excuses to speak to him when she used to visit home years ago.

We chose an action movie for they were so much better than the romantic ones. The whole time, Melissa kept glancing at Ryder, and I kept smiling. *That girl will never change!*

We were standing outside the theatre after the movie was over when Melissa turned up.

"Hey, Ryder! How are you?" She was busy twirling her hair around her fingers trying to look... I don't know, innocent?

"I'm fine, Melissa." Ryder had a strong dislike towards her from the start, way before she became like this.

Xavier and the rest of his friends were busy ogling at other girls when he noticed me next to Ryder.

"Boyfriend, huh?" Xavier asked and sized Ryder almost as if he was his rival. What was wrong with that guy?

"Thought you didn't bend that way." Then the guy showed his true colours.

His friends from the football team had a good laugh at my expense, but the person who was enjoying it the most was the head jock, Easton 'Eugene' Dale. He was the best-looking boy in the school. Even I had to admit that. He was tall with unnaturally huge muscles like the rest of them. He had blond hair that was cropped short and green eyes.

"Whatever, dude. You may make fun of her, but you want her bending for you too." Ryder taunted back, and I glared at him. *Was the bending part necessary?*

"No comments," Easton replied with a sick smirk which I would like to wipe off with my fist.

"Don't you have better things to do, Eugene? Do me a favour and drag your dog outside. He is creating an unnecessary ruckus here." I put an end to the conversation. Easton stiffened at the dog comment, so did the remaining of his friends. Hey, dog wasn't that bad an insult!

He said nothing and left. Xavier followed him too.

Did I mention that I hate them?

After the *conversation* with the school guys, both the boys and I went to the nearby restaurant. It was just a normal café, but it was my favourite place at the mall. The best part about these small cafés was that you can eat how much you want without people staring at you, unlike starred restaurants.

We ordered burgers and milkshakes for a drink.

"Who was that guy?" Broody inquired. He was trying to be indifferent, but I could sense the curiosity underneath.

"Nothing, just a pain of the Earth," I muttered in a bored tone. They knew that I always had problems in school from a younger age but didn't know the cause of the problems. Besides, I preferred it to be that way.

"Nev?" Why did Broody want to know?

"He is among the popular people in our school... and we hate each other," I told him, hatred evident in my voice.

"High school," Ryder commented with a sigh. I rolled my eyes. He himself was in high school a year ago! *Boys!*

We had dinner, and then I went home. I was sincerely praying to God that Ma and Bryan wouldn't be at home when I arrive. I would never recover if I saw something, and I also wanted some alone time. Luckily, God heard my prayers, and the house was empty. *Thank Goodness!*

I got ready to do homework because there were still some left.

This was my life.

I go to school, do homework, go out, do homework again, and sleep

It was not bad, but it was boring. I wanted to do something interesting. Ma said that I should have a boyfriend to keep me entertained, but I was not interested in anyone. Sometimes, I actually thought that I might be a lesbian, but then I wasn't interested in girls either.

Instead of wasting my time, I went to sleep.

I was happy being this loud, rude, nerdy, and bratty girl anyway.

"Miss, I need extra work. I finished the last report you gave me."

The teacher looked shocked for a second before saying, "I need time to decide on the topic."

"Oh, alright. I'll submit my current work after class."

I was only seventeen, a senior, and hoping to finish school as soon as possible with the highest credits.

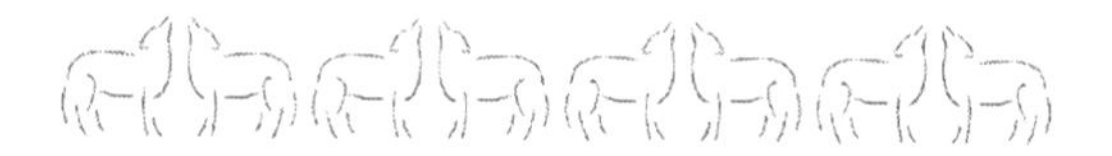

I was in physics class the next day when a message was sent that the principal wanted to meet me. So now, I was standing outside his office.

"The principal wants you in his office," the secretary announced.

I entered the office and sitting there was a man I have not seen in a long time.

Peter Dale was a handsome old man in his early forties. With the same green eyes as his son and dark blond hair, he could give Easton a run for his money. A large smile on his face only made him look more striking. He was way better than Easton behaviour wise.

When he got up, I crashed into his chest. He too wrapped his hands around my back and hugged me. He was the closest thing I had to a father. I let go after roughly a minute.

"Hey, Peter," I greeted him, happy to see him after such a long time.

"Hey, kid," he greeted back. A few wrinkles appeared on his face when he smiled.

We both turned towards the principal who somehow didn't look comfortable. "Mister Davis, can I talk to Miss Huber personally? We have things to discuss." The way Peter spoke, it wasn't like he was asking for permission. It was like he was ordering the man.

The principal left. *Seriously?* I thought we were going to leave, not Mr. Davis.

Peter always had that dominating and commanding personality about him that made everyone listen to him. However, his personality had some flaws, too. Like how Easton always didn't listen to anything his father said and made him sad. Then again, Easton had an excellent talent for making people sad.

I cleared my mind of junior Dale and focused my attention on the senior one.

"Peter?" I was pretty sure that he was not here to chit-chat with me.

"It's nice to see you, kid." I smiled but waited for him to continue. "How is Easton?" The question didn't come as a surprise to me. Easton and Peter weren't that close anymore.

"He is slogging. He is wasting a very important time of his life. He doesn't know what to do and what not to," I answered honestly, knowing that Peter wanted to hear the truth.

Peter's eyes turned sad just like they have been for the past decade. "I don't know what to do. I spoke to the principal. I am here to ask a favour from you, Neveah."

"Yup, sure," I replied, hoping that this statement was not going to come back and bite me in the ass.

"I want you to tutor, Easton. If there is one person he will listen to, it is you." Peter's eyes were so sad that I had no choice but to agree to him.

"I'll try, but no promises," I said and shuddered internally. Me and Easton? That was not much of a good idea. Peter just nodded in an understanding manner.

What have I gotten myself into? Why would Easton even listen to me?

After that, I had to get Easton interested in his studies. The principal told me that he had already informed the teachers. The plan was set. Now, it was time to put it in motion.

Easton wasn't failing or anything, but he wasn't good either. The guy used to get same marks as mine some years back, and my aim was to make sure that happens again.

This was going to be very difficult. We decided that I would start helping him in chemistry since that was his worst. The chemistry teacher would pair me with him for a project.

I spent most of the last period with Peter, so I didn't bother going to class for the last period. Joining the class in the last three minutes would be too nerdy, even for me!

I was going to go home instead of waiting in the library as usual.

However, the scene in front of the school building shocked me to a stop. Melissa was crying her heart out while Alden, who was standing next to her, was glaring at her with pure hatred. His jock friends surrounding them was also staring at her in pity. The girl was crying, but none of those d*cks cared to even console her. *What the hell?*

"Melissa?" I called out.

As soon as she saw me, she came running into my arms and cried on my shoulder.

"Take the bitch with you." Alden looked hurt, angry, and pained all at the same time. What was happening here? Melissa was definitely not a girl to cry over a guy. Moreover, Alden looked like he would beat to death anyone who went in front of him.

"Melissa, what happened?" I asked in a soft and cautious tone, not wanting to hurt her in any manner, and ran my hands on her back in an effort to console her.

"T-take me away," she whispered in my ears. She sounded so heartbroken. I knew her for almost all my life, and I've never seen her so sad!

"Alright, I'll take you." She was my ex-BFF, after all.

"Die, bitch," Alden spat out. He was now pissing me off. There was no damn connection between them that gave him any right to behave in such a way.

"F*ck off, Alden," I spat back.

"Stay out of this, Huber. You don't know a damn thing." Alden sounded even angrier at my interruption.

"Forget it, Nev." Melissa was pulling me to my car.

"Both freaks together! You both deserve no one except each other." He muttered something else too, but it was too low for my hearing. It was probably more curse words. I wanted to kill him but ended up laughing.

I turned back and shout. "You still want Melissa, Alden. Maybe she is a freak, but she is hot! As for me, I have more brains than your team combined. You may call me a nerd, but I call it smart. I'll remember this statement when you fail this year along with your measly friends. To me, you are a failure, a damn big one."

I dragged Mell without waiting for the loser's reply. Just because they looked good and can run like a dog after a ball, doesn't mean that they were Gods.

We were leaving the parking lot when I saw Easton holding Alden back. *Brainless idiots!*

I drove the car really fast, barely following the speed limit. What happened there was confusing me, and I needed to clear my mind. Luckily, Ma was at work, or I would've had to explain what I barely knew anything of.

I made her sit on the sofa and brought her things to eat and coke.

"Spill."

Sure enough, the next statement had me spurting my coke from my mouth on her shirt.

"I love Alden so much."

What?

Chapter 2

Neveah

What?

"What the hell did you say?" My eyes were almost bulging out of their sockets. Surely, my ears were playing tricks on me. *This cannot be happening!*

This was absolutely impossible.

"Are you insane?" I asked her frankly. Maybe I shouldn't have brought her home with me if she was going to feed me this kind of nonsense.

"No, Nev. I do love him." She looked so sad when she was telling me this. Her eyes were brimming with tears.

"How? I mean, when did this happen?" The last time I checked, she was with Easton or Xavier but never with Alden.

"This may sound weird, Nev, but when I saw him today, I just fell in love. It was somewhat like love at first sight." She turned away, not wanting to face me. I just scoffed.

That shit didn't even exist. Love at first sight was a totally stupid concept created by people who were obsessed, and here I thought that she likes Easton and not Alden. When did this crush shift even happen?

I almost felt like laughing but managed to compose myself. I asked her questions just to hold back my laughter. "But why was he so angry? I mean, did you just blurt it out?" Guys got angry at that sort of things. They liked it commitment-free. Well, most of them did.

She turned to look at me and replied. "No, he came to know on his own."

Ah! Great! Guys with telepathic powers!

Okay, this *love story* was turning complicated and impossibly idiotic with every passing second.

"Okay, whatever. Do you want to have anything?" I quickly changed the subject and pointed to the food between us. I so didn't want to know anything more about her *love story*.

She looked around and then at me. "No, I should be leaving. Where is your mom?" Melissa was up before I could say anything.

"At work," I replied as if it was the most obvious thing in the world.

"Okay." She smiled a bit even though I could see immense sadness on her face. I wanted to help her, but I didn't have a single idea what to do.

She was standing near the door in a split second. Well, that was fast.

"I'm sorry, real sorry. I know it couldn't make up for the things I said to you, but still, I am sorry." There was something genuine in her words and expression.

That was unexpected! She wasn't exactly this nice when she refused to be my friend anymore.

"You're right. It couldn't make up for things, but we can try. Promise." My statement wasn't the truth, nor was it a lie.

"Thank you, Nevy." She used my nickname from before, and a ghost of a smile lingered on her face. We hugged and then she left.

I sat back down to do homework. When Ma returned, I was still doing them. To no one's surprise, she came with Bryan.

"Hey, kiddo!" He greeted me with a peck on the forehead. This was kind of becoming a habit, one which I like.

"Hey, Bryan." I greeted back.

"Are you free? Can we talk?" He looked nervous, and I shrugged. "Sure."

We went to my room. It was a bit messy, but it wasn't that bad.

"So, Neveah, I have to say something very important. Here it goes. I love your mom a lot. She's caring and sweet. She is kind with a beautiful heart, but the best part is that she is one of the best mothers I have ever come across." He wasn't even looking at me while saying this and was just gazing at the window behind me. It was almost as if he was reliving a memory.

"You want to marry her," I stated, recognizing the look all the main characters carry in those sappy movies Ma always watched.

Bryan looked at me with surprise before continuing, "No. I mean, not yet. She is still insecure. I want her to be sure about us when I propose. I don't know much about your father—"

He was going to continue, but I interrupted him.

"That makes two of us, and he is not my father. He's just a sperm donor." I corrected him with a hint of malice in my tone. I didn't want to talk about that man at all. Ever.

He smiled a bit at that. "So as I was saying, I don't know anything about your father, but I do know that I want to be your father. You are an amazing child, Neveah. So, will you allow me to be your father?" He kneeled down on one a knee and placed his hand out.

I slipped my hand in his and gave him a smile full of love. "Sure."

Bryan was a good man. Actually, he was pretty amazing. I knew that Ma loved him, and I didn't want them to be apart because of me.

"Thank you, kiddo. This will help your mother open up. Probably, she'll start trusting me more. I owe you a favour." He kissed my hand and got up.

"So you're winning me over to get close to my Ma, huh?" It was meant to be a joke, but Bryan took it way too seriously.

"No, I want to be a part of your beautiful family." His eyes held so much love for my Ma.

"She does love you, Bryan. She is just scared. Don't worry, she will be yours in a short time." I reassured him. I knew my mother better than anyone.

"Come down, people. Food is ready." I heard Ma's call.

"Come on, Bryan." I smiled at him, and he wrapped his arms around my shoulders.

Ma just stared at us with amazement when we reached the dining area. "Okay, so what's going on?" She was trying to be indifferent, but anyone could see the genuine curiosity in her eyes.

"Nothing, just father-daughter bonding," I answered. Ma narrowed her eyes at Bryan while he let out a grateful sigh beside me.

"Let's eat," I said, wanting to break their cheesy stares and also because I was hungry.

"Smells lovely, Gina." Thankfully, he just kissed her on the cheek.

We all ate in silence and after that, I went to my room. I knew Ma wanted to talk to Bryan about my answer, and I didn't want to bother them.

It was late, and I was almost going to sleep when Ma opened the door to my room. "Can we talk?"

"Sure, Ma." She sat on the bed while I stood near it.

"Do you mean what you said today?" she asked, sounding a bit scared.

"Of course. The guy loves you, Ma. Even a blind man can see that."

I could see restlessness and insecurity in her eyes.

I sat on the bed with her and held her hands in mine.

"Ma, it has been almost eighteen years. He is not going to come back, and Bryan is surely not going to leave you. He loves you, and he always will. He doesn't care that you have a seventeen-year-old daughter. He cares about me. He will be a wonderful partner that will be with you in all the situations."

I didn't want to say this part, but I had to in order to convince Ma.

"Maybe I will have a real father this time." I didn't like talking about that man, but deep down, I have always wondered what it would be like to have a father— a person who would be there for me all the time, someone who would tell me that everything is alright when I am sad and who would threaten a guy I bring home. I wanted to know what it feels like to be someone's princess, to simply have a dad.

"Oh, baby." She hugged me, and I could feel wetness on my shoulder. Now, I felt bad. It wasn't her fault.

"It's okay, Ma. The asshole doesn't deserve your tears." I kept my tone low, wanting to keep the resentment off it.

She pulled back and hit me on the same shoulder she was crying on a few moments ago. "Nev." I knew that the 'we don't curse at home' speech was coming, but I was not in the mood today.

"Whatever, I'm going to sleep. Goodnight, sexy lady."

"Goodnight, my stupid daughter," she said and patted my head.

"Hey... I'm not stupid! I am the smartest girl ever," I hollered as she was about to close the door.

She didn't reply and just shook her head as she went to her room.

The next day went smoothly, and Xavier kept his nasty mouth shut, which was kind of a miracle.

At last, it was time for chemistry, the time for the big announcement. We were all completing our notes when the teacher announced the project in which I was to be paired with Easton in order to improve him.

"Easton, you are paired with Neveah for this project." I could practically hear the disappointment of the class. Why were they so sad? I should've been the one who was crying right now.

"This is sad," the girl next to me said. She was the second best at studies.

"Believe me, I know."

What have I gotten myself into?

I was sitting in the cafeteria along with Melissa. We weren't exactly back to being friends, but we did smile at each other. Progress! She was actually eating along with me which was really surprising. She must've been real sad to eat during lunch.

I had seen her and Alden exchanging glances all the time. I didn't know when the connection was formed between them, but I could clearly see a look of want on Alden.

Then why the hell did he behave the way he acted yesterday?

So what she said was actually the truth and not the words of a mentally unstable person like I imagined it to be? I was not calling Melissa mad, but her statement just didn't seem logical.

This was exactly why I preferred being single. Relationships are a pain, and one-night stands are even more painful, especially if you develop feelings for the other person.

A small voice in my mind said that no one would actually go on a date with me, not that I mind it at all.

After we had our lunch, I went to the washroom before the break was over. I was doing my business when I heard two girls talking outside.

"You know, the new alpha is turning eighteen. He will choose a girl today!" Girl number one gushed. Who was the alpha and why would he choose a girl?

"I know, I'm so excited! I wonder who will be the lucky female. Gosh, I hope it's me." Girl number two went on.

"Hey! I want to be her, but we can share." Share what….. or was it a whom? These girls were making no sense. *Whatever!* Who cared what and who they were talking about?

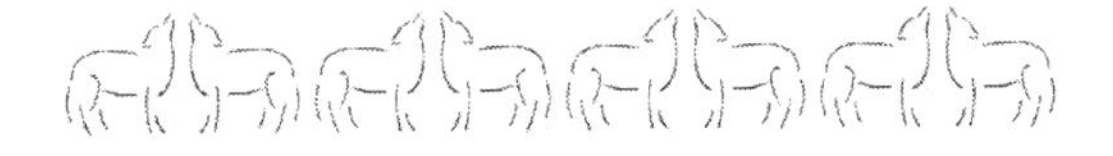

When I returned from the washroom, I spotted Easton in the parking lot along with Alden and Xavier.

Now was the time to execute the second part of the plan. I called out his name and went to talk to him.

"Listen, Eugene, I need marks. The only reason you are paired with me is because you are brainless, and you need marks to pass. Do both of us a favour and don't show up till I tell you to. I'll complete it on my own and just make sure you are with me when I give the final draft."

After I finished my little speech, I expected him to make some snide remark or at least scoff, but to my surprise and shock, I didn't get any of them. So I just turned around and walked away.

I thought that if he felt insulted, he might take up on his huge ego and make a decision of contributing to the project. That so didn't happen!

The guy wasn't even looking at me. He was staring at my lips the whole freaking time. Since when did jocks like Easton start showing interest in me! As I was walking, I heard a growl of "mine" from Easton. *Stupid guy!*

Time for plan B then.

When school was over, Easton was still in the parking lot. God! What did he do here all the time? Clean it?

He was there with his friends when I called out to him. Again.

"Can I talk to you, Easton?" I asked with a disinterested voice.

"Yeah, sure." He seemed happy when I asked, but just as I was about to speak, he cut me off.

"Before you say anything, I want to tell you that I want to help you in this project. No, wait. I have to do this project with you since we are partners, and I can't let you do all the work." Wasn't that supposed to be my line? I pinched the bridge of my nose slightly to make sure that it wasn't a dream.

"Yeah, sure," I deadpanned and started speed walking. What happened was super weird. Since when did Easton start taking academics so seriously?

"Neveah?" I heard Easton call out my name.

"Yes." I turned around, urging him to continue.

"Have a good day ahead." He was smiling so wide that I almost fainted.

"Thank you?" It came out more like a question.

I sped off as fast as I could because the guy was acting crazy. Maybe they had a bet among themselves involving me. Yes! That must've been the case. I decided to just forget what happened some moments ago and concentrate on tonight.

I hurried back home to get ready. Tonight, Bryan was taking Ma and me out to dinner. He asked us to dress classy. When I returned home, Ma was all over the place.

"Ma, what are you doing? Stop and take a deep breath." I made her sit on her bed. "Now tell me, what's going on?"

"I don't have a dress," she cried out. I just scoffed. If she doesn't have a dress, then no one does. I went to her closet to take a look at all her clothes. After some searching, I came up with the perfect dress. It was a knee-length black dress with a deep back.

"Ma, wear this one." I handed her the dress, and she hugged me. "Oh! Thank you, baby, and dress nice," she muttered in my ear in a no-nonsense tone. Ugh! I hated wearing a dress.

I rummaged my wardrobe to find a suitable dress. Ma loved wearing dresses, and whenever she buys one for herself, she buys one for me too. I have not worn most of them, so almost all of them have their tags still on.

I searched and searched and at last found the perfect dress. It was a cream coloured dress with a V neckline that was not deep but not too high either. It showed a bit of my assets. The dress was up to my mid-thigh with a fitting form. I paired it with cream heels, added a bit of makeup, and I was ready. Now, I looked classy.

Night time came and so did Bryan. He was wearing a black suit and looked much like the lawyer that he was. He brought Ma red roses and me, a chain with a locket that he made me wear right then and there. It was beautiful with its topaz embellished locket.

I have never seen Ma look so happy. Seeing her that happy made me happy, too. I went and stood near the car to try to give them some privacy. After talking for some time, they started making out which was utterly gross. "Daughter in here, guys!" I said loudly, waving my hands dramatically in the air.

"Sorry, Nev," Bryan said, and Ma turned into a deep shade of red. "Stop blushing, guys. You both are embarrassing me." Bryan chuckled and led us to the car. Ma and Brian sat in the front while I sat in the back.

We reached the restaurant after some time. The whole way, Brian was holding Ma's hand and was giving her sweet smiles during the traffic jams. The restaurant was beautiful! I looked at Ma, and her eyes said the same thing.

"A table under Walter."

The waitress led us to a table in one corner. To my surprise and dislike, Easton was sitting with some girl and what I assumed was her family. I felt a slight twinge in the chest at seeing him smiling with some other girl. I had no idea where the pain came from, but it was probably just gas problems. I ignored it and concentrated on the food. The bad thing about these high-class places was that you pay high prices for much less food.

I didn't give much thought to the price since I knew that Bryan was loaded and can afford anything on the menu, so

I ordered their meatloaf. When the food arrived, it was just as I expected it to be. It had a bit of meat, and the rest was just a dressing of leaves. I frowned. Noticing it, Bryan got worried.

"Is the food bad?"

"Where is the food, dude? There are only leaves."

Bryan shook his head and went back to eating his food. I guess that was childish, but I was hungry, and there was hardly any food on my plate. I finished the food fast and went to the washroom. Standing there was the girl with Easton. She was really pretty with her blonde hair and hazel eyes. The girl turned to me and smiled. Not giving much thought, I smiled back.

"You are Neveah, right?" How did this girl know my name?

"Yes. Do I know you?" I asked even though I was very sure that I haven't met her before.

"Oh no. I have heard about you. You are pretty famous in your school." Since she was with Easton, I truly couldn't guess her intentions.

"Uh, thank you? I should leave. Nice meeting you." I didn't wait for her to reply and walked out of the ladies' room.

The sight outside was even more horrific. Standing near our table were the couple and Easton. "There she is." I heard Bryan's voice, so I went and stood beside him. Seeing me, Easton flashed a huge smile. I was sure that his jaw would tear if his smile got any wider. "Hello, Neveah. It's such a pleasant surprise to meet you." This was not Easton, the head jock. He was someone else. I knew I should keep my mouth shut, but I just couldn't help it.

"Is it really pleasant for you to see me?" I questioned with a frown on my face. His face fell at that instant, and an itty-bitty part of me felt guilty. He quickly masked his face with an expressionless look and gave a small smile. "Of course, Neveah." He wasn't lying. Since when did this brainless jock start to like me?

"Okay, Mr. Tate, we got to leave. See you sometime soon." The other man and Bryan spoke for some more time and then all of us left.

We reached home, but none of us got out of the car just yet.

"So… " Ma began with a nervous smile on her face. I knew where this was going. "Ma, if you want to go with Bryan to his house, please do so. It's okay, I can manage one night. I am seventeen and can manage a night alone in the house."

"Okay, but you should call me if there is any emergency or if you need anything." She hugged me and pressed a wet kiss to my cheek.

"Yes, Ma." I saluted and wiped my cheek. I got out of the car, and they waited till I had opened the door. I turned back and called out to them as I stood on the doorstep. "Be careful, Ma!" I love that woman.

At last, they were gone, and I had the house to myself.

Chapter 3

Neveah

The house was mine at last, not that I was going to host a party or something. Now, I could watch TV for the whole night and eat junk food. That was something I was never able to do since Ma wouldn't allow it.

I took out all the junk food from the fridge, some colas, and even chocolates. I was hungry anyway since I didn't have much of a dinner at that stupid restaurant. I was never going there again.

My mobile beeped just as I was busting out a rerun of Beauty and the Beast. I almost fell off the sofa when I saw the message.

Unknown Number

You looked beautiful tonight.

I knew of only one soul who saw me that night, and the one who sent this message was definitely not that person.

I replied, *Who is this?* Hoping that it wasn't the guy I was guessing it to be. I got an instant confirmation instead.

Easton Dale.

Was he kidding me? This was one sick joke, so I sent back a reply.

Dude, stop bugging me in the middle of the night and find some other girl to shower your attention on.

This shouldn't be something new for him. He always had girls surrounding him. Somehow, that thought hurt me.

I wish I could do that.

The stupid prick was not making any sense. So I thought that instead of wasting my time on him, I should watch Jay Ryan. Man, he was one hot guy! I kept on checking my phone in between the commercial breaks but didn't receive any other messages from Easton after that.

I spent the whole night watching movies. The next day, I was obviously extremely sleepy and tired. Ma was not back yet, and when I tried calling her, my call went to her voicemail. I hoped she returns by tonight. A small part of me was jealous, but the larger part was very happy for Ma. She had found her perfect guy at last.

Speaking of guys, I had yet to see Easton. Facing him after yesterday's message would make me feel weird, anyway.

I spotted him at the parking lot. Upon seeing me, he gave me a huge smile like yesterday. On the other side, I spotted Alden sucking the face of Melissa's sidekick. Man, payback was a bitch! I used to hear many girls complaining that Melissa was spotted making out with their boyfriends. Now, she was the one watching the guy she loved with another girl.

She was standing alone in a corner, and I felt bad about it. She was always the centre type of girl and never the corner one. I could either enjoy her misery or comfort her. Even though I felt the first option was appealing, that would be too insensitive of me so I went and stood near her.

"Hello, Melissa." My greeting was replied with a heavy sigh.

"Hey, Nevy. How are you?" she said, but her eyes just didn't leave Alden's form.

Before I could reply, she started talking. "I'm such a bitch, right?" There was so much hatred in her tone when she looked at me, but I couldn't figure out if it was towards Alden or herself.

"I would be lying if I say you're not," the ever-honest me replied.

She just shook her head. "I love Alden, Nevy. It is so difficult to live without him." She sounded almost suicidal. I locked my hands with hers and dragged her to the classroom. When the jocks entered, Melissa stiffened. I looked at the door to spot the same girl from before and Alden looking very cosy. When Easton entered behind them, he looked at Melissa with pity. It was a look I had never seen on him before. Thankfully, he didn't look at me, or it would've been awkward.

All our classes passed with Alden roaming around with different girls on his arms. By lunch time, Melissa looked sad and dead. I was getting pretty angry at Alden's behaviour. If he did not want to be with Melissa, fine, but why was he rubbing it on her face?

This wasn't right, and then the bulb in my brain lit up. Jealousy always worked in two ways, so why not try it this way? I dragged Melissa to the washroom. To my extreme luck, it was empty.

"Stop behaving like this, Melissa. It is not healthy." I was on the verge of shouting at her. Why was she behaving so needy for a guy she fell in love with yesterday?

"I can't stop, Nevy. It hurts so badly." She was actually moaning like she was in pain.

"Listen to me, Melissa Archer. I know you love him, and I can also see that he likes you. He's just roaming with other girls to make you feel bad, so why not try his tricks on him?" The plan has already formed in my head. All I needed now were the correct people and the proper amount of acting to execute it flawlessly

"But what if they have the opposite effect?" Her eyes widened, and she looked scared.

I sighed before replying. "I am not going to sugarcoat this. Look, if this works, he will come to you, and if it doesn't, well… it's not like he can be worse than this, right? So why not give it a try?" This was the best way I could sum it up for her. Personally, I wouldn't put so much effort for a guy if he treated me this bad.

Then again, love makes you do weird things.

"Alright." She still looked uncomfortable, but this could prove to be in her favour since most guys were possessive assholes.

"Okay, this is the plan…"

I was standing in the corridor to search for a suitable guy. God must have heard my prayers because Liam walked in the corridor at that instant. He was one of the hottest guys ever

to be born. He was not from the jock group and hated each of them with a passion.

"Hey, Liam! I need to talk to you." I dragged him to a part of the school which was usually empty. At first, he was reluctant, but when I promised to help him in homework, he agreed. *The things you can do with brains!*

School was over, and now it was time to put my brilliant plan into action.

Liam was waiting outside the class along with Melissa.

"You both know what to do, right? Please don't screw this." I warned, and they both nodded. Melissa and I walked ahead while Liam was to enter a bit late.

"Don't you dare screw this up, Melissa!" She just rolled her eyes, but I knew that she listened. I spotted all the jocks in their usual spot in the parking lot. It was time!

We were walking in such a way that I can see Alden, but she can't. Actually, I was walking with Melissa who was yapping loudly to get Alden's attention. Not that she had to do a lot of work. The moment Melissa came out of the school building, Alden's attention immediately turned towards her. At first, he seemed surprised, and then it turned to anger. If the guy was this affected with Melissa, then why didn't he accept her?

We were still walking when Liam came and wrapped his arms on Melissa from behind. "Hey, babe. Are you free this evening?" he flirtatiously said and placed a kiss on her neck.

I discretely rolled my eyes at Liam's overacting and looked towards Alden's direction to see him fuming. If Alden was God, Liam would be in his grave by now.

"Sure, Liam. I'm free whenever you want me." She giggled loudly and sank further into Liam's embrace. I had so warned them about overacting, and yet they ended up doing it anyway.

Alden was ready to kill now. Melissa and Liam were going for a kiss in a slow motion style when Alden walked incredibly fast towards them. Liam and Melissa's lips were just about to touch when Alden separated them.

"What are you doing?" he shouted. Melissa flinched, and Liam cowered under Alden's glare. I rolled my eyes again at this nonsense. You didn't want to be with that girl, yet you couldn't bear the thought of her being with someone else? *How hypocritical!*

I took the liberty of replying since I didn't think the other two were in the state to do so. "Can't you see? They were going to kiss." I made it sound like I was least interested. The moment I closed my mouth, Alden was right in front of me. I was scared.

"What I do is none of your business, Alden. So I suggest you stay away from it," Melissa shouted back at him, and Alden turned his angry glare away from me. *Go, Melissa!* Alden became even angrier. His clenched hands were tight, and his breaths were getting shorter by the second.

Liam and I looked at each other and couldn't help but snicker. This plan was going in the right direction.

Suddenly, the ground disappeared from my feet. I was hauled upwards by a strong force. I looked up to see myself close to Alden with his eyes eerily black. He had an arm around my neck, and the other was pulling my hair. The air supply to my lungs was being cut, and I could barely breathe.

Then Alden dropped me down abruptly. I held my head in my hands and started coughing out loud. I could hear shouting and screaming, but I could barely hear them. I tried to hold on to my consciousness as much as I could but ended up fainting. The last thing I heard was Easton screaming my name.

Easton

Neveah was the only word on my mind since this afternoon! Today was my eighteenth birthday, the day where I am to become the alpha. Today was also the day that my chance of finding my mate increases. It was not necessary that I find her today, but chances were high.

Never in my life did I expect it to be Neveah, the nerd of the school! Actually, not. She was not like those silent blushing girls. She was much more. She was one of those bitchy, arrogant, rude, and irritating girls, and I couldn't help falling in love with her.

Yes, I, Easton Dale, was completely in love with Neveah Huber who completely hates me!

I knew that the attraction I felt for her now was mostly because of the bond between us. Well, for me at least! But I knew that one day, we will both fall head over heels in love with each other.

When I told Xavier, he made fun of her for a total of thirty seconds before I punched him square in the face. No one ever makes fun of my mate.

Now that I had my mate, I was more capable of being a good alpha that my pack wanted and needed. That was what mates do, they provide stability and security.

There was a ceremony in the afternoon to mark the start of my alpha duties. Xavier would also be given the rights of the beta and Alden, the third in command.

Alden, who was a day older than me, had also found his mate, and it turned out to be Melissa, the head cheerleader of the school. I was more than happy when I heard the news because it meant that she would leave me alone at last.

Alden, on the other hand, was depressed. He didn't want her because she had been with many guys. Even though people thought that I slept with her, it was not true. I have never been with anyone from the pack. It would've been weird for my mate and the female if they come face to face. I was to be their leader, not their lover.

I was surprised at the choice of mate for me, but I was not disappointed. I never would. Fate was on our side because she was paired with me for the project. When she told me that she wanted to do the project alone, I was kind of scared. I couldn't be away from her, ever! I was too shocked to protest, though.

But when she came to me the second time, I was ready to protest. I told her that I would help her on the project no matter what. This mate thing was turning me into a love sick puppy and a full-blown wuss, but the worst part was that I actually didn't mind!

The ceremony started at about four in the afternoon. The whole pack was present along with my father, the alpha. The whole alpha family took part in the ceremony, but since it was just my dad and me, it would be over quickly. We were in a big clearing where Dad and I stood in the centre facing each other with the whole pack surrounding us. The elders of the pack who stood in front of us would be conducting the ceremony.

"The time has come. Today is the day when the positions will be passed on to the younger warriors of the pack. Today, the current alpha will retire from his duties, placing his heir in his place. Along with him, the positions of second and third in command will also be handed over. With the blessings of the fates and the Moon Goddess, let the position be handed over," they spoke together. Did these guys rehearse their speech?

"I, Peter Dale, alpha of the pack hand over my title, duties, and pack to you." My father's strong voice rang through the clearing.

"I, Easton Dale, accept the position and the obligation that comes with it. I promise to take care of the pack's every need with the help of my beta and alpha female." I couldn't help but smile when I said the last two words

Neveah would be an amazing Luna. She would be one of a kind! As soon as I finished my oath, the whole pack bowed to me, a sign of respect and a symbol that they have accepted me as their leader to guide and look after them.

The ceremony ended with an amazing meal. That was what guys of my age think about: food and girls. Or in my case, it was my mate, my Neveah.

That same night, I was to have dinner with my cousin's family. Elena was my uncle's daughter. She was my age and a human. Her mother was not my uncle's mate and was just a normal human, so their children also turned out to be one. A child doesn't need to have two werewolf parents to be born as our kind. However, only a child of mates could be born as a werewolf. Otherwise, they would turn out to be human like in Elena's case.

I had promised her that as soon as I become alpha, I would treat her with a party. But she lived a state away, and her parents wouldn't let her come to my town alone. Hence, we had to make do with a family dinner instead.

I was currently sitting with her family at a famous restaurant when I got a whiff of the most amazing smell.

There she was, my mate, Neveah, wearing a cream dress and looking so damn hot! She entered with a man of my father's age who had his arm around her shoulder. Who was he? He had no right to touch my mate. Following closely behind them was a woman who looked like Neveah.

It was Gina, my late mother's best friend! It had been a while since I last saw her. She used to come to our house to console and look after me after my mother passed away. I, however, constantly pushed her away, so she left. I wanted to go and greet her, but I was not sure of how she would react. So I just stayed put.

Gina and the man exchanged smiles. The way they looked at each other reminded me of how mates' meet each other's gazes. It must've been her boyfriend. Deep in my thoughts, I didn't notice that the whole table was also eyeing Neveah.

"Is there anything you need to tell us?" Alex, my uncle, asked me. He wasn't my dad's brother. He was his cousin.

"She is my mate," I announced gleefully.

"Does she know?"

I was too busy looking at the bit of cleavage peeping out of her dress to pay attention to what my uncle was saying.

"What?" I muttered absentmindedly.

"She is human," Elena said.

"Unfortunately, yes." If only Neveah was a shifter like me, we would have been together by now. I looked at her again to find that her eyes were also on me. I could see that she was hurt that I was with some other female. I liked it, and so did my wolf.

I knew that she would have thoughts of me because of the bond. She didn't know the reason yet, and that may upset her. Slowly, the bond would grow stronger, and soon enough, it would be very difficult for us to stay away from each other.

Elena went to the washroom, and Neveah followed after her.

"Want me to introduce you to her mother?" uncle asked.

"Do you know her?" There was no way that he knew Gina better than I did.

"No, but I know the man with her. He heads a law firm. Come on, let's go."

All of us went to his table, and my uncle and the man had small talk. I approached Gina, not knowing how she would react. To my surprise, she simply hugged me like she used to when I was younger, and I wrapped my arms tightly around her.

"I'm sorry," I whispered in her ear.

"It's okay," she whispered back as the rest of the lot stared at us.

After a few good seconds, I let her go, and we patiently waited for my mate and cousin to get out of the washroom. They were taking too long.

I came to know that the man was Bryan and that he was Gina's boyfriend. Neveah and Elena joined us after some time.

Even this close, Neveah looked fantastic. She had red lipstick which made her plump lips look even better. All I wanted to do now was to pin her against a wall and kiss her passionately. If only we didn't have an audience.

"Hello, Neveah. It's such a pleasant surprise to meet you." I tried to be nice, but I didn't think it would work.

"Is it really pleasant for you to see me?"

That hurt. I knew that we were not friends, but she could have been a bit more polite. I blanked my face and replied, "Of course, Neveah." She was trying to analyse whether I was lying or not. I wasn't.

We said our goodbyes and left.

As I was laying in my bed, I was thinking of ideas to get closer to Neveah. One thing was for sure: I couldn't go on long without her.

Neveah Gail Huber, you will be *mine*.

Chapter 4

Easton

The next day was full of drama.

Alden wanted to show everyone that he didn't need a mate, so he was roaming around with a different girl with each passing class. I felt bad for Melissa. Even though I was irritated with her insane stalking abilities, it was just too cruel. The pain of rejection is especially heartbreaking for wolves.

I was not one of those guys who would reject their mate to stay single or to find a more attractive girl. Finding one was quite a blessing already. A mate was a gift of nature, no matter how sappy that sounded.

I had my own issues to work on too, though. I had a pack to take care of. I needed to learn about my pack, their strengths and weakness, and their war strategies, but the most important was for me to become a better leader. I knew that I should talk to my father about all this, but somehow, I felt that I didn't know that man anymore.

We just… drifted apart.

The hardest of my problems were already giving me headaches. I had to make Neveah love me, which was near to impossible. The girl loved no one except her mother.

Also, she wasn't my greatest fan. In fact, I was sure that she hated me, *a lot*. Then again, I couldn't blame her for that. I wasn't exactly the best person to her in our younger days.

We were all standing in the parking lot when Melissa and Neveah came out of the school building. My mate was looking hot in those shorts of hers with her tanned legs showing. I couldn't help but imagine how they would feel wrapped around my hips. I shook my head to clear out the image. *So not happening, bud... at least for some time.*

Neveah had started hanging out with Melissa again after Alden rejected her.

Liam came behind Melissa and started flirting with her. Liam was human and had no idea about Melissa and Alden. The bad part was that Melissa started flirting back with him, too. I knew that Alden rejected her, but flirting with other guys in front of him will surely agitate his wolf. Then again, he himself has been doing it since this morning.

The rest of my pack was watching the show as I watched my mate. She rolled her eyes at the two of them, making me break into a smile. She was standing impatiently, almost like she was waiting for something to happen. Something was running in that brain of hers.

Liam and Melissa were about to kiss when Alden stormed towards them and broke them up.

"What are you doing?" I had never seen Alden this angry.

"Can't you see? They were going to kiss." Neveah shouldn't have replied. This would anger Alden's wolf, and he can harm her. I heard Melissa reply something.

I then heard Liam and Neveah giggle. It was a beautiful sound.

So I turned to look at her again and saw the mischief in her eyes. Then the next thing I saw was Alden choking my mate.

How dare he! Who was he to even touch my mate? This made my wolf very angry. I went to them as fast as I could. I pulled him off my mate, making him lose his grip on her. I didn't care if anyone would see the commotion. She was choking and coughing, and her whole face was red.

Right now, all I wanted to do was kill Alden. I turned to him and started punching and kicking the bastard. He tried to fight back, but he was in no way a match to my strength. I wanted to shift but couldn't, not in front of so many humans.

I was about to finish him off when Xavier and some other guys from my pack pulled me away. I looked at my mate to see her lying unconscious on the floor. This couldn't be good. Why hadn't someone helped her yet?

"Neveah!"

My growl echoed all over the lot.

I snarled at the sight of a panicked Melissa hovering over her. She was the reason all of this happened.

I quickly took her to the hospital and made Melissa call Gina. I never felt this angry all my life. I messaged Xavier to keep Alden in the basement. He was going to die, and he was going to die a slow and painful death.

I also felt anger towards myself. If only I was a better mate, Neveah wouldn't be lying on a hospital bed right now. I should've taken better care of her, especially because she was human. They were weak compared to us.

Gina came after some time with tears on her face. She spotted me in the hallway and came running towards me. "Where is my daughter?"

"The doctor is treating her," I whispered in a grave tone. Fear clutched my heart. I didn't know the extent of her injuries, and that was killing me.

Gina started sobbing. Seeing the pain in her eyes made me want to kill Alden as quickly as possible.

"She will be alright, Gina. She is too stubborn to give up like that," I assured her. I knew my mate, and I also knew she was going to be alright. *Call it a mate intuition!*

She smiled a bit at that. "She is, isn't she?"

"She will be alright," I said it again, more to myself than to her.

Minutes passed, and the doctor finally came out.

"Ms. Huber is alright. She fainted due to asphyxiation. Mind telling me what happened? I see handprints on her neck." I could see where the doctor was going with this. She looked at me suspiciously for a split second. She must be thinking that I was the reason for those bruises.

As if I would hurt my mate!

"A guy tried to choke her, Doc," I said and heard Gina gasp.

"I think you should inform the concerned authorities."

"Don't worry, Doc. I'll take care of this." There was a dark tone to my voice, and I knew that both the ladies heard it. It didn't matter. What matters to me was Alden's death.

He made the biggest mistake by harming a human who happened to be his luna. Such a crime was not to be forgiven.

"Is it possible for us to visit her?" I desperately wanted to see her awake. I wanted to catch a glimpse of her lively brown eyes.

"Sure, but she needs a little more rest. She will regain consciousness after a while." The doctor smiled reassuringly.

"Thank you, Doctor," Gina said gratefully.

"You are welcome. Take care of her and make sure it doesn't happen again." She didn't need to say that. I would always take care of her from now on.

Gina and I went to my mate. She was so peaceful in her sleep. Gina went and kissed her forehead and cheek. I was tempted to do the same, but if Neveah came to know about it later, I would have to pay dearly.

"I should leave now. Update me on her health." The more I stayed there, the more time Alden had to live, and I didn't want that.

"Sure, Easton. Thank you." Her voice was appreciative, and I smiled.

"Nothing to thank."

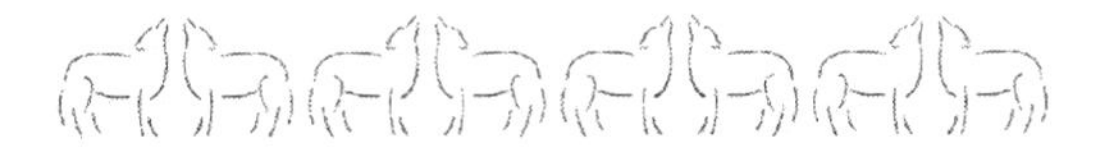

After that, I left for our house. Alden's parents were there along with some people from the pack. They were curious as to what made me so angry. Now, I would have to tell them that I have found my mate.

"What did my son do? You may be the alpha, but you cannot treat my son this way. You have to apologize to him." This was what I have been hearing since I arrived home. My father left the country this morning for some business, so I had to handle this alone.

"Your son did an unforgivable crime, and he will pay for it," I said in an alpha tone, leaving no room for argument.

"Where is he?" I questioned Xavier.

"In the infirmary." I wasn't exactly pleased that he wasn't in the basement, but I let it slide this time.

"Bring him here," I ordered.

We all waited for Alden to arrive. He came in a wheelchair with Xavier and Melissa on his side. Melissa looked exhausted and sad. No matter how wrong your mate was, you couldn't help but love them regardless of whether they showed the love back or not.

"I am sorry, Alpha," he apologized without meeting my eye.

"You are sorry for what?" I spat out, the need to see him dead bubbling within me.

"For manhandling a human." I could sense his anger. He didn't feel bad for his actions at all, he was just frustrated and confused.

"You should be sorry for manhandling your luna, Neveah." I heard Melissa gasp and the guys from school whisper to each other. Mate or not, I couldn't allow a pack member to hurt a human, and for that, Alden had to pay.

He looked at me and scoffed. "What? She couldn't be a luna."

"Are you telling me I can't identify my own mate?" My voice was way too high, and my wolf was on the edge. *How dare he?* First, he tried to kill her, and now he was questioning me?

"I didn't know. I swear… I didn't know." His voice trembled with fear and pain, and the beast in me liked that.

"Do not raise your voice at me, Alden. I am your alpha. For your crime, you are banished from this pack. You are now officially not a part of us." My voice was void of any emotions. He was lucky that I did not kill him. Believe me, I wanted to, but he was right. He didn't know. No one did, and that was the only reason I was sparing his life now.

"No, Alpha. Please forgive our son. He didn't know about the luna. Please, give him a chance. Please, sir." His father dropped to his knees and begged at my feet.

I had no idea what to do. Alden's parents were good and loyal people.

"Alright, he can stay with the pack, but he is not allowed to be near the luna without my permission among other things. Also, there will be a legal action which will go in his records." If he thought that I would leave him alone this easily, then he was mistaken. He was of legal age so he may have to spend time in prison, and that was much better than my original punishment.

My wolf was still angry that I let him live, but I had no other choice. Killing Alden would hurt Melissa which would, in turn, hurt Neveah, and I couldn't let that happen. This mate thing was turning me into a caring dumbass!

"I would like to inform the pack that I have found the luna, but she is a human, so it will take time for her to adapt to our way of life. She will be presented to the pack when she is ready." The pack was happy that I found the alpha female so soon. Usually, it took months and years.

I had to admit, I was lucky indeed.

Neveah

I woke up in a strange place where everything was freaking white. At first, everything was a blur, but after focusing my eyes, I was able to identify Ma.

"Wh-what happened?" My voice was hoarse, and my throat hurt like hell.

"Miss Huber, I am your doctor. Can you tell me, what is the last thing that you remember?" I turned away from Ma to see a middle-aged woman in scrubs.

All the events came rushing in— me asking Liam to help, Melissa and Liam flirting, and Alden interrupting their kiss and trying to kill me.

"Alden."

"Is that the guy who did this to you?" I looked up into the doctor's eyes.

"Y-yes. Who brought me to the hospital?"

"Easton," Ma answered.

Easton Eugene Dale? Wow! That guy was acting really, really weird.

"You should thank him later. He was the one who pulled Alden off you." *Oh, really, Ma?* She was always fond of Easton, and I hated that.

"Do you want to register a complaint?" The doctor looked quite concerned while looking at my neck. I touched it and flinched from the pain. The doctor got a mirror from somewhere, and I inspected my neck in the reflection.

On my neck are big red hand marks. Stupid Alden left bruises on me.

"I need time to think first." I was yet to decide on whether I wanted to take it to the cops or not.

"Sure, take your time, but I suggest that you do. These things are not to be taken lightly. Meanwhile, I'll prepare your discharge papers. You can leave now, but I'll give you some painkillers which I suggest you to take for the next three days." She smiled warmly.

Thank God!

"Thank you, Doctor," I said genuinely.

She smiles again and leaves.

Mom came and sat on the edge of my bed, so I tried to get up and sit.

"Don't stress yourself." I looked at Ma to see dried tears and her face looking dull.

"How long have I been out, Ma?" My voice came out dead.

"Almost three hours. Thank God nothing happened to you. Nevy, do you want to sue him? I can start the legal proceedings."

Suddenly, the door burst open, and in came a flustered Bryan.

"Bryan, what are you doing here?" Ma looked surprised. I took it that she didn't inform him.

"Why didn't you tell me that our daughter is in the hospital, Gina? I came to know from the reception at the firm."

He didn't sound angry, but he was obviously sad. He even said *our daughter*.

"I am sorry, Bryan. I was so scared that I just... I just came here. I am really sorry." She was so going have a panic attack.

"Hey, I understand. It's alright." He hugged her and kissed her on the cheek. I smiled as I observed them. My Ma was no longer alone.

"Are you alright, kiddo? I swear I almost had a heart attack." He smiled a bit but then his eyes turned dark. "What do you plan to do about the guy who did this to you? Lucky thing both your parents are lawyers. We will make sure that he does not see the light of the day again ever."

I raised my eyebrow at that. "Both my parents? Did you two get married or something?"

"Not yet, but I asked her yesterday, and your mother said yes but she has a condi—"

"You have my blessings, Dad." I cut him out. The way happiness crept into his face was unbelievable. Looking at them made me forget my pain for the meantime.

"I will be the best father ever, Neveah, but that is not the condition. She wants to stay in your current house after we get married." I knew why. The house belonged to Grandma. It was the only remaining thing we had of her, and Ma and I loved her very much.

"So what is the problem?" I asked.

"You don't have any problems with me staying with you?" He sounded bewildered. Why would I have a problem with that?

"As long as you both are not loud, I don't mind." Mom blushed, and Bryan smirked.

"Thank you."

I just waved my hand at them, not having the energy to talk anymore.

The discharge papers were issued by then so I got to go home. The school was already informed of what happened, and they advised me to stay at home as long as necessary.

The next day, Bryan was moving in, so the whole house was messed up. I always thought that guys had very few things.

I never realized how wrong I was until today.

Bryan had a whole lot of stuff!

I have never felt that the house was small because it was not. But now, I was seriously doubting the size of the house. We had to turn one whole bedroom into a closet for both Bryan and Ma. The number of shoes that he had was way more than what Ma and I have combined. And not to mention the suits!

At last, all the movers finished the job, and their room was set.

We were going to have a simple family dinner with takeout pizza since we were all too tired to cook. But as we were watching television, the doorbell rang, and Bryan went to get it.

"Hey, kiddo. Some of your friends are here from school."

Friends?

I didn't have friends, and I doubted Melissa would come because she did not even visit me in the hospital, notwithstanding the fact that I was at the hospital because of her. Then again, I was the one who planned it all

I went out to see two people who I never expected to see anytime soon.

Standing outside our door was Easton and Alden.

Chapter 5

Neveah

I was about to shut the door in their faces when Easton pushed it open.

"Neveah, don't shut the door. Just listen to me, okay? Just trust me, alright?" His eyes do look sincere, but I was way past caring.

Trust him? Was he out of out of his mind? First, he brought his friend who tried to kill me to my house, and then he was telling me to trust him?

"No, Eugene. I don't trust you! Get out and take your dear '*I try to kill people by choking them*' friend out of my property before I call the cops." I threatened in a loud voice, but it didn't faze him. I put my hand on his chest to push him away, but before I could take back my hand, he puts his on top of mine. He was now holding my hand hostage.

A small part of me actually liked it, but I instantly cleared my head of such absurd thoughts. "Please leave,

Easton, and take your friend along with you," I whispered in a tired voice. My already sore throat was hurting again from all the shouting.

Hearing all the commotion, Brian and Ma came out.

"What is happening here, Neveah? And Easton, what are you doing outside? Neveah, invite him and his friend inside. Don't be rude." *Ma, this is not the time for you to be the good host.*

Me, rude? Okay, I was, but they deserved it.

"Won't you ask your dear Easton who his friend is?" I looked at Easton, waiting for him to explain.

"Ma'am, this is Alden."

Ma gasped, and Bryan tried to hit Alden.

"Stop, Bryan. We are not like him." I managed to pull my hand away and blocked Bryan.

"Get out and take your friend with you," Bryan growled. I looked around to see the neighbours watching the scene unfold.

"Neveah, you will listen to me for a minute, and you can do whatever you want after I finish speaking," Easton said with so much authority, that I kept my mouth shut. Well, that was a first for me. Even Ma and Bryan didn't oppose.

"Speak, Alden," Easton ordered him.

"L-listen, Neveah, I'm sorry. You have no idea how sorry I am. What I did to you was wrong, and I admit it. What happened was a big misunderstanding. I love Melissa more than anything in the world." I tried to interrupt, but he held his hand up.

"I love her, and I know she loves me too. I just had a problem that she was, well… with many guys. I got so frustrated that I couldn't help falling for her. No matter what I did, I couldn't get past it. So I tried to show that it didn't affect me when it really did. When I saw her with Liam, I was beyond jealous. I wanted to take out my anger on her, but I couldn't bring myself to do so, and there you were making fun of my pain. I am sorry. I shouldn't have lost control. If you want to take any legal action against me, I don't have any problem. So, yeah that's it."

I laughed out loud— really, really loudly!

He was freaking unbelievable.

The best part was when he said that I was making fun of his pain. What about the times when he and his gang did the same to me when they were the ones who caused me pain? That just didn't count, right?

Easton, Alden, Ma, and Bryan were looking at me like I had lost my mind.

"Are you finished, Alden?" I asked in a disinterested tone.

"Yes." He didn't look happy at my response. I would have forgiven him eventually if he didn't make me listen to his little speech. Now, I had a lot to think about.

"Neveah?" Easton was looking at me with an adorably confused expression on his face. *Okay, adorable?* Where did that come from? Anyway…

"I will give my answer tomorrow. Meet me at the diner near the school. I'll call Melissa, too. As for you, Easton. We have to discuss the project."

Alden looked irritated while Easton was visibly elated.

"Alright, Neveah. See you tomorrow in school." Easton bid farewell.

"I am not coming to school tomorrow." I wanted to go, but Ma advised me against it. Easton nodded in understanding, but what he did next shocked me to the core.

He wrapped an arm around my waist and hugged me.

"Goodnight, Neveah."

Curving my lips stiffly, I closed the door and turned to my mother. "I have no idea why he did that."

"I wasn't asking anything," Ma said, but I knew clearly what was going on in her brain.

I narrowed my eyes at her.

"Okay, maybe I would have asked," she said while twiddling her thumbs.

I scoffed and playfully glared at her. "You lie real bad, Ma."

"Whatever," she stuck her tongue out childishly.

The rest of the evening went relatively smooth. We had dinner, and soon after, Ma and Bryan retired to their room while I watched TV a little longer.

I took my cell and messaged Melissa to meet me tomorrow after school in the diner. *So much to do tomorrow!* I took the pills and went to sleep.

I knew I was asleep, but I could feel someone watching me. I tried to open my eyes, but it felt like my eyelids were glued together. *Damn eyes.* I heard some shuffling, so I just stayed still. Then I felt a puff of air on my forehead. Okay, that was definitely someone's breath.

Okay, so someone was standing over my bed. Nothing to worry at all! My sarcasm game was strong.

The breath then shifted to my eyes, my nose, and then my lips. Heck, I could even taste the person! Then it continued to my neck.

The next thing I knew was that a pair of lips was pressed on my forehead. I wanted to open my eyes, but I was scared of what I would see. If the person thought that I was asleep, maybe he or she would leave.

But the next second, I felt the same breath near my lips. They were dangerously close to mine.

I couldn't take it anymore, and I jerked awake.

What the hell just happened?

I woke up and abruptly switched on the light near the nightstand. I looked around the room to find the damned person who was literally breathing down my neck but found the whole room empty. No one was here except me.

Had I imagined the whole thing?

No, it couldn't be. It felt way too real.

I was so confused, and why didn't I open my eyes in the first place?

I came to the conclusion that it was a dream. That was it, nothing else.

Just for the sake of my sanity, however, I searched the whole room— below my bed, in the closet, and even the toilet. It was safe to say that there was no sign of anyone. I looked at the time. It was just over five in the morning, so I stopped trying and went back to sleep.

I couldn't help thinking about those lips, though. They were soft.

Wait, why was I dreaming of a pair of lips? This was so unlike me. It must've been the drugs!

Go to sleep, Neveah, you got to speak to Alden tomorrow.

Easton

I stayed up all night thinking about Neveah. I was very anxious the whole day after dishing out the sentence to Alden. I had to know whether she was alright or not.

I had to find an excuse, so I came up with an apology. I called Alden and dragged him to Neveah's house. When we reached there, I instantly recognised her sweet scent. She was only wearing shorts and a baggy shirt, but she looked good nonetheless— very, very good.

But I didn't understand why she laughed after Alden spoke up. I thought about it for a long time, but I couldn't come up with anything. She told us to meet at the diner. She also reminded me about that chemistry project. If it weren't for the project, I wouldn't be able to spend time with her.

The sight of her bruises and marks angered me again, and I regretted Alden's existence once more.

I couldn't help but hug her while leaving. I just had to make sure that she was alright and in my arms. I saw Gina smile at me and wiggle her eyebrows. Looks like she was able to guess my feelings! Actually, anyone can, except my own mate because she was too dense.

I couldn't sleep, so I went to her house. Her window was left open, and it made it all the easier for me.

And there she was, sleeping like the most innocent thing in the world even though she was far from it. She occupied the whole bed, spreading out like a starfish. She looked beautiful with the moonlight reflecting on her. Her hair was strewn on the pillow, making her look so calm and serene.

I officially sounded like an emotional chick.

I watched over her like a stalker. After about an hour, I just couldn't resist it. I moved closer to her and sat on her bed. I breathed in her scent. It was mouthwatering. Then I pressed my lips to her forehead.

I removed my lips with great care and brought them near hers. I could feel her breath in mine. I wanted to kiss her badly, but I held myself back.

She instinctively raised her lips to meet mine, but I couldn't do it. Not when she was asleep. That would be a huge blow to my ego.

I had to leave. If I didn't leave now, I never would.

I felt her stirring, so I went out of her window and stood on the railing.

Neveah

I wake up late the next day. The dream didn't bother me anymore because I was sure the incident was only a damn dream. I got up and did my chores. Ma and Bryan had already left for work. Thankfully, she had already made breakfast. I could do many things, but I couldn't cook much.

After breakfast, I did some homework and caught up on Ryder and Danny. Broody had exams next week so he couldn't be bothered.

When it was finally time, I got ready and went to the diner.

"Hey, Nev." The manager and owner of the diner greeted me.

"Hey, Stuart." I smiled at him. Ma and I were usual customers in this place.

"Where's Gina?"

"Work. She got engaged." I inform him with a huge smile.

"Great. Who is he and what does he do?" I told him about Bryan, his job, and other stuff. Stuart was like a brother to Ma, so it was alright.

"I'm meeting people from school for a group project." I hated group projects, and this time, I couldn't even blame the teachers. I brought this upon myself.

"Sure, Neveah."

I waited for some more time. Melissa was the first one to come, followed by Easton and Alden None of them spoke anything, so I had to break the silence first.

"I called you all here to speak about what happened yesterday." Alden was about to interrupt me when I spoke again. "Alden, I would appreciate it if you will listen to me first. You can voice out your thoughts afterwards." He didn't seem happy but nodded, nonetheless.

"First of all, what happened yesterday was my fault. I was the one who came up with the '*make Alden jealous'* plan.

Okay, I don't get when you both fell in love and the other stuff, but I do know that Melissa was sad. Wait, no, she looked like she was going to commit suicide." I tried to keep my voice down for the sake of my health but barely managed to do so. "I wanted to help her, so I devised this whole plan along with Liam. What I didn't expect was a murder attempt on me." I explained and took a deep breath to try to calm myself down.

This was the first time that someone has behaved like that with me. It amounted to physical abuse.

"Yeah, I know you are sorry and shit, but I am not here for that," I muttered when all three of them were going to interrupt me.

"I am sorry. I know all of this was because of me," Melissa spoke up.

"It was not your fault," I said, "but I am not here for that. I am here to talk about you and Alden. I am doing this because Melissa is my best friend... no, my ex-BFF! Whatever! And I think it will be better if Easton is here." Somehow, I knew that Easton wouldn't allow Alden to harm me. The thought sounded so ridiculous to me, but something had changed.

I cleared my throat and started speaking.

"Alden, this is for you. One, when you came to my house, you said that you don't have a problem if I hand you to the cops, right? But dear Alden, you mister don't have a bloody choice. I do. No matter what decision I make, you have to go along with it. You are not doing me a favour. You are paying for your damned mistakes. Two, you told me that you don't want to be with Melissa because she was associated with other people. Say, are you pure like white snow? Three, I suggest you keep your good-for-nothing ego to yourself. Four, you are not God, so stop acting like one. If not for you, Melissa had many other options… hotter options, I may include."

I waited for Alden to reply or something, but nothing happened. He was too shocked. Melissa was, too, but Easton had a smirk on his face.

Since I didn't get a reaction, I continued with my speech.

"For you, Melissa. One, choose better people to fall in love with. Two, you are perfect as it is. Love is ignoring the faults, not pointing them out. Three… this is just a suggestion, but I think Alden won't do you any good."

"As for you, Easton." I looked at him to find him still smirking.

"You and I have chemistry to discuss."

As soon as I finished my speech Alden stormed out, and Melissa walked out after some time. I didn't ask her anything. She needed time to think.

"That went well," I murmured.

"Sure, that went well." Easton was still smirking.

"I am alive without any bruises," I said with a smirk of my own.

His eyes darkened when I mentioned bruises. His eyes travelled to my neck and back to my face.

He stood up to leave.

"Hey, where are you going?"

"To the washroom," came his simple reply. His fists were clenched. Something was clearly wrong.

"Go alone," I said to try to lighten the mood.

It worked.

"Yes, ma'am." He even mock saluted me.

"Don't push it, Eugene."

Chapter 6

Neveah

It had been about half an hour, and Easton still hasn't returned from the washroom. I sighed and continued munching on my fries.

Just when I almost finished them, Easton turned up looking haywire.

"I told you to go alone, Eugene." I playfully scolded him. Images of Easton and some other girl doing something in the washroom flashed in my mind.

"Mind your business, Neveah," he growled, not meeting my eye. *Someone is angry!*

"Ouch, that hurt," I said with a pout. As soon as I said that, he snapped his head to look at me and his angry expression melted away.

"I'm sorry." Easton looked so sincere, I almost had a heart attack.

Did I hear it right? Easton was apologizing to me?

Wow! I stood up and placed my hand on his forehead. "Are you alright?"

"What?" He just shrugged as if he was not aware of his own actions.

"You actually said sorry. Of all the times you discouraged, pushed, and made fun of me, this is the first time in all twelve years that you apologized," I stated. Twelve long years of torment and he was saying sorry now.

"I… I did not do those things to you, did I?" Disbelief was written all over his face.

"No, Easton Dale. It wasn't you, it was your doppelgänger." I was shaking with laughter by now. When did he start caring? As far as I knew, I was just the fatherless daughter of his mother's best friend.

He sat down shakily on the chair and put his head in his hands and his elbows on the table. I heard a faint sound but couldn't quite make out what it was.

"Huh?" I realized that he was talking to himself.

"I hurt you," he said as he looked into my eyes, his own green ones full of anguish.

"You're really late. It took you twelve years to realize that? Better late than never, I guess! Anyway, I'm here to discuss chemistry with you," I said with a scoff.

He looked at me for a split-second with a wounded expression before he spoke up. "Do you hate me, Neveah?" Okay, where was this coming from? I thought he was just messing with me like always.

I thought about a diplomatic reply and said, "You are not worth it."

"Your hate?"

I shook my head. "My time."

"Am I that bad?" The pained expression was back.

Ugh! What was wrong with this guy? Why did he want to know whether I hated him or not? "Listen, Easton, it does not matter what I think about you. As I have said before, I need marks, and you need them too, badly if I must admit. So do both of us a favour and concentrate on the project. As for me hating you, I don't. You don't matter enough for me to hate or love you."

I felt guilty that I said it, but truth stings. He nodded in response, but I could see that he was still sad. His usually sparkly green eyes were dull. The worst part was that I was the one who put that look in his eyes.

"Okay. So we need to choose a topic and make a presentation, model, and observation report for it." I quickly changed the topic.

"But we have to do only one of them!" *God!* How did he even manage to pass till now?

"Extra credits." For him to get normal credits were impossible, let alone extra ones.

"Alright, but I feel we should do a project on physical chemistry." Easton's suggestion had me looking up at him in wonder.

"You know what physical chemistry is?" I'm impressed. For a guy who was failing, he sure knew things. He just glared at me, and I sighed in response.

"You are right. There will be a lot of practical work in inorganic and organic. I think we should go with Blocks of the Periodic Table."

"Sure. Now, where should we complete the project?"

"We can do it in my house. It is empty for most of the time, but not today. I am still not feeling well enough to do some serious thinking." I sighed. I was still sleepy. These drugs were messing with me.

We left the place after Easton forcefully paid for my food. I folded my arms and glared at him the whole time he paid the bill.

Just as we were about to go in our different directions, I caught his hand and tugged him towards me. "Don't be so sad, Easton. It's not you."

His lips curved into a trademark *Easton smirk* that the ladies of the school would die for.

The next day, I was busy rummaging through my closet for something appropriate to wear to school when Bryan entered the room.

"Hey, Dad."

"I will never get used to that word," he whispered.

"No one said you had to." I went and hugged him. He kissed my head in return.

"My beautiful daughter!" His eyes sparkled with love for me.

"You are the only guy who says that," I said. I let him go and looked at my closet again.

"You have no idea how happy I am about that fact," he muttered under his breath.

"So, what's up?" I asked him. Bryan was surely not here to pay me a visit.

"Dress fast. We are having a family meeting."

I chuckled. I was going to attend a family meeting for the first time. “Can you choose something for me to wear?”

Surprisingly, he chose a short skirt, a tank top, and a jean jacket. For a second, I thought that he would make me wear a nun gown.

“I’m impressed, Dad. You have good fashion sense.” I patted him on the back in appreciation.

“That’s what your mother says.” He had a sly smirk on his face.

“Gross.” I pushed him out of the room and dressed fast.

Ma and Bryan, I mean, Dad were passionately kissing when I came down. They both jumped apart when they heard my footsteps.

“Get a room.” Ma blushed, and Bryan just wiped his lips, probably of lip gloss.

“So, what’s up?”

“The reason we called you is to discuss the wedding,” Ma spoke after she regained her composure.

“I’m okay with anything, but you are not allowed to choose a pink colour in any part of the wedding.” I hated pink with a passion, and there was no way I was wearing it to any wedding, especially my mother’s.

“Okay, but you have to wear a typical bridesmaid dress.” *Oh, for the love of...*

“I’ll wear it. Okay, people, I’m off.” I kissed Ma on the cheek, and off I was to school.

"You look nice, Nevy." I was with Melissa, who was abnormally happy today.

"Why do you look so happy?" I was suddenly suspicious. Just yesterday, she looked like she was about to commit suicide.

"I thought a lot about what you said yesterday. You're right. He doesn't love me, and no matter what, I cannot change that. So I have decided to live my life the way I want it, and I got to say, that Alden is not at all happy with all this arrangement. He is royally pissed."

And all of that happened in one night?

"Let's hope he keeps his hands to himself," was all I could say to her. How she got over the love of her life in one night was beyond me! Or maybe she hasn't? Upon closer inspection, I could see that she had dark circles carefully hidden by a thick layer of makeup, and her eyes were a little red.

Maybe she hadn't moved on yet. Perhaps she was just trying to be strong. At that moment, I felt a sense of respect towards Melissa.

"Oh, he will. Otherwise, he will kill him," she muttered.

"Who will kill whom?" I asked her while scrolling through my phone.

"No one." She looked uncomfortable, so I didn't pry further. "Have you heard that there is a new hot guy in school?"

"You're unbelievable!" She just recovered for a severe heartache, and now she was already checking out another guy? The disappointment must have shown on my face because she pulled my hand and led us into an empty classroom.

"Nev, I am not what people think I am. I have not been with more than five guys, and I have never slept with Easton." She confessed and waited for my reaction.

Wow! Five was less, right? "That's good… I think, and I don't care if you have slept with Eugene or not." There was no need to tell me such things. That was their personal business. A small part of me was relieved, though. "Let's leave for class."

"Ah! I almost forgot about you being brainy," she said with a smirk on her face.

"With the size of yours, you need mine too." I teased back and watched her smirk fall off.

"Whatever."

Retaliate, baby, but you do need them.

"Class, let me introduce to you a new student from London, Mr. Gregory Lawsin." On queue, a boy who looked like Xavier's younger version entered the room.

Black hair, check.

Pathetic smirk, check.

An overdose of attitude, double check.

"Who wants to show him around the school?" *Thank the teacher's stars!* Almost all the girls were ready, including my dear ex-BFF. For a woman who was going through severe heartache, she was quite friendly! "The girls would show him around, alright." Again, I couldn't keep my mouth shut!

The new guy heard me since I was sitting on the first bench and looked at me in a weird way. I didn't know whether the teacher heard it or if she was ignoring my statements.

"Alright, I'll choose. Neveah, you will be the one." Ah, she heard it!

Oh, for the love of...

"Thank you, ma'am." I didn't miss the way his eyes raked through my figure. Thank you, Bryan!

I looked at him and yawned. "Sure," I said with a sigh. I could actually feel his ego crushing, and it felt so good.

He came and sat beside me because that was the only vacant seat in the class.

"Hello, miss." Now he was irritating me.

I turned towards him and smiled. "Shut up, Mr. Lawsin."

Snickers were heard throughout the room. "Ouch, dude," the one and only Xavier said. The guy just couldn't keep his mouth shut.

"Piece of advice, stay away from her. She is of no use to us guys," he shouted from the last bench. The new guy looked somewhat shocked by this. I turned to Xavier and just winked at him.

"So, what's your name?" I was now walking with the new boy and actually showing him around the campus.

"Oh, come on, tell me your name." This had to the fifth time he asked me.

"Neveah Huber," I answered at last.

"Middle name?" He looked at me expectantly.

"Gail," I replied at once. Otherwise, he would irritate me over it again.

"What does Gail mean?" And here I thought he would shut up. "I don't know. My mother liked it, so she gave me that name."

"All these years, you didn't ask her what it meant? You didn't even try to find out on your own?"

I just turned to him and glared. I left him without an answer and walked towards the cafeteria.

"Hey, answer me." Gregory's voice rang out on the whole café, and suddenly, everyone was quiet.

I ignored him and went to the line. I thanked my lucky stars that the line was not big. I could get my food easily!

I thought that I got rid of the new guy, but then I saw him talking with Melissa who looked very happy. For a second, I was tempted to not sit with them, but I swallowed my childishness and went anyway.

"You have a very good BFF." I knew for a fact that good meant hot. Melissa was hot, and even I was not going to deny it.

"Thank you." He then proceeded to take some food out of my plate.

"Hey! Put that back!" I swatted his hand, and he pulled it to his chest along with my fries.

"But it's just some fries." Gregory scoffed.

They weren't any other fries. They were *my* fries, and no one messes with my fries.

"A piece of info, Gregory, never mess with Neveah's food. She's very possessive about it," Melissa said while wiggling her eyebrows.

"Okay, I won't take it next time."

I glared at him but didn't say anything.

The whole lunch period, he kept on flirting with Melissa and irritating me though I had to say that the guy had a sense of humour.

"I am going to call you Georgy," I told him.

He put an arm around me. "Why?"

"Because I can." I winked at him.

We were walking to our last class, chemistry. We as in me, Melissa, and the new boy. To my extreme bad luck, we were all in the same class. The man up there clearly didn't like me!

"Good afternoon, everyone. Today, you are to sit with your project partners and discuss your respective projects," the teacher announced.

Georgy was sad, I was sadder, and Melissa was the saddest. I went and sat with Easton who was busy shooting glares at the new guy's back. I didn't know that he was a closet gay. *Sheesh!* "I know you find his ass tempting, but can we discuss marks for at least some time, then you can go back to staring at whoever's ass you want."

Instead of looking angry he looked rather happy. "Jealous?"

"Either you are desperate, or you have lost your mind. Actually, I think it is the second option because I have seen you with tonnes of girls. Believe me, all I felt was a feeling of, whoa, wait, I don't feel anything for you. So, where were we?"

I could clearly see his face etching in anger, but that made me feel so good and bad at the same time.

“We will start the project today at your house.” Easton swiftly changed the subject.

“Alright, today at four in my house,” I said.

“I can only come by five. Can we set it an hour late?” He didn’t sound like the cool jock guy he was supposed to be.

What crawled up his spine? Or maybe someone hasn’t. I mentally giggled at that.

“Fine,” I said.

Chapter 7

Neveah

I was cleaning my room after school when the doorbell rang. I opened the door to see Melissa and the new guy standing on our doorstep.

"What are you both doing here?" The surprise in my tone was very evident.

"Well, we were bored, so we came to see you," Melissa replied.

"You actually want me to believe that? And if you both were bored, I'm sure there are other ways of keeping you both busy without me," I deadpanned.

Georgy smiled. "True enough, Neveah, but I would rather prefer spending time with you than keeping myself occupied in other ways." By the time he said the last sentence, he had brought his face very close to mine.

"Was that supposed to be a pickup line?" Even Bryan had better lines than that. He seriously needed to improve his womanizing skills.

"Uh, yeah," he said and flushed a light shade of pink.

"It didn't work at all. Try better ones next time." Then I kissed his cheek because he looked so cute.

"Alright, enough of flirting. Let us in, Nev." Melissa was huffing and puffing.

"Jealous, Mel?" I asked in a sweet tone. I didn't want her to feel ignored by the new boy since she and the rest of the girls in the school were raving about him all morning.

"I'm not the only one," she muttered with a smirk on her face.

"What?" What was with her and her weird statements?

I cleared my mind and invited them in. "Whatever. Come on in."

The three of us settled on the living room couch. We were watching some stupid show when Georgy broke the silence.

"Come on, Nev. Let's do something better," he said out of the blue.

"What do you have in mind, Georgy?" I asked, sitting closer to him to rile up Melissa.

"Play a game? Truth or dare?" He put an arm around me, and we both looked at Melissa expectantly.

She didn't look irritated. Plan failed! "Okay, let's start. We can spin my pen."

"You carry a pen, Melissa?" I didn't mean to say it aloud, but my traitor mouth couldn't stay shut.

"Very funny, Nev," she retorted.

"Actually, it is," I countered back. It was funny. Well, at least for me.

On the first spin, the pen landed on Melissa's side.

"Truth or dare?" I asked.

"Truth."

"Who is your favourite person?" Georgy asked.

"Well, she is in front of me," she said with a soft smile.

Me? Wow!

I couldn't help smiling, and my heart swelled. Well, at least someone likes me.

"Thanks, Mel." She smiled back at me. I got up and hugged her.

"Oh, God! So much love is making my eyes bleed." And the moment had to be interrupted by Mr. Lawsin.

"Shut up, Georgy." Melissa didn't take the interruption too well.

The next turn was on Georgy.

"What do you choose, Georgy?" I questioned.

"Truth."

"What do you think about Neveah?" Melissa asked.

I glared at her.

"She is rude and arrogant but hot, and I like it. I like you… but more like a sister."

"Way to crush my ego, Lawsin." I pretended to be hurt. "Damn my sensitive ego!"

"You guys. Let's get back to the game," Melissa chuckled.

By playing truth or dare with them, I learned a lot of things. I found out that Melissa's favourite colour was grey and not hot pink and that she actually somewhat liked science now. *Shocker!* Her tastes have changed drastically over the years. She was not the Melissa I knew.

I also learned that Georgy was at the top of his previous school and that he was good in track. *Rival alert!* I would have to watch out. We spent the whole time asking silly questions to each other. I got bored with truth, so I chose dare instead. Both of them were still deciding on the dare when the bell rang again.

I was getting up to open the door when Melissa spoke. "Kiss the person on the door."

Was she serious?

"No way." I had a right to refuse. It could be anyone. What if it was Bryan or worse, the postman?

"A dare is a dare, Nev." Georgy added more fuel to the fire. No way was I kissing any stranger. I knew that it was not Ma since she had informed me that she would reach home at ten, and it was only five.

I didn't reply and just opened the door. Standing in front of me was Easton Dale. Why was he here? That was when I saw the chemistry textbook in his hand. Oh yes, the stupid project!

That was when I also remembered the dare. *Dang it!* Should I do it?

Okay, here goes nothing. I took a deep breath and prepared myself.

I pulled down his head and hastily pressed my lips to his. I stiffly kept myself pressed against him for five seconds when his arms encircled my waist and pulled me more into him. My knees almost buckled from the force.

We kissed for almost a minute before I realized where I was and pulled back.

He, however, had other plans. He pulled me back so that our lips brushed again. I squirmed in his arms till he set me free.

"What the hell, dude?" I shouted at him.

"What do you mean by hell? I should be asking that question." There was a pleased smile on his face.

I wiped my lips and was about to reply when a voice was heard from inside the house. "Who's the lucky person, Nev?" Georgy came out. To my surprise, Easton's face suddenly darkened.

"What is going on here, Neveah?"

Before I could answer, Georgy spoke again. "Nothing. I, Nev, and Mel were playing truth or dare. Nev was dared to kiss the person at the door. Luckily, it wasn't her mother or any old guy."

"This was a stupid dare?"

"Ye—"

"Yup, all for the love of a dare. So what are you doing here?" Melissa interrupted me.

"Project." Again before I could answer, Easton did it for me.

I frowned. Why were they answering for me?

"Come in." Georgy invited Easton on my behalf.

I grumbled under my breath. Now, this was just ridiculous.

"We'll leave, Nev," Melissa said as she collected her purse.

"Okay, have a nice day of whatever's left."

She smiled and waved, and I waved back. While leaving, she also winked at Easton who winked back as well!

What the hell?

Georgy, to my surprise, came and hugged me. He lifted me off the ground and twirled. Then he set me back at the same place before backing off.

"What was that?"

"Just a usual goodbye." He smiled and kissed my head before leaving. What a weird guy. I waited on the porch while they were walking back. When I turned around, I caught Easton staring at Georgy with an unreadable expression.

"Would you stop staring at his ass, Easton?" I tried to get a reaction from him.

"I can't help it, Neveah." He was smirking. Every trace of irritation from before vanished into thin air. Plan fired again!

"Come on in." I let him in and closed the door.

"Let's get started," he said in a business-like tone.

"Never thought I would live to see this day," I mumbled under my breath.

"Did you say something, Neveah?" he spoke as if he was trying to imply something. He did this little smirk which clearly showed that he heard what I said. It was practically impossible, though, since the human ear was not that sensitive.

"Nothing, Easton."

We then got to work. For a guy who never listened during class, he had real good knowledge about chemistry.

"How come you know so many things?" I asked bewildered.

"Just because I don't care doesn't mean I don't know." Now, I was confused as to what he was talking about.

"You are absolutely weird, Easton."

He made a big smile when I said that.

"I'm not sure that it was a compliment."

"It is the closest thing to a compliment I can get from you, so thank you." It was true, anyway.

"Okay, enough break time, back to studies." He beamed at me again. He seemed so happy and free. It was so different from the guy I knew and disliked.

We discussed the project after that, sometimes in peace and sometimes with a lot of bickering, and they were mostly started by me. It was not my fault that we were polar opposites. Opposites attract was not true in our case.

The rest of the evening was spent in the same way. I was surprised that he did not complain or taunt me in any form. That was one great accomplishment for him!

It was almost eight in the evening, and I went for a long time without food. "Come on, Easton. It's enough for today. I'm too hungry to think." I went to the kitchen to make something simple. If I was hungry, then Easton must have been starving.

"Hey," I called out to Easton who was still in the hall, "are you having something?"

I heard some shuffling, and a moment later, he entered the kitchen. "Are you actually offering food?"

"I am not a heartless creature like you, Eugene," I answered and went to remove the dishes from the dishwasher.

"I am far from being heartless, my Neveah." I heard a voice in my ear and felt a pair of arms wrap around my waist.

"What are you doing, Easton?" I whispered, his closeness affecting me in a way that it shouldn't.

"What do you think I am doing, Neveah?" His arms tightened around me.

"Easton, stop." My voice came out weaker than I intended it to be. What was happening with me?

"Do you want me to?" His voice dipped an octave lower. Even though some small irrational part of me didn't want him to stop, I turned back to face him.

Bad choice. His face was now dangerously close to mine. If anyone entered the room now, they would think that we were a real couple. "You have thirty seconds to remove your hands from my body before I put mine on yours, and I mean it in a violent way." If he thought that I would not hit him, he was sorely mistaken.

Easton, however, seemed to find my words funny. He moved so that he was hugging me and his lips were near my ear. "I don't mind your hands on me, babe, no matter how violent it would be."

With the ongoing banter between us, I had not paid attention to my surroundings. Just as I was about to hit the rascal in front of me, I heard a gasp.

I turned to the door and came face-to-face with my dear wide-eyed mother. Why did Ma have to arrive early today?

I turned back to Easton to see him smirking at me.

Easton Dale, you are so screwed.

Chapter 8

Dinner was awkward, to say the least. Ma made Easton have dinner in our house. The whole time, my mother was giving me looks, and Easton was smirking at me. I so wanted to wipe that smirk out of his face with my fists.

Luckily, Bryan turned up late. The last thing I wanted was a father's speech, especially if it was about Easton. We were all sitting on the dining table, but no conversation was made. Easton was sitting next to me and was busy gulping his food like a starved person. On the other hand, I was just pushing around the food on my plate. I absolutely had no interest in the food. That was something new for me!

Damn you, Eugene, for taking away my interest from food!

Thankfully, Ma was not saying anything in front of him. Thinking about her reaction when she saw us wrapped around each other in the kitchen was enough for me.

Every now and then, Ma would give me sly looks when she thought Easton wasn't looking. I just breathed and kept a fake smile plastered on my face even thought I had the intentions of murdering the other two people in the room.

Dinner was over at last. Easton thanked my mother for the delicious food. He even kissed my mother on the cheek.

"Why don't you say goodbye, Nev? I'll go inside and clean the table." Her subtle suggestion wasn't lost on me, and I gave her the stink eye.

"Sure, Ma." Right now, some alone time with him was just what I wanted. Not to say goodbye or anything, but to harm him in a very, very bad way.

"Bye, Neveah." I was very sure that Ma was watching us from the kitchen window, so I pretended that I was actually saying goodbye even though I was one step away from killing him.

"Bye, Easton."

He hugged me, and I let him for the meantime.

As soon as I was sure that Ma was no longer watching, I pushed Easton off me.

I took hold of the buttons of his shirt to pull him down so that he was of my height. "What were you doing in the kitchen, Eugene?"

"Nothing." He tried to feign innocence, but I was growing tired of his shit.

Rage boiled through my veins, and I was in no mood for his playboy attitude right now. "Look, Eugene, come near me again and I promise you that some part of your body will be deeply injured." He may not take my threat seriously, but I surely meant what I said, and there would be consequences.

He didn't reply and just kissed my head and left.

Just after giving him a threat, I let him near me. How would he take me and my words seriously?

I just huffed and went back inside.

Time to face the mother!

I quickly escaped to my room while she was cleaning. I knew that she would question me sooner or later, but I felt that later was better because then I could think of some excuses.

I was about to sleep that night when I heard a knock on my door. Oh no, here comes the mother.

"Come in." To my surprise, Bryan entered.

"What's up, kiddo?"

I sat up and made him sit too. "Nothing. I was just about to sleep."

"Okay, but we have to discuss something important." His face turned totally serious. "My parents want to meet you and Gina." I knew that Bryan's parents were the jerky rich kind of people. I also knew that his family was not happy that he was marrying a woman with a child… let alone a teenage child.

I decided to shut my trap on this one. "Alright, that's it?" I didn't say anything else, not wanting to insult his parents. He loved them, and they loved him too no matter how much they hated my Ma.

"No, I know that my family is disappointed, especially my mother. I also know that Gina will not say a thing even if she insulted her. I just want you to take care of that. Just show her… sorry for my inappropriate language… *who the 'head bitch' is*." He did the quotes with his fingers.

Oh, thank God! I wouldn't have been able to keep my mouth shut, anyway. "That's what I will be there for, Bryan." I promised him and thumped my fist on my heart, trying to make a joke out of it so he doesn't get distressed.

"Okay, be ready by seven."

We then talked about some trivial things. Before he left, he gave me a *dad hug,* as he called it, and a usual peck on the forehead. Just as he was about the close the door, he poked his head back in and said, “I heard what happened in the kitchen today.” And with that, he closed the door.

Uhh! Easton Dale, damn you!

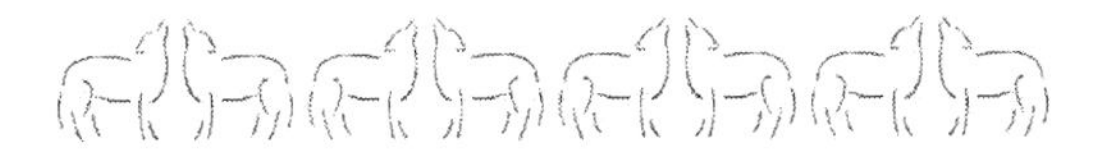

Next day in school was fun. Melissa and Georgy were behaving like two drunk teenagers. It was lunch, and they were running all around the cafeteria bumping into people and making fun of them.

“Neveah, we missed you.” This was the tenth time they shouted it. By the third time, I decided to ignore them and concentrate on my work.

Georgy came and sat with me on our table. “I missed you, Lively.”

“Who is Lively?”

“You, my dear, are Lively,” he replied with a chuckle.

What the hell was he talking about? The confusion must have shown on my face because he spoke up the next second. “I searched the meaning of Gail on the net, and it says that the name means lively.”

“Alright.” So he actually searched my name. That was sweet of him, but before I could reply, he took Melissa, and they were on their way again. I got bored with reading the book, so I started looking around.

My eyes met the one person I wanted to avoid right now, the one and only Eugene!

Our eyes met, and he started smirking. I remembered yesterday's events and my temper flared up. I glared back at him, but my glare did not seem to affect him at all. His smirk only became wider.

Stupid guy!

However, we did not shift our gazes. It was like a competition as to who would avert their gaze first. I was glaring for God knows how long when a pair of arms wrapped around me.

"Hey, Nev! What are you doing?" Melissa spoke, but it was Georgy who wrapped himself around me. Did they have their own private party or something after they left my home yesterday? They sure weren't acting normally.

I turned back to look at Easton who was now conversing with some blonde female who I recognized to be from one of Melissa's old group. I didn't know why, but somehow, I was feeling bad that he was talking to her. Something was wrong with me.

"Why were you staring at each other?" It was Georgy who asked. He looked adorable with that cute frown and pouted lips. He was fully acting like a girl and definitely drunk.

"Nothing." Georgy didn't ask for any elaboration after that.

The whole day passed with me glaring at Eugene at every chance I got.

I was excited to go home because we were going to Bryan's house today. The best part was that I had official permission to be rude and bratty. I never behaved that way unless the situation calls for it, which was the case most of the time.

I only do that in school because people there couldn't understand the normal one.

Ma and I were ready by seven. We were currently waiting for our escort to arrive, who happened to be just Bryan.

Ma looked pretty in a simple grey dress that looked classy but with a hint of sexy. I seriously hoped that there wouldn't be any scenes because no matter how much I would enjoy them, Ma would not. She absolutely loathed the idea of fights and misunderstandings.

Bryan arrived behind schedule so we too reached a bit late. As soon as we passed the massive gates, I was rendered speechless. It wasn't a house, it was a mansion! Their family was in the interior of the town, somewhat near Easton's house, and now I understand why!

"Wow! This is beautiful!" I couldn't even stop my words. Ma, too, looked mesmerized. Who wouldn't be?

Bryan parked his car directly in front of the huge door. A man came running from behind the house and took the keys from him. *Oh god!* They had their own valet!

I didn't have to look at Ma to know that she was a hundred times more nervous than she was before.

I placed a hand on her back to provide comfort. Bryan rang the bell, and the only thought in my head was, *please let everything be alright.*

Mrs. Walter was a woman of gems. She had stones all over her. If she was doing this to show off her wealth, she was highly successful. She made the house help get us some refreshments and drinks. She was also very beautiful. Something in her told me that she used her allure for her own selfish benefits.

Mr. Walter was a relatively humble man. Even though Bryan had told me that both his parents had problems regarding this marriage, his father did not show it openly unlike his wife.

Mrs. Walters hadn't even acknowledged our presence till now and by our, I mean Ma and me. She welcomed her own son with open arms.

My dislike for this woman was turning stronger by each second. I understood that she was a bit upset that her son was marrying a single mother, but at least she could try to get to know my mother. If she still had a problem after that, then something was really wrong with her.

"Hey, Mum." Bryan greeted her. "This is my beautiful fiancée, Gina, and our gorgeous daughter, Neveah. Darling, this is my mother, Claire." He wrapped his arms around Ma's waist, and she leaned into him. They looked so cute together. They were the perfect couple. I smiled at that thought.

"Please make yourselves at home." Her tone and eyes spoke otherwise. This was going to be one long night.

Dinner was served, and it was downright delicious. Claire's food made up for the lost mood though I was very sure that it was not her own cooking. During the whole dinner, Claire made sure that my mother would be looked upon.

The best part came after dinner when the desserts arrived. We were all having custard when the bell rang. Then entered a blonde lady who looked like a model. He had long tanned legs, perfect makeup, and, let's not forget, lots of gems on her. She looked like a walking gem store.

As soon as she entered, she wrapped herself around Bryan, who looked way too uncomfortable. The best part was that she was wearing a golden dress which made her look like a goldfish.

"Rebecca darling, it's so nice of you to drop in here. It's been so long since you and Bryan have been together." Such a cheap move, Claire.

The new girl, Rebecca, replied with equal enthusiasm. "Oh, Claire, come on, families don't thank each other. Do they, Bryan?" She did that fake giggling thing.

Wow! She made good use of the figure of speech, especially with the family part. Ma looked sad before, but now she looked depressed. Luckily, Bryan came to her rescue. "Yes, family don't thank each other." He muttered the family part while looking at Ma. Then he got up from the sofa and embraced her

"Rebecca, I would like to introduce to you my lovely fiancée, Gina Huber, and my daughter, Neveah." I was very surprised when he called me his daughter and so were the other people in the room. Go, Bryan!

Claire recovered the fastest and was trying to engage Bryan and Rebecca in a conversation with each other. What was the problem with these people? I didn't understand. So the want for a glamorous daughter-in-law was more important than her own child's wishes?

After a lot of awkward silence, Rebecca spoke up, "We should go to this party nearby." *Seriously!*

"Oh, yes! Peter's party is going on nearby. We should all go," Claire replied.

What kind of a party would it be if people her age attended it? Oh, yes! It would be a party where all the men would drink and speak of how much money they made while their female counterparts would speak about how much of their partner's money they had spent this weekend.

How boring!

Bryan tried to convince them that it would be a bad idea, but no one paid heed to his words. This showed just how high Claire thought of us. God knows she just wanted us to get out of her house. She could have said it by herself instead of sending us to an unknown place full of strangers.

The party was in a hotel near the mansion. As soon as we neared the place, I recognized it to be one of the hotels owned by the Dale Group of Industries. Peter was a man with his hand on many pies, and hotel business was just one of them. Though I knew the owner, I had never been inside the hotel.

If I thought the mansion was the most beautiful thing I had ever seen, I so have been proved wrong! I have never been to such a classy place in all my life as in this hotel. The whole place was glimmering with broad leather couches, fountains of champagne, and diamond chandeliers. The place looked like a freaking palace.

The people in the hotel looked equally rich. The men were in Armani suits, and the ladies were in designer gowns! I was in total awe of this place.

Now, I understood why Claire brought us here. She wanted to show Ma that we were not worthy of living with her son.

As soon as we entered the hall where the party was being held, Bryan and his father were whisked away by some men and Claire left us to speak with some of her friends. We were left alone with Rebecca.

"Claire is such a bitch, right?" I was surprised to hear such words out of Rebecca. What was more shocking was the scowl on her face. *Excuse me?*

"You have no idea." Ma and I uttered at the same time.

Hearing my reply, Ma gave me the mother glare while Rebecca's scowl turned into a smirk.

"Your daughter is right, Gina. I shouldn't say this, but I have to." Her face turned utterly serious. "Claire thinks that she is superior to others, and she will try her best so that this wedding does not happen. Don't try to associate yourself with her because she won't appreciate it. My best advice for you is to stay away from her."

I thought that Rebecca was just exaggerating, but something in me said that the danger she was talking about was not the typical kind of danger.

It must be something different… something deeper.

Rebecca just gave a polite smile after that and excused herself. Ma had turned pale, and her eyes showed immense worry.

I took her hand in mine and said, "Everything will be alright. Bryan will never leave you."

For the next fifteen minutes, we both stood in one corner of the hall until I heard a familiar voice.

“Welcome, everyone! I hope you all are enjoying yourselves.” Peter’s loud voice rang out through the hall. I smiled. Finally, someone who could show Claire her place.

This was going to be so much fun!

Chapter 9

Neveah

Here I was, standing at a party organized by Easton and Peter.

Peter was a sweet old man… and then there was Easton. I had no words for it!

He was the worst host I had ever seen in my life. He was just standing in the middle with Xavier and Alden flanking him like some kind of royalty!

Surprisingly, Melissa and Georgy were also here. I didn't know that the Lawsins and Dales were good friends.

I also met Georgy's family. His father was a tall man who looked nothing like his son. However, Georgy had the same features as his mother. It turned out that he also had an elder brother who was too professional and boring. Actually, all the members of his family seemed boring. *Poor guy!* No wonder he acted like a crackpot in school!

I was standing with Ma and Rebecca who had joined us again in a corner of the room. It was weird for both of us to be in this place. Though I knew a lot of people, I couldn't leave my mother alone with anyone here. From the looks of the people fluttering about, they didn't seem trustworthy.

Melissa called me over to her, but I just waved back. Georgy had just left after showing his womanizing talents, poor if I must say, to Rebecca and Ma. Oh, he also called Ma a sexy old woman, which was plain gross for me.

Bryan tried to join us, but someone always interrupted him.

After some time, Rebecca dragged Ma into the powder room, leaving me alone. I heard a voice behind me. "Enjoying the party?"

I turned behind me to see Peter.

"What does it look like, Peter?" I scowled at him.

"May I ask what you are doing here?" It wasn't in a rude but in a concerned way. "The beep Claire dragged us here. She wanted to show off that my mother is not enough for her son." I frowned thinking of that vile woman. I didn't even bother to hide the disgust in my voice. It was Peter, so it was alright.

He thought about it for a while before answering. "Ah, Claire! Oh, she is a beep alright. But seriously, your mother is too good for anyone." There was a fondness in his tone, and it felt good to hear that. "Why don't you dance with someone of your age? I can keep Gina company."

"Okay." I excused myself and went in search of Melissa or Georgy. Instead, I found Easton and his crew who were currently surrounded by girls.

So instead of searching for them myself, I decided to ask them. I mean, Easton wasn't that bad.

"Easton," I called out to him. Xavier looked bored, and Alden looked pissed. *Whatever!* "Do you know where Melissa is?"

He was about to answer when some blonde grabbed his shirt and tried to drag him.

Seriously!

I turned to walk away when I bumped into someone. The person turned out to be Peter again. He wasn't alone this time. There were a few people surrounding him just like Easton had before.

"Your mother is with her fiancé, dear." He actually kept Ma company.

"Thanks, Peter." He looked over my shoulder to see his son. I also turned around to see him wrapped around the girl. When I turned back to look at Peter, he had a big frown on his face. Just looking at his face made me say the first thing that came to my mind.

"Are you sure that he is your son?" Peter looked shocked then laughed loudly. His companion looked horrified.

"I guess." The expression on his face made me laugh loudly, too. Looking at me laughing, he got louder. We were laughing for some time before I heard Easton's voice.

"What is going on here?"

Just to piss him off for not answering me before, I replied with a smirk, "I was just asking Peter if he is really your dad, considering he is such a good company."

Easton's face darkened.

"Who invited you and the people with you here, Neveah? Last time I checked, I didn't. Didn't think that you are the type to go to anyone's party uninvited!" He was glowering with anger right now.

My smile vanished automatically. I closed my mouth and looked around to see everyone looking at us, including Ma and Bryan.

That hurt. The worst part was that he continued. "Stop behaving in such an embarrassing way."

Peter seemed still before he spoke up. "I invited her Easton."

He was about to say something else when I snapped out of it. "You know what Eugene? For a second, I thought you had changed, but now I know that some things never change." A traitor tear escaped my eye, and I wiped it off quickly. Why did I even think for a second that I belonged here?

Why did I even think for a second that he had actually changed? The kiss, the smile, *everything* was a lie. I knew that this was going to happen, and it wasn't the first time it happened either. Yet a part of my heart was shattered. What must be the crowd thinking about me? Never had I expected that he would say that in public. I closed my eyes to cut my tears off. I took a deep breath and opened them.

"I am sorry," I murmured, knowing that Easton clearly heard me. I looked up into his eyes and saw the guilt already forming, but it was of no use now.

He put his hand forward to touch my face, but I pushed it away. "Don't," I muttered, and moved away from him.

"Neveah... I… I am—" I shook my head, and he just stood still.

Easton cautiously came near me and took my hand, making sure that I don't run away.

He rubbed my hand with his thumb. "I am sorry," he said pleadingly.

I took my hand from his and looked away. “No, I am sorry.” I looked back at him, and now he knew why I was apologising. His grief-stricken green eyes didn’t leave me as I gestured to Ma that I was leaving. She followed me as I crossed the gate of the hotel. I promised myself that I would *never again* enter any establishment they owned… including his home.

Ever!

Easton

I stared at her during the whole lunch break like a stalker. By this morning, it had spread throughout the whole school that I insulted her publicly yesterday. People were making fun of her. Of course, not on her face, but there were loud whispers in the hallways that everyone could hear.

I had no idea what prompted me to act like that in my own party.

An alpha who insulted his own luna at the celebration of him becoming an alpha was unheard of.

I could still remember the look of hurt and embarrassment in her eyes. I was an idiot for opening my mouth, and I knew that I would have to do a lot of pleading to make up for yesterday.

I knew that she could feel my eyes on her back, yet she pretended that I did not exist. I tried to talk to her this morning, but one look in her eyes made me realize that it was not the time.

Melissa had tried to help me, but she was very much unsuccessful in her attempt. I had utterly no idea what to do since I wasn't used to apologizing. The best option in front of me was a simple, heartfelt sorry. It wouldn't work, but it would be a good start.

I sat in during the whole lunch, thinking of how to do it. The guys were playing football outside, but I was too tired to join them.

I spent the whole night yesterday outside her house, just wanting to see her and feel her presence.

Last night

I wanted to leave just after she had finished ranting.

Shit!

She had just left, and that was when I realized what an ass I was to her and her mother. I heard someone clear his throat, so I turned around. I saw my father looking clearly unhappy with me. The way he and Neveah acted around each other had always made me happy.

After mother's death, my father had become a closed off person. He didn't like speaking to others or spending time with the pack. He rarely talked to me, his own son, but he could talk to my mate. And I have never seen Neveah so happy. Obviously, she hated me, but with my father, she was a singing canary. Maybe that was what made me react like that.

The possessive jackass in me didn't like the fact that she was laughing along with my father whilst avoiding me.

Stupid, possessive a-hole!

I had to bear a big lecture from my aunt and a lot of sympathetic looks from the pack. By last night, everyone was aware of who the luna was.

I was about to leave to talk to my mate when Melissa stopped me. The next words uttered by her crushed my hope a lot.

"Don't leave now, Easton. She will be in a very bad mood."

"What do you want me to do, wait?" I retorted. That was something I couldn't afford to do.

"Yes. At least wait until tomorrow morning. Can we talk alone?" I was definitely not interested, but I knew that she wanted to talk to me about my mate so I agreed.

We went into an empty room. "Spill, and fast," I said in a commanding tone.

"I know Neveah to quite an extent. When we fought in eighth grade, I was not nice to her and said many things. Things which I should not have said and I will regret my whole life." Her voice was brimming with guilt. I had no idea whether to ask her as to why she was speaking such insignificant things or to kill her for hurting Neveah. I was about to interrupt her when she held her hand to stop me, so I let her continue.

"She was there for me when I needed her." I knew she was referring to her and Alden's situation. How could he resist the bond and hurt Melissa while here I was feeling guilty as a sinner because I raised my voice? "No matter how much Neveah says that she can forgive, she never ever forgets, Easton,"

"Even when I speak to her, she pretends like everything is alright, but I know deep down that she always

remembers my words whenever she sees me. I know that she will never forget, and we can never be best friends like before."

"But what you said and what I said were different." I desperately wanted to argue that she and I were different and that Neveah would love me a lot in the future, nonetheless.

"Words are words, Alpha. They hurt the same."

I didn't want to hear any further.

"Leave, now."

Melissa left without another word, but deep down, even I knew that what she said was completely true.

That night, I tried sleeping in all the positions there was, but sleep just evaded me. I knew what was missing! Or rather, who I was missing!

I had to see her.

I had to see her now.

I needed to know if she was alright.

I didn't even put on a shirt before I ran in my human form all the way to her house.

I needed to see her face, her warm brown eyes, and her dark wavy hair.

I reached her house in no time and heard the heartbeat of three people. I climbed up her room. Luckily, the window was open.

Entering the bedroom through the window like last time, I saw that the room was a lot messier. There were a lot of dresses piled on the floor. Some of them were short and would look great on her. I also noticed a picture of her, Gina, and Bryan on her table. There was also a photo of her when she was probably five or so.

My girl looked real cute!

Then my eyes turned to her sleeping form.

She occupied the whole bed like usual. I shifted her to one side and sat on the bed. I saw a slight frown on her face. I didn't like it, so I placed my thumb on her lips to make them even.

I couldn't remove my hand from her. I traced her eyes, eyebrows, cheekbones, and her jaw. It was so soft, unlike mine which was rough. We would fit perfectly... soft and rough together.

The thought made me smile like a retarded person until I realized that she still had to forgive me and that I still needed to come up with a solid plan.

I spent the whole night looking at her. After some time, I slept next to her. Ridiculous, right?

When I woke up early in the morning, I was surprised to see my mate, my girl Neveah, curled up against me. She had her face tucked in the crook of my neck, and her one hand was on my chest while the other was on my arm. We fit. This was what I desperately wanted every day.

Boy, am I whipped!

And she didn't even know it!

I would do anything just to keep her happy, just to keep her smiling.

Sometimes, I wondered if it would have been easier if she was like me. Then again, she was perfect the way she was.

Absolutely perfect!

All these mate talk was turning me into an emotional chick. I quietly pulled away from her, tucked her in, and left.

Now, I had to face her in a few hours with a damn good apology.

I was so lost in my thoughts that I didn't sense someone approach me. I heard someone clear her throat, so I looked up. I got the shock of my life to see Neveah standing near my table. I took in my surroundings to realise that there was no single soul in this room except us. I was so lost in my thoughts that I didn't realize that classes had started already. Maybe that was why Neveah came to talk to me.

She smelled amazingly good today.

I was about to speak when she cut me off.

"Project discussion at five, my house. Don't be late," she said and walked away.

But before she could leave, I wrapped my arms around her from behind.

"Listen to me, please." She squirmed, but I didn't let her loose. If I let her go now, I wouldn't get another opportunity.

"I am sorry for what I said yesterday. I was completely acting like an idiot, and what I said was absolutely wrong. You have the right to come to my house anytime you want. I have no solid reason, but I want you to forgive me," I whispered in her ear, hoping that she would understand.

I waited for her reply, but nothing came out for a minute. This was bad. I turned her around, and her face was void of any emotion.

"You finished, Easton?" Her voice was cold, and I didn't like it.

I reluctantly muttered a yes and let her out of my arms.

She punched me square in the gut.

Damn! My girl can hit!

Believe me, if I was human that would've hurt a lot more.

I clutched my stomach while she spoke, "Never touch me, Easton Dale. As for the forgiving part, go to hell!"

I stood up straight to watch her retreating back. Half of the pain was gone thanks to my super healing.

Time for plan B.

Chapter 10

Neveah

Ma didn't say anything the whole way home, but I knew that she was angry and disappointed. Truth be told, I never expected Easton to react the way he did. I thought about the whole event and what left my mouth, but nothing I said could have made him react this way.

I was actually polite at the party. I didn't want to disappoint Peter. His son may be an idiot, but Peter has always been kind towards Ma and me. He was one of the people Ma trusted with all her heart.

After we had reached home, Ma and I changed into more comfortable clothes and sat on the couch. Both of us were deep in our own thoughts. I put my head on her lap while she was humming something.

Tomorrow was Friday, and after that was the weekend! However, I would have to face all of them tomorrow. I was very sure by now that the whole school would know what happened. I was not scared of the name calling and the gossiping anymore. I was used to it by now. But I didn't think I would have the patience to deal with them tomorrow.

For one second, I couldn't help blaming Bryan, but then I realized that it wasn't his fault that his parents were class A douches, just like Peter has a class A jerk for a son.

Some time passed that way, and I was almost asleep when I heard the loud screeching of tires on our driveway. It must've been Bryan. He had dropped us off and went to his house. He said that he needed to sort something out with his parents.

The door opened the next second, and Bryan came storming in. Boy did he look pissed!

"Hey, Bryan." I greeted in an almost cheerful voice as if the events of a few hours ago didn't happen. I got up from Ma's lap and sat up straight.

"I'm so sorry, Gina. I should have stopped it. I should have—" Before he could continue, Ma stopped him.

She went to him and cupped his face. "It was not your fault, Bryan. How would you know?"

"Seriously, Gina? After all this, you say that it is not my fault?" Bryan sounded sad and disappointed. We all are sad.

Oh, come on! This wasn't his fault. He didn't know that this would happen

If someone was at fault, it had to be Easton. He was the reason for all this shit happening.

Before either of us could talk, another screeching sound of tires was heard.

Who was it now?

After two seconds, a flustered looking Claire entered with her husband in tow. For a second, I thought that she was here to apologize, but one look at her face made me think the exact opposite. She wasn't here to resolve anything. I was sure about that. What did she want now? She got what she wanted! I was insulted publicly in front of some of the most important people in this town.

"What did you do?" She shouted and pointed her finger in my direction.

She went on with her acquisitions, "How could you disrespect him? Do you have any idea who he is?" She didn't even wait for my answer before she went on and on. After some time, I sat down on the couch and started thinking ideas for our chemistry project.

She went on and on before her cell started ringing. Her eyes widened when she looked at the caller id. She hesitantly answered the phone. Whoever was on the phone didn't sound happy. Next thing I knew, she thrust the phone to me. The caller id had no name, so I put it on speaker.

"Hello? Who is it?" I asked, tired of having any sort of conversation with anyone right now.

"It's me, Neveah dear." Peter's clear voice came out of the speaker.

"Peter?" Why was he calling Claire, and why did he want to speak to me?

"Yes, dear," he answered, confirming his identity.

"What's up?" I asked the first thing that came to my mind.

I heard a laugh before Peter spoke again. "Nothing is up, girl, apart from my temper. I just wanted to say sorry for my son. What he did was absolutely disgusting, and I am sorry that I didn't stop it."

"It's alright. I mean, come on, he is Easton. I will be surprised if he didn't do it," I said with a scoff, but my voice broke a bit towards the end.

"Really, Neveah?" he asked, sensing that I was hurt.

"Nope, but since he is your son, I'll have to leave him alive," I simply answered, trying to make a joke of it.

He chuckles through the receiver, and I laughed. It wasn't his fault that he partially created that idiot.

"I'm still sorry," he apologized again.

"It's alright, Peter," Ma replied this time.

"Goodnight, Gina. Goodnight, Neveah."

I cut the call and threw the phone back to a shocked looking Claire.

"Who is Easton to you?" She actually wanted an answer after what happened a few hours ago?

She seriously looked serious, so I answered. "Yesterday, he was my project partner, someone who could be considered as an acquaintance, but as of now, he is the guy I hate."

"No, he must be something more," she told me. She seemed quite sure of her statement.

"He is nothing to me, Claire. If you have finished, get out." I spat at her. My manners were long gone. She didn't deserve any from me, anyway.

"What did you say?" Claire seethed. Ma tried to stop me, but I was tired of Claire's shit, and I needed to get to bed soon which won't happen if she was standing here.

"I said get out. You are the reason I was insulted today. Instead of entertaining the guests at your house, you simply dumped us somewhere. You don't give a damn about my mother or me, and frankly, I don't care. I am tired, pissed, and upset, so I suggest for the third time to take your ass out of our house before I haul it myself."

I take out all my frustration on her.

"Bryan, are you going to let this girl speak to me like this?" She looked at Bryan for support, and I, too, waited for his answer.

"You heard my daughter, mother, and I think that she's right." He stood by me, and I loved it. *In your face, bitch!*

She narrowed her eyes at me before glancing at Ma and leaves. Her husband followed behind her, the same way he came in.

At last!

"It is your decision now, Bryan. I won't see my mother being insulted anymore. I don't think I can tolerate her insulting Ma again."

I was currently speaking to Bryan the morning after the incident. Last night was bad. I wanted to clear things up with him. Ma suggested that I apologize to Claire for being rude, but there was no way I was going to do it. It wasn't my fault!

I was not in any way making him choose, but he had to act fair.

He thought about it for some time before replying. "I'll speak to my mother."

"Fair enough."

He left for work with Ma, and now I have to go to school.

I didn't want to go, but I had to do the project, so I had no other choice.

Things were bad at school, just as I had expected it to be. As soon as I entered the parking lot, everyone started whispering. Some girls shot me glares, but I glared back at them. What was their problem? I didn't try going to their house, right?

This continued throughout the day. Wherever I went, the whispers and name-calling followed me. I was growing tired of it. Easton tried to talk to me before school started, but I was too exhausted to face him. Even Melissa tried to coax me into speaking to him, but nothing worked.

The whole lunch period, he was staring at me. It was plain irritating. After the bell, he was still sitting on his table thinking about God knows what.

I went to him and got straight to the point. "Project discussion at five, my house. Don't be late."

I started to walk away when two arms encircled me from behind.

I squirmed but to no avail. "Listen to me, please."

I stayed still, and he continued.

"I am sorry for what I said yesterday. I was completely acting like an idiot, and what I said was absolutely wrong. You have the right to come to my house anytime you want. I have no solid reason, but I want you to forgive me."

I didn't react, so he turned me to face him.

"You finished, Easton?" I didn't give a crap about his apology. I heard him say yes, and I punched him square in the gut.

"Never touch me, Easton Dale. As for the forgiving part, go to hell!" I ran out of the cafeteria as fast as I could whilst clutching my now hurting hand.

I was waiting for him after school in the library while he has football practice. I had asked Melissa to inform Easton. He came to the library by four-thirty.

We both didn't say anything. We both drove to my home in our cars. As I neared the door, I heard voices. It was Ma and Peter. Just as I was opening the door with my keys, I felt Easton's body behind me.

"I am not sad or embarrassed, Peter, but what your son said would have definitely disappointed Amy."

I heard a rough exhale, and when I turned to look at him, he was gone. His car was nowhere in sight as well. How did he move so fast?

I went in and said, "Easton heard the last part."

Chapter 11

Neveah

The next day was an eventless Saturday. Ma took me to a cake shop to save her from the dilemma of choosing the cake for the wedding.

I had to choose between a blueberry cake with white icing and a grape cake with ivory icing. Do they actually make a grape cake because I have never heard of it?

And who cared if the icing was white or ivory? There was no difference between them. Those colours are practically the same.

So here I was standing amidst cakes in the afternoon, accompanying my Ma.

It was pastry heaven. I could literally smell every ingredient. Okay, not literally, but you get what I say. There was every kind of cake from all over the world in this thousand square foot place.

"So, what should we get?" This had to be the thousandth time I was asked this question.

And this was also the thousandth time I was replying the same thing. "Buy whichever you want, Ma. You are going to eat only a piece, and both of them look the same." And once again, she goes into an internal dilemma.

"Come on, Nev. Tell me which one," she urged,

I could only sigh.

Oh, for the love of God!

Later that evening, I was alone in the house. Ma and Bryan were out again to the cake shop. *Poor guy!* What was wrong with Ma? She was never this choosy or confused before. It was better to get married in Vegas. All you had to pay there was for the liquor charges, and they, too, come cheap.

I was studying physics when I got a call from an unknown number.

"Hey, Nev."

"Melissa?" There was a lot of noise from wherever she was speaking.

"Where are you?" I asked her, my voice turning louder with every word.

"Home," she replied.

"Then why is there so much noise?" I could barely make out what she was saying, and the music was so loud, I could practically hear the lyrics through the phone.

"Oh, I'm having a party," she said casually.

"So?" I should be the last person she should call if there was a party. I hardly attended them. Okay, confession here, I have gone to only one party, and that was two years ago.

All the parties in this town were hosted only by those brainless jocks, and I couldn't tarnish my high reputation by going there. It was just a big no-no. Now, the other part of the story was that I hardly ever get invited. The only person who invited me was Xavier because he wanted to insult me.

Teenage boys these days!

"You are coming." Her voice rang with finality.

"I am not." She should've known that I didn't attend parties.

"I was not asking."

"I was also not asking," I said with a grin. As if she could make me come to the party!

"I promise you, Nev, that if you don't turn up for the party, I will send Georgy to collect you." She threatened.

"Send whoever you want, but I am not coming. And what will he do to me?"

I mean, come on. What could he do? Drag me?

"You should be at my house by ten or…" she paused for emphasis, "Oh, you will be there by ten thirty, anyway."

Ah! Confidence! I liked it. It was just sad that it wouldn't work on me.

"Oh, we will see, Melissa." I scoffed and cut the call.

A couple of hours later, and here I was standing in her house, wearing a blood red knee-length dress and black stilettos with my hair styled.

And yes, I was dragged.

I was peacefully studying for the physics test when I heard a doorbell. I thought that Ma had finally come to a decision about the cake, but no, standing in front of me was Georgy.

He was looking hot! Just because I didn't put that much effort into my appearance didn't mean I couldn't appreciate other people's beauty.

He was wearing tight blue jeans and a grey t-shirt. His hair was styled, and his muscles could be clearly seen. He also had a tattoo above his elbow. It was actually my first time seeing it.

"You got a tattoo?"

"I always had it there. You were the first girl to not notice," he said matter-of-factly.

I just shrugged.

"So, what brings you here?" I asked him in an innocent way as if I didn't know the reason for him being at my house.

"I believe that you and I are going somewhere."

"Really? Because I don't." Two could play this, my friend.

"Come on, babe. We need to leave." He kept pushing me into the house.

"Last time I checked, I am not going anywhere. So I suggest that you take a U-turn and leave the way you came."

He gave me a smug smile in reply. *Stupid!*

He pushed past me and plopped himself on the sofa. "I am not leaving until you come with me."

"Fine. Sit there on that couch the whole time until Bryan returns and kicks you out." I sat along with him.

"Oh, no one is kicking me out tonight. You and I will be leaving this place together." With that, he walked off somewhere inside the house. My mood to study was completely ruined, so I settled for watching TV.

I was watching some silly, meaningless opera show when Georgy came out with two dresses. One was a short red one while the other one was a white backless one. Both the dresses had tags on them.

"When did you buy those? I admit they are good-looking, but I doubt they would look good on you," I said with a smirk while he narrowed his eyes.

Where did he get those from, anyway? He wasn't carrying anything when he entered.

"They are for you, silly, and I found them in your closet." *Really?* I just gave him a blank look.

"You are really ignorant, Nev. Okay. Now go wear one of these dresses and do the normal makeup things you girls do." He thrust those dresses on my lap and shooed me away.

"Dress up and do what?" I grunted. I was not in a mood to play dress up.

He just looked at me for some time, and then took the dress on my lap. *Yes!* He has given up!

He suddenly pulled me up and put me on his shoulder.

"Hey, what are you doing?" My face was near his ass, and the whole world was upside down.

"Put me down," I shouted and pinched his ass.

He yelped and almost dropped me, but luckily, I held on. "You know, if you were some other girl, I surely would have spanked you," he grumbled, and I gave him another hit on the back.

He didn't answer and just dragged me to my bed and pushed me on it.

"Hey, are you going to abuse me?" I tried to get up, but he pushed me back.

"Yup. If you don't get dressed, then I will." He stood with his arms folded in an intimidating manner.

"Please, someone, save me! Please, someone, save me! Why are you doing this to me?"

I clutched my hands over my heart for some extra dramatic effect.

"Don't do this to me," I added.

By the end of my speech, Georgy was laughing uncontrollably. I couldn't help but join him. After some time, we both grew silent.

Before he could speak up, I said, "I am still not coming to the party."

"You are coming." He spoke with so much conviction in his voice that, for a second, even I believed him.

"Nope, I am still not coming," I argued back.

He got up from the floor and sat beside me on the bed.

"Come on, Nev. It is my first party in this town, and I want both of my friends to be there." He sounded so sad and sincere that I nodded my head.

"But to remind you, I am only coming because you emotionally blackmailed me." He had such a huge smile on his face that I also smile back.

"Thank you, Nev. Now get dressed… fast." He kissed my cheek in gratitude, and I kicked him out of my room.

"Alright. Jeez, you are so pushy." I went in my room and dolled up. I let my hair down and curled it at the ends and matched my blood red dress with black stilettos. I also added a bit of makeup here and there. I looked at myself in the mirror after I was finished. In front of me was a fine teenager. I had to admit to myself that this was one of the rare times I behaved like a true hormonal teenager.

I took a black clutch from Ma's collection and threw in all the essentials like my phone, tissues, a plastic bag, and money.

I stuck a note on the refrigerator telling Ma that I was going to Melissa's party. At least, she would be happy that I was leaving the house for something. Ma was always concerned that I didn't behave like 'normal' teenagers. She just couldn't accept the fact that I was far more normal than the others. Just because I was different didn't mean I was abnormal!

I locked the house to find a monster jeep on the side of the road. It was huge, and the floor was almost up to my waist. I couldn't climb up on my own while wearing this thing, so I had to ask for Georgy's assistance.

After I was seated and buckled up, I asked him, "What is your brother doing?"

He sighed before answering. "He was in college, but now he dropped out to assist our father in his business."

"Okay, so is he not coming?"

"Nah, he's too boring. They all are."

I just nodded my head in understanding. I understood boring people for I was one of them.

He drove for some time, and we reached the place at last.

Melissa's house was huge. It was very modern with many expensive items lined up outside the house. I could hear the music from outside the gates itself.

There were people on the lawn, in the pool, and on the roof. Yes, on the roof, too! Georgy chuckled as he followed my line of vision. He was a funny guy, but Melissa was different.

Melissa… well, she had changed a lot. She started wearing common clothes. Well, as common as they could get. Oh, no! She was not someone who would wear skimpy outfits like all cheerleaders in movies.

She was always decent and at her glamorous best. Her clothes probably cost more than my car. She was fashion at its best.

Her father, Arthur, was a successful businessman while her mother, Linda, was a hotshot designer, which equals to a lot of money and free clothes. However, she was never one to flaunt it. Arthur and Linda were busy people, so they never took an interest in what was happening with her life. This was one of the main reasons her hormones spiralled out of control like it did. She wanted to feel loved and cared for, and my friendship was lacking in that department.

She wanted more attention, so she broke up our friendship and turned to those flirtatious boys for affection. Needless to say, it all ended badly, but now she was trying to put herself back, and I appreciated that about her. She could be certain that I would always be there to support her.

As soon as we entered the house, I could smell three things: chicken, alcohol, and sweat. It was the usual party scene. There were tons of people grinding each other, and the ones who weren't, were drinking to their hearts' content.

I saw Melissa on the side with Easton and Xavier standing not far away. All three of them were staring off into space in different directions.

When Melissa saw me, she came bouncing towards me. At first, I couldn't tell what she was wearing due to the disco lights, but I could see it clearly now. She looked beautiful. She was wearing a peach medium-length dress with frills at the bottom. There was also a wide smile on her face which I have not seen in a long time.

"Hey, Nev. I told you that you would come, and see, here you are!"

"Please, I am here because this idiot..." I turned around, but there was no one standing behind me. I searched the room and spotted him flirting with a girl who was giggling overdramatically. "Because that idiot," I said, "blackmailed me emotionally."

"Doesn't matter. All that matters is that you are here now."

I was about to ask her something when I heard a voice behind me.

"Well, what do we have here?"

It was a voice I have not heard for almost two years.

Chapter 12

Neveah

Oh for the love of Pete!

I turned behind to see a younger version of Melissa with her arms around a guy, and that guy just happened to be Alden. *Seriously, Alden. Could you get any cheaper than this?*

I was absolutely disgusted by his behaviour. He was trying with all his might to break Melissa. He laid low for a little while, but now he was back on his game. And he was determined to hurt Melissa again.

At first, I thought that this was just two hormonal people speaking, but both their actions showed that it was way beyond teenage hormones. It was like they were bound by something though both of them wanted to get away from it. Never mind the fact that I had no idea how or when Melissa managed to fall for Alden or how he came to know about it. Complicated, I know.

Now, both of them were hell-bent on staying away from each other. However, Alden seemed to have a different idea of what staying away meant. He wanted to show that he was doing alright without her, that he didn't need Melissa. But deep down, I knew that he loved her as much as she loved him.

But you know what? It didn't matter. What mattered was the blonde bitch he was with.

Standing with Alden was none other than Madeline. She was my dear friend Melissa's younger sister, who was not the best person in the world. The girl had a heart of stone and would sell anyone to the devil if possible. She and I never got along. I have heard her calling me poor more than a hundred times.

"Well, we have a blonde brainless lapdog with a collar on her neck."

Her face fell, and her contacts-covered irises turned dark.

"What are you doing here?" Same dialogue as someone else. I so knew how this would end.

"I am here for the same reason you are here." She had a blank look on her face which was definitely a sign of her inability to understand. Could a person be this dumb?

"The party, Madeline. Look what is going on around you," I said in a very slow and patronizing tone.

"Do I look like an idiot to you?" She sneered at me.

"Yes," I said like it was the most obvious thing in the world.

I heard loud laughs around the room. I turned behind me to see Georgy, Easton, Xavier, and some other people laughing. Man, even Melissa was smiling.

"Get out of my house." Was this seriously happening to me twice this week?

"Enough, Madeline," Easton's voice boomed from behind me.

Oh, come on! Is this kick-Neveah-out-of-the-house week?

I turned back, and before Easton could open his mouth again, I placed my hand on it. "Shut up."

I heard him grumble something under my hand before he removed it.

"Ew! At least wash your hand before you do that. She touched you."

I just narrowed my eyes at her.

"The only person who needs a wash is you, Madeline. If I'm not mistaken, I think your hand has been in many places, and the guy who you are sticking with now has also stuck things to people. Oh, on the other hand, maybe you can exchange things with each other," I said to Madeline. She had mocked me too many times before... not that I stayed silent after that.

"Huh?"

Easton and Georgy were almost on the verge of tears after laughing so much, and Xavier was confused and clueless as usual.

"I am not going to repeat myself. I spoke in English, right, Mel?" I asked her for confirmation.

"Uh-uh. Maybe you should try layman English?" Okay, was she also confused?

"Whatever, loser," Madeline blurted out, but Alden was still staring blankly into space. "Are you going to move from there, idiot?"

"The only one who is an idiot is you."

With that, Alden just ran away from that place. What a coward. Madeline stomped her foot forward and locked eyes with me.

"I'll take care of you later." Her voice was an octave short of a shout.

"I know I'm hot, babe, but I am just not into girls. Sorry." How I managed to say it without laughing my guts out was beyond me.

This time, it was not only Easton and Georgy who laughed but almost everyone in the room.

And Xavier laughed, too. I guess he understood things better when someone was being insulted.

"Okay! I'm leaving now," I announced.

Before Mel could protest, Georgy spoke, "But we just got here." He was almost whining.

"I didn't tell you to come with me, Georgy," I said.

"But why are you leaving?" Melissa asked. She seemed sad.

"Hey, the bet was coming to the party, right? And I did come. I need to go home soon. Ma has this issue of choosing between an ivory and a white cake," I pointed out.

"Aren't they both the same?" Mel replied confused.

"Say that to her, Mel, not to me. Poor Bryan." I shuddered, thinking about all the pain Bryan had to go through to marry Ma.

"Why don't we all go out?" Georgy said.

"Don't be rude. It's her party. She can't just leave," I reminded Georgy. It was her house party for God sakes.

"As if she is doing anything here." He snorted. I turned towards Melissa and raised an eyebrow.

"I'm free to leave, Neveah."

“Really, Mel?” I ask again, confirming.

“Okay, let’s leave, then.” If she had no problems, who was I to protest? Secretly, I thought that she wanted to get away from Alden.

“Who wants to stay with Madeline, anyway?” She scoffed. I didn’t understand that statement.

“Aren’t siblings supposed to love each other and cherish their bond or something?”

“Depends on the sibling, Nev,” Georgy interrupted. I would bet my money that he was thinking about his elder brother.

“Okay?” I said, dragging the ‘ay’ since I was not sure of the statement. I was an only child, after all.

“So, when are we leaving?” said a voice from behind me.

It was Xavier.

What was he doing here? Was he standing there for a long time?

“*We* are not going anywhere.” Georgy gestured between him and Xavier. “Only me, Nev, and Mel are leaving. You are staying here with the others.”

Xavier’s face dropped, and I kind of felt bad.

He went to protest when Easton silenced him. “You better leave before your sister returns, Melissa.” His tone was firm and commanding.

“You take Mel out. I’ll join you soon,” I told Georgy.

He seemed reluctant but got her out after I glared at him. I turned back to Xavier and Easton. “So, which car are we going in?”

“To where?” asked Easton.

“My house, silly.”

"I'll take my car," Xavier replied. He didn't even wait for my nod and just rushed out. I was still unsure that he wanted to come to my house.

Just as I turned around, Easton pulled me back. "What are you doing, Neveah?" He looked very unsure as if I was going to do something to him.

"Xavier wants to come to my house, so I formally invited him, and you can tag along. I promise I won't kick you out," I added with a smirk.

"You will always remind me that I kicked you out, won't you?" He didn't look amused.

"Till the day you die. Wait, scratch that. I'll even announce it at your funeral." And his face broke out into a big smile.

"Come on, lady. Let us leave."

I, Easton, and Xavier rode into the night on his black BMW. The car was nice, I admit. Xavier played an awfully loud song on the radio, Easton was playing something on his cell phone, and I was looking at the passing trees.

I got a message from Melissa that they had reached my house and that there was no one home. So I checked my cell again and found a message that Ma sent to say that they were staying at some hotel.

I called and informed her that there were some people coming over at our home so that she wouldn't get shocked by the amount of waste that I was sure would be piled up by tomorrow morning.

We got out of the car, and I noticed that Georgy did not look happy. I realized that he was being protective of me, and I found that quite funny.

I thought I was the last person he would be protective of.

"Come on, people. Let's go in." I opened the door and made everyone take their seats on the couch and on the loveseat in the hall. I went to the kitchen to see if there were enough leftovers to feed everyone, especially the hulking boys!

I opened the door only to see raw meat, some drinks, and, of course, vegetables. I was too tired to make anything. I was not any good at it, anyway. I decided that it was time to order. I took out the juices and the drink cans. I was washing some glasses when I felt someone behind me.

"You really shouldn't bend in such a dress." There, standing behind me, was Easton in his mighty jock glory. He was here the whole time.

"You really should keep your eyes and thoughts to yourself. Since you reminded me, I am going to change, so wash these glasses and take them out along with the drinks." Easton pouted. "Don't pout and get to work," I chided playfully.

"Yes, ma'am." He saluted, and I giggled.

I went upstairs to change. I put on a t-shirt and knee-length capris, removed my makeup, and tied up my hair. Now I felt normal!

I went downstairs where everyone was sitting stiffly.

"Last time I checked, I am not conducting a funeral here."

Everyone looked at me.

"What?" I retorted.

"We should do something fun." At last, Xavier said something sensible!

Easton and Georgy nodded in approval.

"But what?"

Melissa was about to say something when the doorbell rang. It was odd. Who was it at such a time? I got up and opened the door. Standing there was Ryder, looking utterly drunk.

"Whoa, how much did you drink?" I asked him as I tried to support his heavy frame.

His black hair was disheveled, and his brown eyes looked droopy. "I lost count after the eighth glass." To prove his point he showed me his fingers but instead of eight, they were seven.

I sighed and made him stand at the wall near the door and closed it.

"That doesn't explain why you are here, not that I have any problem with it."

"Daniel kicked me out because his girl was coming over." I raised an eyebrow, so he explained further.

"We rented a flat together near college." That made sense. The college they went to was on the outskirts of town which was far away.

"Can I crash here?"

As if he needed to ask!

"Sure." I went to support him before he fell, but he shooed me away, saying something along the lines of being a strong boy. *Fine, have it your way then.*

He went in while I locked the door. I went down the hall from the porch to see Easton and Ryder glaring at each other.

"Ryder, go to sleep. And Easton, stop glaring at him." I pushed Ryder to the stairs that lead to my room.

Ryder then turned his attention from Easton to the other people in the room. "Hello, Blondie." He greeted Melissa.

"Ryder." She gave a curt nod.

"What happened? No baby this time, huh?" *Okay, enough of it.* I grabbed Ryder's hand and pushed him upstairs. This time, more forcefully.

"Get lost and don't break anything," I shouted after him.

"I won't, Nev. Goodnight."

I sighed again and turned to face my guests.

"Why is he here, Neveah?" Easton's voice rang throughout the whole room.

"None of your business." Why was he even concerned?

"It is my business, Nev. So please answer."

"He's my friend, Easton. I grew up with him and his cousin. He has the freedom to come and go whenever he wants to."

"Bullshit, you grew up with Melissa and me." He remembered that now?

"I was dragged to your house when Ma wanted to go. And please, you merely tolerated me and had your high and mighty ego in the air whenever I came around. All you did was make my life hell by tormenting me." I wanted to say more, but this was not the place.

"I never—"

"Enough, guys." We were interrupted by an angry looking Melissa.

"Okay. Let's watch a movie. Shall we?" I said while raising my hand.

I allowed them to choose. Ma had a huge stack of rom coms, and Bryan brought along a box filled with action and horror movies, so they had plenty to choose from.

They decided on *Sherlock Holmes*. It was a nice movie and not at all boring.

We all watched the movie with interest. On top of that, Robert Downey Jr. looked pretty good for his age.

It was almost two in the morning when the movie finished.

Melissa and Georgy were already asleep in each other's arms on the loveseat while Xavier was on the verge of passing out on the single couch. The only people awake were Easton and me.

We were both on the main couch.

Going to my room was not possible since Ryder was already there.

I didn't exactly mind sharing a bed with him since I have done it a lot in the past, but boy, the guy can kick during his sleep. I was in no mood to get kicked, and sleeping in Ma and Bryan's bed was a big no-no.

It looked like we have to crash on the couch.

"We gotta sleep here, Easton. You take the left side, and I'll take the right."

He snorted and mumbled something. I was sleepy to make out anything of it, though.

"Goodnight, Easton."

"Goodnight, Nev."

Something bright was flashing in my eyes. I felt around for the window to pull down the curtains when my hand came in contact with something hard, which was definitely not what I was looking for. I traced my hand on the object, and it was hard but soft too.

I opened my eyes to see myself trapped on Easton's side. He was on his stomach with his one arm wrapped around mine while the other was below my head. How the hell did I get in this position?

On the loveseat, Melissa and Georgy were cuddled up. They looked so cute.

On the other hand, Xavier was sleeping with his mouth wide open, and light snores were coming off it.

I looked at the clock and realised that it was eleven in the morning. No wonder there was so much light streaming in.

I was surprised that Ma was not here yet. She would've been shocked out of her life at the sight. All the pizza boxes from last night were strewn on the floor along with the juice and beer cans, and not to mention the leftovers.

Lots of work to do today!

I tried to move his hand away, but he was too strong. What exactly did he have in his food?

"Get up, Easton." I tried shaking him as much as I could.

"Sleep, baby girl." His arm tightened around me, and he went back to sleep again. I waited for exactly ten seconds before letting out a high-pitched scream.

Xavier fell out of his chair, and Melissa and Georgy woke up with a start. Even Ryder bounded down the stairs looking utterly confused and concerned.

The one person who looked the least affected was the guy sleeping next to me. How could he be still asleep?

"Get him off me," I mouthed to Ryder.

Ryder and Georgy got to work. In the process of pulling him off me, they pulled him down, and he pulled me along with him.

Just before I was to hit the ground, Easton opened his eyes and pushed his hands to shield my head so it wouldn't hurt.

I laid with him on top of me for a second before he swiftly got up and punched Ryder straight in the face.

"How dare you hurt her?"

Chapter 13

Neveah

"Easton, what are you doing?" I hollered.

Easton hit Ryder, but as soon as he recovered, Ryder hit him back. Even I couldn't blame the guy. I would've done the same thing.

They started throwing punches at each other. I tried to stop them, only to be pushed back by Georgy.

"What are you doing?"

"I am trying to stop them, idiot," I stated.

"You cannot stop him. Let the men do the work." He pushed me further so that I was standing with Melissa. With great difficulty, Xavier managed to pull back Easton, and Georgy was able to restrain Ryder.

"Touch him, Nev," Ryder ordered. He was almost back to his calm self while Easton looked like an angry dragon ready to blow some fire. *Wait, what?*

"What shit are you talking about?" I asked him, bewildered.

"Do what he says, Neveah. Trust me, he's right." This time, Xavier's face was not his usual mischievous one. He was one hundred percent serious.

"Where?" I ask confused.

"Anywhere. Just do it." It was Melissa who answered this time.

What were they talking about? Did they all know something I didn't?

I huffed and went to Easton. When I put my hands to his chest, I felt some weird spark flow through me. *Whoa!* I dragged my hands over his chest. Man, it was hard. I steadied my left hand on his torso while I moved my right one to his face. I looked into his eyes. They seemed darker than their usual emerald green.

"Easton, calm down. It's alright. I'm alright," I gently said.

I felt him tense up before all the tension in his body evaporated, and he hugged me. He kept his hands on my waist while my face was tucked on his neck. Why did I have to be so much shorter than him? We stayed in the same way for a whole two minutes before I pulled away.

"What in the hell happened right now?" I glanced towards all of them. "You all better have the best possible explanation for this ready, and it better be believable." I glared at all of them, but not one of them looked me in my eye. Now, something was definitely wrong.

Ryder gulped and went to make excuses, but I shut him up.

"You are not getting out of this house till you open your mouth." I was pretty much shouting by the end of.

"Fine, but can I talk to Blondie alone?"

I looked at Easton, but he just shrugged so I turned back to Ryder. “You can, and Blondie’s name is Easton Dale.”

“Like I care,” he grumbled. A bruise was forming on his cheek by now. Ryder was mostly worried about his looks and what excuse he should make.

“Shut up, Ryder.”

I thought about sending them to my room when something clicked. I took my cell phone from the table near the couch and told Easton and Ryder to go to my room. I casually followed them as the others stayed downstairs. While I was doing so, I activated the voice recorder and locked my phone.

Ryder sat on the bed while Easton just stood there.

I placed my cell on the study table. “Talk. I’ll be waiting downstairs with the others. No fighting. I like my room the way it is, so please don’t damage it. Am I clear?”

Ryder grunted, and Easton nodded.

“Just don’t take a lot of time.” I closed the door on my way and went downstairs.

I found Melissa and Xavier on the couch and a jittery Georgy pacing around the room.

“You all better have a good explanation.”

“It’s better if Easton explains it,” Georgy said. *Seriously?* You too, Georgy?

He was the only one who didn’t encourage me to calm Easton down, so I thought that he knew nothing. Now, I realized how wrong I was.

“Whatever.” I slumped on the couch between Melissa and Xavier and switched on the TV. We all watched some comedy show while the two idiots talked upstairs.

All I had to do now was wait.

Ryder and Easton returned after some time. I looked at them and found no signs of injury, at least not any new ones. Ryder's cheek was swollen from where Easton punched him, and Easton was sporting a purple eye which was soon going to turn black.

"So... how was the talk? Are you ready to answer me?"

"I'm leaving. Talk to me after you talk to him." Ryder left through the front door with not even a goodbye. *Ouch!*

"We're leaving too, Neveah." Mell, Georgy, and Xavier left after Ryder, leaving me alone with Easton.

"Easton, I don't have the whole day. Just get this over with already."

"I was angry."

That's all?

"Seriously, Easton? Since when did you get angry over me?" Easton Dale cares about me? I'm so not believing that again!

"Since the night I kicked you out of my house."

What has that incident got to do with anything?

"Since that night, I realized that I have been in a very bad way with you, and I regret it… I really do. When Ryder pulled you off me, you could have gotten hurt, so I got angry at him, and you know the rest." He sounded sincere, but it just sounded too good to be true.

"Alright, but don't repeat it again, and we wouldn't have that scenario had you gotten up when I screeched."

"My ears stopped working for a while, woman. Not my fault that I was in shock," he retorted.

"Whatever."

Just then, the landline started ringing. *It must be Ma.*

"Excuse me."

I answered the phone, and it was Bryan. Well, close enough.

"Hello, my beautiful child."

"Good morning, Dad." An automatic smile appeared on my face.

"How was the sleepover?"

I looked at Easton before replying.

"Interesting." You have no idea to what extent, Brian.

"Okay, I just called to say to say that we will be home by noon. You're Mom's tired. She's still sleeping."

"I didn't need that visual, Bryan. I'm scarred." I giggled, and I heard him laugh from the other end.

"Ha, I wish. But we were at the cake shop till ten and then had dinner with a client."

"Oh, okay. See you later. Love you."

"Love you too, my baby." I put the phone receiver down and turned to Easton who had a smile on his face.

"What?" I ask. Maybe there was something on my face.

"Nothing." But still, he didn't stop smiling. "I'm leaving, Nev."

"Okay, bye. Wait tomorrow after school. We need to work on the project."

"Ah, man. I almost forgot about it." I should've been the one crying, not him.

He was leaving when I said, "Just so you know, I don't trust a single word that comes out of your mouth."

I didn't hear any response.

I was patiently waiting for Easton outside the library. Hopefully, he remembered where the library was because half of the population at school didn't.

As I waited for him, I remembered the recording I did yesterday. I was yet to play it. As soon as Easton left, I dashed into my room to stop the recording. I tried to listen to it after I finished my breakfast, but no sooner than I started it, there was someone knocking on the door. It turned out to be Ma and Bryan. They had at last selected a cake, and it wasn't the grape or anything... it was lemon. Not that it mattered, though. Just like I said, I was not going to eat more than one piece.

That evening, we decided on the colour theme of the wedding. Ma, like any other girly girl, wanted pink, but I refused it on the spot.

She had promised that she wouldn't make me wear a pink dress, but if she chose that shade for her wedding, I would be forced to wear the dumb colour. I understood it was her wedding, and that she was getting married for the first time and all... but pink just wouldn't do.

Since it was going to be a pre-Christmas wedding, I felt like red and green. You know, to blend with the Christmas mood, but then we decided that green would be a dull colour, so we had to settle with maroon. I liked that colour, anyway.

We then had to choose the card. It was beautiful. Ma was freaking out even though it was only September, and we still had a whole four months before the wedding.

Next week, we would go shopping. *Sheesh!* Planning a wedding could be a pain sometimes.

I was so caught up in my thoughts that I didn't notice Easton in front of me.

"Finally! I was going to fall asleep standing."

"Sorry, I had detention," he said, not at all looking sorry.

"Yeah, come on." I dragged him in since he was feeling shy and was refusing to come in.

The librarian had shock plastered all over her face. I couldn't help laughing, and she glared at me in return. I never liked that woman, anyway. She was a redhead in her early forties who was more than eager to hit on any guy in school. *Gross!*

She was eyeing Easton closely, but before she could start anything, I dragged him to the chemistry section.

"Did she…?" The poor guy was shocked by the nasty expression on the woman's face.

"Oh, she surely did, but don't worry, you're not the first one," I assured him.

"Just start, Neveah, I just wanna get out," he moaned.

"But we just came in," I moaned back, enjoying his misery. Man, I was so mean.

I smiled at him for some time before I picked up the necessary books and started going through them. We discussed the topic for some time and made notes. I explained to Easton many things, and he too knew a lot of things about chemistry that he diligently explained to me. *Wow!*

After some while, we both got bored, so we went to a nearby diner. I only ordered a cup of coffee while Easton ordered fries, five burgers, and two cokes.

After the food arrived, I started sipping on my coffee when Easton said, "I didn't buy it all for myself. Have some. I know you didn't have anything since lunch, and it's almost six now."

"I like you a lot more now," I said and inhaled the food first before indulging them.

He just shrugged, and we went back to eating.

After paying, which Easton insisted that he would, we walked back to school.

"Why don't you have any interest in academics?" I knew that he was not as bad he was now. During middle school, he was an extremely bright kid — the kind who always did his homework. He was not better than me, but he was close. However, in high school, everything changed.

"To tell you the truth, I don't know. All I know is that my life is a big mess right now, and I have no idea what to do."

"You have to sort it out. Talk to someone if you want to. Talk to me." I took out my hand and placed it on his shoulder. The sad look on his face made me do it.

"Are you vying for the post of my personal shrink, Neveah?" Suddenly, all the sadness from his face evaporated and was replaced with humour. He was hiding things. That, I was sure of. I understood that I was not his best friend and all, but he should've talked to Xavier or even to that jerk named Alden.

I just frowned when he looked at me. When he saw it, he turned his face away.

We both went our separate ways.

While I was driving, my thoughts went to that recording on my phone. I had to listen to it and fast.

I went home to find Ma watching TV, and Bryan preparing dinner in the kitchen, which was strange.

"What is going on here?" I asked.

"Bryan is preparing dinner today." Ma was watching Glee. She was a bit too old to watch that show!

"Should I be scared?" I said loudly.

"Have some trust, kiddo," a voice came from the kitchen. I went to it to see Bryan preparing some pasta. *Yummy!*

I went upstairs and changed into some comfy clothes and came bouncing downstairs. The dining table was set up with candles and fancy dinner set.

"Wow! I'm impressed."

We all prayed and then had dinner. It was the best dinner I have had in a while.

After the meal, Ma and Bryan went to visit some client. These businessmen only have free time late at night.

I went upstairs and closed the door of my room. Then I plugged my headphones on my cell, put them on, and clicked on the recording.

For the first few minutes, there was no sound at all, but after that came a rough voice which belonged to Ryder.

"What is wrong with you?" Ryder's voice was almost a growl.

"What's wrong with me? You're the one who almost killed her." It sounded like Easton, and he was really angry.

"Well, you weren't getting your fat ass up, and she wouldn't even have a concussion. The height of the sofa is damn low," Ryder argued back.

"Doesn't matter, and what are you doing here? It's my territory."

Territory? What was Easton talking about? Was he some gang leader or something? Maybe he was. You never know.

"That's where you are wrong. It's neutral territory, and Neveah was my best friend since a very long time ago. Believe me, I've heard a lot about you from her and Gina." This time, Ryder's voice was almost patronizing in a sarcastic kind of way.

"She is mine." Easton's voice was so loud that I almost took off my headphones. How come I didn't hear this yesterday?

What were they going on about? First, I did not belong to anyone, let alone Easton, and second, when did Ma ever speak to Ryder about him?

"Last time I checked, your second guy Xavier wasn't that fond of her. In the mall, remember?" Ryder was definitely sarcastic. I was sure of it now.

"Don't, Ryder. I'm not in the best mood right now. I am missing my girl. She wants an explanation, and I don't know what to say."

His girl?

"It's better you tell the truth," Ryder said.

"Are you nuts? You and I both know how she will react. I'll be lucky if she leaves me alive."

"Alright, but look out for any intruders," Ryder said.

"Sure," Easton replied.

"Consider my advice, Easton. I know my Neveah," Ryder said.

"She isn't yours."

"I know, dude. I'm just messing with you." I swore I could almost hear a smile in Ryder's voice.

The phone recording ended after that, leaving me confused and shocked. What was Easton going on about me being 'his?' Man, I got to talk to Ryder.

So I sent a message to him. *Hey, we gotta meet.*

Sure, when? Ryder replied.

Come to my house. There is no one here right now.

Alright, meet you in twenty.

Ryder arrived within the next twenty minutes just as he promised.

"What's up?" he asked me nonchalantly. His bruises from yesterday had almost disappeared.

"What is a neutral territory?" I asked in a very sweet voice. Ryder's face went pale within a split-second.

"How… h-how do you?" The poor guy was having a tough time forming his sentences.

"I recorded the whole conversation," I told him.

"You did what?" he blurted out.

"Don't shout. I'm sure you heard me the first time."

"What did Blondie tell you after I left?" I knew what he was doing. He was trying to measure how much I already knew.

"All he did was make excuses," I said truthfully.

"This is regarding you and him, Neveah. I shouldn't come in between this. Just understand that, Neveah." He patted my back affectionately

Oh, great! What were all of them hiding?

Chapter 14

Neveah

The next morning, everything started in the normal way except I ignored everyone including Melissa and Georgy. I was giving them the silent treatment.

I was so angry at Easton and the rest of them. Call me childish, but all of them were hiding something from me, and I didn't like it. I wouldn't have bothered if it wasn't associated with me, but I had a feeling that it is.

I didn't spare Xavier either. Whenever we passed each other, be it in classroom or hallways, I glared at him. Surprisingly, he didn't pass any comments. Talk about unusual!

I was in the cafeteria sitting alone reading some book when I heard the sound of scraping chairs.

The next thing I knew my table was filled with people.

"What the hell, Neveah? Why are you ignoring us?" Melissa asked with an angry tone.

"You really don't know?" I was full-on mocking her and the others in the table by now. By others, I meant Easton, Georgy, and, much to my surprise, even Xavier. I noticed that the black eye Easton was sporting yesterday was almost completely gone. *Strange!* Humans couldn't heal that fast. I, however, decided to push it back. I needed to focus on the issue at hand.

"Stop overreacting, Nev," Georgy said. I snorted and ignored him and turned to Easton instead.

"You're not saying anything?" I questioned him with a smile on my face even though I was fuming inside.

"What do you want me to ask, Neveah?" His eyes were blank, and his expression was guarded.

"I don't know...." I shrugged before continuing, "How about the 'Neveah is mine' line, hmmm?"

All the colour drained from his face.

"Holy God! How did you know about that?" Xavier exclaimed. So he knew about it, too? *Oh, joy!*

"Did your friend say anything?" Easton's voice was cold.

"From the looks of it, he is more of your friend than mine."

When his face turned into an expression of confusion, I took my cell out and switched on the recording. I put my one leg over the other, folded my hands in my lap, smirked at all of them, and channeled a look of superiority in my eyes. After some time, it started.

It was very funny to see all their expressions drop one by one. Call me cruel, but man, I was enjoying the hell out of it. By the time the recording stopped, I realised that the whole cafeteria was silent. It looked like lunch was over! Time goes fast when you are enjoying.

"How?" Easton was at a loss for words.

I looked straight into his eye and said, "You actually thought that I will let you and Ryder talk to each other alone after the way you were trying to kill each other? And let's not forget, that 'touch him, and he will calm down speech' was just plain fishy. I only listened to it last night. This would have happened yesterday if only I had listened to it sooner. By the way, I need to leave now. Lunch is over." I left the four of them in the table visibly shocked.

During all the remaining lectures, all four of them were absent. I had no idea whether to wait for Easton after school. Easton was already failing, he didn't need to bunk off more classes. The others weren't any better.

Being the 'good' person that I was, I decide to wait for Easton... but only for ten minutes. About five minutes into it, a hand came over my mouth. I tried to pull it off or give the person behind me a jab in the stomach, but I always missed.

The next thing I knew, I was being pushed into my own car. After I was in, the person released my mouth.

There, sitting in my car, was Georgy, and the mystery person who had a hand over my mouth turned out to be Easton.

"Can anyone explain to me what is happening over here?" I screeched at the top of my voice, fuming with anger.

"We are going to my house and then we can all talk," Easton replied.

"Sorry, dude, but I ain't entering your house," I said and folded my hands over each other. I was no longer looking at them.

"Why not?"

I knew that Easton was going to get angry when I say the reason, so I tried to avoid it. "I just don't trust you. Nothing personal, Easton, but I just don't trust the four of you," I said instead.

"There is no one at my house right now and hurting you would be the last thing we could think of." He took my hands and kissed them like he did a few days ago.

"I just don't want to go to your house, okay?"

The car stopped, and I realized that we had already reached his house. *Okay, then.* We all got out, and Melissa and Georgy were waiting outside.

"I am still not coming in." I kept my stand and stood close to my car.

"Why not, Neveah?" Easton was getting extremely angry, so I didn't reply. That idiot just wouldn't let it go.

"I just don't want to," I said and snobbishly whipped my head to the side.

"Just shut up and get in." He pulled my hand and proceeded to drag me.

"I will not." I tried to pull my hand out, but his grip was too strong.

He stopped and whispered to me in a hard voice. "Yes, you will."

"No, I won't," I retorted. I didn't feel so confident anymore, tough.

"Why not?"

"Because when you kicked me out, I promised myself that I will never enter your house again."

Shit! I should have kept my mouth shut. I didn't want to say anything, but he just wouldn't let go. Right now, he looked very angry. He closed his eyes for a second, and when he opened them again, they were relatively calm. "Okay, let's go to Xavier's house. It is empty now."

I nodded in reply.

We all walked to Xavier's house since it was only two blocks away from Easton's.

We all sat on at the dining table, but I had no idea what to expect from this so-called meeting. I speculated that maybe Easton had some crush on me since childhood and was suddenly in love with me and that all the people knew that except me. Even in my thoughts, it sounded horrible and well… impossibly impossible. There was no way that was happening.

Alright, here goes nothing.

"So, I assume that I was kidnapped so that you all can explain what exactly happened yesterday, hmm?"

"We are not exactly normal, Neveah," Easton started.

"I knew that," I interrupted him.

Take that!

He frowned, obviously annoyed with what I was implying. Then again, when was I able to shut my mouth?

"Shut up, Neveah, and listen."

"Alright, alright! Jeez, no need to get angry!" I scolded him and pointed a finger at his face. Melissa and Xavier snickered.

"Enough! And you, young lady, will listen to me."

Easton

"Enough! And you, young lady, will listen to me," I ordered.

I had no idea how I was going to explain what I am, that I was not normal, that I was a werewolf.

"Listen, Nev... We are not normal," I started as I gestured to everyone in the room, "Okay? We are..."

I continued dreading this moment, but I had no other choice but to do this. My original plan was to woo her and then slowly reveal the other part of my existence, but my girl was damn smart. Never in my strangest dreams had I imagined that she would record that conversation between me and her friend, Ryder. I didn't even think that she would invite me to her house after the way I kicked her out. No matter what I said, I knew that she would not forget it. Melissa was right.

The best example was when she refused to enter my house earlier. Now, I would have to buy a new house for us to live in.

That was when my wolf conveniently pointed out that there was no way we were going to live together in the next few years. *Stupid Dog!* Now that I had also hit her friend, winning her over would be more difficult. Not to mention that I was not her favourite person in the first place.

I actually never thought of losing control in front of her like that, but the thought of someone hurting her was unbearable for me. I did not have the intention to fight her friend, but he put her in danger. Plus, he entered her house drunk. Intoxicated werewolves were very dangerous. They could cause a lot of damage. What would have happened if I hadn't been there yesterday? God knows what he could have done! So I was already pissed beforehand. The situation just helped me release my anger. I was very satisfied with the blows

I delivered even though the ones I received were just as painful. Luckily, due to a bit of advanced healing inherent to all werewolves, it was now a lot better.

I was so shocked to hear the recording, I finally decided it was better to tell her that I wasn't exactly human, but I would have to leave out the mate part. I would tell it to her when she is more comfortable accepting me. *Damn that Ryder.* He told me to tell her as soon as possible, and here we are!

I didn't even want to think about her reaction. My best hope was that she does not go to the cops or tell any human anything. Luckily, her only friends knew about the existence of our kind. And of course, she wasn't the kind to go around gossiping. She wasn't someone interested in that.

I got myself prepared mentally.

But before I could say anything, there was a knock on the door. The person outside didn't even wait for us to open it and just barged in.

A small boy of about five came running in wearing only small pants. It was Rick, a boy from our pack.

"Can you play with me, Alpha? I just shifted yesterday," he shouted.

Oh, boy!

Neveah

Easton was about to say something about all of them not being normal when a cute little boy came running in. He was about four or five with cute blond curls and sparkly blue eyes and only wore a cute Ben 10 pants. He looked so cute!

He came and stood in front of Easton and said, "Can you play with me, Alpha? I just shifted yesterday."

Somehow, I had a feeling that he wasn't talking about shifting homes.

Before Easton could say anything, the boy spoke again, "Can you come too, Luna?"

Okay, why was he calling me Luna? I didn't think I changed my name. Warning bells were going off in my head. I had a very good idea as to what Easton was going to say, and my brain was just refusing to accept the reasoning behind it.

"Go and play outside, Rick. We'll come soon," Melissa said. The boy just smiled at her and ran at the same speed he entered.

Looking at the shocked and horrified expressions on everyone's face, I took a very impulsive and rash decision to run after the boy. The door was open. As soon as I reached the door, I closed and locked it and took off behind the boy. The boy ran behind Xavier's house and into the forest. I had no idea that there was such a huge forest behind his house, and why does he stay so near it?

The boy had an amazing speed for a four or five-year-old. Even I wasn't able to catch him. We ran and ran till we reached a meadow. It was huge and empty and stretched for quite a distance. It was surrounded by dense trees which probably formed the forest. The boy then ran into the trees, and I deduced that I was not fit enough to run at his speed. *Shame on me!*

Panting from the run, I decided to give my body a much-needed rest and plopped myself on the soft grass. That was when I realized that I was in the middle of nowhere with no idea how to get out. *Great, that was just what I needed!* My mind went through numerous possibilities of what Easton could possibly be. Does that mean that Ryder was one of them, too? At least, the possibility of that stupid infatuation was out of the picture.

But if Easton was not normal, then what was the connection between his 'abnormal behaviour' and me calming him? Last time I checked, I was pretty much normal and human. There was one possibility I kept pushing to the back of my brain. I did not want to acknowledge it, but was it the answer I was searching for?

I sat there for God knows how long thinking about random things. After a while, I removed my cell from my pocket to check the time when I realized that *bam!*

I had a cell phone with me! I could call those idiots!

Why haven't I realised that before? I checked the signal, and surprisingly, it was full.

Yes!

I hurriedly called the person responsible for this big mess.

The phone rang for about five seconds before a voice thundered through it. "Where are you, Neveah?"

Oh, man! Easton sounded angry.

I waited for some time before I replied, "You see, umm… Well, I'm kinda lost in the middle of the forest behind Xavier's house," I stammered out.

"Can you describe the place?" His voice was relatively calmer now.

"Okay. It is a grassy clearing in the middle of the forest surrounded by really tall trees." My knowledge of biology wasn't that strong so I couldn't identify the trees.

"Alright, hold on. Just stay there. I'll come and get you in ten minutes."

"Okay," I replied and cut the phone.

I kept the phone on my side and hugged my knees to myself, waiting for Easton to rescue me out of this mess.

I was just sitting on the grass when I heard loud growls from the forest. I would be lying if I said that I wasn't scared. *Hell!* I was terrified. *What do I do now?* I had to do something.

I stood up shakily when I felt a pair of hands on my hips. I stiffened and turned around to come face-to-face with Easton.

"Oh God, thank you. I was so scared." I put my arms around his shoulders and hugged him. I knew that in any other circumstance, I would have not done this at all. He might probably be one of the things making that strange noise in the forest, but right now, I was too terrified for logical thinking.

He wrapped his arms tightly around me as well and nuzzled his face into my neck. I, too, closed my eyes and felt the panic slowly ebb away.

I opened them after some time and found the other three giving me strange looks. *Ohh!* That was when I remembered the position we were in.

I pulled on Easton's t-shirt and whispered in his ear, "Let go, Easton."

He loosened his arms around me, and we separated, but then he wrapped one arm around my waist. Okay, this was really weird. I cleared my throat and said in a small voice, "Thank you."

He just nodded in reply.

I was looking at Easton when the realisation hit him as to where we were. "What were you thinking when you ran out locking us all in? And not to mention getting stuck in the forest?" he blurted out.

Truth to be told, I was expecting this.

If this was any other time, I would have hastily made a witty comeback or two, but I was too tired right now.

"Not today, Easton, please," I murmured in a dejected tone.

Something in my tone must have done it because he didn't press the matter further. He just nodded and tightened his hold on my waist. "Let's go back."

Surprisingly, all the others were silent. I sighed and started walking when I heard that loud growl again. I immediately turned around, but Easton tightened his hold on me further to a point where his nails were piercing my skin. I hissed out loud at the pain. *Damn, it hurts!* I tried to get out, but it only aggravated my pain. When I looked at him, he wasn't even aware he was hurting me. He had a furious look in his eyes which was currently directed towards the forest.

"Easton, stop! You are hurting her," Melissa said. I thought everyone except Easton noticed that. *Slowcoach.* His eyes widened comically, and he immediately let go as if I burned him. If I wasn't hurting, I would have laughed at his expression.

Just then, the growling sounds were heard from the forest once more. I turned my attention to where they came from. It wasn't that dark yet so I could make out proper outlines.

I saw something twinkling in the forest. I saw many more of them before a pack of wolves came running towards us. I was rooted to my spot and prepared for my death. I didn't get to eat Ma's wedding cake. How would she cope without me? At least she had Bryan now. Oh God, I was about to die, and I was thinking such silly thoughts. What was wrong with me? I braced myself for the pain when the wolves went running to the other side of the forest without even sparing me a second glance. *What the?*

Great! I was sad now because those huge wolves didn't come running to kill me. How much weird could I get? This was just not me. All I needed was to go home and sleep for some time. Oh, how would I love to forget about all that happened today!

I turned back and started walking to God knows where when something nudged my leg. It was a wolf puppy. Actually, it was a pup the size of a German Shepherd. It licked me through my jeans, and before I could react, Easton cursed out loud.

The baby wolf started making growling noises, and suddenly, its fur started to recede. In the place of the wolf was the small boy I was chasing through the forest hours ago.

Oh, my God! I looked at my hips, and there were three long gashes from where Easton held me. No wonder it hurt like a bitch… or should I say dog? Pun intended.

That was when I realised that they were all wolves…

FREAKING WOLVES!

Oh, for the love of...

Chapter 15

Easton

This shouldn't have happened. Neveah was not supposed to find out things this way.

I was at Xavier's house along with Dad, Melissa, Gregory, Xavier and, unfortunately, Alden since he was my third in command.

We were all patiently waiting for Neveah to wake up.

She fainted when she saw Rick shift.

Seriously, I still couldn't believe that Neveah got to know so much on her own. This all seemed so surreal.

I made Melissa call Gina to inform her that Neveah would come home late. Somehow, she didn't question any further, and I was grateful for that. The last thing I wanted was an angry mother on my doorstep. Speaking of parents, my father was shocked when I narrated to him the incident but then started laughing. I saw my father laughing in front of me after a long, long time. He said something along the lines of, ‘keep me in check.’ At least, someone was happy.

The doctor did some tests on her and reassured me that Neveah fainted only due to shock and that it wasn’t serious. I breathed a big sigh of relief after that.

Now, the only thing I needed to worry about was how to answer her questions without freaking her out again. Everyone left after some time, leaving me with an unconscious Neveah.

I held her limp hand and spoke to her even though she couldn’t hear me. “I’m sorry, Nev. I never meant any of this to happen. Just wake up soon. We have a lot to do.”

“Oh yeah, mister, we have a lot to talk about.” I looked down wide-eyed to see Neveah glaring at me. “And let go of my hand,” she added. She snatched her hand away as soon as I loosened my hold.

“Go home now. I made Melissa call Gina to tell her that you will come home late. We will talk tomorrow. Come, I’ll drop you off,” I said before she could speak again.

“Can I trust you not to kill me?” It hurt when she asked that. She was silent, which was very much unlike her. I bet she was scared. I wanted to erase all of her fears, but now was not the time.

“Can I trust you not to repeat the episode of today to anyone?” I asked her in return.

She thought about it for a while. “Yes.”

“Then there won’t be a problem,” I promised. She just shook her head in reply and got up from the bed. As we were leaving the room, I couldn’t help checking out her legs.

What? They were hot.

I took her home in my car and ordered Xavier to call for a pack meeting in half-an-hour. It was very necessary, considering the circumstances. During the whole car ride, she was silent as an owl. We parked near her house, and I turned to her. "Trust me, Neveah. I will explain everything tomorrow after school. Goodnight." Again, she just sighed and nodded.

I turned back the car and headed for the meeting.

Neveah

I laid on the bed thinking about all that happened today.

The last thing on my mind was Easton being a werewolf!

Yes, A FREAKING WEREWOLF… A DOG!

No wonder Melissa behaved like a bitch to me, even though she was my ex-best friend and on the process of becoming my best friend again. This also meant that Ryder had to be one, too. The freaking slimy dog! Wait, then what about Daniel and Broody? I had to speak to them soon.

No wonder I fainted! I was surprised that I didn't try to kill Easton, though. Then again, I was scared. He was a dangerous werewolf, and not to mention an Alpha. The cops wouldn't even find my body if something happened. Easton and his buddies may end up eating me. They were wild animals, after all.

So I kept silent on the whole ride back home. I reached home by ten, and that wasn't even that late. Thankfully, Easton had the presence of mind to inform Ma. Otherwise, there would have been loads of questions about my whereabouts. When Ma asked, I just told her that a little boy was celebrating his birthday and that we were invited to attend.

We sat down on the couch together before Ma began talking. "Hey, I just looked for venues for the wedding." Ma looked so excited, and Bryan smiled lovingly at her.

"Did you find a good place?" I tried to join the conversation, but my voice came out tired and worn out.

She ignored the tone of my voice and continued, "Yes, I found a place. It looks really bad right now, but I am sure that after we clean it out, it will look fabulous." She showed me the picture of a clearing surrounded by lots of trees. Even though it did look a bit dirty, I was sure it would look nice after some cleaning, just like Ma said.

"Appearances can be deceptive," I said out aloud with Easton on my mind.

"Are you alright, sweetie?" Ma looked worried now.

I mentally cursed myself and let out a small fake smile. "I am alright, Ma. It's nothing," I said.

"Alright, if you say so." I was a hundred percent sure that she did not believe me, but I couldn't tell her the truth. She smiled at me, gave me a small peck on the head, and left for the kitchen saying something about leftovers. She tried to coax me into eating dinner, but I lied to her that I had enough food at the party.

Having dinner didn't seem like the best thing for me, especially after what I witnessed. I said goodnight to both of them and went straight to bed.

Before I left, Bryan told me, "You can talk to me about anything, Neveah."

I just hugged him tightly, burying my face in his chest. I was tempted to tell him but decided that I couldn't be selfish and drag him into own problems. I let him go after some time.

"What was that for?" he asked. Well, I was not exactly the most affectionate person.

"Just because I can," I simply told him.

"Alright, then. Off to bed," he shooed me with a smile on his face.

"*Goodnight*, Dad." I blew him a kiss and then shouted, "Goodnight, Ma."

I heard her say goodnight when I reached upstairs.

I looked at the clock on the table near my bed. It was only eleven.

I have been lying on my bed for nearly an hour. My mind just wouldn't switch off. I thought about all the warning signs I missed before the big revelation.

Easton and his buddies were all good looking and unusually buff.

The fact of them all sticking together.

Melissa's bitchiness.

Their healing power, as was shown by Easton's fading bruise.

And Claire's statement of just how *important* Peter was.

Although that didn't explain why I had to touch Easton that day.

I looked at my phone contacts and decided to do it after thinking about it for some time.

"Hello, can you come here?"

Easton

I was currently standing on a podium, addressing the crowd in front of me.

"Good evening, everyone! I am sorry that this meeting is being conducted this late, but the matter to be discussed is very important." I looked around for Rick in the crowd. "Could you please come up here?" He looked scared, but I just smiled at him.

He came up with his adoptive mother.

"I am sure many of you already know what happened." Many of the pack members nodded. Rick's adoptive mother, Sarah, looked scared. I continued, "Since my mate has unexpectedly come to know that we are werewolves, I just want all of you to refrain from shifting in her presence since she is still sensitive about it."

They all nodded in agreement. "That is all. You are all dismissed."

They all went back to their homes and carried on with whatever they were doing.

I picked up Rick and gently carried him in my arms. "Thanks, buddy. You were of great help to me today," I said.

"So does this mean that you are not angry with me?" he asked in his cute baby voice.

"No, buddy. Why will I be angry at you?"

"Momma said I made luna fall."

"No, buddy. She is alright. She was just shocked." I was pretty sure that he didn't understand what shock meant, but I was really grateful to him. I had come to the conclusion that her coming to know about my species through other means was better than me telling her directly. Truth to be told, I was scared of her knowing. Even though Neveah acted all brave, deep down I knew that she would have a hard time coming to terms with the truth.

If this was her reaction to me being a werewolf, I couldn't even imagine her reaction when I tell her that she was my mate and that we were stuck together forever. Things were really going to turn bad for me.

I put down Rick and ruffled his hair. He went back home, preferably, to his bed since it is way past his bed time. I smiled at Sarah and excused myself. I went inside the house to see Melissa, Xavier, Alden, and some other guys in the hall. They were playing some game while Melissa read some magazine.

I sat down and played with them for some time before I realised something. I turned to Xavier and Alden. "I want you to guard Neveah's house. She is in a very vulnerable state right now, and I don't want her to make any bad decisions," I said.

Alden frowned but got up and got out of the house.

I went back to my room and lifted the chemistry book sitting on my bed. I was pointlessly turning its pages when I got a message on my phone.

There is a male wolf hanging from her window, Easton, it read.

Neveah

I waited on the bed in my now pitch dark room. I was afraid that Ma would somehow come to know since I had no experience in this kind of thing whatsoever. I was almost asleep when I heard a soft knock on my window.

I got up and went near it. My eyes went the size of saucers as I saw Ryder hanging from the tree branch near my window. *How?* "Get away from the tree, Ryder. You're going break it." It was quite an old tree, and I didn't think the tree could handle his weight.

"So you are more worried about the tree than me?" he asked in his usual happy tone.

I narrowed my eyes at him. "Obviously, I am not worried about you. You are a dog. Poor tree," I replied in a bitchy tone.

Ryder's eyes widened, and he gave me a questioning stare. I just nodded back.

"It's called a werewolf. Not a dog," he corrected me.

"Same thing."

"No, it is not. Now get away from the window and let me get inside." Ryder was back to his happy self again.

I just sighed and stepped back. I made him sit on the bed and switched on the small light nearby. Then I sat down beside him.

"So, Neveah, why did you call me at this time of the night?"

I sighed again and narrated to him the whole series of events that occurred today. By the end of it, Ryder was laughing on the floor. I frowned at him. That was not funny. This was my life story. Well, not mine, but his actually.

"It is not funny, Ryder. He is a five-year-old child." I just couldn't fathom how he found my situation hilarious. I glared at him, and he stopped laughing.

"You mean, you have not seen an adult wolf?" Ryder asked suddenly. What did he mean by that? Was it important?

"No?" I said, unsure of what to say.

"No wonder! I want to know your reaction when you see one. That is if you are conscious after that." Again, he was on the verge of laughing. I swore if he starts laughing like a hyena once again, I was going kill him.

"What do you mean?" I asked.

"He means nothing," said a voice coming from my window.

"What are you doing here, Xavier?" He was hanging on my window. What an improvement! At least the tree would be safe.

"Easton doesn't want you with him in your bedroom," Xavier said with a stern look on his face. *Seriously?*

"And why do you think I care about what Easton thinks?" Easton was the sole cause for all this. I was happy in my mundane and normal world until he came along. Now, I was cursing myself for bugging him to answer my questions. I felt like a fool for worrying about a world that was not even mine.

"You should if you want to stay in this area," Xavier replied with a frown on his face.

"This house belongs to my mother, not him." Dumb guy. Did he not know this? This area belongs to Easton, my foot.

"Actually not, this area does belong to him," Ryder spoke up from my bed on which he was currently laying on.

"Really?"

"Yeah, it does belong—"

"I understood the first time. It was just an expression, Ryder. Stop irritating me." I cut him out.

He held up his hands in surrender. "But did you really run behind a five-year-old and couldn't keep up with him?" He and Xavier snickered and did an air high five.

"Shut up." I gritted through my teeth. I really, really wanted to shout, but if I did, Ma, Bryan, and the whole neighbourhood would wake up.

He and Xavier snickered again.

"Out, get out! And Xavier, don't you hang from my window again." Now, I was pissed.

"Oh, come on, I was joking." Ryder tried to calm me down, but I was tired of their shit.

"Get out, Ryder."

"Alright, alright we'll leave. Goodnight." Ryder said and left through the window. Xavier followed after him.

I switched off the light and laid on my bed. Just then, the door to my room creaked opened. I immediately closed my eyes and pretended to be asleep. Whoever it was switched on the light again. Then I felt the bed sheet being pulled on me and a light kiss on my forehead.

"Goodnight, kiddo. You are one of the best things that ever happened to me." It sounded like Bryan.

"You know she can't hear you, right?" Ma's soft voice said.

"Doesn't matter. She will know it in her subconscious mind." I heard Ma giggle.

"Silly man! Let Neveah sleep."

Bryan pressed his lips again to my forehead. Moments later, I heard the door closing.

I opened my eyes after I was sure that they had left. For the first time, I was happy that I didn't get to know my father. I fell asleep with a smile on my face.

The next day, I wasn't really in the mood to go to school, but then I got a text from Easton at six in the morning.

Please wait after school in the football ground.

Now, I had no option but to go. Anyway, I was eager to know about wolf-men or whatever they called themselves.

I behaved very properly with all of them during class. I behaved as if Xavier did not hang from my window last night. It was not friendly but cordial. I sat with Melissa and Georgy during lunch. Enough said, it was uncomfortable.

I was pushing my food around my plate when Georgy spoke up. "Hey, how is your friend?"

"You mean, Ryder?"

"Yup."

"Why are you asking about him?" I was still suspicious about his origin. I was not sure if he was a wolf-man too. I was already sure Melissa and Alden were.

"Because I saw both of them leave your house in the middle of the night, and by them I mean, Ryder and Xavier." *Oh, thank God!* He didn't see Xavier hanging from my window. If he saw that, others would have seen it too. What if someone saw it and informs Ma? That would be the last thing I wanted to add to my long list of worries.

"What were you doing at such a time in front of my house?" I asked in a suspicious tone.

"Nothing. Just happened to pass by."

I nodded, but I wasn't fully convinced by what he said it.

"Oh, okay. Ryder and I were having a party which our dear friend, Xavier, gatecrashed." I didn't mean for the statement to come out in a sarcastic way, but I couldn't help myself.

An awkward silence came after that.

"Can I ask you something?" I asked Georgy. I was hesitant and scared of his reaction.

"Sure." He seemed wary too but allowed me.

"Are you… one of them?" It was so pathetic that I couldn't even say werewolf. There was still some part of me that didn't believe that this was happening. Deep inside, I was still hoping that this was all a bad dream.

"You mean a werewolf?" he asked with a teasing smile on his face. This was not funny!

"Yeah."

"No, no. I am just a plain ole human."

Okay... now I was confused and relieved at the same time. If he was human, how come he knew about them? Wasn't it against the rules or something?

"Then how do you..."

"I'll explain sometime later. We can talk about it after you and Easton speak. We have a lot to discuss."

"Okay, alright," I said. We sure did have a lot to talk about.

"We can meet at my home. My brother and parents are both out of town."

"Deal."

By the time I had reached the ground, Easton was already there. He looked tired and irritated, so I decided that it would be best if I kept my mouth shut.

"Should we—" I started but was rudely interrupted.

"What was he doing at your house at eleven thirty in the night?"

How did he know? It must've been Xavier.

I was so going to kill him one day.

"Making fun of me along with Xavier, happy?" I too replied in a rude tone.

"I didn't mean it like that, Neveah. We... we can be unstable sometimes. I was just scared."

He was the werewolf, and I was the human… and he said that he was scared. Talk about irony!

"You are just like him," I said, referring to Ryder. I should be more scared of the fact that Xavier was at my house. For God's sake, I grew up with him. He surely wouldn't kill me.

"I've never been alone with you in your house," Easton contradicted.

"Oh, you have been alone with me. Ma caught us that time you were messing with me in the kitchen," I said, referring to that sad time. Stupid guy trying to get me into trouble!

"Oh, yeah, but you kissed me first."

"It was a silly dare, Easton," I retorted. I didn't want him to even think about it. It was one of my most embarrassing moments.

"It was hot," he said with a dreamy look in his eyes.

"I'm surprised that you actually remember it." I scoffed. Everyone knew about his past. I was sure that he wasn't even thinking about me.

"Now, you're judging me, Neveah," Easton said mischievously, knowing that I knew he was right.

"Sorry," I muttered quietly.

"It's alright. Come, let's go somewhere."

"Where?" I had to go to Georgy's house too. But I couldn't forget about our project. I just couldn't have us failing. Since we have started working together, Easton's grades had considerably improved.

"Somewhere. I can't talk in public."

"Oh! Alright."

We went to the parking lot and got in his car.

We reached the forest near his and Xavier's house. We walked for some time, and then I sat on the grass. He was still walking ahead without knowing that I was not with him anymore.

"Eugene!"

"Don't call me that," he said as he turned sideways. That was when he realised that I was not beside him. The expression on his face had me laughing and clapping my hands like a seal.

"When did you sit there?"

"We passed the place, Easton."

He sighed and came to sit in front of me.

"So, you can ask any questions you want, but before that, I want to ask one question. Are you scared of me?"

"Truthfully, I don't know. I just don't know." I tried to explain it the best way I could. "You know, sometimes things are beyond our control. But I like to be in control with my life, and this...... this is beyond me. I just don't understand it no matter how much I try. To answer your question, yesterday, I was scared out of my life. However, when I saw you in school, I realised that you are still the guy who hated me since we've met. I mean, you are just Easton Eugene Dale. Plain and simple." I ended with a smile on my face.

He mirrored my smile with his own. "I never hated you."

I narrowed my eyes at him. I highly doubted that he was telling the truth.

"Someday, I'll tell you a story."

"Whatever." I shrugged.

Suddenly, I heard growling.

"You all do that in the day, too?" Wasn't it dangerous for the normal inhabitants nearby? And to think that Ma used to bring me here regularly years ago.

"Yup."

"Can I see one?" I asked, remembering Ryder's and Xavier's taunt. I wanted to prove a point right now.

"What? A werewolf?"

"Uh-huh."

"But why?"

"Because Xavier and Ryder were making fun of me saying that I wouldn't handle seeing a fully grown one. So please, let me see." I was practically begging. "Please, pretty please." I pouted and showed my puppy dog eyes.

"I think that both of them were correct," Easton said in a slow voice, probably not to anger me.

"Of course, I can handle it. I am not that weak," I whined. Well, not really.

"I am not saying that you are weak, but facing any wild animal could be scary, you know."

"Sheesh! Alright."

The growls increased, and at some point, my curiosity took over me. I forgot all the questions I had to ask when I saw a tail swishing behind the bushes. I stood up and walked over it.

"Stubborn," Easton muttered under his breath as he followed me closely.

I walked towards the bush and heard similar sounds from yesterday. I got closer and saw a wolf turning into a human. Man, he was hot! I craned my neck to see more of him, but Easton wasn't allowing me to.

Easton's arms were already restraining me. "Hey, let me see! I wanna watch!" I whined, hoping he would comply. But all I got was growls from him. "Oh, come on, East. Stop growling."

I was watching only the muscles of the guy. He was at least ten years older than me. I was sure of that.

Suddenly a pair of hands covered my eyes. "Enough."

"But, East—"

"I said enough," he cut me off. His voice was now much deeper and sharper,

I took his hands off my eyes and turned to him. "What is your problem?"

"You are looking at some other male," he grumbled.

"I will look at whoever I like, and there is nothing you can do about it."

His growls turned more violent, and within a split-second, a huge wolf was standing in his place.

Chapter 16

Neveah

Wow!

My eyes widened as I took in the sight in front of me. In front of me was a huge, and I mean *huge,* oversized wolf baring its sharp teeth in front of me. The wolf's midnight-black coat and looked really smooth and soft. A while back, I thought that Easton may be a light collared wolf because of his hair colour.

"Easton?" I was not even sure it was him anymore.

Learning that the guy I have known throughout my life was a wolf and seeing him as one in front of my eyes were two different things.

No wonder Easton didn't want me to see him in this shape. It was downright scary and terrifying, and I was seriously contemplating running and screaming in the opposite direction.

"Easton Dale, is that you?" I turned around and saw the man who was phasing from before. He sure was hot!

I might have been busy observing the new guy because Easton growled again.

"Oh, stop growling, Easton, and become the blond guy again. It's very weird to look at you like this." Right now, my irritation was winning over my fear. Moreover, it was just Easton, the same guy who always pissed me off. He was impolite, dumb, and a dog… literally!

The animal glared at me with his glowing forest green eyes. I glared back at him, totally forgetting the fact that he was ten times stronger than me. "You cannot defeat me, Easton, wolf or not," I said as I pushed my index finger against his snout. "Now."

He then shifted back to his human form again, but he was still angry.

"Wear some clothes, dude," the new guy standing behind me said. So when any wolf phases back, they don't have any clothes on them. New info! Should have asked Easton about it.

That was when I realized that he was wearing nothing. He walked to the forest behind some trees and came back with shorts on.

I got to say, he looked good without a shirt.

"Like something you see?" His eyes held humour and arrogance as he walked with style and his hands in his pant pockets.

I went and stood close to him. "Yup! Your eyes seem greener now." I pointed my index finger at his face.

The expression on his face was priceless.

"Don't fret. I am not going to blush by just seeing you without a shirt," I said and ran a consoling hand on his shoulder.

"I already have a lot of girls waiting for me. I don't need more." The arrogance was back!

I beamed at him. "That's great. Then you go to them, and I'll get acquainted with the guy behind us."

"You will do no such thing," he said sternly, obviously in a foul mood again.

"You know, you say the wrong things at the wrong time." It was my conclusion after so many years. I couldn't keep my mouth shut, just as he couldn't say the right things.

I heard a low chuckle behind me.

"I'm starting to understand that," Easton replied with a glum look.

"Is she your mate?" The other guy asked. I turned to look at him, but Easton restrained my motion.

"What's a mate? A friend?" I asked. I know the meaning of the word, but it might mean another thing for werewolves, so I brushed it away.

Easton, however, tensed up and glared at the guy. "I'll tell you later."

"Whatever." I tried throwing them off the topic by acting like I didn't care.

"Who is at your house right now?" Easton asked me, ignoring the other guy.

"Right now? Well, no one." Ma and Bryan were at work.

"Great, we're going there." He was already dragging me back to civilization as he said that.

"Ben, please go to my house. My father will address your matter. I have more important things to do as of now." Easton, at last, addressed him. I felt bad that Easton was ignoring him all this time.

"Bye, Ben." I waved at him, much to Easton's annoyance.

"Bye, Luna." He waved back with a huge smile on his face.

"It's Neveah, not Luna." I corrected. Ben, however, only continued smiling at me.

We went to my house. I made some sandwiches for snacks, and both of us sat in the hall.

"So, shall we start?" There were so many things I needed to ask.

"Ask away, Neveah."

"What are you exactly? I mean, are you all werewolves or something else?" Now, that was a dumb question on my part since I had seen him in his wolf form just a few minutes ago, but I asked him anyway.

"I am a werewolf along with many people of this town."

"You mean there are *that* many?" My jaw dropped.

"We comprise a considerable percent of the town's population." Hearing this sent my shock to another level.

"Whoa! Isn't that a bit too many? I mean, won't humans come to know? Just like I did." How come I didn't know what they were until now when I had spent my whole life with them?

"Not actually. In the olden times, werewolves used to occupy the whole town and did not allow any human immigration. But now, we don't have a choice. You came to know about us because I wanted you to know, and not because you wanted to know." His voice held truth.

"I guess that makes sense since I didn't realize for eighteen years that there is something wrong with you people."

"We are not abnormal, Neveah."

"Yeah, you just sprout fur whenever you feel like it. That's it, right?" Who knows? Maybe the next thing I'll know was that vampires also exist, along with witches, elves, and hybrids!

How normal!

"Somewhat yes." He looked a little uncomfortable, so I didn't press the topic further.

We fell into a comfortable silence while eating our sandwiches when I remembered something.

"What is an alpha?" The five-year-old boy called him that. An alpha male or female in the animal world was someone who had a dominant nature. So where did Easton come in? Even though Easton had the traits of a good leader, he couldn't be dominating at all. At least for me.

"I am an alpha."

No shit, Sherlock?

"And I am pi." I actually didn't expect Easton to understand the joke, but I said it anyway with a toothy grin. I continued when a confused Easton kept staring at me. "I know you are the alpha. I heard the small guy really well. I am asking what that means."

"Why were you smiling?" *Seriously?*

"You know, alpha, beta, gamma, pi. Grade two math, remember? They are all Greek alphabets used in math and science." Okay, that turned out to be a joke on me.

"That was lame, Neveah. I understood what you were asking. I was going to inform you of my position then the meaning of it."

"At least I have a sense of humour even if it's bad, unlike a certain someone." Easton didn't have even a minuscule amount of funny bone in his body.

"Okay, enough," he scolded me. "Let's get back to the topic. An alpha is someone who is a leader... someone who leads a group of people or, in my case, a pack of wolves."

I nodded, grasping this small nugget of knowledge. "So, how big is your pack?"

"As of now, two thousand nine-hundred ninety-nine."

"Oh, make that three thousand. We'll have a new member soon," he added after some time,

"Who?" There was a high possibility that I knew the person. Is it Georgy? But he was human, right? I contemplated asking Easton but then decide against it. It wasn't his story to tell.

"You will meet the person soon," he replied with promise ringing in his voice.

"Oh, alright." I stopped eating and started thinking about more questions.

"What's special about you? I mean, you are obviously not human, so any special powers?" I was thinking of Superman or Batman.

"Nothing abnormal, apart from shifting. Our kind's senses are just a tad more advanced than humans. We are equipped with better eyesight and hearing. Also, we are better built and have a bit of healing abilities, but not that much as humans believe it to be."

"Oh, okay." Absorbing this much knowledge was painful. I didn't believe half of it. "So why does Alden not like Melissa?" I shifted the conversation to a totally different topic. I had this feeling that it was somehow related to them being werewolves.

"It's something personal. She may feel bad if I say it to you. You should ask her. I'm sure that she will tell you. You will be able to provide her the companionship she craves right now." His eyes turned sad all of a sudden.

"How do you know what she wants?"

"As an alpha, I can feel the feelings of my pack members. I couldn't hear their thoughts, but I feel their emotions." That was cool and unfair at the same time! Poor Melissa. She was miserably sad, and everyone knew that.

"It's good that you can't hear their thoughts. That would be an invasion of privacy," I stated.

"Believe me, Neveah, when you live in a pack, there is no such thing as privacy. Everyone knows everything."

"Man, that is sad."

"You have no idea. Any more questions?" he asked.

I racked my brain to think of a question. Yesterday, I could think of hundreds, but right now, I came up blank.

"Okay, what is a mate?" I asked, remembering Ben's comment from earlier.

Easton stiffened before replying in a small voice, "I am sorry, Neveah, but it's against our law to tell that to you." That made sense. I was human, after all.

"Okay. So does my Ma know about you all?" I asked, hoping that she didn't.

"I actually don't know. She may or she may not. She was my mom's best friend." Sorrow flickered in his eyes at the thought of Amy. Even I grew sad seeing Easton that way.

"Hey, it's alright." I consoled him by running a hand through his. He caught mine and held it gently but firmly as if I was going to run somewhere.

"It will be," Easton promised, his hand tightening its grip.

"Okay, now enough of the wolfy talks. We have a project to complete. Your old man is so stressed that he asked me for help." There, the secret was revealed! I swiftly removed his hand from mine.

"I don't know whether to be angry or thank him."

"Why thank him?" I was utterly confused. All children hate it when parents tell them to study, including me.

"For trying to improve my educational status in school. Why did you tell me that my father told you to help me? It was supposed to be a secret, right?" He hit the nail on the head.

"So I can give you more homework for all our subjects since you don't do what the teacher tells you to." I had already prepared a schedule for him, and he had no choice but to follow.

"You're serious?" Now it was Easton's turn to get shocked.

"A hundred percent," I replied.

"Now, I am seriously angry." His beautiful face was marred by a deep scowl. I swear, his mood swings were terrifying, and not to mention irritating. I had to ask him about it sometime later.

"Stop acting up, Easton. You act like a girl sometimes." I teased.

"Alright, I'll do as you say."

"At last, you learned that it's no use fighting me." I gave him a smirk.

"Yup," he chuckled as if it was a joke I didn't know.

"Okay, then! Do the practice problems in chapter one of any algebra reference books from the library. And yes, you are searching for the book on your own." I confirmed Easton's worst fears.

"Do I have to?" There goes the scowl again.

"Yup. I want at least ten sums by tomorrow evening. About chemistry, I am bored right now, and I have to meet up with Georgy and Melissa. We will have to put that off for a later date."

"Nev, things aren't looking bright for Melissa. Just take care of her, will you? She was not the best person to you, I know, but you are one of best things that happened to her."

"I will." I nodded in understanding. It was heart-warming to know that he cared about Melissa. "You know, you don't seem that bad now."

"I am the good guy, Nev."

"You weren't good to me for a long time." I couldn't help thinking of all our previous memories together. They weren't all that good, and some of them were bad.

"I was just an idiot who thought that he had everything." This time, I gave him a sad smile and promised that it would be all be alright in the end. It had to be.

"At least you knew your father, Easton. I didn't know mine." Now I was just whining about my own personal problems. But sometimes, I wondered why he didn't want Ma and me. I mean, she was the perfect package. Ma was beautiful, kind, sincere, and intelligent. She was almost perfect. The only reason I could come up with was that he was just one big idiot who ran away from his responsibilities with his tail between his legs.

"Hey, it's alright." Easton wiped a stray tear that managed to roll down my cheeks with his thumb. Why was I even crying for that man? He didn't deserve my tears. He didn't deserve anything at all.

"It will be. Ma is getting married. Things are finally turning good for her. She is happy now."

Easton's fingers were still on my cheek. "She deserves it," he said.

"She does." I took his hand and held it in mine.

"This is one of the very rare times I like the fact that you exist." I smiled, my sour mood from before slowly vanishing.

"I wish I could feel the same way." *There he goes again!*

"And here I go regretting your existence again. Will you drop me at Melissa's house?" I asked with his hand still in mine.

"Sure," he replied with a charming boyish smile.

"Hop in." He dragged me with my hand tucked between his arm.

He played some rock song I didn't recognize along the way and sang along with it. Easton didn't have the best voice, but it wasn't all that bad.

"You've changed," I said, gazing at him while he was driving. He was very nice to me nowadays. That was very strange of him.

"You know, it's been eight years, Neveah."

I just smiled at him and said, "Sometimes, things are difficult to forget, Easton."

I then went back to gazing out at the scenery.

Chapter 17

Neveah

Easton dropped me at Melissa's house. During the way, we decided to ask each other random questions.

"What is your favourite colour?" he asked me.

"Black. Yours?"

"Blue. Favourite dish?"

Before I could say anything, he spoke again, "Don't answer. I know you'll eat anything edible."

"You won't?" I challenged him.

He opens his mouth to say something before he closes it again. "Mine is chicken alfredo. Yours?"

"Cake."

"It's not a dish, Neveah." He looked at me as if I have committed a crime.

"Well, I like cake." I stood my ground. "Favourite movie?"

"*Lord of the Ring* series."

"Mine is *An American Werewolf in Paris*." I couldn't bear it and started laughing. Easton growled playfully at me. "How's that for a werewolf?"

"Nah, I like *Harry Potter* more," I answered truthfully this time.

"Favourite book?"

"Same as the movie."

"Me too."

We continued for some more time till we reached Melissa's house.

Melissa was standing outside her house when we arrived. "Good evening, Alpha."

"Melissa." He nodded back in acknowledgement. We all then stared at each other, not knowing what to say.

"I'll leave now," Easton said when it became too uncomfortable.

"Okay."

"Take care and be home by ten," Easton ordered me sternly.

"Why? Will you be in the woods at that time running a race?" I was curious. They had to phase sometime, right? Thinking about it, I grinned, and a laugh escaped my lips.

"Care to share what's funny?" Easton had a displeased look on his face again.

"Just trying to imagine you people running in a group. So crazy!" Just the thought of it made me want to faint. Seeing Easton in wolf form was shocking to me, let alone a group of them.

"Maybe, maybe not." Clearly, he was teasing me. "Seriously, be back home by ten-thirty at max."

"Yes, Daddy," I replied in a sweet voice even though I was scowling. Who was he to give me a curfew?

"We have company right now. You call me that later, baby." He dragged the *by* for added emphasis.

"Get lost, Alpha." I pushed him away. He didn't even budge. *Stupid strong man!* I pushed him again with two hands, but he still wouldn't move.

He instead stepped forward and hugged me, lifting my body ever-so-slightly. "Bye, Nev."

"Uh, okay?"

He put me back down and went back the other way in his car. I was still shocked at what actually happened. Did he just do that?

Easton never ever behaved that way, especially around me. He never spoke to me much before, and if he did, it was never good things. I understood that he had matured enough, but this was drastic! No one changes this much in a day, no matter what the reason is.

"What is going on, Neveah?" Melissa's question brought me out of my thoughts. She was wiggling her eyebrows.

"Believe me, I have no idea," I replied, sounding utterly surprised.

"Same here."

We both looked at each other and started laughing. Life was so messed up!

"Go sit in the car. I'll lock the door and come."

"What happened to the servants?" I was surprised that their huge house looked empty. They had many retainers, and they were almost always present.

"Madeline is in my room."

I burst out laughing. Now, this I understood. It wasn't like Madeline was that bad, but trusting her would be a very bad decision.

We made it to Georgy's home in record time. He was also waiting outside his house that was just as huge as Melissa's. Man, these werewolves are wealthy people.

I got out of her car walked towards him. "Why are you standing outside your house?"

"So I can escort the two beautiful ladies visiting my humble abode." He took my hand and kissed it while trying to sound charming. I wiped it on my shirt to see his reaction.

"Chivalry is so dead," he muttered under his breath.

I hit him on the shoulder. "Really?" I gave him a pointed look. I was very sure that he was lying.

"My parents are in there." He paused. "They are not a huge fan of humans."

"So?" What could they do?

"Mind you, Georgy's mother is strong," Melissa said from beside me.

"She is a werewolf?" I shouldn't be surprised, but I couldn't help it.

"She is a class A bitch," Georgy spat out. There was so much hate in his voice, it was scary.

Before the conversation could start again, I dragged both of them inside.

I forgot for a moment about how much of a bitch Georgy's mother was. It turned out to be a big mistake.

I entered the house flanked by Melissa and Georgy. The house was huge with cream shade tones and a classy finish. His father was sitting on the couch and sipping red wine while his mother was sitting with a female who had her back to me. As soon as Georgy's mother spotted me, she looked up and growled. "Why is this filth in my house?"

She actually growled! The other person who was with her turned out to be none other than Claire.

Oh for the love of Pete!

"She is my friend, Mother. She is here because I want her here," Georgy replied for me with a strained voice.

Before his mother could reply, Claire started, "Listen to your mother, son. The likes of us are not meant to be mingling with them."

"Talk about yourself. I am a plain human."

Wow! Then how was he not a werewolf? His mom was one for God's sake.

"You're human and your mom's not? How is that possible?" I wondered out loud.

"None of this is your business," Georgy's mom said. What was with this woman? I didn't even know her name for God's sake. So I asked her.

"May I know your name, ma'am?" I asked in the most respectful way possible.

"None of your business," Claire replied for her.

Okay, women, you want to play bitch? Then I am ready. "That's a really bad choice for a name. What were your parents thinking when they named you? Never thought of getting it changed?" I asked sweetly.

"Get out of my house and never come back!" Mrs. none-of-your-business glared. If looks could kill, I would have been dead by now.

"As if I want to stay here. This place is really a house." A *house* not a home. What a pity Georgy had to live here. It was even worse than Melissa's. I walked straight out, not waiting for the other two to accompany me.

When I got out, I bumped into someone. I raised my head and saw a man that resembled Georgy. It must be his elder brother.

"Sorry," he said.

"No, it's alright. I wasn't paying attention," I replied. The guy was looking at me in a very strange way.

I quickly backed away and ran to Melissa's car. I opened the door and slid inside before taking a deep breath to calm myself down.

"Are you alright?"

I jumped and turned back to see Easton sitting on the back seat. "What are you doing here?" I whispered.

"Nothing. I followed you both, that's it," Easton replied matter-of-factly like he hadn't just admitted to stalking.

"Why were you following us?"

Easton sighed. "Just wanted to make sure that you are both safe."

"There is no danger here, Easton." Yeah, Georgy's mother was harsh, but she wouldn't kill me, right?

"Mrs. Lawsin doesn't like you."

That was when it hit me! If Mrs. Lawsin was a werewolf, and Claire was her close friend, she would obviously know about the species. And what about her 'the likes of *us*' comment earlier?

Does this mean that she was one of them, too? Then what about Bryan?

"Wait, is Claire a shifter as well?" I asked him.

"No, she is human."

"Huh? Then how come she knows about your kind? It's against your law, right?"

"It's kind of complicated, but Claire's father was one, but she isn't. That's why she knows about us," Easton explained.

"Oh, okay." It sure was complicated! I mentally noted it down as one of the questions I had to ask Melissa.

"What are they doing inside, Easton? Can you hear them?" He should be able to.

"No, my senses aren't that great. We can just hear a bit more than humans. For example, even when girls talk in a hushed tone, I can still faintly hear them even if I'm in the adjacent room. But I cannot handle more than that. These heightened senses help us when we are in the woods."

Wow! "That's still a lot. It seems exciting."

We both stayed silent after that, and I kept looking at the door, waiting for both Georgy and Melissa to come out. I just hoped that he wasn't getting into a fight with his mother. That was the last thing I wanted.

"Ugh, when are they coming out? Is Melissa chatting with her dear mother-in-law?" I whined. Waiting was so damn boring.

Easton looked at me confused.

"They have something going on between them," I explained.

"Oh, I never noticed that." It was kind of expected from him. Being an alpha must be something big. I closed my eyes and laid my head on the soft and comfortable car seat. I was thinking of random things when something strike me.

"What is a mate?"

Easton stiffened just like last time. "I told you that I can't tell you about it," he said in a hard voice.

"But—" before I could continue, he stopped my words.

"I don't want to tell you." He growled the last word, and I was scared that he would go all wolf right there in the car.

"Jeez, Easton. Don't get angry. It's alright. I won't ask you again, okay?" I held my hand up in surrender.

I opened the door of the car and got out. I couldn't trust him when he was this angry. Why was he here again? Oh yeah, to keep me safe. How safe was he going to keep me if he himself was on the verge of attacking me?

He came out of the car after some time and looked at me.

"What?" I said with furrowed brows. I couldn't help but turn bitchy. "Tell me one thing, do you have multiple personality disorder or is it just really bad, pregnant woman type mood swings?"

Easton burst out laughing, and I just glared at him some more.

"It was a serious question, though. Right now, I am thinking of sticking with the pregnant woman theory."

His laugh quieted a bit. "It's not being pregnant. It is just me being a werewolf."

"Explain."

"Sometimes, my mind and the animal inside me disagree over things, and the result is that we end snapping at the person in front of us."

Listening to him talking about the 'inner animal inside' was very disturbing for me.

Thankfully, Georgy and Melissa came out right at that time. Claire was following them. All three of them were furious.

I decided to keep my mouth shut just in case any of them takes it out on me. Claire left in her car immediately, not even throwing me a single glance. I had to warn Ma against staying with her at any point in time.

"Hey, what happened?" I asked Georgy. Melissa and Easton were looking at one another with a blank expression on their faces.

"Nothing," he replied, but there was too much anger in his voice.

"Do you even hear yourself? You are so angry that you can't even speak properly."

"She was just going on and on about insulting humans even though she is married to one." His hands were clenched into fists. I hugged him. At first, he was stiff but then his arms came around me.

"Thank you," he whispered in my ear.

Before I could say anything else, I was pulled from Georgy into another set of arms. "You should not hug him," Easton said and rested his face on my shoulder. I removed his hands and turned to him.

"And please enlighten me why I shouldn't, oh great Alpha?" No one interrupts my 'friend' time, and besides, it wasn't that Georgy was going to end up killing me. The guy wasn't even angry anymore!

"Because I say so." So typical Easton.

"You don't rule over me, Eugene," I said as I jabbed a finger on his chest, "and you sure don't have the right to order me."

"Sure of that?" Easton moved his face closer, so it was directly in front of mine.

"Very," I seethed and pushed him back.

"Okay, guys enough. I am feeling much better now. Thank you for the concern." Georgy interrupted us, who currently has his hand glued to Melissa's.

"I can see that clearly, sweetheart," I replied in an amused tone as I looked at the two of them in immense surprise. Melissa blushed. Talk about crazy!

Easton coughed in a teasing manner. "Glad to see you happy, Melissa," Easton said.

"Thank you, Alpha." Melissa bowed down to him and looked at Easton with respect.

I just snorted. "Seriously? She bowed down to you?"

"You don't know many things about me. Now, let's get you home." He dragged me as Melissa and Georgy walked hand in hand behind us.

Chapter 18

Neveah

Nothing important happened the next few days, save for Ma choosing the bridesmaid dress for me. It was a simple maroon dress. I also brought golden heels to go with the dress.

It was Friday again, and I couldn't help feeling excited for the weekend. I got ready for school early since I had to pay a visit to the library. I wasn't sure that Easton would do his homework, so I now had to find a book for him myself.

After picking up some books, I went to the parking lot and waited for everyone to arrive. I sat on the hood of my car and went through the books to check for any special or important sums.

I was pretty much looking at the sky when Easton's car arrived. I waited for him to get down. To my immense surprise, a girl of our age got out along with him. She was beautiful! She had a long black hair and a pair of pretty brown eyes.

I pretty much expected him to at least glance at my direction because mine was the only car other than his in the lot, but the guy just left with his companion. *Rude much!*

Playing tutor to a guy like Easton was damn difficult.

I felt insulted, so I also went in and sat in the classroom to get ready for the first class. After some time, Georgy entered with Melissa in tow.

"Hey, guys! Why are you both here so early in the morning?" Melissa wasn't an active member in most of the classes, and Georgy was too intelligent for his own good. Polar opposites do attract!

"I called Gina. She said you left for school early, so we came to talk to you," Melissa answered with a smile. Someone was in a good mood.

"Oh, okay. Sit."

Melissa sat on the chair next to me while Georgy settled on a chair in the next row.

"So?" Georgy started but let the sentence hang in the air. He was probably waiting for me to complete it, so I asked them the one question that was troubling me the most.

"What in the hell is a mate?"

Melissa froze, and Georgy stood up to close the door.

He came back and stood near my desk. I was expecting him to say something, but it was Melissa who answered. "A mate is a gift of nature to the werewolves, the other halves of their soul." When she said the soul part, there was pain laced in it. It was obvious from her tone that Alden was her mate. But I didn't dare ask her for confirmation.

"Hey." I wrapped an arm around her shoulder and turned her to me. "You don't need to say anything if you don't want to. It's alright. I just asked because I figured it had something to do why Georgy is human while his mom is clearly not. That's it." I was getting a bit scared because Melissa looked one step away from crying. I didn't want anyone to cry because of me.

Melissa looked at me with a sad smile on her face. "It isn't your fault, Nev. It's just some unwanted memories," she replied

"Werewolves start finding their mate after they turn eighteen," she continued. "Whereas the most common age for shifting is sixteen, I first shifted at fifteen. That's kind of rare." She looked so proud of herself when she said that.

"That's a good thing, I presume?" I asked. Just the image of someone changing into a wild animal was terrifying for me.

"Very," she replied with a glint in her eyes, her sorrow long forgotten. "It is very rare for a female to shift at such a young age. Well except alphas. Easton shifted when he was fourteen."

"Why do you exactly worship him?" It was obvious that Easton was a God for them.

"Wolves live in a group, Neveah. We need that to survive, especially now that the world is full of humans. We live together to keep our species intact and away from harm, and alphas are our protectors. They spend almost their whole lives taking care of us and organizing things so we don't get into any kind of distress. They keep the everlasting unity within our kind. A wolf without a pack to call home, what we call a rogue, is alone and weak. Being in a pack is a sort of strength. It's assurance that there is someone watching your back for you at all times." She did all the motions with her hand so I understand what she was saying. That's when I realized, Easton was important to them.

"Wow! That's a huge setup you have." I said in awe. Somehow, Easton gained a bit respect from me.

"Yeah," she said.

Georgy was quiet the whole time as if he was in his own world.

"Earth to Georgy! What are you thinking so much about?" I said and waved my hands in front of his face.

"Just things." The way he said it, I understood that these *things* were kind of serious.

"Since you are thinking about some things, can you please enlighten me as to why you are human when your mother is not?"

He didn't answer right away. Just as he was about to, the whole Easton group came in— Easton, Xavier, the new girl, and of course, Alden.

Melissa automatically stiffened next to me, and Georgy glared at her.

"How are you, *darling?*" Alden sneered and stood right in front of us. The nerve of this guy!

Before Melissa could even think of answering him, I spoke. "She was very happy until a second ago, and now you can get lost."

"No one asked for your opinion," the new girl interjected. She was now clinging to Easton like a leech with a smirk plastered on her face. I didn't like it one bit. And apparently, one male was not enough for her. She was staring at Georgy in a not so decent way! That got my ire.

"I don't want to be rude, but this is something between us," I said to her while gesturing to me, Melissa, and Alden.

"Frankly, this doesn't concern you, so I would suggest that you occupy yourself with Easton," I continued. Her smirk fell, and I was the one smirking in the end.

"Oh, and, Easton, these are some books I need you to read and solve." I handed him two books which I brought from the library this morning.

"I am sorry, but Easton is busy with me tonight." The new girl said, clinging a bit closer to Easton.

"Easton, I don't care what you do tonight, but I need you to do the sums by tomorrow. You'll be having a detention today for sure, so do them at that time. Tell the teacher I told you to. I'm sure she won't mind." Who was I kidding? The teacher will probably have a heart attack when she hears that *the* Easton Dale is actually doing some studying in detention.

"Sure, I am free today, anyways. I'll do it." He slowly removed his hand from hers and took the books from me. All of us sat on our respective seats after that since the class was about to begin.

The new girl sat on the bench behind me. She was pissed at me, that much I could decipher. Melissa beside me was in some other world of her own, and Georgy was looking at her with eyes full of love. *Gross!*

I just kept my wandering eyes away from both of them and concentrated on the class.

I was sitting in the cafeteria and having a good chocolate milkshake when a blood-red nail polished hand banged the table. It was only me and Georgy. Melissa was somewhere else.

The whole place went silent, and everyone stared at our table with high expectations of a cat fight. They'd get disappointed. She was literally a *bitch*, after all. I was sure of it. Easton mostly hung out with his kind.

"What can I help you with, Miss…" I trailed off since I didn't know her name yet. The only class she had with me was the one where the teacher didn't bother with introductions.

"Sabrina. Sabrina Bolts." Her impersonation of the famous bond dialogue was an utter waste.

"Neveah," I said.

"I don't care. You need to stay away from him."

"Whom?" I wasn't sure who she was talking about. Was it Easton or Georgy? I was sure she had lewd thoughts for both of them.

"Easton Dale. He is mine!" Just as she said that, Easton entered with Melissa and the rest of his squad.

Easton and Melissa came to our table. "What is going on here?" Easton's voice echoed throughout the whole room. That was how quiet it was.

"Nothing, just your new girlfriend threatening me to stay away from you," I replied and went back to enjoying my milkshake.

"Sabrina?" Easton turned to her with a tight frown on his face.

"I was just telling the truth," she whined.

"Get out and wait at my house at six in the evening." If his tone wasn't furious, I would have assumed that they had something planned.

"Sure, baby. Just get rid of this bitch for us."

Easton's hand balled into fists, and his eyes turned dark.

Ah, shit! He was staring at Sabrina like he would kill her at any moment.

He was about to say something when Melissa interrupted him.

"Listen, babe, and listen good. There could only be one bitch here, and that's me. You know every school has a queen bee, that's me. The mean girl who would destroy your high school life if you mess with her, that's me. So I suggest that you stay away from my best friend and my boyfriend if you want to survive this school. Am I clear?" By the end of her speech, Melissa's voice had turned low and dangerous. I looked at Easton who had a horrible, cruel smirk on his face like he was enjoying Sabrina's misery.

That's bad, even though she was a bitch to me. Pun indented!

"Ye… yes." Sabrina ran out of the lunchroom as fast as she could.

"Man, that was hot!" Georgy said, pulling Melissa near.

Oh, indeed it was!

Easton

I was pissed. I didn't know what Sabrina's problem was, but she was getting on my nerves. She and her brother,

Ben, transferred to our pack some days ago after they had some problems with their last one.

But with the kind of sister he had, I wouldn't be surprised if he told me that they were kicked out of their former pack.

Since this morning, she was hanging onto my arm like a heavy bag I really would love to dispose of. In the parking lot, she hardly let me turn towards Neveah, and I was sure that Neveah was waiting for me, too. The stupid female just wouldn't let me go. Since she was a new pack member, I let it slide and ignored all her lies about us dating. But clearly, she crossed the line during lunch break.

What she did with Neveah today was beyond infuriating. How dare she insult my luna?

I was going to have a long chat with her and her brother in the evening. On top of that, I had homework to do.

When I entered our house, Sabrina, her brother, my father, Melissa, and Gregory were there.

"Good evening." I greeted.

"Good evening, Alpha." They all chorused while my father gave me an acknowledging nod.

"I'll change and come back." I sprinted to my room, my wolf eager to do the homework Neveah gave us. *Bloody whipped dog!*

I came down after some time. My father and Georgy were in some conversation while Melissa and Sabrina were glaring at each other. Man, I loved the way Melissa spoke today. To think that I despised the girl a few weeks ago! She was a good woman, after all. She was just confused then. Now, she had a lot of stability with Georgy. God knows she needed this after Alden.

Rejecting her was harsh, but I couldn't punish him for it since it does not break our laws. Not to mention that it was becoming a common occurrence nowadays. I couldn't understand it, though. How could one reject their mate? I couldn't go on without seeing mine every day.

I looked at Sabrina and her brother and tried to speak in the most diplomatic voice I could muster right now. "May I know what exactly prompted you to act the way you did in the lunch room?"

Everyone in the room, save my dad, flinched at my voice. Wasn't it soft enough?

"I, Alpha... actually it... I m-mean..." she started talking, but it wasn't fast enough. She very well knew that Neveah was my mate. I had already told Ben about her after that encounter in the clearing. On top of it, I had already specified to the whole pack that my mate was human, yet Sabrina behaved this way. I didn't know about her experiences in her past pack, but if she thought that could get away with insulting the luna, she was dead wrong.

"Stop stuttering and speak. I don't have time for your nonsense." I growled, looking her dead in the eyes and letting my inner wolf intimidate her. She was really getting on my nerve right now.

"I was jealous, alright? I mean, she is just a bloody nerd for God's sake. She isn't even that great. The whole time yesterday, your beta was talking about her like she was some goddess when she is just a filthy human," she spat.

"Enough." I roared. "The filthy human is my mate, the future luna of this pack. Say one more word about her, and I'll end your worthless life." I was on the verge of shifting. My wolf wanted out. He wanted the blood of the fool who dared insult his mate.

Just then, the doorbell rang. My father got up from the couch to answer it while I took deep breaths to calm myself down. It wouldn't be good if the person on the door gets traumatised by the sight of a mangled teenage girl. I wouldn't raise my hand at a girl under any circumstances, but I was confident that I could convince Melissa to do it for me. There wouldn't be much convincing required since she looked like she wanted to mince Sabrina to a million pieces for insulting her friend.

The person on the other side of the door turned out to be none other than my mate, my Neveah.

Shit! What was she doing here? Did she hear what I was talking about?

"What are you doing here?" My voice came out harsh, and I mentally slapped myself for raising my voice at my mate.

"I came here to discuss chem. I tried calling you, but your phone was switched off, so I thought *why not drop by here*?" Her voice was loud and clear as if I hadn't raised my voice some seconds ago.

"Sure, let me just take care of things. You can wait in my room." She scrunched up her nose when I mentioned my room.

"I'd rather not come in."

It clicked after two seconds. Was she kidding me?

"Oh, come on. Don't tell me you're still hung up on that episode." What I did was wrong, very wrong, but she shouldn't hold it on me forever. Not entering my house for all eternity was too much.

"It was more than an episode for me, Easton." Her voice was tight and rough. I stood in front of her and raised her chin to look at me.

"I know what I did was very wrong, but you shouldn't punish me forever for it. I am genuinely sorry." I was hoping that this would work. I mean, she had to stay in this house in the future if everything went well.

"Please, honey, it would be great if you come in," my father interjected. For a second, I was shocked. My father was not known for his politeness. Then again, it was Neveah we're talking about. She had a way of making things work for her.

Sabrina was intently staring at my mate. I could feel the malice radiate out of her. I growled low so Neveah wouldn't hear it.

She turned to me the next second, and I uttered a single word.

"NO."

Sabrina flinched and turned to face the others. I could feel her fear. She deserved it.

I turned my attention back to my lovely mate. Neveah seemed reluctant, but she just shook her head and entered.

"Hey, Mell! Hey, Georgy!" They both smiled at her.

"Why don't you wait in my room while I wrap this up?" I requested her.

"Sure." She started walking when she saw Ben. "Hey, hot stuff. So you're a were too?"

My temper soared to the seventh sky, and I wanted to do nothing more than kill him.

"Yup," Ben replied but didn't speak any further. Good for him!

"Neveah." I started, but she interrupted me, "Isn't there any other room available?"

"Why not mine?" My room was pretty big, and I remembered that she loved the view from there back when we were kids.

"It's your room, Easton, and guys aren't exactly known for clean rooms."

Melissa chuckled, and Gregory blushed a bit.

"Oh, looks like I was right," she said teasingly while looking at Gregory.

"Shut up, Nev."

Neveah gave him a big smile and sat next to him. His arm automatically went around her shoulder, and she leaned into him. I felt a bit sad that Neveah wasn't that comfortable with me as with her friend. I turned to Melissa to gauge her reaction. I was surprised that she wasn't angry or jealous for female werewolves were more possessive than the males. Instead, there was only love for her best friend and boyfriend in her eyes. At least, Neveah had two good friends who she could always lean on. That thought made my mind a bit calmer.

One day, I would lose my mind worrying about her!

It was frustrating to be near her yet to be far. Never in my life had I needed anyone. Maybe an exception to it was my long dead mother. I always wanted her near me but not to the extent of what I feel for Neveah now. She was becoming a very crucial part of my existence. I didn't know how long I could go on without telling her what she meant to me, to my pack, and to my family.

"Sabrina, Ben, you can leave. Remember what I warned you about and make sure that you follow it." I shoot my best pointed look at Sabrina's direction. I could feel their fear, but there was something else. There was a sense of confidence in them. Even though it was small, I could feel it. It felt absolutely wrong.

"Come on, Neveah. We got to study Chemistry. You both are free to hang out here or in the game room. It's the second door on the right," I instructed Melissa and her boyfriend.

They both nodded and proceeded to the game room while I lead Neveah to mine.

"Welcome to my humble abode."

"Your room is almost half the size of my house. There is nothing humble in here." Neveah wouldn't be Neveah if she didn't comment on something every once a while.

"Not my fault it's big, Neveah," I politely replied.

"Yeah, yeah. Now let's get started."

We sat down on my bed and went through the plot for the project and divided the work amongst ourselves. I realised that Neveah made sure that most of the important works would be assigned to her. I knew that my grades weren't exceptional, but I wasn't that bad.

Looks like I would have to prove that fact to her!

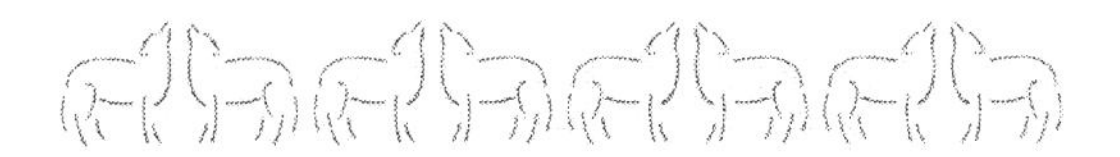

Neveah

We spent a while in his room working on the project. He got bored after some time, so we stopped studying chemistry for today. I walked down to the hall on my own since he had to do something first. He promised to join me later.

Melissa and Xavier were in the living room, but Peter and Georgy weren't.

"Hello, Neveah. What were you and Easton doing in his room?" Xavier asked while wiggling his eyebrows.

Ever since I found out what he was, Xavier's behaviour towards me changed. He no longer made unnecessary digs at me and left me alone for the most part.

"Oh, we were discussing how hot, smart, and cute you are. Easton seemed particularly fond of you." Xavier playfully scowled at my reply while Melissa giggled.

"So are you telling me that you aren't fond of me?" Xavier put his hand over his heart and looked at me with a sad expression.

"Sorry, sweetie. I'm not into gay men," I replied in a patronizing tone.

"Oh, sweetheart, I'll turn straight if I get to be with you." He smirked freakishly.

"Lemme think." My eyes scanned him from head to toe and lingered on his shoes. Man, they were nice! "Nah, I'll pass."

"Ouch, you broke my heart, my fair lady." By this time, Melissa was laughing like crazy. I couldn't help smiling.

"What is going on here?" Easton's voice boomed right into my ears. The idiot was standing behind me.

"Oh, nothing, just trying to turn Xavier straight."

We all burst into laughter once again. Peter and Georgy came in after some time with very serious expressions on their faces.

"Hello, dear. Are you staying for dinner?" Peter asked me.

"I'm not sure. Let me just call Ma and ask."

"Sure, sweetie."

I went to the corner of the room and called Ma. It was Bryan who answered the phone. "Hey, I'm at the Dale residence. They want me to have dinner here. Can I?"

"What are you doing in his house?" Bryan instantly replied just as I had expected.

"Chemistry project."

"Fine, but be back by ten." I checked the watch, and it was eight forty-five. That gave me enough time.

"Alright. Bye. Love you," I whispered in the phone.

"Love you too, kiddo."

Dinner went smoothly. We all said our goodbyes, and I reminded Easton to do his math homework. I reached home at exactly ten o'clock and saw Bryan on the porch.

"Why are you outside?" I gave him a puzzled look.

"Because I can." I gave him a you-really-want-me-to-believe-that look.

"Alright, I was just waiting for you."

I grinned at Bryan, and we both went inside the house.

"I'm going to bed. Tell Ma I love her when she arrives," I said.

"Sure, kid. Goodnight," he said and kissed my forehead.

Upon reaching my room, I quickly changed into my pajamas, curled up on the bed, and waited for sleep to come.

Just before drifting off to sleep, my mind replayed Easton's words earlier.

"The filthy human is my mate, the future luna of this pack."

Chapter 19

Neveah

Saturday was the best day of the week. One more day and Ma will be over with the wedding preparations. Well, it was supposed to be done by now, but with Ma and her planning, it was taking ages!

I got up in the morning, had a long soak in the tub, and dressed up in jean shorts and a tank top. I went downstairs and saw Ma flipping pancakes. *Yum!* "You're in for a treat, tummy," I said to my stomach and rubbed it.

Bryan was on the dining table busily flipping through the newspaper.

"Good morning," I greeted Ma and Bryan and sat on the chair.

"Hey, honey." Ma came and kissed my forehead while Bryan looked up from the paper and smiled at me. Mornings like this made me feel that my family was indeed complete.

“So what’s the plan for today?” I asked, internally hoping that it wasn’t wedding shopping

“You and I are going to the mall this evening,” Bryan said. Mall? I hated shopping!

“Can’t we go somewhere else?”

“Honey, your mother is going to a business dinner tonight. We are free, so I thought that it will be a good time for a father-daughter bonding,” Bryan explained.

“Can’t we have this father-daughter bonding in the house while watching a repeat telecast of *Beauty and the Beast*?” I was pretty much pleading. I didn’t want to go to the mall at all.

“Nope. We are going, and that’s final.” I pouted a bit, but I couldn’t really do anything about it.

The mall it is then!

I spent the entire afternoon studying because I didn’t have anything else to do. I also did a bit of task for our chemistry project. Just because I was helping him, didn’t mean that I trusted him to do schoolwork.

After knowing that he was an alpha and grasping what it meant, I understood that he might be busy. Taking care of people was not an easy job. Somehow, after knowing what he was, I developed some respect for him.

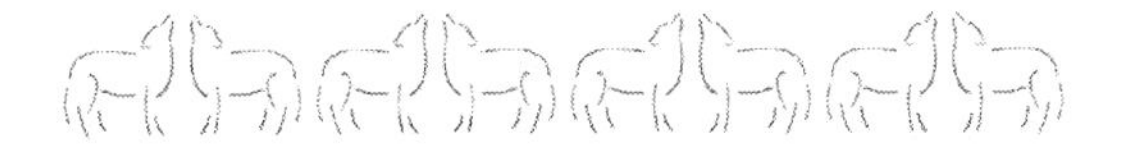

The first place we went to in the mall was the food court. After spending some time munching on KFC, Bryan and I decided to go shopping. Bryan went to Mark and Spencer, and

I went to Forever 21. I didn't like shopping, but I didn't have any choice, so I decided to make the most out of it.

I looked around the racks and spotted some really cool stuff. I took a trolley and put in two skirts, a shirt, a top, and an awesome pair of shorts.

I also checked the jewellery section and spot a long chain with a big wolf as a locket. A laugh escaped my throat as soon as I saw it. I decided to get it. I searched for some matching earrings but found none. I so wanted to see their reactions!

I called Bryan while waiting for the line since I was penniless. The line was long, and my feet were killing me. This was why I didn't like shopping.

Bryan entered with just a small bag, and I felt guilty for shopping so much. Then again, I haven't gone shopping for quite a long time. I just had to make sure that Ma repays him.

We paid for my stuff and visited some other shops.

Bryan and I entered this weird gift shop with all kinds of things available. Well, all kinds of costly things, from a handmade card to a rare diamond. They had it all. Brian wanted to buy Ma something, so here we were.

How romantic!

I went to the jewellery section and asked the sales lady for their most beautiful piece of antique jewellery.

"Are you sure?" The woman didn't believe that I had the capability to buy anything. I couldn't blame her. I didn't really look convincing in a tank top, loose ripped jeans, and a sling bag.

I turned back and pointed to Bryan who was looking at the watches. "Look at that man there. He is my Dad, and he is loaded!"

"Alright, honey." She showed me a huge selection of rings and lockets, but I didn't like any of them. They weren't beautiful enough for my Ma.

"Do you have anything else? Something unique perhaps?" I wanted something different for Ma.

She searched some more and came up with an old worn box. "Open it," she said and carefully placed it on my hand.

I did what she said, and inside were two gems.

One was bright red in colour, and the other one was jet black. Both of them were set on lockets. The red one was covered with a beautiful golden design in the shape of an oval while the black one had a base covering of silver and was in the shape of a thin rectangle. Both of them were beautiful.

"It's so beautiful. Can we buy it?" The saleswoman looked unsure, but I really wanted to buy them.

"I'm not sure. The pendants choose the owner, not the other way around," the saleswoman replied.

"Now, you sound like a person from Harry Potter. The wand chooses the wizard," I quipped and gave her a silly smile. Did she expect me to believe this?

"This may sound like a joke, but it is true. It's not the first time that someone has shown interest in the stones, but no one is able to purchase them due to some unknown reasons. The stones always reach back here." There was an underlying warning in her statement.

"Okay," I replied nonchalantly. "So let it be. Pack the stones, and if I'm lucky enough, I'll be the one taking it home."

"If you are buying it, just make sure that you are the only one to wear it." She warned again.

"But it is a gift for my mother." I was not a great fan of necklaces, anyway.

"It isn't made for her. You will realize that soon."

"Okay, now you sound scary." I grinned at her. Was she always like this or was it just with me?

"Here." She wrapped the old box in a bleak looking paper. "Wear it when the time is right."

I just smiled at her and bolted away as fast as possible. If I stayed with her for a few more seconds, I would have gone mad. I found Brian in the watches section.

"I found it." I handed him the box, but his expression changed as soon as he opened it.

"Where did you get this from?" He sounded alarmed.

"The jewellery section." Wasn't it obvious?

Bryan, however, didn't look that happy with my selection.

"Do one thing. Take it to the former alpha, the senior Dale, and hand these to him." He sounded utterly serious.

"Why will I give him the present I bought for Ma?" Was he nuts?

"Here, take my card and pay for it and hand it over to Mr. Dale as soon as possible." He removed his card from his wallet and put it in my hand. I stood still, not knowing what to do.

"Are you sure?"

"I am sure, Neveah. I am doing this for a reason. We will talk tonight." *Oh, man!* A lot of people wanted to talk to me nowadays.

"Fine." I reluctantly took the card from his hand and made my way to the counter. I seriously liked the ruby locket a lot, but if this was what Bryan wanted, then what could I do?

Bryan had to go due to some urgent work. The lockets were now safely tucked in my bag that I held close to myself. I still didn't understand what was so special about them. Sure, they were beautiful but nothing more.

I ended up at the food court again. Three hours of shopping made me tired. I ordered a meal from McDonalds and was happily munching on the awesome fries. Seriously, there were no better fries in this whole wide world than the ones made at McDonalds.

A shadow came over my plate. I looked up to see Ryder standing beside my table.

"Hi." I got up and gave him a hug. It felt like ages since I had seen him when in reality, it had just been a week.

He returned my hug with equal enthusiasm. "Hey, Nev."

"Come sit down." Ryder sat beside me on one of the chairs.

"You're alone?" I was hoping that Dan and Broody were with him. I kind of missed them. They were too busy to even message me.

"Yup. They both are drowned in piles of homework," he said.

I frowned but cheered up quickly. At least, Ryder was here.

"So what's up?" he asked and stole a fry from my plate. I glared at him.

"Nothing, just school." Then I remembered something. "Hey, are you part of Easton's pack?" I lowered my volume when I started speaking about Easton's 'family.'

"Uh, no."

"Oh, so you are allowed to be without one?" I asked, remembering Melissa saying something about rogue wolves.

"Yup. Being in a pack gives you security. If a member of the pack gets into trouble, it is Easton's responsibility to rescue him or her. However, they will still back me up in the case of an emergency but not at the cost of their pack members."

"Alright, but why didn't you join a pack?"

"Because I don't want to be a part of it. Being in a pack puts a lot of responsibilities on your shoulders, and you don't have much freedom. Privacy is rare in there." I remembered Easton's statement.

"Yeah, Easton told me about it. That sucks big time," I chuckled.

We talked and had fun for some more time before I remembered that I have to go to Easton's house. "Hey, do you have your car?"

"I do. Why?"

"I need a lift to Easton's house. I came with Bryan, but he left early. I have no means of transportation now," I told him.

"Alright. Let's leave."

Ryder dropped me off at Easton's house and drove off. I told him that I will tell Easton to drop me home and that he need not wait.

I rang the doorbell, but no one answered. I waited for some more time but still got nothing. Since his house was empty, I went to Xavier's house nearby.

No one answered there, too. Did they all have some get-together kind of thing? The whole street sounded empty and silent.

I was thinking of a way to go home when I heard some sound from the woods behind Easton's house. I pinpointed the direction of the sound and started walking towards it. Halfway through, I started praying that I don't encounter things I saw the last time I was here. Being in this forest never ended up good for me!

I walked some more and came to an open field where hundreds of wolves stood.

Fuck my luck!

This was worse than last time. All the wolves were huge and mighty-looking. At the top of some rocks was a big black wolf who I recognised as Easton. He was growling, and the wolves growled back. This was really crazy. The growls got louder and louder, and I started panicking. The only thought in my mind was, *I am not supposed to be standing here.*

I started backing away when a wolf spotted me and growled.

Shit! What do I do now? I took one step back, and the wolf growled louder. At that instant, all the others stopped growling and turned to look at me with their big glowing eyes.

Easton jumped down the rocks and started running towards me. The sheer terror of what was to come shut my senses one by one. The last thought that entered my mind before everything went dark was, *Easton is going to kill me because I made him do math sums.*

Chapter 20

Neveah

There was a light source from somewhere which was disturbing my sound sleep. Was it Monday already?

Someone was shaking me. I moved my hand to hit the person. My hand hit a curved surface with as much force as possible. The sound of the slap echoed throughout the room, and the next instant, there was the sound of people laughing.

I tried to open my eyes and stop the noise. I didn't want to get up. I was still sleepy. I rolled to face the direction of the sound and opened my eyes. There were many people standing in front of me. Nearest to me was Melissa with Peter and Xavier behind her. So who did I hit? I turned my head to the other side, and there it was!

My hand was on Easton's ass!

Wait, what?

I removed my hand immediately and tried to stand up. As soon as my feet touched the ground, my legs gave away. I was about to fall when Easton caught me in his arms!

Such a rom-com movie moment!

"Are you alright?" he asked concerned. I just nodded, unable to make any coherent sentences.

Easton dragged me back to the thing I was sleeping on. Wait, why was I sleeping with these people watching me?

That was when everything came back to me.

Oh, my! That was one horrific sight for any human to witness. Didn't they realize that anyone can pass through the place, and their secret will be out?

I just sat still for some time to collect my thoughts. I looked up again, and there were many people cramped in the room. I looked around to see that it was Easton's bedroom, and I was in his bed! Easton had both his arms on my shoulder with a worried expression on his face. I shrugged his arms off my body.

"Are you alright?" He repeated the same question from before.

"I guess," I replied.

"What were you doing there?" I was about to answer when I recalled what Bryan had told me.

"Where is my bag?" I asked Easton. I just wanted to deliver the box and leave.

Easton turned to the other side of his bed, picked up my bag from the table, and handed it to me.

I searched through it and came up with the box. I handed it to him immediately.

"A gift, for me?" Easton's surprised expression made me chuckle. Why in the world would he think that I would give him a present!

I shook my head sideways. "No, just open it."

Easton tore the paper with haste. The moment he saw the box, he dropped it on the bed. "Where did you get this from?" His eyes were turning dark. *Oops!* It looked like he was angry! Ok, was he going to shift or something?

I turned to Peter for help.

"Let us leave them alone," Peter just said, and everyone left including Melissa and Xavier.

I begged with my eyes to Melissa to not leave us alone, but she just went outside.

Such a traitor!

What were we? A newly married couple to leave us alone? I looked at Easton again. He was now staring at the box as if he was trying to burn it with his eyes.

"Easton?" I called aloud to make sure that he was still with me and not in some other world.

"Where did you get this from?" His eyes somehow turned a shade darker, and I regretted addressing him.

"I, uh… got it…" I tried answering, but my words failed me when I looked at Easton's eyes. They were damn scary, and all coherent thoughts flew out of my mind.

"Answer fast." His loud and deep voice reverberated in the room. Gosh, he sounded so not like Easton. Come on, Neveah, speak! Say something!

"I went to shop in… at…" I started speaking slowly. I was careful with my choice of words.

"It's obvious that you have brought this from some sort of store. I want to know from which and who sold it to you." He gritted his teeth while speaking to me.

"She didn't sell it to me, Easton. She said some things which were—"

Again, Easton interrupted me. "I don't want to know what she said. I only want to know two things. Am I not clear?" he growled, and his face was inches away from mine. I was pressed to the headboard of the bed with Easton hovering above me.

For the first time in my life, I was scared of Easton. For the first time, I actually understood that Easton was a werewolf and an alpha male. I could feel the power radiating from him from all over me.

My heart was beating triple times faster than normal. I was scared and angry at the same time. How dare he shout at me like that? He may be some alpha, but I was not meant to obey him. How dare he scared me like this? Despite my fears, I was furious, and this anger pulsed through my veins. I pushed Easton off me with all my strength. God alone knew where I got the strength from, but as soon as I pushed Easton off me, he fell to the floor with a big thud.

"You know what?" I stood up, took the box from the bed, and went to his bedroom door. "We will talk when you are capable enough to do so."

Easton's eyes turned back to green as he stood up with his face stretched into a frown. "Neveah, I—"

"I am not in the mood to hear anything. Save it for later." I turned and left the room.

I went to the hall to see their whole 'family' stuffed inside the room. I went to Peter and placed the box in his hand.

"Neveah, what…"

I didn't even wait to listen to him. I just opened their front door and shut it after me with a big bang so that the joints creaked. It was Peter's fault anyway for leaving us alone. I didn't even care that I acted rudely.

I stormed out of the house and waited in the street when I realized that I didn't have any way to reach back home. I walked a safe distance from his house and sat down in a nearby park. They had special lights for night time which made the park look Avatar-themed and utterly beautiful. I looked up at the starless sky to see a big full moon. I cursed it and the people who worshiped them. My mind started forming unwanted thoughts.

I started thinking about my life before all this werewolf thing happened. It was so peaceful. Back then, it was only me and my dear books, and nothing else! I realised that I didn't want to be a part of all these supernatural stuff. I just wanted things to be normal like the way they were before.

I sat for some more time and watched children playing before I called up Ma.

She answered the phone after three rings. "Hey, are you at home?" I asked her. If she was not, I would have to be homeless for some more time.

"Yup." I could hear the loud buzz of the vacuum cleaner in the background along with the television. "I am cleaning. What happened?"

"I need you to pick me up from a park," I said, hoping she won't ask me anything. I was in no mood to answer her.

"Why are you sitting in a park, and where is Bryan?" When did God ever hear my prayers?

"Long story. I'll tell you later. Please, Ma."

"Okay. Give me the address and don't go anywhere." Even though Ma didn't argue any further, I knew that the lawyer in her was dying to interrogate me.

"Okay." I told her the address and cut the phone.

I sat there and waited, just as she said. I got bored, so I went and sat on an empty swing. I looked at the sky again.

"And now I find you beautiful," I muttered.

"It is indeed beautiful!" A familiar voice came from behind me.

I dipped my head low to see the person upside down.

"What do you want, Easton? Can't you leave me alone for some time?" Just like that, my somewhat happy mood turned crappy again.

"I just want to talk about what happened earlier." He sounded sincere, but I wasn't in the mood.

"But I don't want to. It's your personal business, Easton, and since when did you start sharing your personal things with me?" I asked in a disinterested tone.

"Since I knew how important you are to me." I looked at him and let out a sarcastic laugh. That was one shitty line.

"Really, Easton?" He was pushing me on the swing while talking.

"Come on, let's go somewhere," he said. As if I was going to listen to him.

"I can't. I have to wait for Ma. I called her to pick me up."

"You don't have your car?"

I shook my head. "Nope. I went to the mall with Bryan, and he had to leave early. I bumped into Ryder, so I asked him to drop me off at your house."

Easton stiffened when I mentioned Ryder.

"You don't like him?"

"Not much."

"Because he is not a part of your pack?" He raised a brow. "I asked him today at the mall," I said.

"You could say that it is one of the reasons." He was blatantly lying to my face.

"Whatever you say." It wasn't my place to ask him for any reasons.

"You don't believe me?" There was an expression of surprise on his face.

"We both know that you are lying."

"How do you know?"

"I don't know. I just knew." He just nodded.

"So where were we?" Easton seemed eager to resume the conversation, all the surprise gone from his face.

"You wanted to talk to me." I reminded him.

"Then we will meet tomorrow to talk."

"Fine, but we will meet in the school library. You have improved a lot, but we have to make sure that you are consistent with it." Not to mention the project. I have finished half already, but I was not going to mention it to him.

"Fine, tomorrow at ten in the morning."

"Okay. Bye, Easton."

Easton just smiled, and I half-heartedly waved at him, eager for him to leave me alone.

"Bye, Neveah."

We were back, and Bryan was not back home yet. I desperately wanted to talk to him.

"Neveah, come on honey. Let's have dinner. Bryan said he will be late." Somehow, Ma did not ask me anything. She was just disappointed that Bryan left me hanging. I just told her that Ryder dropped me off at Easton's house for the project and that I had a fight with Easton and Xavier there, which was a very normal thing.

"I'm not having anything. I already ate at the mall. I'm going to sleep."

"Alright, honey. Goodnight." Luckily she didn't pry any further.

I kissed her cheek and went upstairs. "Goodnight, Ma."

I went to bed thinking about all that happened today. Eventually, sleep took over.

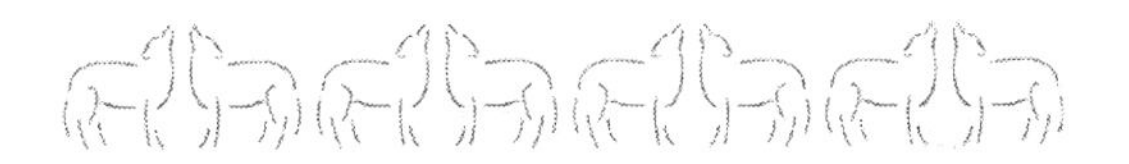

I got up the next morning at seven. It was very early for a Sunday! I just couldn't sleep anymore. I sat down on the dining table with a coffee mug and the newspaper in my hand.

Bryan came from their room after some time. "Good morning, kid. Get down from the table. There is a reason why there are chairs kept near this table."

I glared at him. He didn't say anything after that.

"Okay, what happened yesterday?" I asked when I couldn't keep silent anymore.

"Come on, let's go for a walk."

"I can't. I have to get ready to go to the library to work with an idiot on chemistry." I was still pissed off about yesterday.

"You do realize that he is an alpha, right?"

I nodded. I wasn't surprised that he knew what Easton was. I already deduced that yesterday, based on his careful and guarded expression.

So, instead of beating around the bush, I just went ahead and asked him. “Bryan, are you a werewolf?”

“Come to the lawn. We cannot risk your mom hearing. I will answer you there,” Bryan said with a serious expression.

Chapter 21

Neveah

I patiently waited for Bryan to answer my question.

"I am a human. Well, as much as I can be considering the blood flowing through me," Bryan replied with a heavy sigh.

"What blood?" I asked. There was something else, too?

"I am not entirely human. We do have werewolf blood in our family," Bryan stated carefully, examining my reaction.

"Oh, who is it? Wait, I know. It's Claire, right?" I exclaimed, remembering the conversation at Georgy's house. *Bloody bitch!* Literally!

"Well, it is more of my dad than my mum." That old man? He seemed decent and relatively normal compared to his wife.

"Wow, I really liked your dad," I murmured while looking down at the ground.

"You don't like him now?" I looked up at Bryan to see if I had offended him by insulting his parents.

However, he was just grinning at me.

"Frankly, I don't care much about either of your parents." What? It was the truth. His parents were already against Ma and their wedding. How cruel!

"Both my parents have werewolf blood through their veins."

My mouth hung open. *Seriously?*

"Then how come you are not one?" I questioned.

"You do know the concept of mates, right?"

"Yup." The word mate left a weird aftertaste in my mouth as I remembered the whole Alden-Melissa controversy.

Melissa made it sound like mates were a blessing while the actions of her own mate said otherwise.

"Well... The only way a child will be born a werewolf is when he or she is a product of the union of mates. Only a pair of mates with at least one werewolf gene can give birth to a werewolf."

"Okay." I nodded my head as I tried to process the new information.

"So your parents are not mates?" That was the only conclusion I came up with.

"Actually, they are just humans." Bryan's reply left me baffled. Looking at my confused and distressed state, Bryan sat down on the grass and took my one hand in his.

"Nev, what I am trying to say is that both my parents are humans. Humans don't have mates like werewolves. My parents are not werewolves, but they do have a special connection with each other because of their ancestry." He explained slowly.

"I still don't get it, Bryan."

"Okay, let me tell you my family story."

"Okay, go ahead," I said.

Brian took a deep breath and started. "My family has been living in this land for centuries, just like all the werewolves here. My maternal grandfather was Xavier Crowney."

"Why does he have the same name as Xavier, Easton's best bud?"

"Because Xavier is my cousin."

I scoffed. "Are you sure? I mean look at him and look at you. There is so much difference between you both."

"Xavier is probably my second or third cousin. Believe me, there is not much of blood connection between us, let alone that of character. And stop interrupting me, Neveah. Let me complete this topic and then you can ask questions."

"Alright, alright," I said, waving my hand in a dismissing motion.

"As I was saying, Xavier Crowney was my maternal grandfather. He was a powerful man in the werewolf world. He was the beta of his time, just like his namesake is now. Betas are the next strongest people after the alpha. Mind you, Alpha's are very powerful.

"My grandfather had a mate, but she died in an epidemic before they could have a child. So, to continue the beta bloodline, he married another werewolf from the pack. They had eight children who all turned out to be human. Xavier's grandfather was the first child, and my mother was the last. Xavier's grandfather mated a she-wolf which is possible only if you have wolf blood in you. So his family was, once again, fully a part of the pack. They hoped the same fate for my mum, but it didn't. She fell for my dad. He was from another pack and was a human with werewolf blood like my mother.

"Since they met, they had a mate-like relationship. We realized that because of such a strong bond between them, they would have been mates had they been born werewolves. Since I have werewolf blood too, they were hoping that I would be mated to a girl of the pack. That didn't happen, and my mother has been furious since then," Bryan explained.

"This is damn confusing." I closed my eyes and laid on the soft grass. My eyelids suddenly felt heavy. All the information that Bryan had given me today was exhausting to process. *Gosh!* They had such a complex system.

I opened my eyes to see Easton standing above me.

"What are you doing here?" I shrieked.

"What are you doing laying on the grass by yourself?" He cross-questioned, moving away from me. Easton offered me a hand, but I declined and got up on my own.

Did I fell asleep? I stood up and dusted off the dirt from my bum. "Can't you properly answer one question, Easton?"

"It is nine forty-five, Neveah." Oh, you gotta be kidding me! But Easton's expression was quite serious.

"Come in. I'll be ready in ten minutes." Easton, however, refused and assured me that he will be fine in his car. Instead of arguing further, I ran inside the house to get ready.

I ran into Bryan. "Why didn't you wake me up?" I scolded him.

"You needed that nap, kiddo. That's why." He was right. I did need that small nap. I quickly ran into my room and took the shortest bath possible. I wore a long, lime-green skirt and a full-sleeved white top and left my wet hair down to dry naturally.

When I reached the kitchen, Ma handed me a tiffin box with my breakfast and kissed me. I informed her that I would be back by six and after which we can go for some more wedding shopping.

Did I mention that I hate it?

Easton was standing near his car, playing with his phone. Usually, I don't notice a guy's clothes, but Easton looked really good in white jeans and peach shirt. Only he can pull off girly colours and actually look good in it.

"Come on, alpha. Let us leave." Easton gave me a weird look but didn't say anything.

I munched on the sandwich Ma had packed as I looked at the trees and houses passing through the window. I had told him to take the long route so I could finish eating my breakfast before we arrive. Easton had proposed that we go to a park, but I declined. I didn't want to waste that much time. I wanted to get over with this as soon as possible.

"Did you finish the report I told you to make?" The only thing I trusted Easton to do was to make the report, for which I had already made a spare. It was not that I didn't trust him. It was just that I badly needed the marks.

"Kind of." I turned to him and gave him a suspicious look. I only gave him one work, and he didn't even complete it! Did he have any intentions of graduating this year?

"What is left?" I asked warily. If he didn't do anything, I couldn't put his name on our project.

"I'll show you once we reach the library."

I just sighed and looked ahead and continued munching on my sandwich.

We reached the public library after some time. I got out and waited at the entrance for Easton to park his car. Knowing him, he wouldn't enter the library alone.

'It will tarnish my reputation,' I mentally quoted Easton.

Poor me to have to put up with him!

"Hi, Neveah," I heard a voice near my ear. I turned back, and there was Broody. I made a toothy smile and hugged him close. "Hi, buddy! I missed you."

"Not my fault babe. You were busy with Ryder and a certain alpha." He smirked and winked at me.

"How do you know?" I had doubts about Daniel since him and Ryder were brothers, but I wasn't sure about Broody. Man, this felt like I was in some paranormal novelette.

"Ryder told me. To answer your question, I am just a plain human with werewolf friends like you."

"Thank God! At least someone is not a wolf. You won't believe me. I feel weird sometimes like I am not the normal one," I said, pushing his hair which was on his face.

As soon as I touched his strands, I was pulled into a pair of arms and my back collided with someone's hard chest.

"MINE!"

I whipped my head and came face to face with none other than, His Highness, the oh-so-mighty alpha, Easton Eugene Dale.

I turned back, crossed my arms on my midriff, and looked at him. "Care to explain what you said now, Eugene?"

"I, Nev, I……." he stuttered, frantically searching for words while I grinned at him.

"Let us take this conversation somewhere else, Eugene."

My smile turned into a frown when he didn't react. Easton looked scared. Never in these seventeen years of my life have I seen Easton this frightened.

"Nev, let me explain."

"I know. That is why I am inviting you to go somewhere else so you can explain things in private," I said and turned to Broody who was smirking at me.

"What?" I asked. Did he know something I didn't? Judging by his expression, I think the answer was yes.

"I'll leave now. Take care, Neveah." Broody gave me a hug and kissed my cheek before leaving. Luckily, Easton was silent, unlike the last time.

"Come on, Easton. Let us talk."

We were back at the forest. I tried to talk Easton out of it, but he just wouldn't budge. He said something like 'it needs to be done there.'

We are now walking through the forest. Well, he was walking, and I was more of dragging myself. I was too tired to walk any further.

"How much more, Easton?" My feet were aching. We were walking for the past thirty minutes.

"We are near."

We both walked for some time before we reached a cabin in the middle of literal nowhere.

"Can you tell me why we are here alone?" I was sure that Easton would not manhandle me. He just didn't have it in him. Then again he was an alpha, which got me a bit paranoid… just a tiny bit.

"I am not going to do anything bad to you, Neveah," Easton assured me. He still had an anxious expression on his face.

"I know you won't hurt me physically, Easton."

He sighed and opened the door of the cabin. The inside was beautiful. Though it looked uninhabited, it has been properly maintained. The whole theme of the house was red and cream, and everything looked so prim and proper.

Easton pointed at the red couch for me to sit while he sat on the cream chair next to the sofa.

"My dad built this for my mum. She loved coming here. She used to say that it gives her some peace. I, too, come here whenever things go bad," Easton said in a sombre voice. It was almost like he was reminiscing the past.

"So something bad is going to happen now?" I asked quietly.

"Wish you weren't this smart," Easton murmured to himself.

"I am not going to beat around the bush, but let me just say it the right way." Easton looked up. His green eyes were shining like polished emeralds.

"You know about soul mates, right?"

"Yeah, I do," I replied cautiously.

"Well, it's just that you're mine."

That was when everything, all the information I have gathered until now, registered in my brain. It all made sense.

Easton

Neveah froze after I told her what she was to me. Honestly, I had expected some shouting, slapping, and scratching, but my mate was still as a rock. It was close to a minute now, and she hasn't even uttered a single word.

I knew that this was all my fault.

I was eager this morning to meet her and sort out what happened yesterday. It was not my intention to get angry or shout at her.

But seeing those lockets after such a long time awakened an anger within me which I buried at the back of my mind long ago. Everything seemed fine for a long time, and then something like this happened.

I obediently completed the whole report, save for a few minor points. I was excited to show it to her. I was sure that she would love it. Some sort of appreciation from my mate would be appreciated.

She looked beautiful in her skirt and top today. Just as expected, she told me to take her to the public library. I understood that she didn't want to come to my house. Whenever she goes to my house, I always end up shouting at her. It was better this way.

I went to park the car, leaving Neveah at the stairs of the library. The sight I saw when I returned was definitely shocking for me. She was standing too close to a guy. I knew that I had seen him somewhere. After some thinking, I remembered that he was one of her three friends from her old place. All four of them used to be together. I usually didn't allow Neveah near me because she was a human. Now, I regretted that foolish decision more than ever.

The guy with her was also human. From the scene, I could understand that she liked him. He made her smile. That was something I was yet to do. When she got too close to him for my liking, I snapped.

I should have had more control over myself. I couldn't do it, and I snapped terribly.

I regretted saying the word I shouldn't have in any circumstance.

On my birthday, I had mixed emotions on whether I wanted a mate or not. Never in a million years did I expect a mate like Neveah. At first, I didn't even know whether I should be happy or sad. The thought of me with Neveah in a romantic relationship was disturbing at first. Then, I realized that she just might be the right match for me.

She was smart, strong, independent, stubborn, protective, and blunt as the back of a knife. She had all the qualities a luna must possess. She said what she wanted to anyone and didn't even feel bad about it. I was responsible for her character shaping up this way. I wasn't a very good child and was often mean to her in our pre-teen days. It was a long time ago, but I knew that she still holds it against me. Only God knew if she would ever forgive me.

Now, I had some hope for us… that there would be an us.

The fight at my house was partially my fault.

Those lockets once belonged to my parents. They symbolized the union of the alpha pair and the prosperity of the pack. How in hell Neveah managed to lay her hands on them was beyond me. The pack had been unsuccessful in searching for them for years, and my own mate ended up bringing them to me.

Right now, all I was hoping was for Neveah to still consider having some sort of a relationship with me.

Chapter 22

Neveah

All this was one big joke, right?

Easton's going to stay silent for some time then burst out laughing and say that all this was just an elaborate prank. *Please, someone, tell me all this is a big joke!*

However, Easton's face said otherwise. All of these were real. I was actually Easton's mate.

Neveah Gail Huber was officially the mate of Easton Eugene Dale!

How did this happen?

Easton sat down in front of me and held my hands in his. "Say something, Nev. You are scaring me."

So I asked the only question that was on my mind. "Are you sure that I am your mate, Easton? You didn't get the wrong one?"

"Well, the fates did give me the wrong one, but I think she was the right one all along." Easton smiled and kissed my hands.

Okay, it was one thing for Easton to say that I was his mate and a totally different thing to say that he liked me. On top of that, he was being romantic to me. I was somewhere between awed and disgusted.

"But... but how will this work, Easton? I am a human, and a relationship between us would be totally weird and awkward." I shuddered at the mere thought of it.

"It will work, Neveah. At first, I wasn't sure too, but now, I am."

"I'm not," I replied, trying to be the sensible one. "I don't even like you that way."

"You will soon. A mate bond is difficult to resist," Easton retorted.

"But Melissa and Alden..." I tried justifying.

"They will love each other forever, Nev, even if they aren't together. They will always have a bond even if Alden has rejected her."

"If the bond is strong, then how could Alden reject Melissa?"

"I don't know. But I am not like him. I can't imagine my life without you, Neveah. It just isn't possible for me." Easton said all of this so smoothly, it was suffocating. How could he easily confess such things? I didn't think it will ever be possible for me.

"I am still not sure about all this." I was still reluctant to admit that I am actually Easton's mate.

"It will be. We will take it slow, Okay?" Easton said in an almost pleading manner.

I sighed. "I don't like this, but I know how much a ans to a werewolf judging from Melissa's experience. So I am willing to give us a chance, but we start from friends, alright?"

"Sure, baby," he replied and pulled us up so that we were standing face-to-face with my hands still in his.

"Eugene?"

He was going to take us back but looked at me when I called out his name. "What is it, babe?"

"We are not a couple yet, and I suck at romance." I pulled out my hands and pushed his chest away.

"That's alright. I think I am romantic enough for the both of us." He gave me a sly smirk.

"Okay, enough of this. We need to talk about the project." I changed the subject before it got more awkward. I still had to ask him what he had left out.

"Yeah, I got to show you something. Let's go." Easton seemed excited and dragged me through the forest. I let him do so. I didn't want to damper his happy mood.

We got into the car. He said that he would show what he had prepared at the library, and I nodded absentmindedly. I was preoccupied with thinking about the pros and cons of this so-called relationship. It was still difficult for me to adjust being so nice to him. We were always fighting as far as I could remember.

Half of my mind was sure that this wasn't going to work while the other half still had hope. I didn't even know whether I wanted this or not.

"Come on, Neveah. We are here." I got down and saw the storefront of a restaurant.

"What are we doing here?"

"Well, it is two pm, so I decided that lunch would do us well." Just as he mentioned food, my stomach got excited. *Food!* How could I forget food?

"Let's go."

We both ordered pizzas with savoury toppings.

"You know, Neveah, you can talk to me. Don't overthink things, they lead you nowhere," Easton said just as I was having a piece.

"First, stop talking with your mouth filled with food, Easton. It is disgusting. Second, if I want to talk to you, I will. Believe me, I don't need any invitation."

"Now, that's the Neveah I know. I am relaxed now since you're doing the normal thing by shouting at me. I thought that maybe you had fallen in love with me, and we would be one of those love-sick couples."

"Don't flatter yourself, Easton. I will really be sick in the head if I am in love with you by now."

Easton smirked, amusement visible in his eyes. "I like it when you shout at me. Not many people do it. It's very hot."

I mentally face palmed and looked at him through narrowed eyes. He looked at me, too. Our staring contest was interrupted when my phone rang. I opened the lock to see Bryan's message.

My mother is throwing her birthday party at seven in the evening. Be home by five. It's just you and me going.

Oh God, what sins did I commit to deserve this party slash punishment? The last time we were in a party definitely didn't end well, and the reason was in front of me. "Easton, did you know that we were mates that night you had a party in your house?"

"Yup, I have known since my eighteenth birthday."

"Then why the hell did you shout at me that night?" I asked him with a raised brow.

Easton blushed as soon as I asked the question. His face, neck, and ears turned red. Never in my life have I seen Easton blushing so much. Wait, I haven't seen Easton blushing, period!

"Wish you hadn't asked that," he muttered, suddenly finding the pizza interesting.

"Oh, come on, it is just a normal question. I think I deserve an answer as to why I was treated so badly that night,"

Easton sighed. "I was jealous."

Okay, wait, pause. I was sure I heard it wrong. Easton and jealous? "Come again," I said.

"I was jealous," he said more firmly this time.

"What?"

"I was jealous, alright?" he almost shouted.

"Oh, I heard you the first time. I was just shocked," I replied.

"I didn't like it that you paid more attention to my father than me," he muttered and looked down.

"Are you being serious, Easton? You were jealous of your own dad? Shame on you. For the record, I will always prefer Peter's company over yours. The guy is amazing."

Easton growled lowly at my reply. I put my hand over his mouth so the others wouldn't hear. "What are you doing? You are surrounded by humans," I hissed. How could he be so irresponsible? I couldn't tell anyone, but he could growl like a wolf anywhere he wanted?

"Sorry, wolves are very possessive. They are very territorial of their possessions." Easton tried to explain.

"You don't own me, Easton."

"Well, in my world, I do. I own you, and you own me. That is what the bond is all about."

I didn't reply and just shifted my attention to my food. It was damn good. After we had the pizza, Easton paid the bill. Usually, I would have argued, but he made me walk to and fro a forest so he could pay for my nourishment in exchange.

"I have to leave by four-thirty. Got to go to a party." I informed him once we were seated in the library.

"That party at your grandma's house at seven?"

"She is not my grandma." Who would want a bitch like her for a grandmother? "How did you know about the party?" I asked, secretly hoping that he's been invited.

"I am invited along with many others from the pack."

I fist pumped the air. *Yes!*

"Oh, great! I have to look at your mug there too." I teased him.

He pulled his chair closer to me and said, "Please, honey, I have the best-looking face in the whole town. No one stands a chance against me." That was true, I guess! Georgy and Xavier were equally good-looking, but Easton was a bit better than them, and this was not the mate bond talking.

"Whatever. Now, show me what you did for the report."

"Here is one-half of our report. The other half is still in the process. Watch it at your house," he said as he held up a CD he pulled out of his bag.

"Okay." I guess it was good because Easton looked pretty proud of himself. I just nodded and placed the CD in my bag. We discussed some other parts, and I explained to him some concepts.

After that, we moved on to physics and math. Those were subjects he needed help on. History and economics were subjects he would have to do on his own. I couldn't help him in those.

We were at the library till four forty-five where I forcibly made Easton do the math sums. He was surprisingly good at physics! He might've been better than me.

I reached home by five thirty. Ma was already getting ready to go somewhere, and Bryan was nowhere to be seen.

"Why are you not coming to the party?" I asked Ma.

"As you can see, I have to be somewhere else. Besides, I don't want to come," she tried justifying herself.

"And it is alright for me to go to that bi—buffalo's party?" I changed my words in the nick of time. Ma never liked it when I swore.

"Bryan will be there with you always. Easton, Melissa, and her boyfriend will be there, so you can be with them. Just wish her happy birthday, give her the gift I have packed, and come back."

I wish it was that easy!

"Fine, I'll get ready."

I was at the party all alone with Claire advancing towards me. I cursed my Ma, Bryan, my friends, and my so-called mate who was busy chatting up with some blonde with great shoes. I smiled at her as she approached.

"Hello, Neveah," she cooed in her irritating voice, trying to sound loving.

"Hello, Claire. Lovely party you have here. You look beautiful," I said as politely as I could muster. Claire was wearing a peach dress which complimented her looks. She barely looked like a woman of sixty-five. She looked way younger.

Her eyes assessed my looks. I could proudly say that I actually looked like I belong in this party, unlike the last time. I was wearing a flowing dark green full-length dress with a slightly plunging neckline. My hair was curled and placed at one side with numerous shiny pins. I had a really costly pair of pearl and diamond earrings dangling in my ears, too. I had applied a bit of eyeliner and mascara and a dab of a maroon lipstick. To say I looked good would be an understatement. I had to thank Ma for the dress and jewellery.

"Thank you, dear. Where is Bryan? I swear he came to attend her mother's party, and I haven't met him yet," she said with fake sorrow. I just grinned at her.

Lying beeping bitch, you sent him to talk to some ultrathin redhead model to keep him busy, and now you are complaining? Bryan was still talking and laughing with her. Gosh, he could be such an idiot sometimes!

"Come on. Since you are alone, let me introduce you to my friends." Claire started speaking again without waiting for my reply and proceeded to drag me behind her. We went to the other side of the hall filled with old ladies.

Tight dresses, check.

Thick makeup, check.

Shimmering diamonds, check.

Botox injections, double check.

All looking forward to insulting me, triple check.

Among the ladies were Georgy and Melissa's mums. They didn't look particularly happy to see me. Why couldn't I have a shy best friend whose mother loves me? Just why? Almost all mothers hate me!

"Hello, ladies. This is Neveah, my son's daughter." *Daughter?* I did have a feeling that this was not going to end well.

"Hello, Neveah," Mrs. Lawsin greeted politely which had my eyes twitching. Why was this woman being so sweet to me? Wasn't she angry last week that I was not a wolf like her? I decided not to think much about. "Hello, Mrs. Lawsin," I greet back.

"It's Gabrielle," she replied curtly.

"Not my fault that you didn't seem very keen on introductions the last time we met." *Damn my blabbering mouth!*

The only sound I could hear was gasps and snickers.

I didn't know I was talking that loud!

Chapter 23

Neveah

I forgot that most of the people in this party had better senses than regular humans. There was utter silence, and everyone was looking at Gabrielle and me.

"You little bi—"

"I wouldn't complete that sentence if I were you," someone interjected from behind me.

I turned around to see Easton walking towards me with a frown on his face. He was wearing grey suit pants and a white full-sleeved shirt that was rolled up just below his elbows. Attached to his collar was a green tie which matched his eyes and, somehow, my dress.

He wrapped his arms around me, hugging me from behind. I glared at him, but he just winked and kissed my cheek.

"Hi, babe." Easton smiled at me.

"Easton, what did I say about calling me babe?" I reprimanded him.

"Sorry, baby." Easton smirked at me and looking all smug.

"I am a big girl, Eugene." Well, two can play this game! His smile dropped when I addressed him with his middle name.

"Sorry, my big girl. Honey, we can do this when we are alone. We have an audience right now." He kissed my nose and turned to Gabrielle. I forgot that we weren't alone. How embarrassing!

"Care to explain why my luna is being insulted?" Gabrielle's eyes narrowed at me, and Claire looked like she was about to faint. Looking at their expressions, I decided to have some fun.

"Nothing, Easton. We were just getting started off with the introductions, right?" I turned to Claire and smiled at her.

"Yes, Alpha. The luna is right. She is a luna, and they are always right, right?" Claire was mumbling nonsense by this point, so I cut her off.

"It's okay, Claire. I am not always right."

"Nope, my mate's always right. She is the best, right Gabrielle?" Easton kissed my temple this time. Oh, now he was taking it too far! I looked at Mrs. Gabrielle Lawsin and waited for her reply.

"I am not bound to you, Easton. I don't have to respect that filthy human," Gabrielle's reply shocked me. I didn't expect her to be this harsh.

Easton pulled himself away from me and was standing in front of Gabrielle in a second. "Never ever disrespect my mate in front of me." Easton looked two seconds away from killing Georgy's mum. Even though she tried to show that she wasn't affected, her eyes gave away her fear.

"It's the truth, and you know it!" *Oops!* Wrong thing to say.

Easton's growl echoed throughout the huge room. Even I was terrified. This was not the Easton I know. The Easton in front of me was someone else. He was the Easton, the animal, the alpha. That was when I realised that all the people in attendance knew about werewolves or are one themselves. Besides, I didn't think Claire would invite humans.

"One more word and you are dead. You may not be a part of my pack, but you are on my land. Disrespecting your leaders won't help you leave this place alive. You may have killed your mate, but I won't allow you to hurt mine."

Shit! Gabrielle killed her mate? Gabrielle gasped, and she looked like she was about to cry. On top of that, Easton was still in front of her, snarling. Why didn't anyone pull him off? I looked around to see very few people, most of them I didn't recognise. Peter was standing at the side, looking all calm like this brawl wasn't happening in front of him.

I realised that no one was going to mess with Easton when he was this furious, so I decided to take matters into my own hands. I went near him and placed a hand on his shoulder. He turned back so fast that it was unreal! His eyes were black, and he looked really angry. But as soon as he understood that it was me in front of him, his expression softened.

"Leave, Easton." I tried to be as stern as possible. He didn't say anything and kept staring at me. I grabbed his hand and started dragging him with me. "Let's leave. We have attended enough of the party." I almost succeed at dragging him outside.

We were near the door when Easton turned to all those who were present. "Make sure that something like this doesn't happen again. My mate won't be there the next time to save anyone."

When we reached the threshold of the mansion, almost everyone was standing there: Melissa, Xavier, Alden, Bryan, Georgy, and his brother among other people.

"Maybe you should go in," I told Georgy.

"Not necessary. She will be coming out, anyway." When Georgy mentioned his mother, there was distaste in his voice. I didn't like it. They may not be close, but I felt that she needed her sons this time.

"Just go in. She needs you. Believe me!" I tried to convince Georgy, but he was adamant about it, so I just left the topic there.

"I should go home, Dad. You can stay the night," I said to Bryan.

"We both should leave. It is getting late, anyway." *Great!* Even Bryan didn't want to listen. I looked around for Easton, but he was nowhere to be seen. "Let's leave," I muttered.

We were both silent the whole car ride. I was sure that Bryan would have heard what Easton said about the luna part, not that I knew what that meant.

"What actually happened there, Bryan?" I wanted to know how everyone in the party was evacuated after Easton got angry.

"You tell me, Neveah. What happened there? You told me that you don't know much about mates, yet you have one?" Bryan sounded really angry and was gripping the steering wheel tightly.

"Easton told me that I am his mate this afternoon."

The car fell silent. I glanced at Bryan after some time and saw guilt written all over his face.

"Sorry, kiddo. I shouldn't be this angry with you. It's not your fault."

I wasn't able to reply. What should I say, anyway?

Since I didn't say anything, he started talking. "My mother should not have done that. I warned her not to do anything, but she didn't listen."

"I'm sorry too."

"Don't be. You are the only reason my mother and that other woman are alive. Had you not pulled Easton off, he would have surely ended up killing them."

"But why didn't anyone do anything to stop them?"

"They insulted a luna and disrespected an alpha. That is a punishable offence in their world," he said.

"Okay, what's this luna thing?"

"You don't know?" Bryan chuckled.

I hit him on his arm. "No, I don't. I forgot to ask Easton."

"A luna is the female leader of the pack. Usually, it is an alpha's mate. Alpha's rarely reject their mate. The pull is too strong to resist."

"You know, I actually don't find the pull strong enough." I didn't feel any sort of connection with Easton.

"So, are you with Easton because he forced you? To feel the connection, you have to be a werewolf."

Oh! That made sense. "Easton didn't force me into anything. We are not even together. It was purely for your mum's benefit." I snickered, thinking about Claire and Gabrielle's expressions. I felt a bit bad, but I was happy for the most part. At least she would start treating Ma in a better way.

"Don't tell Ma what happened at your house."

"I don't need to, kiddo. She knew that something might happen, but she was confident that you are strong enough to take care of yourself, and of course, I was there with you."

"Please." I scoffed. "You were talking to some hot redhead model the whole time, leaving me alone with Claire."

"She is my cousin."

Oops! We didn't speak further, and just enjoyed the ride back home.

Once I was home, I directly went to my room and changed my clothes. The heels and the restricting dress were killing me.

I changed into pajamas and sat on the bed, browsing my Whatsapp for any messages. I saw a message from Melissa.

Wow! It came out good.

What came out good? I replied.

Melissa sent me a photo as the next message.

This. I didn't take it, but I do have the photo.

I waited for it to load and there it was— the perfect picture!

I giggled uncontrollably before collapsing on the bed. I let out a small laugh again, thinking about the picture. Gosh, it was so hilarious. It was a picture of Claire and Gabriella with shock on their faces. Claire even had her mouth wide open! The image was probably taken when Easton announced to the world that I was the luna.

I sat down on the bed for some more time before I remembered about Easton's CD. I switched on my laptop and put the CD in the drive.

There were a slide presentation and an animation. I gotta say, both of them were perfect.

To say that I was amazed was an understatement! This was something I never imagined from him. I opened my phone and sent him a message.

The CD is amazing, East.

I waited for a reply, but I didn't get one. So, I flopped back on the bed and looked at the ceiling. I thought about the things Easton told me today. Somehow, I couldn't get my mind away from it. I just couldn't digest the thought of Easton and me as a couple. Me and Easton hugging, kissing, making out, grinding, and then—

"Hi, babe."

I turned to my left to see no one. I shrugged. It must've been my imagination. How pathetic that I actually imagined Easton's voice! What was wrong with me?

"Turn, sweetheart."

I turned around and got shocked to see Easton lying beside me. I placed my hand over my heart in efforts to calm it down. "What are you doing here?" I whispered when I felt better. I wanted to yell at him, but I couldn't risk getting caught with a guy in my room.

"Oh, well, my mate told me that she finds me amazing for the first time in my life. So I felt like I had to see her and thank her," he smirked. I rolled my eyes at his stupid reasoning.

"Well, you could have thanked me on Monday." Did he have to sneak into my room tonight when there was a high probability that my parents were downstairs? "How did you even get in?"

"Well, it's not the first time I sneaked in," Easton said casually before realising what he said. He bolted up and looked at me.

"What do you mean the first time?" How many times had this happened? I didn't even know about it till now.

"Can we forget that I said that previous statement?"

"Of course not, Easton," I replied. "How many times has this happened?"

"Well, you see…" he started and kneeled on the bed beside me. I too got up so that I would be in the same position as him.

"Easton?" I said in a threatening voice. He scooted closer to me, and his hands encircled my waist.

"Baby, I've just come in once and—" I panicked and pushed him off me. He landed on the bed with me on top of him since his hands held on to my waist.

I tried to loosen his grip, but he just tightened them more. "Easton, let go," I hissed. I was really pissed off. First, he barged into my room and now were lying on my bed with him under me?

Just who did he think he is? Oh, he was the bloody alpha. And not to forget, my mate.

He probably understood that I was angry, so he loosened his arms and moved so I was now under him. "Calm down, Neveah. I came in your room the first time I kicked you out of my house. The guilt was eating me alive. I hurt Neveah, my mate. Do you know how unacceptable that is? So, I came to your house and saw you sleeping. You are an angel when you sleep you know? You look…" Easton looked around, searching for words, "divine. Yeah, divine is how you look. You are not that girl who behaves her best to stop from hurting, even though she is the best." He laughed a bit after that. "You are not that girl I… I hurt." He sounded so broken when he whispered the last part.

Easton shifted so that we were lying sideways with my head on his shoulder. I looked up to him, but he wasn't looking at me. His eyes were on the ceiling.

I had no words to say. What should I say anyway? Thank you that he realised he hurt me when we were children or sorry that I was not the mate he wants? I remained silent as I laid my head on his chest and closed my eyes.

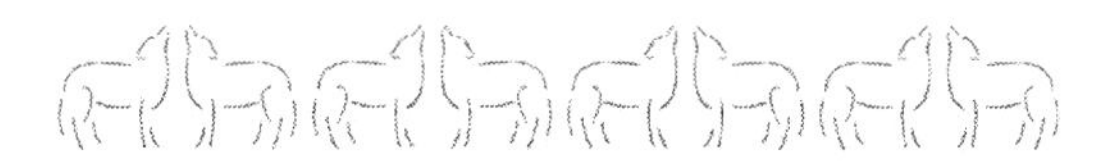

When I opened my eyes, it was already morning. I felt two arms around me. I opened my eyes to see Easton sleeping soundly with me still on his chest. I tried to get up, but his arms were tight around me. I wiggled around a bit and was freed at last.

I went inside the bathroom, did my stuff, and came out to find Easton missing and my window wide open. I sighed and went downstairs to find that both Ma and Brain weren't there. I looked at the clock and saw that it was only seven thirty am. That was very early.

I sat on the couch and tried to read the newspaper but failed. I only read three words before Easton entered my mind. Why did he leave so early? A part of me was happy, but the other half wanted to talk to him more.

I let him spend one whole night with me in my bed, and this was how he ran away. I should have kicked him out. Then again, after his confession, how could I?

"What are you thinking about so early in the morning?" I snapped out of my thoughts to see Ma hovering over me.

"Easton asked me out," I blurted out without thinking. God, why did I say that?

I looked at Easton who was avoiding me since this morning. It was Monday morning, and we were sitting next to each other in chemistry class. The project was due tomorrow, and the teacher made all the partners sit together so we could make the final touches, or in Xavier and Alden's case, the starting touches. I was very sure that they were going to fail chemistry.

"Why did you leave, Easton?" I decided to do the talking since Easton wasn't going to do the honours.

"Later, Nev. Not now." I let it go and sat quietly for the whole one hour.

During lunchtime, I was sitting with Melissa and Georgy as usual. There was complete silence on our table. I cleared my throat to get their attention. "Why is everyone silent?"

"Well, someone didn't tell me that they already knew about being the alpha's mate," Melissa said in an overly dramatic voice.

"He only told me yesterday afternoon. There was a party after that so I didn't get to tell you. You do remember what happened last night, don't you?" I regretted saying that immediately.

"Georgy, I didn't mean to say that." I looked at him. Surprisingly, he didn't look angry or annoyed.

"My mother is at fault here, Neveah."

"Still, Easton shouldn't have done that." Easton was partially guilty, too. It was utterly wrong of him to announce other people's secret in public.

Suddenly, we heard a high-pitched voice which was somewhere between a shriek and a laugh. I saw the girl who Melissa had threatened some time before. She looked really pretty. However, the position she was in wasn't that great.

She was standing between Xavier and Alden and was currently leaning towards Easton who looked like he was in la la land. "Easton, are you listening to me?" Her screech could be heard from anywhere in the room.

"I can't believe her." Melissa snorted.

"Hey, you were the same before." I reminded her, knowing for sure that she wouldn't feel bad. If there was one thing we share, it was honesty.

"Hey, I never went to anyone. They all came to me." Georgy just smiled at her, and they were all lovey-dovey again. I averted my eyes from them and glanced at Sabrina. Our eyes met, so I smiled at her.

What she did was beyond my expectations. She snarled at me, pulled Easton, who was currently having his lunch, and kissed him.

What the fuck?

Easton pushed her off him. The next thing I knew, he was pulling me off my chair and dragging me towards his table. At that exact time, the bell rang.

Everyone left for their classes except Easton and a few people from his pack. "Sabrina, what the hell were you thinking?"

"Oh, come on. She is just a human. I look so better than her."

"Oh please, you look like a chimpanzee! You should stick to the likes of Alden who has a very small—" I didn't let Melissa complete her sentence.

"Melissa, don't be harsh. She is beautiful." I smiled at her. She really was. "But you know what? I don't think Easton has enough energy left after last night."

We know nothing happened, but Sabrina didn't, and she didn't need to.

Chapter 24

Neveah

There were a whole lot of laughs, gasps, and hooting. Melissa and Xavier looked shocked, and Georgy smirked.

"Please, baby, we both know that I am ready for anything right now," Easton said and wrapped his arms around me. I could almost hear the smile in his voice.

"Shush, Easton, or I may have to drag you to the nearest closet," I warned him, not lifting my eyes from little Miss Sabrina.

"Or we could always go home. My bed is much better than yours," Easton said. As if I would! *Dream on, Easton, dream on.*

"I am not the one who needs to pass this year. We both have to go to class right now." I was serious. He couldn't afford to miss more classes. "You should return to class, too. The principal is not so liberal about bunking lectures," I said to Sabrina.

She huffed and left.

"Remove your hand, Easton. She is gone," I ordered.

"Sorry, babe."

I gritted my teeth and kept the smile on my face. I would handle this when we were alone. "Okay, the show's over. All of you, get back to your classes."

"Yes, Luna," everyone chorused.

They all left, and only me and Easton were in the huge room. Before Melissa left, she gave me a look saying 'we got to talk.' I shook my head and smirked at her.

"I am sorry, Neveah. I didn't mean to kiss her. She kissed me, but I didn't kiss her back. I swear." Easton looked really nervous.

"Hey, it is alright. You didn't know she was gonna do it."

He looked a bit relieved after that. I went back to my table to get my bag. We needed to get back to class and fast. When I turned back, Easton was standing in front of me.

"Where are you going?" he said as he blocked my path. Man, he was huge. I only reached his shoulder.

"Take a wild guess, Easton," I said, giving him a distasteful look.

"Don't be such a nerd, Nev. Half of the class is already over. Why don't we just stay here and talk?"

"About what?" I asked.

"About yesterday evening."

I thought about it and decided that it was actually a better idea than waltzing into a class this late. We sat down on one of the tables. "What do you want to say, Easton?"

"I don't think you appreciate the fact that I announced you as my mate yesterday in the party."

"It's alright," I said, shaking my head. "It was kind of obvious that everyone knew that we are mates except for Claire and Gabrielle." Easton turned pink, confirming my hunch.

"What happened yesterday in your house…"

"Oh, I should have kicked you out. I got the feeling that a guy ditched me after a hot night in bed even though nothing happened and you're not that hot," I said casually, knowing that Easton would rile up after hearing the *hot* part.

"Oh please, honey, I am sexy, and I know it."

"I am not here to talk about your hotness."

"I know, sorry. Do you have any questions to ask?"

"Why did you leave yesterday morning?" I went for the obvious. That was one question that I wanted to ask. Deep down, I wanted to know if he did want to leave.

"Oh, nothing, honey. When I got up, you were in the shower. While I was thinking about joining you or not, I detected an irritated feeling from my dad and got a call from Alden. He said he had something to discuss. So I had to leave. Besides, I thought you would be angry if I stayed."

"Oh, I… uh... I thought you didn't want to be with me so you left." That was the only answer that came to mind. Otherwise, why would a guy, who broke into my house, leave as soon as I was out of his sight?

Easton looked shocked by my answer. "Baby, I swear I wanted to stay, but I couldn't. I'm sorry if I hurt your feelings."

"No, it's… don't say sorry. Why did Alden want to talk?" I changed the awkward subject, wanting to know what that a-hole wanted to talk about.

"He wants Melissa back."

Really, Alden? Can you get any more cliche?

"What?" He was very sure that he will never need her when he rejected her, and now he wants her back?

"Yup, you heard me right. He said that he repents all he did and wants to start a new life with her," he continued.

"But she is already with Georgy!"

"Believe me, babe, you can't be happier than me. All we did was kiss a few times, and she was stalking me," Easton piped in, looking relieved.

"Definitely didn't need that mental image, East!" What he did with his past partners was none of my business. Frankly, I didn't want to know.

"I was just saying. Besides, I have not had any sort of relationship with anyone from the pack. Just so you know."

"Why the hell should I know that?" I didn't need to.

"Because we are mates," Easton stated as if it was the most obvious thing in the world.

"Okay…" I didn't know what else to say. We sat in silence for some time before something struck me. "You know the cute boy who shifted in front of me?"

"Yeah, Rick?" Easton urged me to go on. "Well, Melissa told me that you people shift for the first time when you are in your early teens or something. Then how come the guy shifted when he was that young?"

"I don't know exactly, but we have a theory. In my generation, males with strong blood shifts at the age of thirteen to fifteen and females by seventeen. What I said was for strong blood like Alphas or Betas. The ones with the least powerful blood shift the last."

"Hmm, okay, so Melissa has some strong blood?" I remembered she was proud of the age when she shifted.

"Ah, Melissa! Yeah, her mother is a beta of another pack," Easton explained. "We were expecting her to mate Xavier, but she ended up with Alden, who is after Xavier, rank wise."

I just nodded my head, trying to take in all the information.

"Okay, so as I was saying, blood determines when you shift, but nature also plays an important role. During my dad's time, they start shifting at eighteen, and during Grandpa's, it was twenty-one. We theorise that it was because there were many of us back then. Now, the number is dwindling, and we need to get stronger fast. There are hardly fifty thousand of us in the whole world."

"But why are your numbers decreasing?" Surely, a species' population wouldn't dip that low without some external force.

"Mates," Easton answered.

"But how?" I said, baffled.

"Many of us are rejecting our mates now. We can't have a werewolf child unless the child is a product of mating. That is why mates are important to us, especially those with strong blood. Because Alden rejected Melissa, and she most probably won't take him back, her werewolf bloodline will be lost. That is unless Madeline had a child with someone from our pack."

Wow! But how is this connected to Rick? Easton answered my unspoken question.

"Rick is an orphan, we have no idea of his parents. He was found on our land four years ago as a small baby. He is now almost six. Due to our decreasing number, there is pressure on our existing generation to fill that gap, so they shift early. However, no child can shift that early unless he has really strong blood. Our only conclusion is that both his parents must have had alpha blood which is really, really rare."

I don't know why, but I felt bad for Rick. The poor boy lost his parents so young.

"This is all so big. I mean, your system is really complex." I sighed. Me being his mate must've been a big thing to him. "Do I mean a lot to you?" I asked.

Easton took my hands and placed them on his lap. "More than my life. More than anything in this world," Easton said, looking into my eyes and giving me a small, sincere smile.

"You know a yes would have sufficed?" I tried to remove my hand. I wasn't good with this romantic stuff. It made me uneasy.

"You're not into this stuff, right?" Easton asked holding my hands tighter.

"I… I've never had this kind of experience before. I'm used to being alone. Having friends itself is a great thing for me." I admitted, still feeling uncomfortable.

"It's alright. There are firsts for everything." He loosened his hands at last.

Soon, the bell rang for the next period. We both got up and went to our classes.

"Babe, we are going on a date at seven. I'll pick you up. Dress classy," Easton called out, just as I was about to enter my class.

"Never," I said out loud, knowing that he could hear me perfectly.

All I heard was a chuckle in reply.

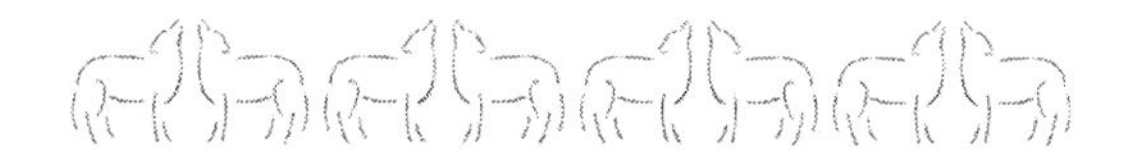

It was six forty-five in the evening, and I am all dressed up. At first, I thought that I shouldn't go. He didn't even ask me properly. He just shouted it out for everyone to hear. All my class heard it, especially Melissa and Sabrina.

Melissa was upset that I didn't tell her anything while Sabrina looked plain furious. One look from Melissa made her lower her head and do her own work, though.

I thought of how Easton was trying so hard for my attention. After what I heard this afternoon, I decided that he did deserve a chance. Also, I accidentally told Ma yesterday that Easton asked me out. *So convenient!*

Her first reaction was surprise, but after which she said, "That's so cute!"

God alone knows what was so cute about it.

So here I was, standing on my front porch at exactly seven pm waiting for my dear date.

Chapter 25

Neveah

I stood outside my house for exactly seven minutes before doubt started plaguing my thoughts. Was he really going to come or was it all a big joke? It wasn't the first time Easton would have a good laugh at my expense.

Then why did he say that I was his mate? I was doubting that right now, too.

No, it couldn't be. Otherwise, Easton wouldn't have told his pack and everyone else that we were mates. Calm down, Neveah. There must be a good reason he was late. He was a busy person, after all. His pack might have needed him for something

I hoped that Easton wasn't making a joke out of me again, but it wasn't a new thing for him and his buddies. Despite my mind's protests, I couldn't help thinking of an unpleasant memory from the past.

Eight years ago

I was eight years old back then. It was Easton's tenth birthday, so everyone was there. Melissa, Xavier, and rest of Easton's buddies were nine like them. I skipped second grade, so they were all with me in class. I never liked them, though.

All Xavier and Alden did was make fun of me. They always did that. I didn't know why they don't like me. Melissa was my only friend. She always talked to me nicely.

That day, Melissa was looking pretty in a blue princess dress just like the ones from Disney, and I was wearing a yellow dress. Ma said that it made me look pretty, but Xavier laughed at me as soon as I entered Easton's house. I hated him the most.

Aunt Amy and Ma were talking about something, and I was sitting next to Melissa. She was talking about this new Barbie movie she saw on TV.

"I am going to the kitchen to drink water, Melissa," I said when I suddenly got thirsty.

She nodded, and I left.

I was washing the glass I used and turned around to place it back in the cupboard when Easton and his friends blocked my path. Xavier grabbed my free hand.

"Let me go." I didn't want to hear what they had to say. It was something bad. It was always something bad about me.

"Come on, Neveah, you look like an ugly duckling. You look like Donald Duck," Xavier hissed, and the others laughed.

"Ugly, ugly, ugly," all of them shouted except Easton. He never said anything to me, but he laughed at me all the same. My eyes watered, and my tears were freely flowing down

my cheeks. "Oh, Neveah is crying! We should tell her daddy, but she doesn't have one," Xavier said again.

I started crying more and ran to the room where the party was. I went to Ma, hugged her, and cried in her dress.

I could hear Aunt Amy shouting at Easton. I glanced at him slightly from Ma's dress. He glared at me with scrunched eyebrows, so I hid my face back.

Unconsciously, a few tears leaked from my eyes, and everything around me became a blur.

I blinked my eyes to find Easton's car approaching my house. I rubbed my eyes as much as I could through the eyeliner and the mascara. Easton parked the car in front of my house and got out. He was looking good in his white shirt and black jeans. I smiled at him so he cannot tell that I was sad.

He kissed my head and looked at me. "You look beautiful." I was wearing a knee-length black skirt and a blue top. I matched it with black flats and earrings. I took the effort to blow-dry my hair too, leaving it in its natural wavy state.

"Same to you," I complimented him back. He took my hand in his, and we walked towards his car. I was silent the whole ride. I was not in the mood to say anything.

"Are you alright?" Easton asked me, looking concerned.

"I am fine," I said even though my tone said otherwise.

"If you say so," Easton stated. He was not convinced but didn't say anything after that.

"Where are we going, Easton?" We have been driving for almost an hour now. I have to be back home by eleven.

"It is a surprise," Easton replied. Well, it seemed like the surprise was too far from home.

We drove for another five minutes before Easton stopped in front of nowhere. The place seemed like a plain highway surrounded by trees on both sides. There was nothing too special in it to plan a surprise.

"Is this where you kill me and bury my body near one of the trees?" I teased him.

"No silly, as if would harm you." He pulled me out of the car and took us into the forest. Thank God, I'm not wearing heels.

We walked through the forest until we came to a huge house that looked like a palace. That was how huge it was. The whole place was decorated with lights and beautiful vines hanging on the pillars of the mansion.

"What is this place?" I was awed by the whole set up.

"It is a casual werewolf meet where all of us socialise once a month. It is strictly for werewolves and their mates."

I sighed. Easton brought me to a party. Didn't he know that I am not the party type?

He led me inside the mansion. I was dazzled by the amazing architecture and expected some party like the one at Melissa's house. This party, however, is totally different. There was a huge room with all people dancing and laughing. It was more of a get together than a party. There were unfamiliar people everywhere. All were enjoying themselves.

"Like it?" Easton whispered in my ear from behind me and placed his hand on my waist.

"I think, but I don't know anyone," I whispered back.

"That's alright. I'll introduce you to people." Easton assured me then held my hand in his. We went to a couple who were busy dancing to their own tune than the song.

When we got closer, I understood that they were both drunk. The guy looked as good as Easton, and that was saying something. His wavy hair, bright blue eyes, and gentle face made him look almost heavenly. A gorgeous redhead totally rocking a short black dress stood next to him.

"Hello, Callum. Hello, Eva." He gave the guy a man hug and a pat on his back and kissed the hand of the girl like some gentleman, which he clearly wasn't.

Eva gave a high-pitched shriek, "Easton, my baby." She came forward and gave Easton a long hug. I removed my hand from his and stood a bit away from them. She left his arms after some time and looked at him, checking him out.

I seriously thought that she was going to kiss him just like Sabrina. What she did was something I never expected in a million years.

She pinched his cheeks!

Easton tried to pry Eva off his face, but she just pinched him harder. After some time, Easton gave up and huffed, closing his arms over his chest.

Eva finally left his cheeks alone and looked at me. I quickly put my hands on my face. She laughed at my reaction. "Who is this hottie, Easton?" she asked him, and gave me a wink.

Easton rolled his eyes. He came towards me and enveloped me in his arms. "This is my mate and luna, Neveah Huber." Eva's grey eyes brightened when she heard the word mate.

"About time, Easton," Callum interjected.

"Thanks, dude," Easton replied. "This is Callum and his mate, Eva. They are the alpha pair of the next state."

“Hello.” I stretched my hand for a handshake, but she pushed it away and hugged me. The hug was really awkward as I had Easton glued to my right and Eva hugging me from the front. I was sandwiched between the two. Seeing my misery, Callum pulled his mate off me to give me some room to breathe. He smiled at me.

“Nice to meet you, Luna.”

“Just call me Neveah. Luna is really weird,” I said. Callum grinned in return.

“So, Neveah, how old are you?” Eva asked me. We were seated near the bar section with Easton still plastered to my right.

“I will be eighteen next month,” I answered before sipping on my wine. It might be odd for some, but I find wine really tasty. Easton and Callum being boys were gulping on beer bottles.

“She is not legal yet, Easton, you cradle robber.” Eva snickered while looking at my mate who looked displeased

“I am only eight months older than her,” Easton stated flatly.

“Just joking, Alpha. Chill. Come on, Neveah, let’s dance.” Eva didn’t even wait for me to answer and pulled me to the dancing crowd.

There was some silly song going on and people loved it.

Both of us also started moving. I took dancing classes till I was sixteen, so I was saved right now from making a fool out of myself.

We lose ourselves in the world of dance for some time. A fast beat Spanish song came on. I looked at Eva and mouthed, "Wanna dance salsa?"

Eva's lips curled into a huge smile. We both started dancing, and I got to say this, Eva was an awesome dancer. We both moved our hips, and damn, it was fun.

We danced throughout the whole song. Once it was over, I quickly realised that everyone at the party was looking at us. Easton was on his feet looking at me with his mouth open. I went to him and closed his mouth.

"That was fucking hot," Easton blurted out. "My nerdy girl, I didn't know that you were so sexy."

I winked and went full-on cliche. "There is still so much you don't know about me, Eugene."

I suddenly felt thirsty. Must've been from all the dancing. So I went to the bar again and took a big gulp of water from a glass lying around on the counter. Well, that was what I thought. It turned out to be vodka. Damn, it burned! Who in the world kept vodka in such huge glass? They are meant to be taken in shots. But it was too late, so I drank the whole thing, anyway.

I then went back to the dance floor where Eva and Callum were dancing. Easton, however, was missing. I turned my head around to look for him and found him next to a guy I didn't recognise. He looked at me, too. I grinned at the happy coincidence.

After some time, a pair of hands slipped around my waist. I automatically knew it was Easton. Don't ask me how. I just felt it.

We danced in that position for some time, and the song changed again. It was retro. All the girls formed an inner circle, and the boys formed the outer one.

The dancing began, and everyone moved like they were high. Well, at least I was, thanks to all the vodka and wine. I danced with random people who I don't even remember anymore. My last partner was Easton. I danced with him in a romantic number.

I placed my hands on Easton's shoulders and swayed to the music while Easton placed his hands on my waist.

The song was about to end. Easton pulled me closer to him till our noses were touching. I closed my eyes, and a second later, I felt his lips on mine. It was a short, sweet peck, but it was a kiss and my first proper one.

I opened my eyes and found Easton looking at me intently.

I smiled sheepishly and rested my head on his neck. I was feeling shy all of a sudden. That was uncharacteristic of me.

Easton was making me feel all giddy and girly.

And I didn't really mind.

Chapter 26

Easton

I explained everything about Rick and my blood to my mate, and she seemed to take it in the right way. I was expecting that question, anyway. Things rarely escape my inquisitive Neveah.

There was one thing she still hadn't figured out, and I was hoping that she never would.

After I was done telling her everything, the bell rang and our time alone was over. I wanted more time with her, so I asked her out on a date.

"Babe, we are going on a date at seven. I'll pick you up. Dress classy."

The manner I asked her out was way out of line. If there was one thing Neveah really cared about, it was her reputation in the school. Embarrassing her in front of the class was a big no-no.

She turned around two seconds later. I was already way ahead of her, not wanting to face the consequences of my rash action.

"Never" she announced, but I pretended to not hear her.

I was hoping with every fibre of my body that she would be ready when I pick her up. The last thing I wanted was to be stood up by my mate.

I skipped the remaining classes. I went straight home to find Alden and Gregory having a heated argument outside my house. Melissa was standing at a safe distance with my father.

"What is happening here?" I didn't need an idiotic argument from these two now. It was time I put an end to this.

"He stole my mate from me," Alden growled.

Gregory growled back in return. "You rejected my Melissa, you piece of shit. She doesn't want you anymore."

Alden's temper flared up and went into the first stage of shifting. Gregory, on the other hand, couldn't shift since he was obviously not one of us. No matter how strong he was, he couldn't take on a werewolf.

"Okay, enough both of you," I commanded. I was tired of their bickering. "Alden, Gregory, and Melissa, all you are going to come inside my house. We will talk like decent people and solve this issue once and for all."

So the three of us sat down at a table in the living room. My Dad was on the couch, and Melissa was pacing on the floor. She looked anxious, something I have never seen on her before.

"Okay, let us start. I am not going to leave this place until we decide a solution for this problem. But I want to make one thing clear. Whatever the outcome of this talk will be final, and all three of you must accept it. I will accept no whining afterwards."

All three of them had sour expressions on their face. "Am I clear?" This time, there was more authoritativeness in my voice.

"Yes, Alpha," all three of them replied. My own pack didn't listen to me unless I behave in such a way which was quite worrying. However, I decided to put it at the back of my mind for the meantime.

"Alden, just reply with yes or no. I don't want any explanations."

Alden nodded in defeat.

"Did you reject Melissa as your mate?"

"Yes, but—"

"A yes or no will suffice, Alden," I cut him off. I had no interest in his reasoning, and I was not the one he should tell them to. I turned to Melissa. "Did you accept his rejection?"

"Yes, Alpha," Melissa replied.

"Alright, and now you are dating Gregory?"

"Yes."

I didn't even know why I was doing this. Everyone in this room knew that Melissa was not going to accept Alden again.

Alden growled lowly at Melissa's answer until I commanded him to shut up. Wait, I knew why I was doing this. I was doing this so Alden finally accepts that he was now mateless, and he could do whatever he wants with it.

He had already denied our pack of a potentially strong pup, a future successor to his position. The least he could do was to shut his trap up and be a worthy third in command.

"Alden, do you want to accept Melissa as your mate again?" I kept my tone professional even though I was already bored to death. Good thing they couldn't sense my feelings. It was the other way round.

His oh-so-obvious nod said it all!

"Melissa, will you accept Alden as your mate?"

"Never," she spat out, hate and anger evident in her eyes. It should've been pretty obvious for Alden that no girl would accept a guy back after he had insulted her to hell.

"No, Melissa. I want you back. Please forgive me." Alden got up and kneeled in front of Melissa. Her expression softened for a second and then the glare was back.

"It's never going to work, Alden. It would be better if we behave like mature adults."

Alden stood up to his full height. He growled and punched the window behind her, shattering it to pieces. Gregory went to stop him, but I grabbed him by the shoulders in time and told him not to go any nearer.

It was a problem between mates, and it would be better if they resolve it by themselves. Melissa jerked as the glass shattered behind her, but she didn't look scared. She didn't need to. No harm would come to her as long as my father and I were in the room.

Alden moved away from her and proceeded to thrash my TV and the glass table near the couch. He didn't spare my wall either and put a big ass dent on it.

Mature, my ass! This was getting out of hand.

There were only a few ways by which a rampaging wolf could be fully calmed down. I chose the easiest way. I went to him and smashed the back of his head on the wall with so much force, it dented the wall. Then I pushed him back, and his face hit the floor.

His eyes opened wide for the shock. His face scrunched up, and he moaned a bit before his eyes rolled back and closed.

I nudged him with my leg to see if he was conscious.

"Just get someone to take him to the hospital and someone to replace this stuff. I want it done by tomorrow," I told my father when he didn't move. He was very much alive as proven by the strong heartbeat I could hear beneath his chest.

My father nodded and picked up his phone. Beside me, Gregory and Melissa were silent. They weren't surprised. They shouldn't be. Just because I was a puppy-dog guy in front of my Neveah, didn't mean I was the same to everyone. I could be scary if I wanted.

I dismissed Melissa and Gregory and went back to work. After dealing with some pack matters, I went to talk to my father.

"I am going on a date with Neveah," I announced. My father stopped reading and looked at me, visibly shocked.

"Why is she going on a date with you?" The fate my father had in me was overwhelming. *Thanks, Dad!*

"We are going on a date because she is my mate and she couldn't resist me anymore." Okay, the last part was a lie. If anything, Neveah couldn't feel the bond just yet. She's human.

"Treat her right, son." My father stood up and clasped his hands on my shoulders. His eyes expressed deep regret.

I smiled back in return. Before exiting his office, I noticed a picture of him and my mother on their wedding day twenty years ago. She looked beautiful with her long dark hair and warm brown eyes, just like my own mate.

My mother was the most beautiful woman I have ever seen. With her kind nature and easy going attitude, she was a hit among the pack members. She was easily the best luna the pack has ever had and the strongest wolf in my opinion.

I had confidence in my heart that Neveah would be just as good. She was amazing, and I am proud of her.

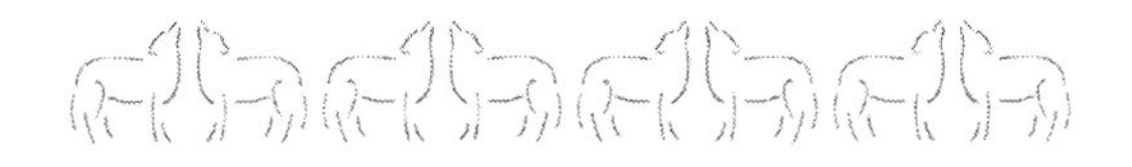

After the party, we reached my house, and my mate was terribly drunk. Not only did she look so flushed, but she was smiling way too much. *Silly girl!* You could tell that I was enjoying the sight of it. My Nev was too grumpy most of the time to smile in my presence. I decided to take her to my home because it was late and I didn't want to disturb her parents.

I parked the car just outside my door. Neveah was already limp before I could open the door. She was about to fall, but I caught her in time. She looked at me and grinned. I smiled back at her. Then suddenly, she pushed herself towards me and kissed me sloppily on the cheek. I somehow managed to remove her from my face and keep her steady on the ground.

I opened the door and carried Neveah to the living room where many of my friends from school were lazing around. My house was a meeting ground of sorts for them.

Everyone was shocked when they saw a drunk Neveah. Melissa was also there. As soon as she saw Nev, she stood in front of us with an angry expression on her face. "What did you do to her?"

I didn't appreciate her rudeness towards me, her alpha, but I had to let it go. She was just concerned about Neveah.

"Nothing, she got drunk," I stated. Melissa didn't seem so thrilled about my response.

"I can clearly see that, but I wanna know how she ended up like this. And why are you bringing her here? You should take her back home."

Melissa was already pulling Neveah out of my arms in no time, but I wouldn't allow it.

"No, she is staying the night with me." It was a direct alpha order.

"Easton, you're not—" I didn't even let Melissa finish her statement.

"Not all mates are like the one you had," I retorted. I knew it was harsh, but I would be damned to let anyone think that I would take advantage of my mate in this situation.

Melissa paled, and her eyes started to glaze over with tears. *Shit!*

"Easton, man—" Before Xavier could say anything more, Neveah hit me on the head.

"Say sorry, Easton." I was amazed that she was still conscious. She looked pretty much normal now except that she was swaying.

"She insulted me," I argued.

"No, you hurt her."

"I didn't," I shouted the last part. By now, my dad and the other important people in our pack were crowding the area.

"That's your problem," Neveah said. What did I do?

"You never know how much you hurt others. How much you and your friends hurt people." I wanted to apologise, but before I could speak, she continued.

"Oh, I know. You don't do anything, Easton. You never do anything. You just stand there like the great leader you are and allow Xavier and Alden to do the dirty work. You just stand there and laugh at people's misery." Neveah was shouting loudly and looked seconds away from crying.

I was shocked, to say the least.

She shakily moved away from me and continued. "You know, you asked me if I was alright in your car earlier. You know what? I wasn't feeling alright. In fact, I was sad. You know why? Because I was thinking about what happened on your tenth birthday and how you and your friends made fun of me that night."

She then turned to Xavier. "You were right, Xavier. At that time, I didn't even have a father. I had no one to complain to, no one to tell me that it wasn't my fault… that it was not my fault I didn't have a father. But Melissa has me, and I will not allow any of you to hurt her anymore."

I was too shocked to do anything. After her outburst, Neveah's eyes closed, and she fell.

Chapter 27

Neveah

"Come on, Neveah. Get up. We have to leave for school." I heard a faraway voice trying to disturb my peaceful slumber.

"Get up, Neveah! You don't want to be late for school, right?" The voice didn't sound like Ma. It sounded different and masculine.

I opened my eyes and found myself face-to-face with Easton.

"We need to leave for school." His voice wasn't loud, but I felt like my head was going to burst any second. My whole body ached, and I was dead tired even though I felt like I have been sleeping for ages.

"Not so loud." My voice came out as a croak. That was when I noticed the pain in my throat.

What happened last night?

Then the events of last night came back to me. Easton and I went to that party and met Callum and Eva. We drank.

We danced. Easton kissed me. And then I came up with a blank! I cannot remember a single thing about what happened after.

I looked around the room. Why am I at Easton's house?

"Why am I here, Easton?" He didn't reply. He went outside the room, and I just watched his retreating back. What was up with that?

I tried getting out of his bed, but my body cried out in protest. I honestly felt so weak, and my head was throbbing in pain.

Easton returned after a while with a massive tray full of breakfast, a glass of orange juice, and two pills.

"Go to the bathroom and wash your face and mouth," Easton said, refusing to look in my eyes. I would have probed the matter further, but I was too tired to do anything.

There was only one door in the room which wasn't the closet, so I went in there.

I stood in front of the full-size mirror in his bathroom. I looked like death herself. My face was pale, and my eyes were bloodshot. Not to mention that my makeup was all smeared. I washed my face with cold water, and my head hurt more as I bent my head.

"Neveah, there are towels at the cabinet near the shower. Take one. I have clothes for you. I will leave it here in the bed. Come out then eat your breakfast. I'll leave now," Easton said in a low voice, and it caused my head to pound faster.

I opened the door to respond since I couldn't shout but Easton was not in the room anymore.

I sighed and went back in the shower. The warm water was soothing. It helped me relax my sore muscles.

After I was done, I had the huge plate of breakfast and popped the pills. Easton returned when I was combing my hair.

He had showered and was well-dressed. The same thing couldn't be said about me. The red tank top I was wearing was two sizes smaller, and the skirt was just to my mid-thigh. They were surely Melissa's clothes. How Easton got them for me this early in the morning, I didn't know.

"Uh, you look good." Easton, being the guy he is, was looking at my legs while saying this. I cleared my throat to get his attention away from them.

"No, Easton, I look like I am wearing some stick thin girl's clothes. You couldn't find anyone other than Melissa?" I sat down on the bed and worked on removing the tangles in my hair.

"How do you know that it is her clothes?"

"I know Melissa, Easton," I replied. It was the most obvious thing in the world. She was my BFF. Well, used to be. So I surely knew her fashion sense and the clothes she chose.

He just shrugged and told me to get ready in another ten minutes.

I left my hair as it was and went to his living room to find that it was empty. Wow! In fact, the whole house was empty, which to my recollection had never happened till now. I walked out to the patio to see Easton near his car. He had my bag pack with him. I sat in the car, and off we are to school.

"Do my parents know that I stayed the night?" Easton didn't look at me and just nodded his head.

"Bryan didn't have anything to say about it?" Bryan was not so comfortable with my whatever-it-is with Easton. I highly doubted that he would have let me stay the night.

"I spoke to Gina, so I am not sure what your step-father has to say on the matter." Easton still didn't look at me and was firmly gripping the steering wheel. If he pressed it any tighter, the thing was going to break. I pushed my aching muscles to the limit and placed a hand on his shoulder to try to loosen his tension. He stiffens for a second and then relaxes.

"Did anything happen last night?" Something must have happened last night because Easton was sounding and acting in a very different way.

"No, nothing happened." Easton was lying. His anxious tone was a dead giveaway. I said nothing.

It was really weird in school today. All his pack mates didn't look at me at all. It was like they were avoiding me on purpose.

Even Xavier was behaving really strange. He didn't look at me and didn't comment on anything I did.

By lunch, I was ready to pull my hair out in frustration. I sat next to Melissa for lunch who looked upset.

"Do you, by any chance, know what happened last night?" My question seemed absurd to me as soon as I said it. How would she know what happened on our date? However, her answer surprised me.

"Yes. You were drunk yesterday, and you scolded Easton and his group," she said.

"Scold?" Why in hell will I scold him? The date was really good. I remembered having a lot of fun with Callum and Eva.

"Uh… Easton said something to me which were kind of true and harsh, but true nonetheless. I teared up, so you shut him up and told him that you are going to protect me because you didn't have anyone to do so for you. You revealed that you were bullied by Xavier and his friends. I'm sorry, Nevy. I didn't know." *Shit!* Melissa didn't know anything about Easton and his friend's wrongdoings.

Xavier was smart like that. He never made fun of me in front of others when we were younger. It was always when I was alone. He knew that Melissa will always defend me.

Wow! Drunk me was not a good thing. "Is Easton angry at me?"

"More like angry with himself," Melissa replied.

"So are you all on some avoid-me operation?" Easton surely had something to do with this. Otherwise, his people wouldn't be ignoring me. Leave the ignoring part, they started gossiping after I left the place.

"No, we're just ashamed."

"Even Xavier?" I couldn't help asking for he was my main tormentor. I wanted to know how he felt after I blurted out his bullying ways in front of important people from his pack.

"Especially Xavier." *Wonderful!*

"Good," I replied, sounding satisfied.

"Good?" Melissa asked.

"Yes. It is high time they repent their actions." I knew very well that Easton and his buddies could hear me. My hatred towards them had slowly died down, especially to Easton. But to forgive them so easily would be wrong. They had to pay for their cruelty.

They made sure that there wouldn't be a future Neveah-Xavier pair.

Georgy joined the table after some time. "How are you, ladies? I heard that someone had a lot of fun yesterday." He wiggled his eyebrows suggestively.

"Did you hear what happened after that?" I so wanted to wipe the smirk off his face. How did he come to know now?

"No." Thank, God! It wouldn't stay that way for long, though. So might as well give him the answer.

"Well, you can ask anyone in the school." I was pissed at the fact that it had now spread throughout the school. I was never getting drunk again. One night of embarrassment was enough.

"Oh, I'll ask him later." The smug expression on his face told me that the *him* was Easton.

"Whatever." I brushed him off. I was more interested in the food.

Georgy didn't like being ignored, being the stud he was. He hooked his arm around my neck and pulled me towards him, but not roughly. I shrieked because I was startled. The whole lunch room turned towards us, and Easton was in front of me in a split second.

"What happened?" Easton asked. Alden and Xavier were behind them.

"Nothing," I replied and went back to my food. I wasn't in the mood to speak to them.

"But you just screamed!" Easton looked seriously worried.

"I was just surprised. I am alright now," I said.

Easton didn't say anything and just stared at me for a long time.

"Are you sure that you are alright?" he asked.

"Just go already." I sighed and glared at him.

Easton left along with his buddies, and everything was normal again. I continued with my food.

"How was the date?" Melissa asked me quietly. There was the gossip queen I knew.

"It was really good," I answered truthfully. It would be wrong of me to say that it wasn't good. Honestly, I enjoyed myself last night.

"Well, he did one thing right," Georgy muttered. "He is a decent guy, and I have seen many shitty guys in my life to know the difference."

"Ah, if you say so." I didn't push it further. I have come to a conclusion that Georgy didn't have a happy childhood. Something told me that it was worse than I was expecting it to be.

"I'm leaving." Melissa interrupted my thoughts.

"Okay, bye." I had the next lecture free along with Georgy. Georgy and Melissa said their goodbyes, and then it was only me and him in the lunch room.

"Want to go somewhere?" Georgy asked me.

"But we only have one free hour, and I have one assignment remaining."

"Come on, nerdy girl. Stop thinking about the school work for some time. Let's go somewhere. The place is nearby, and you will love it." The excitement in his voice almost convinced me.

I agreed after some more persuasion, and off we went. Georgy parked on a highway, and we got out.

"Where are we going?" I inquired.

"There is a place nearby, just at the start of the forest. We are just going there to relax and talk."

"Okay."

Georgy guided me, and after five minutes, we reached a beautiful place with apple trees and a small waterfall that formed a medium-sized pond.

"Wow! How do you know about this place?" I asked him. I have been living here all my life, and yet I didn't know about this beautiful place. That was such a shame.

"Well, I do know the owner," Georgy said smugly.

"Who?" I asked, excited to know about the person who owns this piece of heaven.

"You," Georgy replied.

I burst out laughing. That was one lame joke, but why was I the only one who was laughing?

"Finished laughing?" He grinned at me.

"Oh, come on, what you said was funny." I didn't even own my car. It was registered in Ma's name, and she was the one who paid for it. And now Georgy was saying that I owned this small piece of paradise?

"Well, I don't find the truth funny." Georgy still had that smug expression on his face. Oh, so he was not lying?

"Really?"

"Yup, the owner of this land is Easton. As his luna, you own it too."

Wow!

Chapter 28

Neveah

Wow!

I was a partial owner of this land. That was if Easton and I got together. That was something I was not sure off, so I decided not to think about him and spend some time knowing things about Georgy.

We sat down on the edge of the pond. I removed my shoes and dipped my legs in the water which was pleasantly cold. Well, that was one good thing about wearing a skirt! Georgy came and sat beside me but didn't put his legs in the water.

I looked at him and asked him straight on. "What was your life before we met?"

Georgy didn't look surprised. "You know, this is why I like you. You are so honest and always straight to the point. You don't hide things."

"I am in the happiest phase of my life right now," he continued. "You and Melissa are a big part of me being happy.

From the outside, I have a pretty normal life with normal parents and older brother. But things are really different in reality. My mom hates all of us. She wasn't like this before, and this didn't happen in one day... it just happened... s-slowly and gradually."

I didn't say anything and just gestured him to continue. If I stopped him now, there was a probability that he wouldn't open up to me again.

"My mother is the daughter of an alpha whose pack is based in the UK. She was mated to the alpha of the nearby pack. His pack wasn't huge, but he was a respectable man. He was pretty much a decent guy until he met some other she-wolf and cheated on my mom with her. Naturally, my mother confronted him about it. Somehow, the fight escalated, and the other she-wolf tried to kill my mom. Her mate didn't even try to save her, so she got angry and killed both of them."

"You mean, she killed two people at a time? But how was she able to kill an alpha? Aren't they supposed to be super strong?"

"Yes. My mother has alpha blood too, and she is highly trained. She is believed to be the strongest female werewolf in the world."

"Wow!" Gosh, I seemed to be saying that word a lot! "Okay, continue."

"Well, all of this happened to her in the last year of high school. After that, she went to Germany for college. That was where she met my dad and had my brother a few months later. They got married after a few years and had me."

"Well, that seems pretty much normal," I commented. It was nothing like mine.

"Yeah, and that is where you are wrong. My mother was never in love with my dad. Sure, she liked him, but she did not love him. She is still in love with a man she killed. She is plagued with the guilt of killing her own mate and marrying another guy afterwards."

I gasped. How was that even possible? She must have loved him at some point in time. She married him and had two children.

"I thinking your mom is lying. You just can't live with someone for years without falling in love with them," I stated.

"If she was human, then maybe she was lying. But she is a werewolf and apparently, they can't survive without a mate unless that mate rejects them outright. It is actually a miracle that she is alive for so long," he said with a cold look in his eyes.

Was he not concerned about her life? I could do many things, but living without my Ma wasn't one of them.

"Enough of this talk. It doesn't matter that much, anyway. So tell me about your story. Why do you hate Xavier and Easton? How about your dad?" I mentally winced. Talking about *him* brought a great deal of pain to me.

"I know nothing about my dad. He bailed out when he learned that Ma was pregnant. Xavier and Easton.... they are the reason I am like this."

"Like what?"

"A snotty, rude, and insecure bitch," I said while looking at the water. I didn't want to look at him. I didn't want to see his reaction.

"You are not..."

I gave him a sharp look. "Don't you even complete that sentence because I know that it will be the biggest lie of your life."

He grasped my shoulder and made me look at him. "Neveah, the way I see things, you are a normal teen with normal teenage issues. Sure, you are rude sometimes, but only to people who deserve it. You are honest and kind. You are even capable of opening your heart to people who did you wrong. Look at Melissa. You hadn't spoken to her for a long time, and yet you were the only one who stood with her in her dark times. That to me is not the traits of a bitch."

I smiled at him, feeling happy.

"Those traits are reserved only for my girlfriend," he added and winked at me. I chuckled. Oh, Melissa was a bitch alright!

"Easton and Xavier?"

"Well, they were the people I used to dislike the most in the world." The past tense was appropriate. I surely didn't hate Easton now.

"But you all were kids back then, right?"

"Believe me, I was the only kid at that time. The rest all were spawns of Satan. They just needed a reason to tease me. You must be thinking that they were kids too and couldn't do that much. Well, they can do a lot. I was their main target. Well, actually it was Xavier and another guy James, but he isn't here right now. Ma was struggling with me. Sure, we had money, but she was tired emotionally, and her only support system was Amy. Amy Dale, as in the angel who birthed my devilish mate." I winced, thinking about those dark times with them.

"I have heard a lot about her," Georgy muttered quietly.

"She was one the best people in the world," I informed him. "Xavier and his buddies loved to demoralise me, and at that age, I took it all *very* seriously. Me being fatherless was one of the topics they loved the most. The others were my lack of height, my nerd qualities, and my inability to stay without crying. Of course, I have moved over some of them."

"You know the worst part in all of that?" I asked him a question to which he obviously didn't have an answer.

"Easton never said anything, ever. He would just look and laugh at me while his friends made fun of me. His expressions hurt me badly. He can glare, you know? And his glare hurts a *lot*. He might not say anything, but his eyes told me how unwanted I was and how much he considers me as a waste of space."

I poured out all my worries, sorrow, and frustrations. "It is because of them that I doubted myself growing up. It may not be visible from the outside, but I sure am an insecure mess. Right now, everything seems nearly perfect, but I feel like it is all going to end someday. I'll just wake up, and all my happiness will be gone."

After I had finished, we both stayed quiet for some time. I placed my head on his shoulder, both of us busy in our own thoughts. It was when my mobile started ringing that we were pulled out of the trance.

I quickly looked at the time and was shocked. It was way past an hour. I quickly stood up and put my shoes on. I pulled Georgy and told him to hurry up. The last lecture was over, but I needed to get my car before they locked up the main gate.

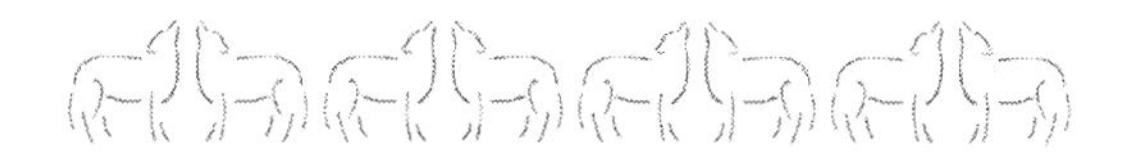

We reached the school way past closing time, but luckily, people were still there. Georgy parked the car, and I quickly got out.

Some of Easton's people who were still in the parking lot raised their eyebrows at the sight of me jumping out from some another male's car. Easton didn't look pleased too, but who in hell cares?

"I got an A plus on the Math test," he said.

I was about to smile and congratulate him when Melissa said, "And you got a B-plus."

I looked at Easton not knowing whether to kiss him or to kill him. The second option seemed better right now.

How in the hell did Easton manage to get an A plus and I got a B? I have never gotten a B-plus in all my life. This was so not fair. Anyone but Easton.

Be the bigger person, Neveah, and just congratulate him, my conscience said. He deserved it. I took a calm breath to try to control my temper

"Congratulations, Easton," I said with a tight-lipped smile.

"You are so not happy with the result." He teased. My annoyed mood didn't seem to affect him.

"And that is not the only test he's got bigger marks than you," Melissa added. If I wasn't heartbroken before, I sure was now.

"What do you want me to tell you? That I am ecstatic? That would be the biggest lie of my life. I am currently plotting your death in a thousand different ways." There was no reason for me to be lying to Easton. He would find out that I was lying, anyway.

"I am happy that you are not happy for me. I would have questioned your sanity had you pretended otherwise." Easton then hugged me for God knows what reason. I didn't protest, the guy deserved that after I insulted him and his beta in front of everyone.

What must they be thinking about me? Or worse, what must they be thinking about Xavier and Easton? This reminded me that we needed to talk about this morning.

"Easton, we need to talk, and we need to talk now," I told Easton after he finished hugging me.

"Okay, let us go to your place. I am in serious need of privacy," Easton muttered. I didn't blame him. People came and go all the time in his house.

"Okay, let us leave. Bye, Mell. Take care. You too, Georgy baby," I shouted to the couple who were busy making out. As soon as I did, they broke up and glared at me.

"Can you just get lost?" Georgy shouted back. Instead, I just went and hugged him. I wrapped my arms around his waist and pressed my face to his chest. His arms came around me, and he kissed my head.

"Thank you," I muttered in his chest. It was muffled, but I knew he heard me.

He hugged me tighter and let go after some seconds. I turned to Melissa and winked and off I was to my house with Easton driving my car. When I asked him what about his car, he shrugged and said that someone from his pack would bring it back to his home.

I dumped my bag on the dining table for which surely Ma was going to give a lecture about. I was tired, so I just let it be. I made Easton sit on the couch while I went to the kitchen and heated some leftover pasta from yesterday.

I sat on the couch and gave him one plate of pasta while I took the other one. We had the food in silence after which I washed the dishes.

"I am sorry about last night. I shouldn't have said those things in front of so many people." I started off the conversation since Easton was silent. Easton didn't say anything, so I continued.

"Why was everyone ignoring me this morning?" It was annoying and very irritating.

"We were not ignoring you. We were just giving you space. We thought that you would not want to speak to us."

What he was saying seemed logical but at the same time weird.

"I don't speak to anyone but Melissa and Georgy. When people avoided me, it was noticeable to all the humans in school, and that is not normal," I argued with him.

"Don't think so much about it, Neveah. They don't care and nor they do have the time to explore, and no, it isn't your fault. I was expecting that, anyways, just not in front if everyone." When he said that, I felt guilty. All of it should've been dealt with personally. Then again, I was drunk. If I were in my proper senses, I would have never said anything.

"Did Peter say something?" Easton smiled when I mentioned Peter.

"He just kicked me out of the house. It's effective starting tonight" Easton wasn't even looking at me while saying this, and he didn't have any sad expression on his face.

"Why did he do that? Where are you gonna stay?" Never did I expect Peter to react like this.

"Oh, I am crashing at Xavier's place. My father said quote, 'you are not to enter this house until my daughter forgives you.' So I am to ask your forgiveness, and then I am allowed to enter the house." Easton mentioned all of this casually as if this wasn't a serious issue.

"Why aren't you worried?" He should be. Any logical teen would be. Then again, he was an alpha. Anyone on his pack would surely make a place for him in their houses.

"Because I know what dad said is right. So, Neveah, I want to ask for forgiveness for all the bad behaviour of mine over the years. I know that you won't forgive me right now, but I just want to at least try. I hope that over time, you will forgive me. I also promise that I will do all that is possible to earn it and be a good mate to you." He sounded so sincere that my heart melted. Well, not exactly!

Easton's speech left me baffled.

"I guess we can give this relationship another try," I replied. I owed that to him for trying to make this work between us.

"Really?" I nodded at Easton's question. "Thanks. This is way better than what I was expecting."

I just smiled at him.

"Oh, and the elders of my pack want Xavier to be removed from the beta position," he said while leaning towards me.

"Can they do that?" I was surprised. Easton was giving me shocking after shocking news.

"Hell, no. I am the only one who can issue the order. So, I want your opinion."

"Can I express my opinion in front of your elders or whoever they are?" I had to make sure that Xavier was not expelled. Besides, he was a kid then. Well, a demonic kid but a kid, nonetheless. Punishing him for his wrongdoings was only my decision, not others.

"Sure, if that is what you want."

"Great. Just gather all the elders and Xavier tomorrow at your place, okay?" The earlier I sorted this out, the better.

"Will do," he said.

There was the sound of the front door opening. Bryan walked in a few seconds later and paused. He was glaring at Easton.

"What is he doing here, baby girl?" Bryan didn't look happy. He looked like he could murder Easton any second.

"We are just talking." I felt guilty. Bryan was just looking out for me. I didn't even come home last night. God knows what he must be thinking about me!

"Talking, huh? I am very sure that you both were talking all through last night?" Bryan questioned in an accusing tone. I couldn't really blame him.

"Nope, I was the only one talking." I explained to him all that had happened yesterday. His anger seemed to amplify when I mentioned my past experience with Easton and his buddies, but he didn't interrupt me.

"Is he treating you right?" Bryan asked me with Easton in front of him. He knew that I would tell the truth even if I hurt Easton in the process.

"Yeah, Dad. He is surely improving. We have decided to make this work."

Bryan seemed satisfied with my answer, so he didn't press the issue any further.

Ma also arrived later in the evening. Easton stayed for dinner, joking that he actually doesn't have a home to go to.

After Easton had left, I sat down to do math and tried to find out where I actually lost the marks. When I mentioned my and Easton's marks to Ma, all she did was congratulate Easton.

What about your own flesh, dear mother?

I was doing a sum when there was a knock on my window. Easton was sitting on the tree branch. Well, more of hanging. I sighed and opened the window.

He let himself in and sat on my bed.

"Can I spend the night here?" he asked a bit sheepishly.

"Why?" Wasn't he crashing at Xavier's?

"Xavier and his family are having a bonding time going on, and it felt really uncomfortable. I didn't want to impose myself on the, so here I am," Easton said. He was now comfortably lying on my bed with his shoes on.

"Oh, okay. But you got to leave early in the morning just like last time."

"Great, thanks." He then closed his eyes and pretended to be asleep.

"You're welcome and remove your shoes."

Chapter 29

Neveah

I was still doing the math sums on my study table, and Easton was on my bed, staring at me with his shoes off. I finished it up and stared back at him. How did he get an A?

I closed my book, went to my bed, and sat near him. "How did you get an A, Easton?" I asked.

He pulled me by the waist so I was lying beside him. I turned my body to face him. "What did you do Easton? Did you copy?" I said accusingly.

"You really think I cheated?" He asked.

"I don't know," I told him truthfully.

"Well, do you remember the math book some days before?" I nodded. "Well, I solved the whole book."

Bloody hell! Even I have not solved the whole book. It was a four hundred page book. "When did you get the time to solve the whole book? I didn't even know that you are interested in math," I muttered.

"I am not interested, but since my mate told me to do so, my wolf won't relent. I ended up solving the whole thing. Besides, it was not that bad!"

"Your wolf?" Aren't they the same person?

"We are the same person. We are one, but we have conflicting opinions sometimes. Frankly, my wolf is a whipped dog, pun intended."

"And you're not?" I tricked him into answering the question.

He smirked at me, knowing my intentions. "Well, not as much as him."

"Nice." I moved closer to him. My head was on his arm now, making it a pillow for me.

I was about to ask him something else when there was a knock on my door. "Neveah, goodnight baby." We both looked at the door and then at each other.

Thank God my door was locked. I tensed up but stayed still. Usually, Ma comes in, and we talk, so now I had to make some excuse to stall her.

"Goodnight, Ma. Now shoo. I need to solve math sums and find where I lost my marks. Love you." I shouted with the most normal voice I could muster.

"Okay. Fine. Love you too." I heard her footsteps fade away. I sighed. That was close.

"Nice save," Easton said and pulled me back to him.

"You're lucky she didn't realise that something was wrong. Actually, you are lucky that it was Ma and not Bryan." The thought of my stepfather finding out that his daughter had a boy in her bed was scandalous in itself.

That reminded me of something. "Easton, don't answer if you don't want to, but why didn't Peter remarry or even date anyone after Aunt Amy's death?" It was almost a decade since she passed away, but I have never seen Peter look at some other woman.

I didn't even remember Amy's body being buried. "What exactly happened to Aunt Amy, East?"

"She was murdered. We never got the body. We just saw a lot of blood." His voice was hoarse.

"When one of the mated couple dies, the other one feels like they have lost a part of themselves as well," he continued. "It is a void which can never be filled. The other mate could try to date. It's just that my father wants to live with her memories as his companion," Easton stated solemnly.

That was so sad. Having mates was both a boon and a curse.

"Did he try to find out who killed your mom?" I whispered, trying not to sound like a nagging person.

"Of course, he did. He is still trying but to no avail. It was like she just disappeared." He explained with a far off expression on his face.

"Then how are you sure that she is no more?" If no body was found, then there might be a possibility that she was alive.

"No, dad says that mated couples knew when the other one dies. So, I didn't question him any further."

I snuggled a bit in his chest. He was really warm, and that felt really good. "It's okay, Easton. She must be really proud of you now."

"About what?" He wrapped an arm around my waist.

"That you got an A." I tried to cheer him up.

"Whatever you say. Now go to sleep."

"Yes, sir. Goodnight." Easton pulled the comforter over us before uttering a silent goodnight to me.

"Neveah, wake up. You have to go to school." I heard Ma's voice. I didn't want to wake up. I snuggled closer to the warm body beside me.

I opened my eyes to face Easton's face. He looked so serene while sleeping. I stared at him for about two minutes before shaking him awake.

"Wake up, Easton. We have to go to school." I was not angry that he didn't leave.

He opened his eyes after my third attempt.

"Morning, Nev." He greeted with a small smile on her face.

"Morning, East." I greeted back.

"Come on, you need to leave." I sat on the bed and pulled him up.

"Get up, Neveah," Ma shouted again, "and wake up Easton, too."

I gasped. I went and opened the door, and there she was— my innocent mother giving me a dirty smirk. "How did you know?" I snapped at her looking horrified. It was not fair.

"Mother's intuition."

"Good morning, honey. I made chocolate pancakes, your favourite. I also picked up some of Bryan's clothes which will fit you. It is in my room. Go there and have a bath. You know where you can find the other things." The woman smiled cheerily before disappearing downstairs.

"Did she have a strong drink this morning?" Easton was still staring at the door with an amazed expression on his face.

"I think. Come on, Ma has made your favourite food," I said with distaste.

"Now now, honey, don't be sad that Gina loves me more than you," he said with a smug look on his face.

"Just get lost." I pushed him out of my room and got ready for the day.

My mood during the whole day at school was turning from bad to worse, and the reason for it was none other than Easton. When I told him that he should concentrate on his studies, I only meant for him to pass, not to get better than me.

In all lectures, Easton kept answering all the teacher's questions. Not only that, he managed to come second in class in history. Of course, I scored more, but that didn't mean that I was not insecure. Georgy was a competitor I could handle, but Easton was threatening my positions. That, I could digest. I kept glaring at him the whole time, and he just kept blowing me kisses. All the teachers were impressed with him. One of them even commented on how my love was improving Easton.

Love, my foot!

I had to do something. I couldn't just give up my position, especially to Easton.

Think, Neveah, think.

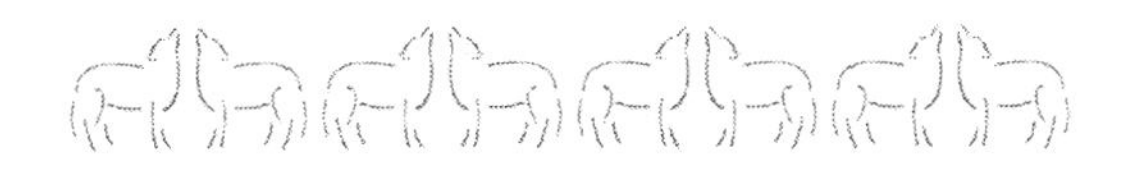

We were currently in the forest waiting for all the elders of his pack and Xavier to arrive. Easton was standing and looked far off while I decided to sit on one of the high rocks. Since I was currently not doing anything, I thought of observing Easton.

The loose jeans and the oversized cream shirt somehow managed to look good on him. Breakfast this morning was a simple event of Ma gushing over Easton and totally ignoring me. Thankfully, Bryan had to leave for some conference early in the morning, or he would have had a heart attack for sure.

After some time, a group of seven really old people walked over to us accompanied by Peter, Xavier, and Alden.

All of them stood in front of Easton and greeted him. I went and stood beside him, observing all the so-called elders who were doing the same to me.

"Okay, today we have assembled here because my mate has something to say about Xavier and the position he holds in the pack. Would you like to start Elder Jack?" Easton mentioned to one man,

"As you wish, Alpha." The man stared with his report. "As said by the luna herself, the pack beta, Xavier, is being accused of bullying and misbehaviour with the luna through the years, and we have—"

"Then shouldn't the alpha be accused too since he was equally guilty? Why only them when there are many others I would like to add? Because of their bullying behaviour towards me, you may punish them, but what about the others? There are many who went through the same rough experience, which I am very sure is instigated by some of your pack. What are you going to do about them?" I cut the old man short.

The old man didn't like the fact that I cut off his speech. That much was obvious from the expression on his face.

"We will look into that matter, young girl. We will solve one matter at a time," the oldie Jack replied to me in a patronizing tone, as if I said something terribly wrong.

That angered me. "Why don't you raise the children in your pack properly instead of advising me?"

The elder seemed shocked by my behaviour. Well, it was not my fault that he was a bloody hypocrite. He was finding faults in others when he himself had the highest fault!

"That is not the right way a luna should speak!" One of the guys from the seven told me. I wasn't paying much attention to the other elders, but they all seemed outraged and disappointed.

"And how do you know how a luna should behave? I believe you haven't been one," I replied easily. My own mother had never told me how to behave, and this man was going to teach me? I knew that I didn't have an easy going nature, but I was rude only to those people who were unjust to others.

Beside me, Easton was laughing his guts off. "You only laugh at others. What kind of best friend are you, Easton? Help your friend." I told him, yet that only made him laugh louder.

"He doesn't need any help. He has luna on his side. Besides, he has told me that he won't accept any help from me." Easton told me whilst looking at Xavier who was looking back at him as if having some telepathic conversation.

"Are you nuts, Xavier? Or do you want to get away from Easton? Not that I could blame you for it." Xavier laughed at my question. Even Peter had a smile on his face.

"No, Neveah, I kinda with the elders."

I went to him. "Do you think that I will let you off so easily? Stepping out of your position will not do me any good.

Believe me, I have my own ways of making you suffer," I announce in a threatening voice. At least now the elders will leave him alone.

"That kind of voice is not appropriate and not appreciated." Elder Jack gave his insignificant opinion just as I finished my conversation with Xavier.

"Your presence is also not appreciated, but did I say anything?" Hadn't he figured out by now that I didn't like him?

"Will you let her speak to us in such a way, Alpha?" another Elder demanded.

"No. Enough, Neveah, and all the elders, my luna is not entirely wrong. There are many who are bullied by many from our pack. It is our duty to teach the younger generation proper behaviour." Easton's voice was final, and no one argued after that.

"Let us leave. Xavier, your punishment is five hundred hours of community service," Peter announced. Xavier gulped as Easton and Alden snickered and gave each other a high five.

The whole meeting seemed pointless with the final decision made by Peter himself. Should have done that the first time!

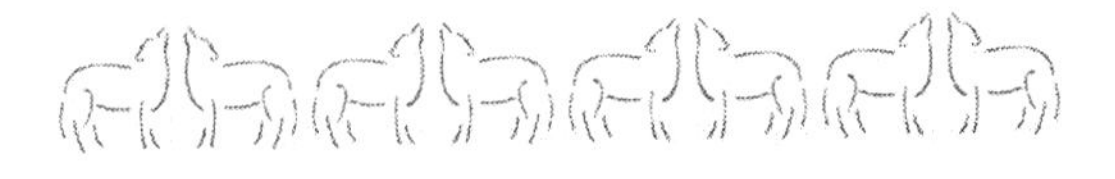

After the meeting at the forest, I ended up at Melissa's house.

Georgy was the one who greeted me at the door. "What you doing here, Neveah?"

"Last time I checked, this is Melissa's house." I pushed him and entered the house to find Melissa applying nail polish on her toes.

"You, out." I pointed to Georgy.

"Mel, she is kicking me out." He complained, giving my best friend his puppy dog eyes. Melissa softened, but I was immune to his charms. I looked at Melissa and gave her a sad expression myself.

"Then kick yourself out," Melissa said, and Georgy's face dropped. I gave a small shout of victory and went to the couch where she was sitting and gave her a high five.

"Fine." He left the place but not before sharing a long kiss with my BFF.

"You seem happy, Mel," I commented while looking at the constant smile on her face.

"I am really happy." There was such a big smile on her face that I smiled with her too.

"How did this happen?" I mean, one day she was sad that her mate rejected her, and the next day she was holding Georgy's hands. It was all so fast.

"I don't know, Neveah. It just happened. On the day he first came to our school, we met again at a pack meeting. We talked. He knew what happened to me all thanks to that jackass of a mate. He approached me, and there was a lot off attraction," she stated with her mind far off as if recalling all those moments. "I know that this may not be permanent. A guy like him won't be tied down to a girl like me, and I know that. It's okay if he wants to leave, but I know that he won't hurt me."

"I don't think that he is going to break off with you anytime soon. So don't worry so much. Besides, you are the head bitch, honey. Worrying doesn't look good on you." I tried consoling her.

We both looked at each other and started laughing. "Forget that. I heard that someone was really rude to the elders."

"Pshh, I was just explaining things to them in a not-so-nice way. Who are these elders, anyway?"

She shuddered in distaste when I mentioned the elders. "They are the oldies that are jobless and love to boss around even though they are of really weak blood. Once, one of them actually hit on me. He was lucky I didn't kill him."

And they were criticizing me about my behavior? Bloody hypocrites! "Did you tell Easton or Peter?" She better had brought it to their notice, or I will.

"Nah." Melissa just brushed it off. "They will end up dead very soon. Easton will probably hire goons to do the job. Everyone is fed up with them. Thankfully, Easton has not appointed any more elders."

I let out a relieved sigh. They will be gone… soon.

Melissa's smile turned evil. "I heard he spent the night in your bed. I want the details."

How did everyone know everything? This was so not fair. Even Ma came to know, and she wouldn't tell me how.

"Easton only spent the night in my bed, Melissa," I stated clearly. To watch the smile fly off her face was comical.

"Oh come on, something must have happened!"

"Nothing happened at all," I said with a voice that ended that subject.

We then spent some time talking about really insignificant stuff, and things were back to normal. Just like when we were kids.

Before leaving, I hugged her. "You are still my best friend, Melissa, and I am happy that we are close now," I said.

She pulled away. "Thanks, Nev. You're the best and my best friend."

Well, seemed like I had two best friends apart from my boys and a possible boyfriend even though he was yet to ask me. I still didn't know if I wanted him to, but I surely liked Easton now.

There I said it.

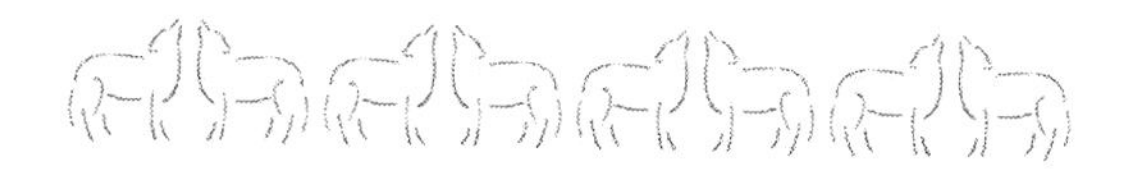

I reached home after some time. Ma was alone and making some pasta dish, again! I was tired of eating pasta. A growing girl needs some variety in her food, not the same old stuff over again.

I went to her and stood by the stove.

"So, how was the date?" she asked

"I didn't go on a date today." I clarified. She must have assumed that I went on one since I didn't inform her that I was going to the forest.

"Then where did you go today?"

"I had to sort out some things with Easton and after that, I went to Melissa's house. We then spent some time together. It was good, just like olden times." I felt really happy about that.

She turned to me and smiled. "That is great! So what happened last night?"

She too?

"Ma, nothing happened! Okay. N-O-T-H-I-N-G" I spelled out the word. What kind of mother was she? Shouldn't she be shouting or at least criticizing me? Instead, here she was asking me about last night.

"Okay, okay. Why did he come here, anyway?" The smell of pasta assaulted my sensed and even though I was bored of it, the food was food.

"Nev?" Ma's voice snapped me out of my daydreaming of the food. "Don't know much. He just said that he and Peter had an argument. Peter got angry and kicked him out," I answered.

"That is sad! I hope they sort it out soon. So where is he staying at?"

"Xavier's place."

"Okay, now get freshened up and let us have dinner." She pushed me out of the kitchen, and I went to my room and showered.

Just as I was going down to have dinner, I looked at my bed for a moment.

I am not allowing Easton on the bed again, I thought.

Chapter 30

Neveah

Ma and I were having dinner quietly when the doorbell went off.

"I'll get it." Ma was almost finished with her food. She ate so little! Or maybe I ate a lot? The second one seemed more correct.

Ma entered with a shirtless Easton carrying a small holiday bag. "Why are you here?" I asked Easton who was busy inhaling the food in the kitchen. No wonder Ma made so much food. When I asked her about it before, she just waved it off saying I would eat it all. As if I could eat a big bowl of pasta!

Now I knew why!

"Neveah, don't be rude to our guest. Besides, aren't you happy that you can spend more time with your boyfriend?" Ma's questioned casually.

"He is not my boyfriend," I shouted at the top of my voice. I am sure that everyone within a five-mile radius would have heard me. Ma even closed her ears with her hands while the stupid idiotic alpha just stood there smiling.

"Yet, Gina. Yet." He simply opened his bag and put on a shirt he pulled out from it. He then took the whole bowl of pasta and sat near me. The whole time, I was standing with my mouth open.

"Neveah, give the poor boy a break and finish your food," Ma said.

I grabbed my meal and went to my room where I sat alone on my bed and finished it alone.

I was angry at Easton for spoiling my dinner with Ma. I haven't spent some quality time with her in a long time. She was always with Bryan, and I had my own problems. This was supposed to be a perfect time to have a mother-daughter bonding. It was just Ma and me, like the olden times! I just missed my mother, and Easton had to spoil the only time I was getting with her.

"Can I come in?" There was a knock on the door followed by Easton's voice.

"No," I said, but he came in, anyway. If he wanted to come in that bad, then why ask me?

He sat on the bed next to me and removed the pillow I was clutching on. "I brought dessert." He then opened the box of a very famous pastry shop that made the best cakes in the world.

As soon as he opened the box, the smell tickled my senses, and the alluring shape of the creamy, chocolatey cake tempted me.

I took the spoon next to it and went to take a bite when Easton pulled the box away from me. I stared at him accusingly. "Give it back."

"My cake, my rules. Now, say the golden word." He spoke to me as if he was scolding some ten-year-old child. I considered telling him to go to hell and to take the cake with him, but my stomach wouldn't comply.

"Please," I said, drawing out the *e*. He looked at me with scrutinising eyes before taking the spoon from my hand and feeding me a piece of it himself.

"Open," he told me, touching the spoon on my lips. I did as I was told, and the reward was amazing. The taste exploded in my mouth, and all I could do was thank my mate.

"God, this is amazing, Easton!" My voice came out muffled because of the piece of heaven in my mouth.

"You're welcome." He then continued feeding me the cake. When only one bite was remaining, he took the spoon into my mouth, and I opened it wide, but he just took the spoon away.

I made a whining sound while he smiled. "I will give you this cake only if you answer my question truthfully, okay?"

I nodded.

"Will you be my girlfriend?

I pondered on the question before saying a soft yes.

He made it clear that I was his soul mate, so why bother denying?

I was on the bed while Easton was on the floor. Yes, Easton was sleeping on the floor! There would be no point to my vow if I couldn't even keep it for one night!

"Are you asleep?" I asked him.

"Nope."

As soon as he said that, I rolled to the edge of my bed so I could see him clearly. "What do you think of the thing I said to the elders?" I propped my head up on my elbow.

"They needed it. I wanted to tell them off myself, but if I said something, they would say that I was protecting my best friend, which I was clearly not." He was on his back with his hands under his head, staring at the ceiling.

"Thanks. I thought I had offended you or something." His eyes assured me that none of that happened.

"Can I ask you something?" Easton asked in a quiet voice.

"Hmm."

"Are you really angry that I am here?" he asked.

"No, it's just that I wanted to spend some time alone with Ma. We don't get to hang out at all. This is all new for me. I am used to it being just the two of us. Now that we are both busy with other things… I just miss my mother." I explained to him. It was never my intention to make him feel like an uninvited guest even though he was.

"Okay. Goodnight, Neveah," he muttered quietly.

"Goodnight, Easton," I whispered back.

The next morning, Easton was gone. I found a sticky note on my table.

Have pack business to attend. Will meet you in school.
Love you,
Boyfriend.

I smiled from ear to ear. Boyfriend! Easton Eugene Dale calling himself boyfriend! Who would have guessed? And love you? Already?

I quickly got ready for school. I ended up wearing some white mid-length dress which I found at the top of my rack. My guess was that it was Ma's. I didn't remember buying any white dresses recently. I matched them with a pair of white ballet flats and a white pearl bangle.

I was trying to push some books into my locker when a pair of arms came around me. I turned to see none other than Easton in front of me.

"Hello, my beautiful girlfriend." He greeted, and everyone in the hallway stood still. Over Easton's shoulder, I saw Sabrina glaring at me. *Wonderful!* The girl was staring at me with so much hatred that it was irritating. A plan quickly formed in my head.

"Hello, my dear boyfriend." I greeted him and pressed my lips against his.

Easton didn't kiss me back at first, probably because of the shock. As soon as his surprise wore off, his arms tightened around my waist, and he pushed me onto the locker.

He tightened his grip even more that it almost hurt, and he tangled the other one in my hair.

I put my arms around his neck, pulling him in more

His tongue traced my lower lip, but I denied him entry, very well aware that we were giving the students a free show. He growled lowly, and I pushed him away.

I pulled my lips away from his and opened my eyes. I found myself staring at Easton. His eyes were dark, and his lips were red and swollen.

"What was that for?" he asked me, his voice husky.

"For everyone to realise that you are mine."

He smirked at me and kissed my forehead. "Come let us go to class."

I shoved all my books inside and closed the locker. He took my hand in his, and we walked to the classroom amidst all the gossip and staring. Some distance away, I saw Sabrina glaring at me with flaming hatred.

This time, I just smirked at her. It was a smirk of victory.

I ended up sitting with Georgy who was giving me sly looks every two seconds.

I was so tired of it that I laid my head on the desk. After a few seconds, there was a tap on the bench.

I raised my head to see the teacher glaring at me. "Did you finish the paper you have to submit?"

"I submitted it almost a month ago." In fact, I have submitted the next paper, too. Clearly, she didn't remember. Well, not my fault.

"Okay," she grumbled and left. Beside me, Georgy was in hysteria. I shushed him with great difficulty. All the jocks at the back of the class including Easton snickered.

I laid my head back on the desk and waited for the lecture to be over.

Lunch was no better. All the while, people were staring at our table. The younger girls would stare at my table, then Easton's, and then start giggling. The sound was getting on my nerves. Not to forget, my BFF and her boyfriend were giving me the looks every two seconds.

All I did was kiss a guy! It wasn't like we were seriously making out or something! To top it all off, all the people I knew from his pack would smile at me whenever they saw me. Melissa said it was them celebrating the love of the alpha and the luna.

Just as I reached home, I got a message from Easton that we were going on our second date today.

I replied, telling him that I would be ready by seven.

Where are we going? I typed.

Just for a movie and a simple dinner, he replied

Okay.

Since we were just going to go for a movie, I dressed casually. I wore simple blue jeans and white tank top with a dark blue knitted jacket. It was cute and comfy. I paired them with the flats from earlier and left my hair open, styling it in their natural waves.

I was waiting outside my house, and Easton was, thankfully, on time this time. He parked his car near me, and I got in. Easton was dressed casually, too. His faded dark jeans and dark green shirt suited him. The green in his shirt brought out the green in his eyes.

"You look nice," I complimented as I got in. The top three buttons were undone, and the sleeves were folded till his elbows.

"Thank you. Wish I could say the same to you." I ignored the all too familiar comment and made myself comfortable in his car.

"Which movie are we going to see?"

"Some romantic comedy," he answered, turning all his attention on the road. I made a face when he mentioned the genre. I wasn't a big fan of romance.

"Did you already get the tickets?" I inquired. If not, we could go somewhere else.

"Nope," Easton answered, quizzically looking at me.

"Great! So can we skip the movie part and just go straight for the dinner?"

"Why?" Easton asked and then turned his attention back to the road.

"I thought you already know that I am not a huge fan of romantic comedies. I am more of an action girl," I told him.

"I actually didn't know that." He sounded sincerely sorry, but it wasn't his fault. There were many things he didn't know about me. This thought led me to a brilliant idea.

"Easton, is there some road nearby where very few vehicles pass through?"

"Yes, but why?"

"Well, this is my surprise, alright? So just take us there." I ordered.

"So dominating!" he muttered. I punched him in return, and he cried out. I knew for a fact that my punch could not have hurt him. He was so much stronger than me.

Easton parked the car on a road where there were absolutely no vehicles around except his. I got out of the car and made him get out too. He asked me what we were doing to which I didn't answer. I hoped that he realized how irritating it was when people keep things from you, even if it was for a lovely surprise.

I sat on the car bonnet, and Easton stood in front of me. "Now, will you tell me what we are doing here?" There was a hint of irritation in his voice. I smirked but answered as he was getting restless.

"I've decided that we should get to know each other," I declared.

Easton gave me a weird look. "You actually brought me here for this?"

"Then what were you expecting?" When his eyes raked through my legs, I got my answer. "Forget it, I already know the answer."

"Well, you were the one who kissed me this morning!"

"I… I wanted to get rid of that girl!" I almost shouted, referring to Sabrina.

"What girl?" Easton appeared confused by my anger.

"Sabrina." I deadpanned. Was he so unaware that she was trying to woo him again? Or he knew but was not bothered?

Realization shone on his face at my mention of her name. "I had warned her before. Looks like I have to talk to her again."

"Whatever! Let us get to know each other!" I wasn't here to talk about her.

"But I already know many things about you!" Easton said.

"No, you don't," I argued. He may know the basics but not a lot of them.

"I do."

"No, you don't." I was sure of it.

"You love your mother and Bryan. You like the fact that you have the highest marks in school. You like every other colour except pink. You like to wake up on the right side always. You enjoy driving. You hate winter. You hate people who are show-offs and people who use their status to put down others. You are always honest and to the point, and even though it could be hurtful, it is endearing at the same time. You are a fierce lover and a fighter. You are amazing, Neveah."

I was the one amazed right now. He knew so much.

"Let us not forget about your precious Jay Ryan and your favourite food namely chocolate ice cream, strawberry donuts, blueberry cakes, stuffed..."

"Okay. Let us go to dinner." I hopped off the car.

Dinner was amazing. At first, I thought we were going to end up at some posh restaurant, but Easton surprised me by taking us to a street filled with rows of small and homey eateries. I was surprised that I didn't know about such a place.

We enjoyed each other's company, and I filled my stomach to the brim. I didn't have to be worried about being not ladylike in there!

We drove back to my street. As we got near my house, I noticed that all the lights were off. I didn't want to sit inside the house alone, so I invited Easton in.

He agreed, and he parked his car in our driveway.

Easton was kissing my neck when we managed to open the door. I clutched his head and widened my eyes.

"Amy?" I screeched.

“Why kill the mood, babe?” His lazy voice penetrated through my shocked state, and I turned his head to the couch.

Chapter 31

Neveah

There she was, Amy Dale's ghost sitting on my couch.

"Who are you?" Easton stood in front of me in a protective stance. He was growling now. I looked around the room to look for something sharp before realising that Easton was a werewolf and could easily protect me.

Then something struck me. Amy's dead body was never found! Could she be…?

"You forgot your mother, son?" Amy's tone was soft. She looked changed and somehow different.

"My mother died eight years ago," Easton replied suspiciously. I clutched his arm, seriously considering the possibility of ghosts. If werewolves exist, why couldn't they?

"I am your mother, Easton. Alive. In the flesh." Amy opened her arms wide expecting her son to hug her. Easton sniffed and stiffened.

In one second, Easton was in front of her. He pulled her from the couch and hugged her. I was still shocked that I held on to the door for support.

Amy started crying, and Easton looked at her like he had seen the dead! Technically, she was supposed to be dead.

"How in the world?" I asked when Easton let her go.

"I am very much alive." She smiled at me, but I found it really difficult to smile back. Besides, her smile… it seemed different. There was something off.

"It doesn't matter. All that matters is that she is back." Easton ended our conversation. He was very defensive, and his eyes said it all. I didn't blame him. He was meeting his mother after eight years, the same mother he thought dead until recently… the woman he had mourned for so much time.

"Of course, I just… Oh, forget it." I went to her and hugged her. She hugged me back tightly. A bit too tight, but I let that slide too.

As soon as she was out of my embrace, Easton was pulling her out of the house with one hand, and the other one was pulling me.

"Let's go home."

I quickly shut the door. Easton and Amy were already in the car by the time I had finished locking up the door.

Amy was sitting near Easton while I sat behind in the middle so I could see both of them. Easton was driving when she turned to me. "So, both of you are together?" She smiled at me. I gave her a small smile in return.

Easton turned behind and winked at me. "She is my mate, Mom."

I pushed his shoulder. "Look at the road while driving." I reprimanded him, but I didn't miss the flash of uneasiness in Amy's eyes. This was not going to end well.

But she was quick to smile widely at her son. "That is great!" But somehow, her voice was different again.

"Thanks, Mom." Easton looked so happy that Amy was back. It was years since I have seen him this happy. He was even happier than when I accepted him as my boyfriend and mate. It was not that I was jealous. I was just scared of the outcome.

Because if Amy was alive, why didn't she come home? Why after so many years? Why now?

We reached his house to find it empty. Easton speculated that the pack might be having a meeting.

"Aren't you supposed to be there when there is a meeting?" I asked.

"Well, yes but I was given an exemption for our date." He smiled cheekily at me.

We ended up walking to the forest. It was dark, but then it was suddenly bright. There were lanterns on the trees, making the place light up like a fair. Upon seeing us, Peter stood in a defensive stance along with the rest of his pack members.

"Why are you here?" Peter snarled at Amy. Easton and I were shocked.

"How did you know she is back?" I asked Peter before Easton could say anything.

"Trackers informed us. She has been in town for the past one and a half days. This was why we have a meeting here today. So my mate understands that she is no longer welcome here," Peter growled out, and his eyes turned dark.

The rest of his pack members looked at Peter in confusion. What made him hate his mate so much?

I have seen the love between Easton's parents firsthand. They were in love as much any couple could be in love with each other. So what changed? The hatred in Peter's eyes was too much.

"What are you saying, Dad? Aren't you happy that Mom is here?" Easton went near Peter, but he just moved back.

Peter removed an old piece of paper from his shirt pocket. As soon as Amy saw the letter, she visibly paled.

"Don't believe it, Easton, please. I had my reasons, I swear," she begged him. Her eyes were wide with fear and tears were streaming down her face. Easton's expression hardened.

She was talking like she had betrayed them. Easton growled at her and roughly snatched the letter from Peter.

With every word he read, Easton's eyes turned darker. He stared at Amy with the same hate as his father. This was so not going to end well.

Easton turned to Amy and angrily said. "Get lost. Never, ever enter my land again! This is the order of the alpha."

Amy broke down and sat on the forest floor. I stood still for some time, shocked at the event occurring in front of me. I was desperately hoping that this was all a bad dream… that I would wake up with Easton on my bed.

I went to comfort her, but before I could get even a foot near her, Easton pulled me back. "Don't go near her."

"Easton, what are you saying? She is your mother!" I tried to defend Amy. I didn't know what Easton read in that letter, but I was sure that it must not be that bad. Easton could never hate Amy! She was the one Easton loved the most in his life.

"She is no mother of mine!" He growled and tightened his grip on my shoulder. I wanted to tell him to lose it, but he didn't look normal yet. His eyes were coal black, and he had small claws instead of nails.

Behind him, Amy was sobbing, and Peter looked miserably sad. The rest of the pack members were looking at Easton and Peter in pity.

"Peter, I don't know what happened, but she is your wife, the mother of your son. Don't treat her this way," I pleaded, but one look in his eyes told me that he was not going to forgive his wife anytime soon.

I turned to Easton and placed a hand on his cheek. "She is your mom, Easton. Just listen to what she has to say, please?"

Easton glared at Amy and was about to say something when Amy spoke up.

"I don't need you to come to my defence. I can take care of myself," she spat at me. Easton tightened his hold on me, so much so that his claws dug into my flesh.

"Do not ever speak to my mate like that! Otherwise, the consequences will be severe," Easton warned sternly. Amy didn't reply and let out a loud sob.

No one said anything for some time, and the whole pack started speaking among themselves. They all looked at Amy, not knowing what to do.

My arm started hurting because of his claws, and I wriggled away from his hold. He started sniffing me. Easton immediately let me go and looked at my arm. There were three long gashes, and there was blood flowing out.

"Baby, I am sorry. Let me take you to the hospital!" He started to pull me.

"No, it's okay. You should talk to Amy and sort things out." I tried pushing Easton away from me, but he just ended up pulling me near him.

"Let us leave. My father will take care of things." Easton ripped a piece of his shirt and tied it on my arm.

As I was being dragged away, I looked back at Amy. The expression on her face will haunt me for years!

What was in that letter?

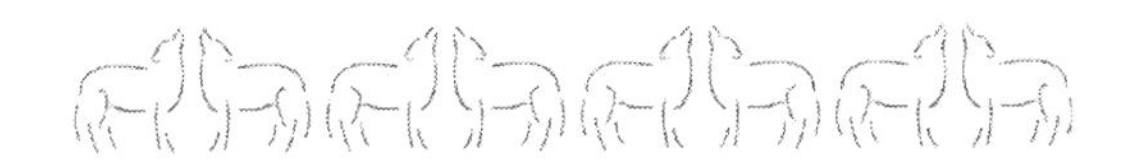

Thus, our second date ended up with me in the hospital. Easton took me to a doctor who was a part of the pack so people wouldn't get suspicious at the gashes.

Dr. Adam said that the wounds weren't that deep so there was no need for stitches. He just cleaned the wound and patched it up. The whole while, Easton didn't say anything. He had a blank expression on his face.

I knew that deep down, he was distraught with his mother's actions and guilty about the wound that he caused me. He needed to know that I didn't blame it on him.

"Doc, can you give us a few minutes?" I politely requested.

"Sure, Luna." He looked at Easton with a sympathetic expression and left the room. Even he knew that their former luna was back.

I looked at Easton who had his eyes on the ground. He was not even meeting my eyes. I took my good hand and cupped his face. I then brought his face to mine so we were staring eye-to-eye.

"It's alright, Easton. I am perfectly fine." I moved my injured hand to show him that I was alright. I internally winced at the pain it was causing me.

"It is my fault. I hurt you again."

"Don't carry this guilt around, Easton. I don't blame you. You would have known by now if I am blaming you," I muttered, trying to get him to laugh.

Easton didn't even look like he cared about my sense of humour.

"Hey, it's okay. I don't know what Amy has done, but I do know that she loves you and that you and Peter should give her a chance to explain her point of view." Easton tried to interrupt me, but I didn't let him.

"Let me just finish. If there is one thing I know about Amy, it is that she loves you and Peter a lot. You were her world. She was one of the best mothers in the world. If she has done something bad, she must have done it under her free will." I tried reasoning.

"I know… I know that she loved my Dad and me, and that is why it hurt so much." His expressionless mask was replaced by a look of betrayal. Whatever Amy has done must be severe.

"I mean, if she had any problems, she could have spoken to my dad, or the elders, or anyone she wishes to. But no, she decided to fake her death and abandon her husband and son just like that. Did she even think of how it was going to affect Dad and me?" he said more to himself than to me.

"Do you know my father was never the same after she left? He was utterly heartbroken. He has never ever looked at any woman besides my mother. Despite what she has done to him, he was always faithful. Why is she back, anyway? Couldn't she stay wherever she was? I finally had some stability in my life, and she ruined it again." Easton's expression turned angrier, and I traced his cheekbone with my thumb to calm him down. I then titled his head and placed a kiss on his cheek.

"The food at the date was amazing. You know what I want after good food?" I whispered in his ear.

He shook his head.

"A good night's sleep." I get up and got down from the bed at Dr. Adam's office and intertwine my good hand with Easton's hand.

"Let's leave. All this drama and blood loss has made me tired."

We left the room and spot the doctor pacing in the corridor.

"Thank you, Doctor," I said.

"It is my pleasure to offer my service to you, Luna." He looked at our hands and grinned. I beamed back at him.

As we were walking towards his car from the hospital, I decided that this was the right time to ask him.

"What was in the letter that Peter gave you?"

Chapter 32

Neveah

"What was in that letter, Easton?" I asked him as we were walking towards his car. He stiffened when I mentioned the letter. He turned to look at me, and we stopped walking.

"Not here, Neveah." He looked around as if searching for someone.

"Okay." We didn't discuss the topic any further.

During the ride back to my home, Easton had a tight grip on the steering wheel, and his jaw was clenched. I wanted to calm him down a bit, but I didn't know how to do it. In the end, I decided that it was better if he had some time alone to think.

We reached home, and Easton helped me get out carefully. As we were about ten steps from the front door, I pulled his hand with my good one.

"What am I going to tell Ma?" I definitely wasn't going to tell her that her best friend was back and that Easton had banned her.

As soon as I mentioned my injury, Easton's expression turned guilty.

"Hey, it's okay." I tried reassuring him. He smiled at me, but the smile didn't reach his eyes.

"It is all because of her." He was back to being angry again.

I just sighed since I didn't know what was actually there in that letter. Until I know what was written in there, I couldn't reply to his statement.

When I rang the bell, Ma answered. I thought that she would be asleep since it was quite late, but she looked cheerful.

"You won't believe this. Can you guess who is back?" Her eyes brimmed with happiness.

Please don't be who I think it is.

"Who is it?" I asked Ma

"Amy."

Oh shit!

Before I could reply anything, Easton pushed Ma carefully and was inside my house in an instant.

There she was! Amy Dale was on my couch again!

And this time, she was angry. All of it was somehow directed to me.

Easton growled low in his throat, and Amy looked away.

"Calm down, Ma is in the same room," I muttered to Easton. The last thing I needed this night was to go back to the hospital if Ma fainted.

"Did I not tell you to go back from wherever you came from?" Easton snapped at Amy. I pressed myself closer to him before he could shift. Already, his eyes were turning black.

This time, I went behind him and clutched his right hand in mine.

"You are not a god, Easton. Remember, I am stronger than you. I am your mother." Amy stood up and took a step forward.

"I have told you that you are no mother of mine." Easton's temper was getting shorter by the second, and Amy didn't seem far behind. I was starting to experience palpitations from the heavy tension in the air

"Easton, don't speak to your mother like that and don't you dare shift and break things in my house," Ma exclaimed.

That was when I had a heart attack.

Amy and I turned to look at Ma who was busy looking at Easton with a stern expression on his face. She looked pissed.

"You know?" a male voice asked, and it didn't sound like Easton. I turned to look at the door to see Bryan with a suitcase and an open mouth.

"Of course, honey. Come in. I want to introduce you to my best friend." Bryan looked at me as if asking me, *what the hell is going on here?* I just shrugged. I didn't know the answer myself.

I loosened my hold on Easton and laid my head on his back while looking at the scene in front of me. I was tired and wanted to go to sleep, but I didn't think that it would happen anytime soon.

Ma went on with the introductions. A few moments later, Ma and Amy were already gushing about Ma's ring like they haven't been apart for the past eight years. *Seriously?*

"Are they actually doing what I think they are doing?" I muttered into his Easton's ear as I wrapped my uninjured hand around his waist.

"Yeah, I guess," Easton muttered back, looking unsure himself.

I yawned, and Easton noticed the tired expression on my face. "Come on, let's go to bed." He wound his one arm around my waist, and the other below my knees and lifted me up bridal style.

"I am taking my mate to bed," Easton informed all three of them. Right then, Ma noticed that there was something wrong with my hand

"What happened to my daughter, Easton?"

"Why don't you ask your best friend?" Easton answered sarcastically and didn't even wait for Ma's answer.

He placed me on the bed, and I snuggled into the sheets. "We'll talk tomorrow, Nev. Goodnight," Easton said.

His gentle voice was the last thing I remembered before drifting off to sleep.

I woke up with a strong urge to go to the bathroom. I tried to move, but something was holding me back. I opened my eyes fully to see Easton's arm on my waist. I tried removing it, but his grip was too tight.

"Easton, get up." When I got no response, I tried a bit louder.

"Hey, Easton, get up!"

Easton moved his head from the pillow to my neck. "Stop moaning my name, or I won't be responsible for the consequences." As soon as he said that, I shut up.

I tried to wake him up with other methods. I tried tickling him, but he wasn't ticklish. I then did the only thing I could think of.

"Easton, my arm." As soon as I said that, Easton was up in a second.

"What? What happened? Is it hurting? Did I crush it? Is it bleeding?" Easton was frantic, and he looked ready to pull me up and take me to the hospital.

"Easton, calm down. It is alright. I just said that to wake up. I wanted to go to the bathroom. And yes, your hand did apply a bit of pressure to it, but my shoulder isn't hurting, just a bit uncomfortable." I admitted. He glared at me.

"You almost gave me a heart attack for a second." Easton accused me.

"Easton, we need to talk. You still haven't told me what is in the letter." I reminded him.

"Later, after school."

"Easton, you cannot avoid this topic forever." I tried convincing him, but he wouldn't budge.

"I am not avoiding it, just putting it off for now. My reaction when I say things may not end up good, so I want to do it when we have a lot of time on our hands." I didn't understand any part of his excuse but let it go.

The only way he was going to tell me things was his way.

Easton went back home after our small argument, and I got ready for a long day of school. When I went down, only Bryan was there on the couch with a newspaper and a cup of coffee in his hand.

"Where's Ma? And what about Amy?" I asked him.

"Amy left last night after telling what happened to your hand, and Gina is still asleep." I nodded and went to sit near him. "This reminds me that I need to have a talk with your boyfriend." Bryan was in full on dad mode.

I just smiled at him lovingly. "Sure." He smiled back.

"I made blueberry pancakes and coffee. Go have your breakfast."

"Thanks, Dad." I kissed his cheek and went to fill my stomach.

The day dragged on in school. Half of the school population was part of Easton's pack, so everyone was talking about Amy's return after so many years. I saw many pitiful glances thrown towards Easton. I was around ninety percent sure that it was irritating him.

Easton wasn't there during lunch. I tried calling him, but he didn't answer. Easton remained absent for the rest of the day, too.

At last, it was the last lecture of the day and still no Easton. Xavier was following me throughout the day. After my drunken confessions, Xavier hasn't tried to talk to me even once. I was about to get into my car when Xavier came and stood beside me.

"Hey, what happened?" I asked him.

"Easton's told me to guard you," he replied with downcast eyes.

"Figured that much. Get in the car," I ordered, and he complied. During the first three minutes, there was no talk in the car which was very weird. Xavier, just like me, wasn't known to keep his mouth shut.

"So, you're angry at me?" I broke the silence.

"No, just at myself." He still didn't look at me while replying.

"I like it when the person I am talking to looks at me," I told him, and a small smile graced his face.

He didn't say anything during the next ten minutes of the ride. I parked my car and hopped off with Xavier on my heels.

"Can I come in?"

"Sure." I opened the door and let myself and Xavier in.

"So, you want to say something?" I asked him.

"Yeah. I got so much to tell you. First, I want to say thank you for protecting my position, and I am so sorry for all the things I did to you when we were younger. I know that sorry doesn't mean anything, but that's the only thing I can give you. Also, a promise that what happened to you will not happen to anyone else as long as I am the beta of the pack." Xavier sounded so sincere. For a second, I thought that my ears were deceiving me.

"I... I really don't know what to say. It is nice that you are apologizing to me, but it's not easy to forget. I am trying, and I promise to forgive you. I just don't know when," I sincerely replied.

"Thank you for telling me the truth. I will be the best beta of the pack," Xavier promised and hugged me.

If I had a list of the most awkward hugs, then this would surely top the list. I just patted on Xavier's back twice. He let me go and smirked at me.

"That was awkward," he muttered

"Very," I admitted.

"Okay. I'll leave. Easton will be here soon."

"Where is Amy?" I asked him as he was about to leave.

"I don't know, actually. The guards saw her crossing the territory border early this morning. I don't know if she will be back."

"Okay, thanks," I replied.

Instead of waiting for Easton, I decided to make myself something and do my homework. I let the corn boil while I did the homework at the dining table.

The bell rang when I almost finished the essay. I opened the door and let Easton in.

"Hi." He greeted me with a peck on my cheek.

"Hey, come in." I made him sit in the dining chair, and I went to the kitchen to see if the corn was cooked. I removed the corn and added some diced onions, tomatoes, and carrots.

I put some for me in a bowl and gave the remaining to Easton. "Thanks," he said. The way his face lighted up looking at the food was fascinating to watch.

We ate the food in silence. After we had finished, I made Easton do the dishes. The guy was looking so tense that I thought that doing the dishes would distract him.

"Now, are you going to tell me what was in the letter?" I swear, my patience level was hanging by a thread.

"Yeah." Easton looked so uncomfortable. I placed a hand on his shoulder to give him some support.

"It's okay. I'm not going to judge you or Amy."

He took a deep breath and started speaking. "My mother left because she felt that we were holding her back. She wanted to do something in life. She wanted to explore the world, and she couldn't do that if she was with my father. She didn't have the decency to reject my father in the face. She took the coward's way and did it using a letter. A bloody letter!"

I sat down on the couch because I seriously needed some support to hold on to. "Are you sure?" That was the first thought that came to my mind.

"Yeah. That is why it was so difficult for me to accept that she doesn't want me. All my life, I thought that she was the best thing in the world, and now I came to know that she doesn't even want me. I doubt that she ever loved me. Maybe it was all an act!" Easton shouted, his eyes turning black.

"She forged her own death. She didn't even have the courtesy to tell me that she was leaving."

"But you said mates feel when the other dies. How is that possible if she is alive?" I voiced out.

"She must have been almost dead. Or did something that made her go into a comatose stage. Her being alive explains why Dad was alive so long after her fake death." Easton's voice was so loud that it was scaring me now.

"Easton, sit down. Please." I pleaded.

When he sat on the couch, I hugged him to calm him down. "It's okay, Easton."

"It's not okay, Neveah. I hate her, baby. I hate her." Easton's voice broke down. He wasn't just crying, he was devastated.

"No. You don't hate her." I tried explaining. I let him go and cupped his face in my hands.

"Sometimes, you fall tired, Easton. You feel like you haven't done anything. Sometimes, you just want to get away from things. The same must have happened to Amy. She must've felt suffocated. No matter what, you can't change what others feel, Easton."

Easton placed his hands over mine. He didn't look a bit convinced by my statement. "It's not that she left. She made a fool of me and Dad's feelings. Do you know how many days I have cried wanting my mother? How many days I wished that I could be with her when I was young?"

"I know—"

"No, you don't. No one does, so stop advising me," Easton cut me off with a sharp and final tone.

I didn't say anything after that.

I just watched his back flexing in a not so normal way. I just hoped that he doesn't shift right now, not because he would destroy the house but because I had no idea how to calm a werewolf in its wolf form.

Easton turned to me after some time and sat on the couch again.

"I am sorry, baby. I knew that this would happen. That is why I didn't want to tell you anything. Do you think I should forgive her, Neveah?" Easton asked me.

"Forgiving her is up to you, but you should let her explain. She does owe you an explanation," I replied after thinking it through.

"Thank you." Easton pulled me on his lap and kissed me. At first, it was just a simple peck, but then he deepened the kiss. Not having much experience in that department, I went along with Easton's pace.

We broke up to catch our breaths. Before I could even take two full gulps or air, Easton's lips were back on mine again.

When I was getting dizzy, Easton proceeded down my neck. I wound my fingers in his blond locks tightly. His one hand went to my waist, and the other tilted my neck so he could get more access. He nibbled on the skin, and I let out a sigh of pleasure.

"Ahem," someone said and cleared his throat.

I quickly pushed Easton off, but only managed to put a distance of a few inches. I looked at the door to see Bryan standing stiffly, anger clouding his eyes. I looked at Easton to find his lips swollen, and his pupils dilated. He took a deep breath and released me from his lap.

"Hi, Bryan." I gave him a small smile and an awkward wave.

He looked disappointed, and I felt bad. I got up to go to him, but Easton pulled me back.

"Stop making my mate feel guilty. She did nothing wrong." Easton ordered Bryan who looked unimpressed with Easton's words.

"I know. It's just that I am not ready for Neveah to leave me." *Aww.* I ran to him and hugged him tightly.

"Love you, Dad," I exclaimed.

Then I was pulled from Bryan by none other than Easton.

"Enough of hugging," he muttered.

I looked at him with a raised brow. *Seriously?*

"So why are you here, Alpha?" Bryan asked Easton.

"Do I not have the right to be here?" Easton answered with a question of his own.

"No, it's just that your parents are having a huge fight right now."

Oh shit!

Chapter 33

Neveah

Oh shit!

"How do you know?" Easton asked

"Gina told me. She called some time back. You should go there," Bryan answered and shrugged

"Want me to come?" I asked Easton. He didn't look too keen to face Amy.

"Will you?" He asked me hopefully.

"Of course." I entwined our fingers and smiled at him.

We reached his house to see Amy throwing the crockery at Peter. This was such a married couple scene. Ma was standing on one side of the room with a smirk on her face. Thankfully, there was no one else around.

"Enough," Easton roared, and both of them stopped midway, halting all their movements.

"What is going on here?" Easton's voice was full if authority. Peter didn't seem intimidated by his son, but Amy sure seemed that way.

"We are trying to solve our problems," Amy argued for which Easton just gave her a flat look.

"I can see that, but if you want to solve your problems, you do it outside my house. So get out!"

"Don't talk to my mate that way. She is still you mother," Peter shouted instinctively.

Easton laughed. He actually laughed! He went and stood in front of Amy.

"My father may forgive you. He is your mate, and he cannot resist you for long. But let's make one thing clear. I am not forgiving you no matter what! For me, my mother died when she decided that I was a burden to her." There was a vow to his statement, and I didn't like it.

"You were never a burden. You are my son, my baby. How can you even?" Amy had tears flowing down his cheeks by now, and Peter looked at Easton the same way Bryan was looking at me some time before.

"Easton, remember what I told you?" I said.

He turned to look at me. He sighed and turned back to his mother.

"I want an explanation. I want the exact reason why you left. If you can't give me that... then I... I don't think I will ever forgive you." Amy nodded at Easton's request.

"I was tired, Easton. I was twenty-eight, and I had done nothing in my life. I didn't even go to college. All I did was cook and clean. I wanted to do something fruitful. I wanted to study, to work, and to roam around the world. I could have never done that if I stayed." Amy sounded desperate, and Easton looked unimpressed.

"And who stopped you from doing those things? You could have gone to the town college, could have gotten a job wherever you wanted. We can always go for vacations," Easton stated.

"Your father..."

"Dad would have allowed you. Hell, you don't need his permission. You are your own person, and you can always make your own decisions. I have a mate you know, and I can tell you now that I will never stop her from doing anything she wants. All I want from her is her smile, and I will do anything for that."

I felt so happy after hearing that. Amy, on the other hand, was not that happy. No one said anything after that. Ma was standing in the corner with a blank look on his face.

"We need to talk, Amy," Peter said, breaking the silence.

"I am moving out," Easton said before Amy could reply.

"Why would you do that?" I asked Easton. His face gave nothing away.

"You will forgive her sooner or later, Dad, and I don't think I am ready for this change."

"But you can't leave your dad," Amy reasoned out, trying to convince her only son to stay.

"My dad died the day you left. It's just my father now." With that, Easton sprinted to his room. Peter looked guilty, and Amy was utterly heartbroken.

I went after Easton because standing there with them didn't feel right. I opened Easton's room and found him packing up stuff.

"So, where are you going to go?" I asked him, leaning in the door.

"We have a lot of land. I'll build a house on any one plot," he replied without any hesitation.

"Are you sure you are doing the right thing?" I knew that it was his decision, but somehow I have a feeling that this wasn't right.

"I can't, baby. I can't live with her… at least not this soon. I need to think about this for some time." I went to him and sat on the bed.

"This is soft." He chuckled at my statement. I wasn't trying to coax him into staying anymore. I just liked the bed. "Well, it will take some time to build a house. Till then, where will you stay?"

"Well, I am hoping that my lovely mate will come to my rescue…" he chuckled.

"And Bryan will end up shooting you," I concluded his sentence.

"I can talk to him." He tried reasoning while dropping all his clothes into a bag from his closet.

"Easton, come here." I requested. I patted his bed, gesturing him to sit on it, and he did.

"Bryan considers me his daughter. He just wants some time with me. I can't deny him that because soon I'll be off to college. Then maybe, things won't be the same again. He won't get this time again," I explained. I too wanted to spend some time as someone's daughter.

"I know." He wrapped an arm around my waist. "I have a house two streets from here. I'll have it cleaned so I can move in there."

"What about food?" I being me had to ask this question. Easton smirked at me before giving me his answer. "I may not live with you, but I am coming to your house for my dinner. For lunch, there is school, and I can make breakfast. I am not that of an invalid."

"Great." I removed his arm and got up from the bed.

"Where are you going?" he asked.

"Home." Where else was I going to go?

"Okay, bye. I have to continue packing." He stood up and kissed my forehead.

"Bye." I quietly shut the door and walked downstairs.

Amy was on the couch looking sad with Ma trying to console here. Peter looked irritated and was pacing the room back and forth. "Ma, let's go home." It was better if we left. This way, maybe there was a chance that Easton would speak to his parents.

"Wait in the car. I'll come in afterwards," Ma replied sternly, leaving me no room for arguments.

"Okay." I left. After some time, Ma joined me. As soon as she was in the driver's seat, she scolded me. "Neveah Gail, what you did there was completely unacceptable. I thought I raised you better than this."

"I thought you were more intelligent than this," I retorted. Ma's eyes narrowed, a surefire sign that she was annoyed!

"What do you mean?"

"I proposed that we leave so we can give the Dale family some time alone. There may be a chance that Easton would talk to his parents in private," I explained.

Ma blushed a bit. "My bad, honey. I am sorry."

"It's cool. I know it's not easy being the mother of such an awesome child."

"Okay, now stop exaggerating."

I pouted and looked outside the window as Ma started the car. It's been a lot of time since we spent some time alone like this.

Easton

I sighed after my mate left me alone in the house with both of them. I quickly packed my clothes in a suitcase and my other stuff in boxes. I had already called up Xavier to make sure that someone cleans the house by tomorrow evening. I would most probably go to Neveah's house for dinner. I had to inform Gina about it.

I wanted to live with her, but she was not ready. I couldn't blame her. What sensible person would want to move in with her boyfriend of two days? But soon, I will make her love me.

I didn't want to meet my parents. I considered getting out through my window, but I was not a coward. So, I decided to face them. Nothing much could go wrong than it already was.

My father was sitting on the couch, and my mother was making dinner. This was our usual schedule before that woman left. It looked like things are back to square one again.

Just yesterday, my father cried betrayal, and today, he was watching her making dinner. Did he have anything called self-respect? That woman left him and made a fool of his feelings and mine. Now he was forgiving her this easily and this fast like the past few years didn't happen?

Everything might be the same for them again, except for one small thing. I was not going to play a part in this happy family. As soon as I entered the hall, my father looked up and smiled. This was the first time my father actually smiled at me since Amy left. There was one time he smiled when I told him that Neveah's my mate. Other than that, he usually remained expressionless.

After Amy left, the man pretty much shut out everything and everyone. He busied himself in pack business. It was like I never existed and now, eight years later, I did? So, I didn't smile back. If he could ignore me for years, I sure could ignore him for hours.

Amy came out from the kitchen with a spatula in her hand. "Come, baby, I made dinner. It's chicken Alfredo, apple pie, and vegetable cutlets."

"I am still moving out." Her smile vanished when I spoke. She was about to cry, I knew it. If I was the old Easton, I would have killed the one who made my mother cry. I was a mamma's boy then, and knowing that she deceived us was a huge blow for me.

"At least try to forgive me. I am trying, Easton. Just give me a chance." She pleaded. It broke my heart to see her this way. My mother was never sad. She was always a happy person. My father was the grumpy one.

"I can't. At least not yet," I told her truthfully.

She nodded her head in understanding. The wound she left was too deep.

"Well, can you at least have dinner? You can leave after. I promise I won't stop you." I didn't want to hurt her anymore, so I agreed. Who could decline this delicious food, anyway?

I called up Neveah to tell her that I was not coming for dinner. She squealed when I told that I am having dinner at my house. Well, ex-house. Neveah most probably thought that I have made up with my mother. I hated to break her heart!

Dinner was awkward, to say the least. The dishes were tasty, but the mood was definitely bad. Amy tried making it better by starting off conversations on random topics, but it always failed. She too kept quiet after some time.

As soon as my mother got up to pick up the dishes, I sprinted outside. I didn't want to wait there anymore.

I parked my car in an empty space three houses from Neveah's. I quietly ran to her house and snuck into her room. It was empty. I heard the noise coming from downstairs. They were having dinner. It all sounded happy, and I wanted that for myself. I felt bad knowing that Neveah had to grow up without a father.

I swore to myself that if I ever met that a-hole, I was going to kill him. Whoever he was, he didn't deserve Gina. Gina was the sweetest person I have met, and Nev's father must've been mad to ditch them.

I plopped on the bed and made myself home while waiting for my mate to grace me with her presence. She entered the room after some time and did not look surprised at all. She just took her night clothes with her and went to her bathroom. She came back wearing some shorts and a tank top.

I whistled as I looked at her legs. "Hot, babe!" She just glared at me and got a thick comforter and a pillow from the top of her closet. She placed it neatly on the floor. "Sleep."

Was she serious? "Why should I sleep on the ground?"

"Because I am saying so!" she said and pushed me off the bed. Luckily, I managed to hold on to the bed a bit so I didn't fall flat on my bum.

"Baby, seriously, tell me!" I pleaded with her. I wanted to know if I did something wrong unintentionally.

She blushed. My mate blushed!

"It is really silly. It's just that everyone knew that we slept on the same bed, and it was embarrassing." Well, it was silly but much better that what I expected it to be.

I got up and sat on the bed with her again. "Neveah, baby, will you promise that you will talk to me if there is any problem between us or if you don't feel comfortable with anything I do?" I wanted this promise from her. Things between my parents went wrong because they weren't comfortable speaking about things.

Miscommunication causes a lot of harm!

"Don't I always?" Neveah asked me, laughing lightly. She was right. My mate was never one to hold up things. She always spoke her mind, and I loved it about her.

"I know you do, but please give me this promise." I was desperate. I never wanted to lose my mate.

"Yes," she whispered. Neveah must have seen something in my eyes.

That night, I slept with a smile on my face and my mate beside me in my arms.

Chapter 34

Neveah

I was standing on the left side of the stage which was erected especially for this ceremony. Ma was standing on my left and Bryan was with his parents. Claire's behaviour was less hostile than it was before, but Bryan's father was pretty much the same silent man.

We were currently listening to Easton speaking on the podium. He was delivering a speech about the improvement of the pack. Of which, I obviously had no idea of! Amy and Peter were sitting on the chair some steps away from where the mike was placed.

They looked like the perfect happy couple they were before. All resentment seemed to vanish, much to Easton's disappointment. My mate still lived on his own and was still not on speaking terms with any of his parents. He moved out from his home to his new house exactly a week before.

Our life had been pretty much the same. Easton still spent his nights with me which was now public knowledge, much to Bryan's displeasure. But sleep was all we do.

Two days ago, we were on my bed when Easton asked me.

"Neveah, I want to introduce you to my pack," Easton said while playing with my hair. We were both lying on my bed after a very tasty dinner.

"Introduce me? As in what do I have to do?" I think almost everyone from their pack already knows about me. Especially after my drunken episode!

"There will be a small party, just the pack, and the important people. I was thinking of inviting Gina and Bryan too. I am sure that they would love to," he explained.

I thought about it for some time. "Sure, but make sure that it is on a weekend," I answered.

"Then we can organize it this Saturday," he offered, and I panicked.

"Do I have to dress up or something? Do they actually approve that I am human? What if they protest? And... what—" Easton stopped me mid-sentence by kissing me.

I forgot about my worries and kissed him back. We kissed for some more time before he moved to my neck. He pushed my tank top from my shoulder and kissed me there. I curled my fingers in his hair. He moved back to my lips, and this time, they were fast and rough.

He pulled his lips back after some time. I held his face close to mine and kissed his nose.

"We need to stop." Easton's voice was rough and husky.

"Hmmm," I sighed. I let go of his face. He laid his head back on the pillow, and I laid mine on his chest.

"Baby, don't think much about the meeting. All I will do is formally introduce to them that you are my mate. They already knew that you are my mate the day Alden hospitalized you. I also informed them that early that you are a human. No one has any problems with you," he told me while I was drawing patterns on his chest. "But since it is a party, you will have to dress pretty and look more beautiful than you already do."

"Sure?" I confirmed again.

"Yup, all they want is a Luna... preferably one who will stay with them." Easton tried to make a joke out of it, but it was hard to miss the anger in his tone.

"Well, it is a good thing I am going to the local college. I can be back every weekend," I told him.

"Didn't you get accepted anywhere else?" Easton asked. He cupped the back of my neck and pulled my face up so he could see me better.

"Well, I thought that if I become luna, I can't go to a college far away." I doubt that Easton was going to college because both Peter and Amy have not attended college.

"Of course, you can. I am going to University of Florida." How in the hell did he manage to get accepted there?

"Well, that's great because I got accepted there, too. I am not trying to be rude, but how did they accept you?" I was genuinely curious.

"Football scholarship." Figures.

"Okay, but what are you going to study?" Easton had never shown much interest in any subject.

"I was thinking about Mechanical Engineering." Well, his physics was good nowadays. Actually, he was many times better than me.

"I am going to take up accounting, maybe even law," I told him. I wasn't sure, but I knew that I wanted a career in the commerce section. I am good at math.

"That's great. I'll look for some apartments nearby."

I got up and sat on the bed. "We're going to live together?"

He also got up and sat next to me.

"Yeah, is there a problem?" Easton was so casual about it like the matter was not much of importance.

"What about that part where you ask me to move in with you? And this time, a cake won't do the job." I warned him. I wanted a proper proposal.

"Okay, I'll do it later. I need some time to think about it. Anything else?"

When I shook my head, he pulled us back to lie on the bed.

So, here we were. In two days' time, all the preparations were finished. Everything was set for the party of the year.

When Easton told me that there will be a party, I expected something like Claire's. Of course, in a more humble way. But this was so different. On the outskirts of the forest behind Easton's house, a stage was erected. The place was kind of a clearing. On the right side were rows and of tables of food for the buffet. On the right side was the DJ setting up his equipment.

"This the progress the pack has made in the last few months..." Easton continued.

I wasn't listening to the speech anymore. I didn't mean to insult him, but I barely understood what he was saying, so I stopped listening.

"The main reason why we have gathered here is for the luna ceremony. Today, I introduce to you all to my mate, my love, my Neveah." At last, he said something I have been waiting for a long time.

He gestured me to come to the stage. Well, he didn't mention this anywhere. Thankfully, I decided to dress up really good. I'm wearing a floor-length white gown with a strapless sweetheart neckline and a beautiful gold necklace. Off course, I borrowed them all from Ma.

I went to stand with him, and everyone cheered. The loudest was Georgy and Bryan. I waved and smiled at them and then at all the others. *Gosh!* There were so many of them.

"Does anyone want your luna to say something?" Easton screamed in the mike. There was a chorus of 'yes' from the crowd. I glared at Easton. If he wanted me to give a speech, he should have informed me before, not this late.

I smiled at them again and then at Easton. He was so going to pay for this. I took a deep breath and started my impromptu speech.

"Well, I wasn't informed that I have to give a speech." I started with the obvious. "I also have to say that I am not good at giving speeches except when I am lecturing Easton."

The whole crowd was laughing at that. "I also have to say that I am very approachable except when I am hungry. I tend to get moody when I am hungry. Just a warning."

"I don't know how many people believe that I can be a good luna because I honestly don't," I stated. I could see Sabrina staring at me with a disapproving look as if I was not worthy of the title.

"But I promise I will try. All I need is your support because, frankly, I have no idea what Easton spoke about during the last few minutes, but I am willing to learn. I just need a good teacher, and it is not you, Eugene." I informed him, to which he simply laughed along with the rest of the pack.

"So that's it. I am just waiting for the food. Doing make up tires you a lot!"

With that, I stepped down the stage. There was a huge round of applause.

Ma smiled. I could see that she was proud of me. "That was great."

"Ma, it was lame, and we both know it." Apparently lame was not a good word because there were huge growls after I said that.

"What did I do?" I looked around confused.

Melissa who was standing next to Ma said, "Rule one. Don't insult yourself in front of the pack. They will think that it was their fault." I raised an eyebrow at her. I turned to the pack and asked them. "Did I do or say something which I shouldn't have?"

"You shouldn't insult yourself. It means that you are insulting our faith in you," a guy from the crowd spoke up.

I just ohhed at it.

"Then what if I insult Easton?" I asked the same guy. Before he could reply, a pair of arms was around me.

"You can do whatever you want to me, baby," Easton whispered seductively in my ear.

"Maybe I will take up on that offer," I answered back without turning, and he tightened his arms around me. I gave a sly smile to Melissa.

"Then can you bring me food? Didn't you hear when I said that I was hungry? You should pay more attention to your mate." I reprimanded him in a playful way.

"Oh, I'll take good care of you." He gave me the same sly smile I gave Melissa. "And since you are hungry, and I am such a good mate, I am going to bring you food." Easton was off then.

I turned to the pack and asked, "So, does anyone want to talk to me?"

After a yummy dinner, the DJ was playing a soft track to which Easton and I were moving. When I said moving, I meant literally. It was almost impossible for me to dance in these high heels. Also, the dress I was wearing was too long for me to do any kind of decent moves.

"That was very sweet of you," Easton muttered in my hair.

"What did I do?"

"You helped Jane. She looks happy. I have been trying for a long time to make her smile." As he said that, we both gazed at the petite girl surrounded by a number of children.

Jane was a handicapped member of Easton's pack. According to Easton, she lost her parents and her left leg in an accident a few years ago. Since then, she has been a silent girl. She never spoke and never showed any emotions in her delicately beautiful face. A few moments ago, she approached me, and we had a heart-to-heart talk.

I was alone enjoying my ice cream with chocolate syrup when Jane came up to me saying that she wanted to talk. I agreed and noticed the limp in her left leg.

"So what's up?" I asked the only question that came to my mind. I wanted to ask her about her leg but refrained from doing so, fearing that she would start crying.

"I just want to talk to you, Luna." She sounded scared.

"Sure, and call me Neveah. Luna is just not that cool. Don't be scared. I won't eat you, promise." I tried cracking a joke, hoping that she would feel more comfortable after that.

Jane did smile to me. It was really short but sweet. "I want to be normal."

"Well, you are normal," I stated, but she didn't seem convinced.

"Well, this is where I should say that I understand and that things well get better. But the fact is that I don't understand what it is to lose a leg, and things aren't miraculously going to be okay. You need to work for it."

Jane's expression dropped from a blank face into a deep grimace.

"What do I do?" She was desperate, and it was very visible.

"I don't know. Frankly, this is your life. I myself had no friends long before. Don't feel bad, but you spent your whole life alone. If you suddenly get up one day and tell yourself that you want to have truckloads of friends, that is not

going to happen, but you can always start with me. You don't find friends. You just get them." Gosh, that was deep. Even for me.

I could see that Jane was not impressed by my speech, but honey, truth hurts!

"Oh, so will you be my friend?" she meekly asked.

"Sure," I replied and gave her a huge smile.

"Thank you." She gave me a hug and went to the children she was babysitting.

"I am awesome, dear mate of mine," I responded with a smug smile.

Easton looked at me lovingly. "I know that. I am just happy that now everyone knows it too."

It usually ended up really awkward for me whenever he said things like this. I had no idea how to respond to them. So I took the easy route and simply kissed him.

We were currently driving back to my house. It was almost one am, but somehow, I wasn't tired. There was some stupid song on the radio. This ride reminded me of the one I took with Melissa yesterday. I smiled thinking about it.

"A penny for your thoughts?" Easton's voice brought me out of that episode.

"Just thinking about some other ride."

"Tell me."

And so, I told him.

Melissa was driving to Georgy's house, and since it was on the way to Easton's new house, I requested her to drop me there. She switched on the radio, and there was some famous boy band song playing. She sang the whole song along with them.

I grimaced at her attempt to sing. Well, it sounded more like a cat's screech especially when she went high pitch.

"Melissa, I love you and all, but can you just shut up?" I pleaded with her. I would rather watch Bryan make out with Ma rather than listen to her attempt at singing.

"Don't be rude!" She scolded me and carried on with the song. I narrowed my eyes at her.

"Look who is talking." I gave her an unimpressed look. Melissa was the mean queen of our school.

"Now you are really being mean," she muttered.

I glared at her. She was the last person on earth who should say that.

"Melissa, please, I beg you. Just shut up." Thankfully, she did stop singing and switched off the radio.

After some time in silence, I asked her, "Melissa, how did you and Georgy start dating?"

That was something I have been waiting to ask her. She had told me before that they just got together.

"It is a long story." Melissa was obviously trying to avoid the subject.

"I have time. I don't mean to pry, but I really want to know." Her expression changed when I said that, so I quickly amended. "It is okay if you don't want to tell me."

I just wanted to know how she moved on so fast. Easton always made mates seem something precious. Very precious, in fact. He kept telling me that living without one's mate was difficult. He always made soul mates seem like a big deal. Sure, we did have a connection, but I knew that Easton's feelings for me were way deeper than the ones I had for him.

"No, it is okay. You are my best friend and my luna. I can always tell you things. It's just that I don't want you to judge me."

"When have I ever?" I asked her. I never asked her the reason she stopped talking to me years ago, and I never asked her the reason she came back to me. This would be the first time that I was actually asking her something.

"We met that day you introduced us to each other in school. Well, at that time I was recovering from the fact that my mate rejected me. He was the hottest guy I had ever seen. He was better than my mate." She was totally in a faraway land.

"Yeah, he is hot. After that?" I was getting desperate here.

"We talked. The day you both met, his mother was introduced into the pack. She was not a member because she has strong alpha blood. She just lives like a lone wolf. Many are out there. Georgy approached me and talked about you. Gosh! I hated you at that moment." I laughed at that. Somehow, Georgy was very fond of me. I too loved him like an elder brother I never had.

"We talked and we talked the whole night. Somehow, with time, our relationship gradually developed. He removed all traces of Alden from my mind. It is like Georgy is my mate," she said with a smile filled with love.

"Yeah, I see that every time you both are free." They are always over each other. It was cute but gross at the same time.

"So, what's going on between you and Easton?" Melissa gave me a look which said spill. This was one conversation I was so trying to avoid.

Easton was moving around a lot on the bed. We both couldn't sleep. He said that he wasn't tired, and even I was not sleepy. So I decided that we should go somewhere after ignoring Easton's suggestion of tiring ourselves some other way.

We were in the same place that Georgy took me some time before. I didn't know the address, but once I mentioned the place to Easton, he seemed to recognize it easily. He shifted into his lovely black wolf form and let me ride on his back.

I sat on the grass waiting for Easton to shift back. There was some rustling sound and then Easton emerged from the woods looking like a modern and hot version of Tarzan.

I whistled looking at him. He just smirked back at me. "So, why did you bring me here?" he asked as he sat beside me on the soft grass.

"Well, you weren't sleeping, and you weren't letting me sleep either, so I thought that it might be better if we do something productive."

"Baby, we could have done something *really* productive on your bed. Not that I mind the grass." Pervert. He just gave me a wolfish smile, literally.

I sighed and went directly to the topic. "I want you to talk to me about Amy." He stiffened when I mentioned her.

"There is nothing to talk about."

"Easton I know that…"

"I said there is nothing to talk about," he cut me off. This time, there was a lot of anger in his face. I flinched back at his loud voice.

His eyes immediately softened when he saw that I was scared of him.

"I am sorry. I didn't mean to be loud or to scare you." He apologised.

"It's okay, but we do have to talk some time, one way or the other."

"I know. But for now, all I know is that I am not ready to forgive her." We sat in silence for some time. He put his arm around my shoulder, and I laid my head on in the crook of his neck.

"You know, I love you," he softly said after some time.

I looked up into his eyes and saw only love just as he said.

"If I tell you that I love you, it will be a lie, but I can assure you that I am getting there," I replied truthfully.

"That's enough for me." Easton kissed my head. I once again retreated to his neck. He wrapped his other arm around me, and I wrapped my arms around his waist.

We both sat there in each other's arms looking at the full moon with the water shining from the moonlight in our feet

Who would have guessed?

Epilogue

Neveah

"Hurry up, Easton, or we are going to be late."

He was busy straightening his tie while I cursed that it would somehow strangle him.

"At least pretend to be happy, baby," he said to me while admiring his looks in the mirror.

"Shut up." I wanted to sit on the soft bed and miserably cry my heart out, but I composed myself.

You can do it, Neveah. You are not weak.

"Sorry. Let's leave." I got up from the chair I was sitting on in Easton's new house. I grabbed my purse and mobile phone on the table near his bed. He drove the car in total silence for I was too pissed to talk to anyone.

"I can back out if you want," Easton said softly.

"As if that would make anything better. I wanted to win it on my own." I snorted. He giving up wouldn't do me any benefit except hurting my ego.

"What do you want me to do, Neveah? I don't want you to be unhappy."

I looked at Easton and sighed. What do I do with this guy? "Stop the car, please." He did as I said with a worried expression. He stopped the car by the side of the road. We both got down, and I hugged him.

"You know I am happy and proud and everything else, but I am just sad that the cause of your happiness is misery," I muttered in his chest. He laughed, and I felt the vibrations.

"You don't know?"

"What?"

"Your happiness is also mine. If you are sad, my success doesn't make any difference." I snuggled more into his chest, feeling guilty as hell. I decided that if Easton could be sad for me, I could be happy for him.

"Let's go. I have to cheer for you," I exclaimed.

He pecked my cheek, and we got in the car.

Ma and Brian were coming to the venue directly. Today was the day of our graduation, the day when we are officially out of school. I was so going to miss that place.

Easton parked the car next to Melissa's new pink car. "You know, I kind of pity Georgy," I muttered.

"I *actually* pity him. As if being with Melissa isn't enough! Poor guy!"

I swatted his arm. "That was mean, Easton."

"So you are mean all the time, Nev." *Ouch!* I was not that bad, right?

"I am mean only to those people who deserve it," I proudly stated. And most of them included his jock friends.

"Whatever." He just nodded, not wanting to argue with me.

Ma and Bryan were standing at the entrance along with Amy and Peter and other bunch of people. To all the humans, Amy Dale left her husband because of some personal problems by faking her death, which was exactly what happened. They just didn't know the finer details.

Easton squirmed and tried to remove his hand from mine when he spotted them. I glared at him. There would be consequences if he left now. I was going to make sure of it.

I mean, things are way better than they were. Easton had started speaking to Amy again. Actually, all he could say was hello, but something was always better than nothing.

It took me a lot of effort and bribes to get him to say that, and I was not going to let go of his progress. "Be polite, East," I managed to whisper in his ear by standing on my toes.

He glared back at me but then his eyes softened. He once told me that it was very difficult for him to deny anything to me, so I planned on using that for things like this.

"I hate you." Easton quickly realized what I was doing to him. I smirked.

"Hate you too, honey."

I somehow managed to drag him near our parents. They were all talking animatedly about some yoga technique to reduce weight.

"Hello." I greeted them with a warm smile while Easton just grunted.

"Hello," Easton muttered when I squeezed his hand hard. His voice sounded stiff whenever he spoke to Claire.

Speaking of Claire, we have started to form some sort of relationship. She did not consider me her granddaughter. That would be very weird if she did. She didn't love Ma and me, but we share a cordial relationship.

Last Saturday, we all went to dinner together, and even Easton tagged along. Gabriella still hated me. Just a little less than she hated Melissa. Part of me was still scared to talk to her. Somehow, she still seemed very intimidating to me.

"I'm leaving." Easton didn't even wait for my reply before he was off like his ass was on fire. I so needed to talk to him about manners.

"You're trying, and that's enough," Amy said with a small smile as her eyes followed her son. Peter nodded in agreement.

Amy was no longer cruel to me. She wasn't angry at me, just frustrated. So, she directed it all to me. But we have talked, and she was back to the normal Amy Dale that I loved.

"That was one of the shittiest lines I have ever heard. You and I both know that you want to hug him and then smack him," I said. Amy sighed before smirking at me.

"Oh no, honey, that's just you," she replied. *Sly woman!*

"I meant his cheek." I clarified.

"Which one?" She was back with another answer. There were loud laughs in the parking lot. I was sure that everyone heard what Amy said, and those who haven't would have been informed by now.

I glance at Easton who was now standing with Xavier and his mate, Jessica. To say that Jessica hated him would be an understatement. Easton and I started out that way, but believe me, they were a few times worse than us. But that is a different story.

Easton looked at me and winked.

"You know, I always wondered why Easton acts like an idiot sometimes. Now, I understand that the apple doesn't fall too far from the tree," I said. Easton and Amy's smile vanished.

"You know, I called you both idiots." I reminded them, trying to reduce the tension.

"They aren't reacting because I had called them that hundreds of times before you did," Peter interjected, and there was another round of laughing.

"Okay, enough. It is time," Ma called out.

We all rushed inside. Every parent wanted to sit in a great spot where they could cheer for their children.

I collected my graduation cap and gown from Melissa which was, thankfully, navy blue in colour. I quickly put it over my teal knee-length dress and put the cap on my head. I had my hair in a ponytail, so I didn't look that bad.

"You look good." Easton's mouth was near my ear, and he wrapped his arms around my waist.

"Thanks," I replied looking at him.

"It's going to be okay," he comforted me, looking all sad.

"It is okay. All I have to do is share the valedictorian place with you," I muttered softly.

Ladies and gentlemen, you have heard that right. He topped the class!

I remembered being heartbroken when the principal gave me the news.

Both Easton and I were seated on the sofa in the principal's office waiting for him to arrive. Easton had received a call from him early this morning saying that he wanted to meet my boyfriend and me. Since I was just next to him on the bed, I butted in and told Mr. Davis that we could meet today. It wasn't probably the most decent thing to do.

"Is he coming today?" I was bored with sitting and doing nothing. I tried playing with Easton's phone to distract me, but to no avail.

"He better be coming in a few minutes." Easton had a pack meeting to attend, and I... well, I had a TV program to catch.

The door opened after some time, and a flustered looking Mr. Davis entered. "Hello, Mr. Dale and Ms. Huber. I have called you here to inform you about something very serious and important."

What did Easton do now?

"I have to inform you, with a great amount of surprise, that Easton was selected as the valedictorian of your class. Ms. Huber, you did score the highest in five subjects, but Easton wasn't lagging far behind. Also, his final score in PE was way more than yours, making his total slightly higher."

What?

"Are you serious?" I was standing up now with Easton still in shock.

"I'm afraid that the answer is yes."

"But that is just not possible! I mean, he is Easton Eugene!" I looked at him and realised that it was wrong of me to say such things. I pulled him up so that he was standing.

"I love you, Easton. You are not dumb, but frankly, I am way better than you."

"I know, that's what I am shocked about! What about my reputation?" Easton replied. He really did look concerned.

"Your reputation? What about mine? What will people think of me when they hear that you scored more than me?" I all but shouted at him then looked at the scared principal.

"Is there some way that people won't know about this?"

"Actually, I think all the board members already know."

I was about to lunge for him, but Easton stopped me before I could do anything crazy.

"Does anyone other than them know?" Easton looked relatively calm.

"No, but I actually called you here to tell you that this year, we have decided that both of you will be valedictorians. It won't be fair on you, Neveah, if we don't do this."

I calmed myself and sat down on the sofa again. There was no other way around it. "Fine, go ahead with the preparations."

"But, Nev—"

"It's okay, Easton," I cut him off.

I spent the next couple of days mourning with lots of junk food and Beauty and the Beast reruns. Those were the only things that made me feel normal and somewhat happy.

When I told Ma about this, she laughed, and I cried. Well, not literally, but yes, she did laugh, and Amy laughed, too. She could hardly believe that her son could achieve something like this.

Everyone else was also shocked.

Their reactions didn't make me feel any better at all.

All of us stood in line. One of the teachers called out the names, and Mr. Davis took his place on the stage where he was to hand over our diplomas. The graduation ceremony officially started.

As soon as Easton climbed up the stage, there were loud cheers from the crowd. But the loudest of them all was me. Come on! I was his mate after all.

"You did it, Easton," I shouted at the top of my voice.

"I do it every night, honey," Easton shouted back.

"No, honey, you did it every night until yesterday. No more from tonight." The colour drained from Easton's face.

There were a lot of *oohs* and *aahs* from the crowd. Some other teacher pushed him off from the stage. It was just the second name, and the crowd was howling. Literally!

The ceremony went on, and my name was called out. Again, there were loud cheers. I smiled at Mr. Davis and almost snatched my diploma from him.

I looked at the crowd and saw Ma and Bryan cheering loudly with Amy and Peter. Melissa and Georgy, who were doing wacky things with their hands, were beside them. Even Xavier was cheering for me. The most shocking thing was Claire was also smiling and clapping for me in the corner of the hall. Of course, the loudest was my mate, Easton.

I smiled at all of them, got down the stage, and ran directly into Ma's arms.

"I am proud of you, my baby. I am so proud of you." She kissed my head, and I didn't let go of her for some time. After that, I hugged Bryan who said the same thing. I did the rounds, hugging everyone who I considered part of my extended *family*.

At last, I went to Claire.

"Thank you," I told her. I was somehow happy that she was here.

"You did well." She shook my hand and kissed me on the cheek. I stayed still for some time, trying to make sure that this was real. Then I quickly cleared my throat and replied with a small thank you.

The principal shushed us all and gave the farewell speech. Now, it was my turn. Easton refused to give a speech, saying that him being a valedictorian is a big embarrassment to him.

"Hello, everyone. I am here to… well, say goodbye. First, I would like to thank Mr. Davis for allowing me this opportunity even though I am not, surprisingly and much to my embarrassment, the first choice for this. I just wanted to say that sometimes, we don't end up with what we expect. This will happen many times in our lives, but we shouldn't give up. We need to fight because the day we give up that is when we lose everything. I would also like to say that we should not always think logically because there are a lot of things beyond logic and underneath nature that are yet to be discovered. I would like to thank all the teachers, Mr. Davis, and all the non-teaching staff for helping us to graduate. Yes, I am sad that the title 'nerd of the school' is no longer rightfully mine. Hard as it may, I hereby bestow the title to one of our own, Easton Eugene Dale."

All eyes turned to Easton, and he blushed. Everyone was laughing at my sorrow, but it didn't feel that bad.

We all threw our caps in the air, took tons of photos, laughed, cried, and cherished the memory of our last day in school.

Can't get enough of Neveah and Easton? Make sure you sign up for the author's blog to find out more about them!

Get these two bonus chapters and more freebies when you sign up at supraja-ir.awesomeauthors.org!

Here is a sample from another story you may enjoy:

KRISTEL JUURIK
PURR,
KITTEN

CHAPTER 1

It looked like our world, felt like our world and even smelled like our world, yet somewhere in the middle of the forest, a girl sat in a tree who was anything but from our world. She was preparing for another long day, but an uneasy feeling settled in the pit of her stomach. It was because of the birds.

In every forest, birds acted like an alarm. Every once in a while, one chirped, and another one would answer on the other side of the forest. It meant the night would be safe. There were only two times they fell silent: they went to sleep with their chicks under their wings, for which the bugs threw a party to celebrate their safety. The second time they stayed quiet was when they flew away. And for them to fly away from their homes, they had to be frightened.

The girl knew the forest like the back of her hand, and the birds belonged to that knowledge. She knew they should already be sending off their first chirps, but they had remained silent for the longest time now. She craned her neck to look up through the thick branches above her head and saw the few last birds taking off. They were escaping, and the girl knew so should she but was glued to the branch.

When she finally saw what had the birds in a frenzy, she knew they weren't fast enough for what was coming but were high enough. Wolves of every size ran past her so fast, but the speed wasn't what startled her. It was the amount of them and the time. What was a pack of wolves doing in the middle of the night running around like the fire was chasing them?

In fascination, she grabbed onto the branch above her head and leaned forward to look closer at them. She hadn't seen strangers of her kind around for so long. There may be a pack some distance away, but she was familiar with them. This one was all new to her.

Even from the distance, she saw the fire of determination that was ablaze in their eyes and cocked her head to the side. Eventually, she felt the scent they carried after themselves: a strange mixture of honey and freshly cut grass. There could have been a completely different combination, an even weirder one, but it fascinated her in a way no other scent could.

'Leave.' The single voice in her head ordered, and she flinched. She didn't expect her own wolf spirit to speak up although she was the same one amongst them two. At least, she knew the right things to do.

'I can't, they're right there.' The girl threw back.

'Of course, not right now, dummy. As soon as they're gone,' the wolf-spirit said with annoyance, and she rolled her eyes. Sharing the mind and sadly, a morphing body with an animal was conflicting. A voice always kept her company and not always was it a good thing. The spirit tended to be more on the annoying side than anything else, and it didn't help with the girl being so stubborn because eventually they always ended up

arguing. Sometimes over a matter that needed action more than debate.

She was a werewolf, *but not the kind you saw on TV or read about in classical novels*. Moon hardly had anything to do with her shifting into a large, hairy beast, and instead, it was more attached to her self-control and dominating emotion.

She stayed back in the shade of her hideout while the pack ran by. They ran straight towards South like an attacking arming. As that startling thought crossed her mind, she slipped from the thick branch under her feet and plunged down.

'Idiot!' The girl ignored her wolf-spirit and instead focused on hanging onto the branch above her and not falling down in the middle of an attack. The pack was an army after all, and it was headed straight towards the pack she knew about. She had personal experience with an attack of that kind, and it was panic that engulfed her as she thought of the pack's future. The last wolf of the army was out of her sight when she finally dropped down next to the tree and rubbed her burning palms. They were red and sore, but she rubbed them more out of habit and in an attempt to relieve the pain.

Her gaze was still stuck on the South, heart beating a tattoo against her rib-cage while the earth seemed to disappear from underneath her, ready to swallow her up in the violent events and raging fires again.

'Move.' The spirit reminded her, but she was frozen to spot. *'Kathryn, move!' And Kathryn did. She ran in the direction of her own private haven, somewhere she always thought she'd be safe at, except that night. She had major doubts about her safety not to even mention the safety of that pack. It felt like as soon as she took two steps away, the*

screams broke loose, and she froze again right in the middle of a run.

"I can't," Kathryn whispered and then gulped. '*I need to help them.'*

'You can't, there's nothing you can do.'

'I can't just turn around and flee again! The situation is different this time, I can fight.'

'But you'd be fighting alone.'

Kathryn couldn't believe that and instead began jogging forward. '*I wouldn't be fighting alone, I'd be fighting on their side. I can help.*' She broke out into a sprint while her wolf-spirit got restless.

'You're selfish, Kathryn!'

'I am not selfish, I am doing this for them.' Kathryn shot back.

'You aren't taking me into consideration. Do you think I want to fight? And, do you actually think we can fight this battle alone and actually survive?' Kathryn ignored a half of her completely. She was determined to finish what she started already, and she could only finish it at her destination.

She was so sure that she could do it. But when she reached the border of the pack, all she could see was an orange glow towards the heart of the pack's land. Fear made her freeze, and her bravery flew away like a light feather in a storm. Her wolf-spirit was right as it usually was, but she wanted to help so badly. Even though Kathryn wanted to continue and help, she knew that the pride, as well as anger and annoyance the other half of her felt, was justified. Her wolf-spirit knew she was perhaps one sentence away from convincing the one in charge of their feet and that body to turn around and run.

'You know what this pack is like, and they attacked at night like your pack was attacked. You can't battle against them, especially since by now you'd be fighting them alone. This one wolf battle against an army is, so far, the stupidest thing you've ever come up with.'

Kathryn let those words guide her away from the pack, and she ran a bit of time before letting her wolf overcome her, and she shifted mid-sprint. Dark brown fur sprung to cover her entire body and throw away the shreds of clothes she had on before. Kathryn was then left into the observer's role as her wolf took the lead and ran away from their almost death scene.

Although the emotions that drove Kathryn towards insanity began to fade again and rational thought reminded her that her wolf was once again right, she couldn't help but feel like she had betrayed that pack. It was a while back, but still, that pack hadn't turned down a chance to help her when she needed it.

Acknowledgements

I would like to thank my cousins who were the first ones to encourage me to write.

A big thank you to Faith and Le-an of Blvnp Publishing for being so supportive.

The biggest thanks goes to Wattpad and my laptop, without whom this wouldn't be possible.

Love it or hate it, let me know!

Leave a review on Amazon or Goodreads!

About the Author

My name is Supraja Iyer and I am in my third year of Engineering.

I live in Mumbai, India.

Also, I have been reading books since the age of six when my mother introduced me to books, making reading a daily ritual.

Writing is something I do to escape studies and I never thought my book will get published.

When not studying and writing, I watch movies late night and eat junk food.

52039160R00240

Made in the USA
Columbia, SC
25 February 2019